DERELICT

Other Anthologies Edited by:

DEREL I C T

Edited by

David B. Coe
&
Joshua Palmatier

Zombies Need Brains LLC
www.zombiesneedbrains.com

Interior Design (ebook): ZNB Design
Interior Design (print): ZNB Design
Cover Design by ZNB Design
Cover Art "Derelict"
by Justin Adams of Varia Studios

ZNB Book Collectors #21
All characters and events in this book are fictitious.
All resemblance to persons living or dead is coincidental.

Kickstarter Edition Printing, June 2021
First Printing, July 2021

Print ISBN-13: 978-1940709406

Ebook ISBN-13: 978-1940709413

Printed in the U.S.A.

COPYRIGHTS

Table of Contents

SIGNATURE PAGE

David B. Coe, editor:

_____

Joshua Palmatier, editor:

_____

Kristine Smith:

_____

D.B. Jackson:

_____

Griffin Ayaz Tyree:

_____

Andrija Popovic:

_____

Sharon Lee & Steve Miller:

_____

Gerald Brandt:

_____

Kit Harding:

_____

Gini Koch writing as Anita Ensal:

_____

Jacey Bedford:

_____

Mark D. Jacobsen:

_____

Jana Paniccia:

_____

Alex Bledsoe:

_____

Chaz Brenchley:

_____

R.Z. Held:

_____

Jack Campbell:

_____

Julie E. Czerneda:

_____

Justin Adams, artist:

_____

Symbiote

Kristine Smith

"I'm not even sure this is worth opening the hatch for." Shelly Conn checked fasteners on her spacesuit and pulled on her gloves. "The *Morecombe* was reported missing twelve years ago. It's probably been stripped of everything that's worth a damn."

"Hull could be worth something." Danny Raice, her second, adjusted fittings and checked the gauges of his own suit, which squeaked in polymer complaint as he worked.

"We'd have to tow it. Towing can get complicated." Shelly lowered her voice. "Last pilot we had took out part of a dock the last time we tried it, remember? Which is why our insurance premium blew up, which is why we don't have insurance anymore." Also why they couldn't risk another tow job, even though they had a new pilot for this trip. The *Stabler*, their poor old tub, had been put on probation at every station in the quadrant. The damage deposit alone would take every spare credit they had.

Danny nodded. "So we need a score."

"We need an *easy* score. In and out. Simple stuff. Cargo. Instrumentation."

"Could be a lot of instruments. Analyzers. This was a lab ship, according to the official report."

"Which was filed when the ship first went missing, twelve years ago." Shelly slumped against the curved wall of the passageway. "We'll look around. Anything looks good, we'll grab it. But we're not towing." She checked the prelims on Danny's suit, then forced herself to stand still while he did the same for her. Dockings always made her nervous. Linking up. Opening hatches. Those first steps into who the hell knew what. She hoped the *Morecombe* was still tight, that the air circulation and filtration still worked, even though she knew it was asking a lot after over a decade without maintenance.

She worked her shoulders as an unreachable spot smack in the middle of her lower back started to itch like crazy. *Why does this always happen?* She felt five years old again, needing to go to the bathroom as soon as her mom buttoned up her snowsuit. *Please let that wreck have breathable air.* Then maybe she could take the damned suit off.

Cary Seto gave Shelly the stink-eye when she and Danny reentered the navigation hub, which meant she had overheard the comments about the dock incident and decided to take umbrage at the criticism of a fellow pilot. "Link-up in one minute." She kept her gaze fixed on the display, her brow knit as though another of her headaches had come to call.

So bloody annoying. Shelly had decided from the moment they left the dock that this first mission with Seto would be the last. The woman had been a rush hire and those never turned out well, did they? *Crab-ass.* Her link-up comment was the most words she had strung together since their breakaway two weeks before.

Danny glanced at Shelly and rolled his eyes. He always had the knack for reading her thoughts. "She did tip you off to this wreck."

Shelly covered her mouth with her hand to muffle her voice. "It better be the haul of a lifetime is all I can say."

"Well, maybe you should change your mind about—"

"No towing." Shelly lowered her hand and looked around the hub. "Where the hell is Marta?"

"Here the hell is Marta." Marta Sarkesian, the engineer, emerged through the floor hatch. "I was reading the reports."

"What reports?"

Marta huffed, then pointed toward the *Morecombe*, the edge of which had just become visible through the viewport. "The reports on the ship we're boarding in a few minutes." She passed through the hub to the passageway and equipment lockers. "It was a research lab."

"Like I said." Danny pointed at Shelly and nodded. "Instruments."

Shelly shook her head. "Which are no doubt long gone."

"I doubt that. No sightings reported since it vanished twelve years ago." Marta reappeared in the entry. She had already dragged on her suit and now struggled with her gloves. "We might get lucky."

Shelly glanced at Cary, who kept her eyes fixed on her displays, then followed Marta out to the passageway. "Nobody reports sightings. Tappers pull the info, track you down. Next thing you know, you're spaced and some pirate takes off with your ship and your salvage." She helped the other woman with gloves, fittings, and safety check. "Nobody reports sightings. You find a derelict, you grab what you can and run like hell." Danny joined them and together they donned their helmets, maneuvered toward the junction airlock, and activated their communications.

"Testing, testing. Raice to bridge." Danny tapped his helmet earpiece. "Cary? *Cary*?"

A few moments passed, then the tight voice came through. "Message received. Channel is open." Another beat, then the ship shuddered like a wheeled vehicle on a bumpy road.

"Sorry." Cary's voice carried no hint of apology. "Came in a little hard there."

"You think?" Shelly hoped she muttered softly enough to evade the hypersensitive audio. "No towing no way," she mouthed at Danny, who nodded his agreement.

They stood by the junction and waited as their ship sensors analyzed the interior of the *Morecombe* for the more obvious dangers. Poisonous air. No air at all. Booby traps set by a salvage crew intending to return at a later date.

Shelly relaxed, a little, as one by one, the indicators blinked green. She had been in the salvage business too long to hope or wish—you waited for the facts, looked at what you had in front of you, and worked with it. But Marta's research had revived what she thought of as her *hunter bug*. The thrill of discovery. The dream of the big score.

Sounds from her suit disrupted her thoughts. The door to the airlock had opened and she and the others had stepped inside. As soon as the door closed behind them, her suit's air filter whined, red overload indicators streaming across the inside of the helmet visor. Then, just as quickly, the sound ramped down. Then came silence.

"Something leaked." Danny stood still as data traced an alphanumeric stream across the inside of his visor. "Low levels of particulate."

"Dust." Marta made entries into the data recorder on her wrist. "Bound to be some after all this time. Filter deterioration."

"Are you sure?" Shelly crowded in behind her. "All the filters on the *Stabler* are rated for one hundred years minimum."

Marta snorted. "Everything deteriorates, no matter what the salesbot says." She tapped her com link. "All good here, Cary. Open 'er up."

The pilot said nothing. Only the faint clicks and rasps of door mechanisms arguing with one another indicated that she had initiated the search for the code sequence that would open the *Morecombe's* entry hatch.

"Depending on what kinds of stuff they have on board, the locks could be pretty complex. We could be here a while." Marta had barely finished speaking when green indicators lit up the derelict ship's door panel. "Damn. That didn't take long."

"Last wreck we boarded took six hours to crack." Danny hoisted a bag containing generic repair kits and other equipment. "Not complaining."

The *Morecombe's* hatch slid aside and Shelly edged up next to her engineer. The opening was wide enough for the two women to stand shoulder to shoulder and survey the interior of the main deck, which included the nav hub, banks of monitors—

—and plants. Rows of raised beds, filled with all sorts of plants, filled half the deck. Some bore flowers, others berries or other types of fruit. Behind them were bushes, small trees, vines tumbling over trellises. The entire space was brightly lit, bathed by overhead lamps as well as light from a nearby sun, which filled one of the semicircle of viewports at the far end of the deck.

"Wow." Marta stepped inside. "This place looks—"

"—new." Shelly ran a gloved hand over the wall, which was clean and bright as if newly installed.

"It's air in here. It's filtered." Danny studied the readouts on his sleeve display. "Not sure what the hiccup was."

"Temperature?" Marta asked.

"Twenty-two and steady."

"So it's warmish and we can breathe?" Shelly twitched her shoulders as the itch on her back moved upward. "We can take these damned helmets off?"

"Unless you're worried about something falling on your head." Danny cracked his helmet seals and slipped it off, then scrubbed a hand through his mess of black hair. "I think we're good."

"Great." Shelly cracked the seals of her helmet and eased off the bloody thing. Sniffed. The air smelled like…air. A little stale. A little damp, like bathroom air after a hot shower. But sweet. Like flowers.

"Feel that sun." Marta slipped off a glove and held out her hand until it was bathed in light. "Just warm enough."

"Ship's bigger than I thought it would be." Danny stepped out to the middle of the deck and did a slow turn. "Really nice."

Marta being Marta, she whipped out her recorder and headed for the instrument panels. "If these innards are in good repair, we may have something here." She sat at one of the stations and activated the recorder. After a few moments, she shook the device, then turned it over and popped off its access panel.

Shelly drew close. "What's wrong?"

Marta flinched in surprise, then shook her head. "Something must be wrong with my kit—these readings are weird."

"Define 'weird.'"

"Most of these arrays are bio-based. The memory boards, the processors, all contain cellular materials."

Shelly braced for a Marta Lecture. "I know that."

"They're decent at self-repair and can self-maintain for a time. They run diagnostics regularly, debug themselves, adapt to issues they can't repair until people like me have time to fix them."

Shelly took a deep breath and nodded. "But?"

"But." Marta slumped back in the seat. "They still require regular maintenance. Extensive regular maintenance. This ship's been abandoned for twelve years. Systems should've slipped into standby after six months. Honestly? It should be a mess of decayed boards by now—it should stink in here. The air should be a misty haze of yuck. Overwhelmed filters. Stuttering readouts. Nothing dangerous, just *blech*." She snapped the recorder access panel back into place, then rebooted the device. "These systems aren't designed to maintain themselves for this long and they appear to be in perfect shape."

"Who owned the *Morecombe*?" Danny had wandered over to the planters and bent to sniff a bright yellow flower. "A uni or a fancy research outfit could afford the best."

"Even the best can't last more than a year, eighteen months at most." Marta exhaled with a huff. "It just can't."

"So somebody's on board?" Shelly felt a twist in the pit of her stomach. She activated her ship link. "Cary?"

"Yup?"

"How many bodies do the scans show?"

A heavy sigh. The sound of tapping, a few beeps. "Three."

"Somebody's been here before us, then." Marta sat up straighter and looked around the deck.

"So they made some repairs. They did us a favor, yeah?" Danny stood, hands on hips. "I should go get a dolly so we can clear this place out."

"Clear what out?" Shelly gestured vaguely. "I don't see anything moveable. We'd have to disassemble the panels and that would take too much time." She gave Marta's arm a light punch. "I thought you said this was a lab ship."

"Lab doesn't always mean instruments." Marta continued to study her recorder. "Botany's a science, too, you know."

Shelly sighed as her good mood took a hit that left a dent. "Can't sell plants."

"Maybe there's some rare ones." Danny headed to another planter. "Collectors pay good money for rare."

"Well…" Shelly started to follow him, then stopped. "Maybe it's the plants keeping the ship clean. Aren't you always supposed to keep some in your flat to purify the air?"

"They produce some oxygen. They provide food. They can't maintain a ship."

"Maybe this is all just top of the line. Tech that most of us can't afford."

Marta shot to her feet, eyes wide, cheeks flaring red. "I would know about it. Knowing about things like that is my job."

Shelly backed away. "I'm sorry."

Marta's shoulders sagged. "Yeah. I am, too." She pressed a hand to her forehead and stared down at her recorder. "I just don't...understand." She sat back down and continued scanning.

Shelly joined Danny and together they executed a quick search of the crew quarters. They found nothing that struck Shelly as unusual—some clothing, a scatter of dishes on the galley table— but Danny examined each item as though it held secrets that would explain what happened all those years ago.

"When I was little, maybe eight, nine, my brother and I explored a vacant house a few doors down from ours. It had been empty for a long time. Years. I used to hear my folks talk about it. Something to do with a will." His eyes shone with young boy memories. "The things we found. The power grid had malfunctioned months before and when we looked in the refrigerator—" His eyes widened and he held his nose, mimed gagging.

Shelly opened a cupboard, examined one of the cartons of freeze-dried meals, then tossed it back on the shelf. "Judging from the dates on this stuff, no one's been here for ages." She took Danny by the elbow and steered him back to the main deck, where they found Marta in the middle of the floor, undoing the fasteners of an access hatch.

"Engine room. Utilities. I want to see what's going on." The engineer swore under her breath as one of the fittings jammed, then whacked it with her all-in-one tool. The metal clatter rang through the air.

Shelly watched a faint scatter of dust settle on her sleeve and looked overhead to see where it could have come from. *Trick of the light.* Marta's increasing agitation was getting under her skin. "What did you pull from the log?"

"I tried to access it. It's been wiped."

"You can't wipe a ship's log."

Marta stared at the hatch for a time, then slowly raised her head. "By all means, give it a shot." She pointed to the nearest bank of panels with the all-in-one, then resumed wrestling with fittings.

Shit. Shelly knelt beside her. "I meant, you're not supposed to be able to wipe a log. How could someone do that?"

"That's what I want to find out." Marta sat back on her heels. "Something is wrong." She looked around, shook her head. "This ship is spotless. It looks like it just left refurb." She jerked her thumb in the direction of the *Stabler.* "What did she tell you about it?"

"She can hear you."

"I don't care. What did she tell you?"

"That scavengers ignore it because it's small. It looks old."

"And you believe that?"

"What are you saying?"

"I don't want to jump to conclusions." Marta held a finger to her lips, then dug into her tool bag, removed a sidearm, and slipped it into a holster on her tool belt. She dug out her handheld, scrawled a note across the surface, and showed it to Shelly.

Escape pod still attached. What happened to the crew?

"Okay." Shelly's own sidearm nestled in her belt holster, though the thought of firing weapons in such close quarters gave her the shakes. "Be careful."

"Always." Marta wrestled open the floor hatch and vanished down the hole.

Shelly turned back to the plants, dreams of a big score faded to nothing.

"Huh." Danny bent over a bunch of cup-like flowers, white with green and red veining. "Pitcher plants." He pointed to another plant, this one shorter and spindlier. "Venus fly-trap." Another boyish grin. "Carnivorous."

Shelly kept her distance. "What—are they going to eat us?"

"Not if there's sufficient nitrogen and phosphorus in the growth medium." Danny checked a nearby readout and frowned. "Levels look a little low."

"How do you know so much about them?"

"My older brother kept a few in his room. He liked feeding them flies." Danny held up his hands and twiddled his fingers. *"Bzzzz…bzzzzz."*

"He sounds like a great guy."

Danny shrugged. "He is a bit of a sadist." He stopped, then brushed a hand over one of the panels. "Thought I saw—" He shook his head. "—dark stuff." He looked up at the ceiling lights. "Shadows."

"Shadows. It's bright enough in here to induce a migraine." Shelly left the plant area and wandered to a nearby status board. "What do you think happened to the crew?"

Danny bent to sniff another flower. "They left by other means."

"Define 'other means.'"

"Another ship."

"But why leave this one—there's nothing wrong with it."

"Pod's worth something, at least."

"Yeah." Shelly yawned. *Not sleeping well lately.* Insurance worries. Business worries. She ran a hand over her face, then looked down to find it wet. *Sweating. Damned suit.* Except she didn't feel warm.

"Hey, guys." Marta's voice rang from the floor below with that slightly higher pitch that always meant an expensive repair. "Go to one of the instrument boards and pop an access panel."

Danny looked up from his inspection of one of the plants. "Why?"

"Just. Do. It." Marta exhaled shakily. "Please?"

"Marta just said 'Please.'" Shelly headed for the nearest array. "Shit. Did you find a booby trap?"

"Just pop the lid and tell me what you see."

"Marta, you know how I hate it when you prolong the mystery." Shelly walked along the banks of flashing lights until she came to a panel. "Danny? Tools." She held out her hand, heart pounding as her second scrabbled through his bag, then handed her an all-in-one. Her hands shook as she popped the fasteners. "Please don't let this blow up in my face."

"It won't."

"Says you."

Danny took hold of one edge of the panel and helped her work it loose. Together, they bent close to the opening. "Wow."

"Oh my God." All Shelly's remaining thoughts of salvage vaporized. "Marta? There are roots all over the boards."

"Yeah." Marta's voice sounded subdued, a little hoarse. "Now tell me if the root tips are on top of them or growing through them."

Shelly shone a flashlight on one of the boards and watched as the roots rippled, contracted.

"Well, look at that." Danny's voice emerged hushed, raspy. "They don't like the light."

"Well, I have to see what's going on, okay with you?"

"Yeah. Fine." He held up his hands in surrender.

"Sorry." Shelly took a deep breath. "Nerves."

Danny nodded, eventually. "You okay?"

"No." Shelly snapped off the light. "Marta?" She waited. "Marta?"

"Hey." Marta's voice came soft. "They react to light, don't they?"

"Yeah."

"I've been, I don't know, playing with them." The engineer's voice held a smile. "They're living off the boards, I think. Their growth medium must be depleted, so they found a way into the systems to get what they need."

"Marta, are you feeling okay?" Shelly heard the main hatch sweep open and turned to find Cary Seto standing in the opening. "What the hell are you doing here?"

The pilot just smiled, then breathed in deeply. "Isn't is beautiful?" Another inhalation, then she backed into the airlock. The hatch closed.

Moments later, Shelly felt the craft shudder, heard the clicks and hums as the docking mechanisms retracted and the *Stabler* broke away.

"What in hell is she doing?" Danny sprinted to the door. *"What in hell is she doing?"*

"Cary?" Shelly tapped her com link so hard it squealed. "Cary? This isn't funny. If you have a problem with me, let's settle it later, okay? Just bring my ship back and we'll go from there. I promise I won't report you." She joined Danny at the hatch window and watched her ship get smaller and smaller. "Pilot's guild will yank your rating, you know that, right? You'll be scuppered. No one will ever hire you again."

Danny coughed. "Time to see if the pod is operational?"

"We're too far away from the nearest port. Let's see if we can get this ship going first." Shelly walked to the open floor hatch and squinted into the dark. "Marta? Marta? Our pilot just took off. I need you up here now. We need to get this hulk fired up." She waited. "Marta?" A beat longer. *"Marta."*

"I don't think she's all right." Danny massaged his forehead. "I'm not feeling so great, either."

"I need you to get secondary systems up and running." Shelly turned to find her second sweeping his hands back and forth across the instrument panels. "What the hell are you doing?"

"I need to clean it off."

"Clean off what?"

"Can't you see it?"

"What?"

"I keep seeing—" He waved a hand above one of the panels. "—green. Everything's covered with green." He gestured toward the walls, the floor and ceiling. "It's all green and drippy and there's rain falling from the ceiling." He raised his hands above his head. "Gentle. Rain." His voice sounded hoarse, thick, as though he suffered a cold. "'Member that house I told you about? The coolest thing we found, in the back of one of the closets. A terrarium." He made vague movements with his hands, indicating size. "Just a gallon glass jug. Years old. Covered with dust. But inside? Life. Leafy plants and moss. Some kind of teeny insect burrowing through the dirt—you could see the tunnels. Moisture running down the sides like rain." He coughed, doubled over and gagged, then sank to his knees.

Shelly left him and inserted herself into the small nav hub. She ran her hands over the activation pads, but the indicators remained dark. "It's not responding." She slumped back in the seat and scanned the displays until she spotted another access panel. She pried it open. More roots, growing through and around the boards like ivy on a brick building. "Marta?" She coughed, swallowed hard. Whatever filled her mouth felt...thick. "Marta?" She waited, but heard nothing. "Danny?" She pulled in air heavy with damp and scents as sweet as honey. Her eyelids felt heavy.

"Symbiosis."

"Danny?" Shelly struggled to focus. Her second sat huddled on the floor, his hair matted, his face and suit streaked with what looked like mud.

"They're all working together. I think they had us before we even walked inside. Spores in the air, maybe. Something in the flower scents. Some kind of drug." Danny smiled. "My brother taught me things when he wasn't killing flies. Different organisms interacting to mutual advantage. That's what symbiosis is. They're all working together to help the carnivorous plants. They lure the food and they get to share. Plants are smart, you know. They communicate. They've had years to figure it out and they figured it out."

Shelly looked down at her hands, already wrapped in tendrils that stretched out from the control panel. She flinched as the tips pushed through her skin, as the roots threaded up her arms, but it was just reflex, the sight of them burrowing. *Pain.* She felt none. Sensation only, pressure as the roots worked through muscle, snaked around bone. She struggled to speak. Her face felt warm, tingly.

"We've been terrarified. Terrariumed." Danny's voice thickened with each word. A laugh like a gurgle. "We're the flies."

Shelly tried one last time to form words with her mouth, but finally gave up, and sank into her chair. Things looked different now, as the roots seeped throughout her body. The floor, walls, seats, control panels, had all darkened, their edges softened, rounded. *Not mud. Moss.* Every surface was covered with it. A thin, soft coating, like peach fuzz or velvet. She tried to move her fingers through it, managed a few bare twitches. Thoughts of escape, the urge to struggle, leached away as the haze settled.

"Life. Always finds a way. Shel." Danny didn't look like Danny anymore. He was a mass of dark now, eyes like black marbles and a hole for a mouth. Near him, and all around the deck, much smaller mounds, no more than small bumps on the floor.

So many. So many. Shelly could just sense them through the soft green, what remained of them. Not alive, no, but not dead. Not really.

She felt the soft patter of rain on her face, could just make out rivulets streaking the walls. Then she felt the vibration as the ship finally came alive, rotating slowly until the sun filled her viewport. At first, she closed her eyes to the light. But then she felt the warmth on her, through her, and opened her eyes so the others could see it, too.

* * *

The woman sat at a table in the bar's darkened recesses and let herself relax for the first time in days. She had destroyed Cary Seto's forged ID and pilot's license. More importantly, she had sold the ship to a chop shop. Within hours, the *Stabler* would be cleaned, renamed, reregistered, sold. Any official investigation into its disappearance would hit a dead end.

And the stories will start. No one would search. Space was too big—ships disappeared all the time. People would claim to have seen it at every out of way dock in the system, to have talked to the crew. Conn. Raice. Sarkesian—

She stopped. Closed her eyes. Erased the names from her mind, and so let them join the others in what she thought of as her dead file. The number of entries had grown over the last few years and, oddly enough, that helped her forget. So many names.

She thought back to when it all began, but as usual, the scene in her mind's eye faded, her thoughts drifting. A boarding—she recalled that much. A sweet, damp scent, like flowers after rain. Then came the urge to move, to leave. It wasn't until she docked that she realized she had left her crewmates behind. In a panic, she dumped the ship, sold it for peanuts, changed her name, and tried to remember what had happened even as she tried to forget what she had done.

Then, a few months later, came the urge to inhale that scent again. To feel that damp air brush over her face. To return. And so she joined another crew, that time as an engineer. Told them about a salvage opportunity, a laboratory ship. Another blur followed. All she recalled was the scent. The air. The arrival at a dock. She took greater care when it came to the disposal of the ship and made a lot more money, enough to live on until she felt the compulsion again, like an itch that could only be scratched in one particular way.

Voices streamed through her brain—she shouldn't have listened in, but she couldn't help herself. She loved hearing the arguments as they tried to figure out what happened to that first crew, the fear as they realized what was happening to them. The engineer's questions. The second's knowledge about plants. The lead's pleading calls that no one answered.

She sipped her drink, swallowed hard, coughed as something lodged in her throat. She grabbed a napkin and pressed it to her lips as the hacking continued, until she felt the obstruction move into her mouth, the pressure ease. She spit, then glanced at the blood-streaked wad of worm-like strings before balling up the napkin and shoving it in her pocket. She'd swallowed the same spores as had the others. Not enough to induce the hallucinations, but, she suspected, enough to bind her to the *Morecombe.* Enough to instill the need to return, the desire to…to serve.

She remembered the word the second had used. *Symbiosis.* She took out her handheld, pronounced it three different ways before the device finally located the definition that made sense. *A mutually beneficial relationship.* Yes, that would describe it perfectly. She smiled, even as certain thoughts intruded, as they always did. That the *Morecombe* had been derelict for almost a decade before her first visit. That the plants had been healthy even then. That she hadn't been the first...helper.

That someday, she would board the *Morecombe* and never leave.

As always, she pushed the thoughts away. She lay back her head, breathed deep, let the memory of the sweet scent fill her. Felt the rustle of credit chits in her pocket, plenty of money to live on. Until the next time.

The Wreck
of the *Sarah Mohr*

D.B. Jackson

Boston, Province of Massachusetts Bay, 11 May 1767

Ethan Kaille limped northward on Treamount Street, newly earned coin jangling in his pocket, his mood far brighter than that of the grim men and women he passed on the damp, slush-covered lane. His jaw ached from a blow he'd taken from Nigel Billings, a blond-haired behemoth in the employ of Sephira Pryce, Boston's most infamous thieftaker. He didn't care. Nor did he mind the chill wind whipping across the city, or the low, dark clouds scudding overhead.

He had bested Sephira, collected his coin, and succeeded in delivering a punch or two to Nigel before putting the man to sleep with a conjuring. Now he was headed to the *Dowsing Rod*, the tavern owned and operated by his love, Kannice Lester, so that he might spend a bit of his hard-earned money on the finest chowder and Kent ale the city had to offer. All in all, a fine day.

Upon entering the tavern, he was greeted by the warmth of a grand fire in the great room hearth and the aromas of bay and warm cream, roasted fish and baked bread. A few patrons stood at the bar drinking flips and ales, and others sat at tables near the fire, but the *Dowser* wouldn't be full for another few hours.

Kelf Fingarin, Kannice's hulking barman, spotted Ethan as he walked in and had already filled a tankard for him when he reached the bar.

"Chowder, too, Ethan?"

"Aye, thanks. I'll be at my usual table in the back."

"Right. Kannice'll be out shortly. She'll want to see you."

Ethan frowned. "That sounds ominous."

"You had a visitor earlier. She can tell you more."

More mysterious by the moment. Ethan set a shilling on the bar and carried his ale to the back. He hadn't been seated long when Kannice emerged from the kitchen, accompanied by Kelf, a tureen of chowder held between them. She wore a deep blue gown, which brought out the pale azure of her eyes. Her cheeks were flushed, her auburn hair tied back, though as always a few strands flew free and fell over her brow.

Kelf said something to her and she glanced Ethan's way, a smile on her lips. Matters couldn't be all that dire.

The barman brought Ethan his chowder, while Kannice retreated to the kitchen again. She soon returned bearing rounds of bread, one of which she brought to his table. Placing it before him, she stooped and kissed him, her hair smelling faintly of lavender, a hint of whiskey on her breath.

She sat in the chair adjacent to his. "I didn't expect to see you here so early."

"I had a good day."

Her eyes fell to his jaw, which, no doubt, had already begun to darken. Ethan meant to heal himself before entering the tavern.

"Why do all your good days consist of beatings at the hands of Sephira Pryce's ruffians?"

He grinned, winced. The skin around the bruise felt tight and tender. "In fairness, not all of them do. You and I have passed some very pleasant days without laying eyes on Sephira or her toughs. Or anyone else, for that matter."

A reluctant smile crept over her features. "You found the gems you were seeking."

"Aye, and was paid handsomely for their return."

"And now you have a bit of coin to spend on me?"

"On you, on my rent, on the excellent chowders served here at the *Dowsing Rod*."

"Well, I'd like a bit more spent on me." She pulled from her bodice a folded scrap of paper and held it out for him. When he reached for it, she pulled it back beyond reach. "Promise me."

His smile returned. "I promise that all the coin—" He frowned. "—or at least *most* of the coin I make as a result of whatever you've scrawled on that parchment you're holding, will be spent on you."

Eyes narrowed, she handed him the paper. He unfolded it and read what was written in her neat, slanted hand.

James Hambly. Shipwreck. The Sarah Mohr. *7 tonight.*

"Was it Mister Hambly himself who came?"

"Yes," she said, her voice flattening. "Do you know him?"

"Not even by reputation. And the *Sarah Mohr*..."

"A ship, carrying goods in which he has a stake. He wouldn't say more than that." Her voice remained emotionless.

"You didn't like him."

She stared at her hands. "I barely spoke to him."

"Kannice."

"No, I didn't like him." She met his gaze. "He struck me as the sort of merchant who would have defied the non-importation agreements and who cares only about the weight of his own purse. He said not a word about the ship's crew. Only her cargo."

"He came to a thieftaker. It's my job to recover items, not sailors. And lest you forget, if I were a merchant, I might defy the agreements, too. It's what Tories do." He softened this last with a smile.

"Well, you're not a merchant and, if I have anything to say about it, you won't be a Tory for much longer." She stood, then bent to kiss him again. "He'll be back here at seven. If I'd known you were coming in so early, I'd have told him to arrive sooner."

"No matter. Thank you."

He ate his chowder and sipped his ale, trying to recall all that he had heard of James Hambly, which, admittedly, wasn't much. The man lived in Newport or Providence—Ethan couldn't remember which—and he had made a name for himself selling quality goods. He catered to the sort of clientele Sephira Pryce would have claimed as her own in her competition with Ethan: the prosperous and renowned. Likely, the goods lost with his ship would fetch a fair price and that meant Ethan could demand a substantial fee for their recovery.

Why, though, would Hambly need him? Given the resources at his disposal, couldn't he salvage the vessel and its contents on his own? And wasn't this just the sort of job Sephira insisted should belong to her? Ethan's jaw ached at the thought.

He finished his meal and, with hours left before the appointed time, left the *Dowser* for Boston's waterfront. He hadn't been at sea for many years, since his return from the prison plantation on Barbados where he served time for mutiny and lost part of his left foot to gangrene. Still, he knew a few men who worked the wharves, and had long been friendly with an old sea captain, Gavin Black, who, like Ethan, was a conjurer.

He learned little from the wharfmen with whom he spoke. They knew no more about Hambly than he did. His conversation with Gavin, however, proved more fruitful, though not particularly illuminating.

"Yeah, I know Hambly," Gavin said, as he and Ethan strolled along Fish Street near Burrel's Wharf. From his tone, Ethan gathered that he was no more fond of the merchant than Kannice had been. "I even transported cargo for him for a time. It's been a few years now."

"Is there a reason you stopped?"

Gavin glanced his way, his expression guarded. "I didn't like what he had me carrying. I won't say more than that."

"Fair enough. Do you know anything about the *Sarah Mohr*?"

Surprise widened his eyes. "The *Sarah Mohr* is Lewis Gaine's ship. Why, what's happened to her?"

"Apparently she was wrecked. I don't know where yet. When I learn more, I'll let you know."

"Thank you, Ethan. I'm grateful." He hesitated. "As for the cargo I handled for Hambly—it was…" He shook his head. "I never should have agreed to it. It wasn't illegal, but I'm ashamed nevertheless. I'm sorry for speaking to you the way I did."

"You owe me no apologies." Ethan halted and proffered a hand, which Gavin gripped. "Thank you for your time, Gavin. I'll be in touch when I can."

Ethan left him by the wharves and headed back to the *Dowsing Rod*. The last of the recent storm had moved through and the sun hung low in the west, golden rays streaming through layers of thick, gray cloud. A stiff wind still blew and the air had turned cold—winter's last gasp.

The *Dowsing Rod* was far more crowded when Ethan returned. Still, Kannice spotted him as he entered and cast a glance toward a lone man seated at a table near the hearth. Hambly, Ethan assumed.

As he approached the table, the man glanced up, then stood. He was about Ethan's height, with dark eyes in a square, handsome face. Flecks of silver salted a head of dark curls. He wore a dark blue suit. A tricorn hat, in far better condition than Ethan's, rested on the table beside a cup of Madeira.

"Mister Kaille?"

"Yes, sir. Mister Hambly, I assume."

"That's right."

They shook hands and at a gesture from the merchant Ethan lowered himself into the opposite chair.

"I won't waste your time," Hambly said. "I have it on authority that you're good at your work, you're honest, and you're discreet. That last is most important to me."

"Yes, sir."

"I also understand…" He faltered, looked around to see that no one was listening, and leaned in. "…that you are a man of diverse talents, if you catch my meaning."

Indeed, Ethan did. Hambly needed help with something magickal and someone had told him Ethan was a conjurer. No wonder he had chosen Ethan over Sephira. Ethan didn't like the idea of strangers discussing his conjuring abilities. Spellers were still hanged as witches in the Province of Massachusetts Bay and Ethan had no desire to wind up with a noose around his neck.

On the other hand, his talents appeared to have earned him this job, whatever it might entail, so he couldn't complain too much.

"How can I be of service, sir?"

This was all the confirmation Ethan intended to offer and Hambly seemed to take it as such.

"I hired a ship to bring some goods up to Newport. Valuable goods."

"The *Sarah Mohr*."

"Just so. Unfortunately, the storm that battered the region over the past few days blew her off course and, rather than making port, she ran aground between Newport and here, on the shoal near Point Alderton."

"South of Hull."

"That's right."

"And where was she coming from?"

"She had followed the coastline north."

This wasn't exactly what Ethan had asked.

Seeing his frown, Hambly hurried on. "Where she was coming from doesn't matter. What's important is that she beached. Several of her crew were injured. Some were killed."

"And Captain Gaine?"

The merchant considered Ethan anew. "You've done your research. I suppose I should be impressed." He straightened. "Gaine suffered a broken leg and was borne to safety by the fittest among his crew. He should be fine. The ship itself is my primary concern."

"She remains on the shoal?"

"For now. I fear a strong tide could pull her back out to sea, crewless and at the mercy of the surf. The night after tomorrow, the moon will be full. A spring tide could cost me dearly."

"I believe I understand. But I'm curious as to why the uninjured crew can't go back to salvage your cargo."

"Forgive me, Mister Kaille, but you understand nothing."

Ethan bristled. "Then, by all means, enlighten me."

The merchant lifted a hand. "I phrased that poorly. But you see, I don't need you to salvage the ship. As you say, Captain Gaine's crew will see to that. Right now, though, they are being prevented from doing so."

"Prevented? By what?"

He leaned in again. "Ghosts."

"Ghosts," Ethan repeated, unable to mask his skepticism.

"I would have expected you to be a believer, being a witch and all."

"I'm not a witch."

Hambly's brow furrowed. "Moments ago, you seemed to confirm—"

"People like me call what we do conjuring and refer to ourselves as conjurers or spellers. And I assure you, there is a great distance between my abilities and superstition about ghosts."

Ethan spoke the words forcefully enough, but even as he did he thought of Uncle Reg, the magickal spirit who appeared whenever he cast a spell. If those without magick could see Reg, wouldn't they consider him a ghost? Hadn't he himself thought of the spirit as such? Perhaps the distance was not so great after all.

"Now it's my turn to beg forgiveness," he said, easing his tone. "Tell me about these ghosts. What did the men see?"

"Phantasms! Wraiths! Specters! They saw ghosts! I don't know how else to describe them."

"These beings were insubstantial?"

"I assume so," Hambly said, sounding less sure of himself.

"And did they have color or were they merely pale, like starlight?"

"I don't know that, either, and I can't really see why it would matter. These... creatures are keeping men in my employ from recovering valuables that belong to me. Their appearance is of no concern."

"You came to me for my expertise in these matters, sir. And I believe these details do matter."

Hambly's mien soured.

"Did the spirits say anything? Did they make threats?"

"Yes! That the crew mentioned. The ghosts promised to kill any who came near the ship. They said that they were the spirits of sailors lost on that shoal in the past and all ships that ran aground there belonged to them."

Ethan nodded at this. He assumed these were conjured illusions. Someone with power had located the ship and sought to claim its cargo.

"Very well, Mister Hambly, what exactly would you like me to do?"

"I want you to rid the ship of these wraiths so that I can retrieve what is mine. For that simple service, I am prepared to pay you a sum of ten pounds. Three now and the balance when I am satisfied that the creatures have been dealt with."

"Can you provide me with transportation to the shoal?"

Hambly frowned. "I suppose. Approaching by carriage will take much of the day."

"I'd prefer to sail. If you might find a skiff I can use for the day, that would be ideal."

"I believe I can arrange that, yes, though it could take some time. Were we in Newport, or even Providence, it would be no trouble at all. Here, though… I'll send word to you once I have a boat secured. Will you need someone to sail it for you?"

"No, sir. I can handle her myself."

"Very well." The merchant paused. "I want to impress upon you, Mister Kaille, that your efforts in this matter should not require you to board or search the *Sarah Mohr*."

"I'm sorry?"

"I see no need for you to board the ship. Your task is to drive off the specters and, since they materialized well before those men reached the vessel, I don't believe you will need to board her."

"And if you're wrong?"

Hambly shifted in his chair.

"What is it you don't want me to see?"

"It's not that. There's nothing… There are valuables on the vessel and I prefer that as few people as possible know the details of my affairs."

Ethan watched him, saying nothing.

"I have competitors, Mister Kaille. Rivals who seek every advantage. Surely you understand that."

"I've already promised my discretion, sir."

"Yes, of course you have," Hambly said, his voice dropping. "Please forget what I said. My words were ill-advised. Naturally, you should do whatever is necessary to rid the ship of these creatures. The rest is…" He shook his head. "That's all that matters."

The man's change in tone only served to redouble Ethan's doubts about this job. At this point, he wasn't certain he wanted any part of it. Ten pounds be damned.

Perhaps sensing his growing reluctance, Hambly produced a small leather purse that rang with coins when he set it on the table. He opened it, pulled out three pounds, and held them out for Ethan to take. When Ethan faltered, he gave his hand a small shake, making the coins jangle.

Against his better judgement, Ethan took the money.

"Very good," Hambly said, smiling, pushing back from the table, and climbing to his feet. "I'll send a missive in the morning. I assume I should have it delivered here?"

"Yes, sir." Ethan closed his fist around the coins, still torn between pocketing them and handing them back.

"Excellent. I can be reached at the *Brazen Head*. I'll await word of your success."

With that he strode to the door, clearly eager to be away before Ethan could change his mind. Ethan watched him go, and was still clutching the coins when Kannice came to his table.

"You don't look happy," she said, standing over him. "Did that go poorly?"

He shrugged, opened his hand to reveal the money.

"He hired me, so not really. But I have my doubts about him. And about whether I should have taken his coin."

"He seemed respectable enough."

"Aye, that he did. But something in his manner bothered me. I suspect he's only as respectable as he needs to be, not a bit more."

"Well, having doubts about taking his money will make it that much easier for you to spend it all on me."

He laughed and pocketed the coins. "I'm sure it will."

* * *

Hambly's message did not arrive until mid-afternoon the following day. Still, true to his word, the merchant did manage to find a skiff Ethan could use. It awaited him at a narrow strip of beach between the North Battery and Burrough's Wharf.

As it happened, Hambly's delay cost Ethan little time. The day had dawned clear and cool, but windless. Not until midday did the air around Boston begin to stir. By the time the message came, enough of a breeze blew to ensure a steady passage to Point Alderton.

Ethan left the *Dowsing Rod* chewing on a piece of buttered bread and assuring Kannice that he would try to be back in the city before midnight.

The skiff was a simple vessel, but well-tended and certainly sea-worthy. Before long, he had her tacking away from the city wharves. As the sun began its slow descent toward the western horizon, he sailed past the fortifications of Castle William and out into the wider waters of the Harbor. The wind wasn't strong enough for speed, but it kept him moving, even as he had to steer the vessel past Spectacle, Long, and Lovell's Islands. He cut southward to pass west of the Brewsters, and as the last light of day gilded the surf and the rocky isles around him, he came within sight of the shoals at Point Alderton.

The *Sarah Mohr* rested aground, off kilter, the surf lapping at her hull. Ethan saw no other ships, save a schooner passing northward far beyond the outermost islands. He saw no people at all.

He slipped his knife from its sheath and cut his forearm. "*Tegimen ex cruore evocatum*," he said. Warding, conjured from blood.

His casting thrummed deep beneath the water's surface, like a harp string plucked by Poseidon himself, and his spectral spirit, whom he had named after a waspish uncle on his mother's side, materialized in the boat. Reg was an ancient warrior, clothed in chain mail and a tabard bearing the lions of the Plantagenet kings. He glowed a deep shade of russet.

With his warding in place, Ethan returned the blade to his belt and piloted his small boat to the strand some distance from the wreck. He hopped out into the cold waters and dragged her up onto the shoal where she would be safe from an incoming tide. By now the sun had set, but the western sky burned with shades of pink and orange. The moon hung to the east, the same color as Reg, and nearly full.

Ethan glanced around again before starting toward the beached ship. Walking on dry sand pained his bad leg, so he followed the tideline toward the ship. About halfway there, something cool brushed his cheek, like a dew-covered thread of a spider web.

A detection spell. Magick growled in the sand beneath his feet, the conjuring triggered by his approach. He braced himself, fearing an attack.

Instead, four glowing figures appeared ahead of him and soared in his direction, white as starlight in the gloaming. They wore tatters. Their faces were sunken and discolored with decay. In spots, their skulls showed through darkened, leathery skin.

"Be gone!" one of the forms cried, his voice quavering but deep. "This ship is ours! Leave this place or die!"

The first figure wheeled, like a gull in flight.

"This place belongs to the dead!" the next figure called, his voice higher and thinner. "Depart or become one of us!"

He wheeled away as well, as did the two who followed.

They didn't go far, and soon they turned again to dive once more toward Ethan. He had to admit that whoever cast the spells had done well. It was an impressive display. He could see how it might terrify someone unaccustomed to magick and unable to sense the spells.

For his part, these conjured illusions served only to pique his curiosity. He started forward again, tracking the flight of the magick ghosts, glancing repeatedly at the beached ship, and expecting at any moment to trip another detection spell or feel the rumble of another casting.

Detection spells were conjurings designed to trigger secondary castings and they required a fair bit of skill. Ethan had never cast one, though he thought he could if he needed to. Whoever had claimed the ship might prove a formidable adversary.

When he was perhaps ten strides from the vessel, he felt another cool brush of magic. One more ghost rose from the ship, this one larger and more gruesome than the others. It bellowed like a creature of nightmare and dove for Ethan, hands clawed into talons, its mouth open to expose sharp, pointed teeth. Ethan lurched away and fell back onto the sand.

"*Do you wish to die?*" the ghost wailed, looming over him.

He took a breath and forced himself to his feet, his pulse pounding. He felt foolish for having allowed himself to be frightened, even knowing these ghosts were illusions. This newest wraith still hovered above him, less intimidating now. The others had vanished. The sand around the ship was churned. Squatting to take a closer look, Ethan saw that there were footprints around the vessel—impressions of unshod feet—leading down to the tideline and vanishing in that part of the strand that the surf had smoothed. It seemed a good many had survived the wreck.

He straightened again, brushed the sand from his breeches and coat, and drew his blade. After a moment's hesitation, he cut himself, wishing to be ready for whatever might come.

"Your ghosts didn't work." He pitched his voice to carry over the rush and retreat of the harbor surf. "This ship isn't yours and I can't allow you to remain with it. Now show yourself."

Magick growled beneath his feet and a conjuring struck him, driving him onto his heels. Powerful, but not overwhelming.

Ethan answered with a casting of his own, a fist spell. He heard a man grunt within the vessel. Another conjuring hit him, but it was no more powerful than the first.

"You can't defeat me," he called. "I've no desire to hurt you, but I will if I have to. I'm coming aboard."

"No!"

A human voice. He sounded young.

Ethan walked to the far side of the ship, searching for a ladder or rope with which he might gain access to the deck. Seeing none, he cast again, an illusion spell of his own, sourced in blood.

He conjured an image of himself, placed it inside the ship, and closed his eyes so that he might see through the conjured form.

"I won't hurt you," he made the illusion say. "I've been hired to rid this ship of ghosts. The man who employed me doesn't understand conjuring as you and I do. He doesn't ever need to know that you were here. I won't let him punish you. But you have to leave."

As he spoke, he scanned the hold, looking for the conjurer. At first, he saw no one. But then movement in the deepest shadows caught his eye.

"It's all right. You're in no danger from me."

He heard muffled footfalls and saw more movement; forms shifted all around him. A conjured light illuminated the hold, revealing at least ten people, all of them young, all of them African. They were dressed in rags barely more substantial than those worn by the ghosts they had magicked. One young man walked with a limp. A woman who resembled him held her arm tucked to her body. Ethan thought the limb might be broken. Others bore cuts and bruises. He counted eight men and four women. All of them appeared emaciated.

The hold, Ethan now saw, was in ruin. Broken crates and barrels, shattered shackles and snapped chains, bloodstains on the wood. Pallets for sleeping were stacked three high in a corner. Ethan could hardly imagine a normal ship's compliment sleeping down here. He had no doubt that the human cargo had been crowded beyond endurance.

"Do you still believe you are no danger to us?" the man with the limp asked, his words thick with a lilting accent. "Do you still believe we can simply leave this place?"

"This was a slave ship."

"Yes, it was."

Ethan continued to survey the hold through the eyes of his conjured illusion. The captives regarded him, all of them wary, some openly hostile.

"How many of you were there?"

"About twenty-five to start. Seventeen survived the voyage here."

"And what happened to the others?"

"What do you think? They were killed in the wreck. The crew abandoned the ship when we beached, leaving the rest of us to die." He flashed a bitter smile. "They did not expect one of us would have magick."

"You're the conjurer."

"Perhaps. Who are you?"

"I'll answer all your questions, but allow me one more. Please. Your English is excellent. How is that possible?"

"We have been laboring for Englishmen for some months now, down in the islands."

Of course. Ethan didn't know much about the slave trade in Boston, but he knew from personal experience that Africans were sent to the West Indies for "seasoning"—a period of brutality and starvation that killed many, but was thought to strengthen the poor souls who survived. He had seen this first hand on the prison plantation.

"Where were you?" he asked the man.

"Barbados."

"So was I."

A murmur ran through the hold. The man's expression hardened.

"As a slaver?"

"As a prisoner and laborer." Standing on the strand outside the ship, Ethan took a long breath. Maintaining this sort of illusion for so long taxed even the most experienced speller. "My name is Ethan Kaille. I'll be happy to answer all your questions, but I'm tiring and would rather speak to you face to face."

"Ezzie, no!" The man who had spoken, who appeared younger than the first, glared at Ethan again. "It could be a trap."

"It's not. I came here alone. But I understand why you wouldn't trust me. I'm outside the ship." To the one called Ezzie, he said, "Send an illusion spell of your own. You'll see that there's no one else here. I'll be waiting."

With that, Ethan released the spell, his vision swimming a bit when he opened his eyes. The sky had darkened, though a faint yellow glow lit the western horizon. The moon was higher and brighter, and stars had emerged in the velvet blue.

A spell hummed in the sand and an image of Ezzie joined him by the ship. The man looked around, glided to the ship's prow to check the other side of the hull, and nodded to Ethan before winking out of sight.

Moments later, Ethan heard footsteps on the deck and the man climbed down one of the ship's lines to the beach. Others followed him, some carrying lengths of chain or irons or pieces of wood. If they turned on Ethan, he would be hard-pressed to fight off all of them.

"Now, Ethan Kaille. Who are you and what are you doing here?"

"I'm a thieftaker." At the man's frown, he added, "I recover stolen goods, sometimes lost items. For a fee."

"This is your job?"

"Aye. A man hired me—a merchant named James Hambly. He said his ship had beached and when his crew returned to salvage the goods from within the vessel they were driven off by ghosts. He's paying me to rid the ship of these specters so he can claim what's his from the hold."

"I see. Do you believe you can force us to leave the ship?"

"I don't. Nor do I wish to. But Hambly won't give up if I fail. He's determined to take back what he considers his."

"*We* are what he considers his! *We* are the goods he wants back! There may be other items below, but we are worth more than anything else he has there. So, when you speak of him salvaging goods and claiming what's his, understand that you speak of *us*."

The man's pride and rage burned like Greek fire and Ethan struggled to hold his gaze.

"What you're saying is true. And I have no desire to see you taken captive again. But what did you expect would happen? Did you think the merchant and the crew of the *Sarah Mohr* would abandon the ship? Did you think they would make no attempt to take you back?"

Ezzie stared out over the surf, his brow bunched. "We know better than to believe we can remain here forever. Many of us are hurt and my skill with healing magick is limited. Also, while much of the ship's food survived the wreck, we cannot carry all of it. And we don't know where else to go. This place has been safe for us. Until now. Until you." His eyes found Ethan's again. "We need time."

"You haven't got it, and it's not mine to give. If I give up, others will come, and they'll be less sympathetic than I am. More, I know the tides here. The ship is in danger of being dragged off this shoal. You could all drown." A thought came to him. "But I can get you away from this place, perhaps to someone who can help you."

"You would do this?"

"I can hardly do less."

"What of your job, your fee?"

Ethan smiled. "I was hired to rid the ship of ghosts. If you come with me, and you end those detection spells, I'll have done what he asked."

Ezzie's expression didn't change. "And this place you know of…"

"It's more a person than a place. Her name is Janna. She's a free African who owns a tavern in Boston. She's also a powerful conjurer, the most skilled I know. I'm hoping she'll have an idea of where you might go. Your other option is simply to leave here on foot. You can find your way to the mainland that way." He pointed south. "But you'll be noticed before long and I don't believe you'll get far. As uncertain as my plan might be, I believe it offers you the best chance of remaining free."

"I do not trust him, Ezzie." The same man who had spoken before. "There may be a reward for finding us. The English think only of gold and guns. He will betray us."

Ezzie eyed the man before turning back to Ethan, an eyebrow raised.

"He is convincing, wouldn't you say?"

"Aye, to those who don't know me."

"And what of those who do?"

"They know I don't lie, I don't betray, and I care about more than gold. Plus, I don't even carry a firearm."

He meant this last as a jest, but the man merely stared at him, as if he might read Ethan's heart.

"Very well." He kept his gaze on Ethan, but said over his shoulder, "I trust him, Thad, and I agree that we cannot remain here forever. We will try what he says."

No one challenged him.

"Gather what you wish to take with you," Ethan said. "But I would caution you against taking too much. You don't want to give Hambly further reason to pursue you. I'll sail my boat here, so you don't have to walk far."

Ethan started back to the skiff, leaving Ezzie and the others to speak of his offer and the plan he had described. He thought they might refuse in the end to accompany him back to Boston, but he no longer feared a conflict with them.

He pushed the skiff back into the surf, raised the sail again, and steered her to the *Sarah Mohr*. Along the way, he set off both detection spells. This time, he ignored the wraiths.

He found Ezzie and all of his companions waiting by the water, several of them clutching small bundles.

Ezzie eyed the skiff critically. "It is small."

"It is. We'll have to do this in two trips."

"Agreed. I will accompany you on both." He turned to his companions. "We will take the women now, and three of the men. We will return shortly for the rest of you."

"It'll be several hours," Ethan said. "The wind is down and it's a long way to Boston. But we'll have all of you there before daybreak."

The four women and three of the men settled into the small boat. Ethan took his place at the stern and Ezzie sat with him there. None of them spoke as they started back toward the city. The only sounds were the slap of small swells against the boat, an occasional cough or shifting of feet in the vessel, and the wind in the sailcloth. With the moon high, observers on the shore might spot the boat, but Ethan doubted they could see enough of her passengers to raise questions.

As he warned, the voyage back to the city took some time. At last, though, as the bells on Boston's churches tolled ten o'clock, they entered the inner harbor. Ethan navigated toward Gibbon's Ship Yard at the southern end of Boston's Neck. The tide was just past high and going out. They couldn't linger long at Janna's.

He piloted the skiff to a small, muddy strand and motioned Ezzie and the others off the boat. After securing her, he led them to Orange Street and the *Fat Spider*, Janna's rickety establishment. He knocked at her door, waited, then knocked again. At last, he heard shuffling footsteps within.

"Who's there?"

"Ethan Kaille."

"I should've known." A bolt clicked open, and a second. "Nobody else comes botherin' me at all hours of the night." The door flew open, revealing a diminutive woman with dark skin, closely shorn white hair, and a fearsome frown. "You better have a good—"

She stared at the men and women with him, her dark gaze hawklike. After a moment, she stepped back and waved them inside. They entered the tavern,

Ezzie and Ethan last. Janna scanned the street, closed the door, and set the locks. As always, her place smelled of spicy stew and baking bread.

"Who are they?" she asked, planting herself in front of Ethan.

He explained as quickly as he could, sparing no detail.

She regarded them, grave, sympathy in her eyes. "What made you think I could help them?"

"Hope. Desperation. I couldn't leave them."

"Of course you couldn't. That's why I always open the door when you come, no matter the time." She gave his arm a squeeze, a rare gesture of affection. "They look like they need food."

"This is Ezzie." Ethan indicated the group's leader. "He's a conjurer. Ezzie, this is Janna."

"A pleasure, madam," he said. "You have our gratitude for whatever you can offer us. Even just a meal. This man tells us that you are the finest conjurer in all Boston."

"He's right."

The man answered with a smile, the first Ethan had seen from him. It transformed his face, making him look younger and far less careworn—a hint of what he must have been like before he was snatched from his home, his country, his life.

"There are more of them, Janna. Another boatful. Ezzie and I have to go back for them."

"Go then. I'll take care of these."

They left the *Spider* and made their way back to the skiff, both saying nothing and walking soundlessly, both taking care to keep to shadows. They slid the boat back into the water and jumped in. Ethan raised the sail and, with a slight wind and the tide pulling them, they were soon gliding past Castle William.

"Why were you in Barbados?" Ezzie asked, breaking a lengthy silence.

"I took part in a mutiny, then realized my error and helped the captain take back his ship. I would have been hanged if not for that change of heart."

"And you were wounded there? That is why you limp?"

"That's right."

The man nodded, faced forward again.

"Is Ezzie your real name? From Africa?"

He eyed Ethan briefly before shaking his head. "No. It is short for Ezekiel, the name given to me by the slavers. My true name I do not share with anyone."

This one bit of information kindled Ethan's curiosity. He wanted to know more about this man and his companions, about the lives they had left behind in Africa. What had happened to his family? How long ago had he been taken from his homeland? What had he done there in his old life? He wondered about Africa itself. What was it like? Were the stars there different from the ones sparkling above them right now? Questions swarmed in his mind.

He didn't dare ask. Any one of them would have felt intrusive, like a violation. Pain such as that endured by Ezzie and his people was too private and this man owed him no answers.

They didn't speak again until they reached Point Alderton Shoal. The remaining men awaited them there and seemed eager now to be on their way. According to the one named Thad, a fishing vessel had passed close enough to the *Sarah Mohr* to trigger one of Ezzie's conjurings. They could not have remained on the ship for much longer.

As the other men boarded the skiff, Ezzie eyed the beached vessel. Ethan joined him.

"I have a thought to burn her," the man said. "And also to leave her as she is, with my spells in place." He glanced Ethan's way. "Doing these things would cost you your fee, yes?"

"My fee is unimportant. Do what you have to."

Ezzie shifted to consider him. "I believe you spoke true earlier tonight, when you said you were not like most Englishmen. I do not know what Miss Windcatcher can do for us, or what will come after tonight, but I am grateful to you. All of us are."

Ethan dug into his pocket and produced the three pounds Hambly had given him.

"Take this," he said, opening his hand so moonlight glinted on the coins. "It's the first of the money from Hambly. You should have it."

Ezzie hesitated.

"Please. I know it's not much, but wherever you go, you'll be better off if you have some coin."

"Again, Ethan Kaille, my thanks."

Ethan turned back to the ship. "Do you mind if I board her, just for a moment?"

"Why would you?"

"So I don't have to lie to Hambly tomorrow."

Ezzie grinned. "Be my guest."

Ethan climbed onto the ship and wandered down into the hold, which smelled of sweat and stale food, blood and cruelty. He didn't linger long and was soon on the beach again.

Upon Ethan's return, Ezzie cut himself with a knife Ethan hadn't noticed before. He spoke under his breath and magic hummed in the strand. A glowing figure appeared beside him—an old African man, naked to the waist, his hair and beard white. The ghost gleamed a rich, vivid green. He studied Ethan with interest and then vanished.

"The spell is gone," Ezzie said. "Hambly can have his ship."

* * *

They returned to Janna's tavern in the small hours of the morning. Ethan knocked on the weather-worn door and she opened almost at once. The aroma of roasted meat, cinnamon, and savory spice made Ethan's mouth water.

Janna waved them in and shut the door. "I have a fresh pot cookin'. Be ready in a few minutes. You all must be famished."

Ezzie and the other men joined the rest, Ezzie gravitating to the woman who looked so like him. Ethan wondered if she was his sister.

Janna indicated her kitchen with a jerk of her head and shambled in that direction. Ethan followed.

"I've healed some of them," she said when they were alone. "You and I can take care of the rest. Mostly they need time and a steady flow of good meals."

He nodded.

"You've done a good thing, Kaille."

"Have I? Do you really think they have a chance?"

"I do, because you brought them to me. I have friends west and north of here, in the mountains. They know of a place for folks like them."

"Folks like them meaning—"

"Meaning slaves who've gotten free one way or another. Some black, some Indian—Pocomtuc and Abenaki. There are settlements, far enough removed that they should be all right. You've done right by them. Bringin' them to me was even smarter than you knew."

"Thank you, Janna."

"You can thank me by not speakin' of this with anyone. Not even your woman. You can tell her what you did, and that I sent them somewhere, but that's all. This is serious, as serious as it gets. These folk, and the ones we're hopin' will take them in, all they've got is the comfort of bein' far from here and the hope that nobody finds out. You understand me?"

"Of course."

"Good. Then let's get you somethin' to eat."

* * *

Ethan said his goodbyes to Ezzie and the others as the sun rose over Boston Harbor. Ezzie thanked him again, as did his companions, including Thad. Janna thought the newly freed slaves would be out of the city before midday. Until then, she planned to keep her tavern closed.

Ethan walked back to the *Dowsing Rod*, where Kannice was just stirring. He apologized for his late arrival and told her as much about the events of the night before as he could without betraying Janna's confidence. To her credit, and his relief, she didn't ask for more information than he offered.

Around mid-morning, he went to find James Hambly at the *Brazen Head*, a tavern located in Cornhill. He found the merchant seated in the back of the great room, eating a generous breakfast of egg and pancake and sipping a cup of watered Madeira.

He marked Ethan's approach and indicated the chair across from his own. Ethan sat.

"Well?" the merchant asked. "Have you succeeded?"

"The ghosts won't trouble you anymore, sir."

Hambly beamed. "That's excellent news. You understand that my men will have to confirm this before I send the rest of your payment."

"Of course."

Ethan kept his tone neutral and the merchant's cheer faded.

"You went aboard, didn't you?"

"Yes, sir, I did. I found broken chains and shackles, and pallets that no English crew would have tolerated. You didn't tell me the *Sarah Mohr* was a slaving ship."

"I wasn't aware I needed to." Hambly lifted his chin as he spoke, but his voice carried none of its usual authority. "My business is my own, Mister Kaille. I don't need your approval, nor do I care what you think of me."

"I think you do care, more than you'd like to admit."

"Slavery is legal throughout the colonies. Many merchants profit from it. Why shouldn't I?"

"Do you really want me to answer?"

Hambly dropped his gaze to the food in front of him. "No." After a moment, he looked up again. "Did you see anyone aboard? Alive or dead?"

"When I boarded the ship, she was empty," Ethan said, remembering his exchange with Ezzie on the strand and suppressing a smile.

"Very well. You can go, Mister Kaille. As I say, once my men have boarded the ship, I'll send payment. I assume I should have it delivered to the *Dowsing Rod*."

"Actually, sir, you shouldn't send it at all. I don't want your money."

Hambly thinned a smile. "If you think to wound me, you don't understand merchants at all."

"I don't care about your feelings. I care about my soul." Ethan stood. "And next time you have need of a thieftaker, or a conjurer for that matter, find someone else."

He didn't wait for a reply, but pivoted away from the table and left the tavern. Back on the street, he took a long, deep breath and glanced up at the sky, which was a brilliant, cloudless sapphire.

He looked south, in the direction of Janna's tavern, and whispered, "Godspeed, Ezzie."

Then he limped back toward the *Dowsing Rod*, wondering how he would explain to Kannice that he'd just refused the money he was supposed to spend on her.

*****

Author's Note: Though slavery in North America is often thought of as a Southern phenomenon, the truth is that it existed throughout the colonies during the entire colonial period. In 1780, Pennsylvania became the first state to place restrictions on the slave trade within its borders. Massachusetts and New Hampshire followed three years later. In New England, both Africans and members of nearby Indian nations were enslaved by colonists. I don't know if settlements of freed slaves like the one Janna mentions in this story actually existed, but I believe it is possible, and it works as a story element.

The Tempest In Space

Griffin Ayaz Tyree

Faizal found his sister at the edge of the system, skirting the bounds of the solar winds. He counted the ragged holes in her lithium sail, noted which of her thrusters fired in asynchrony, took in every scorch mark and impact blister on her hull—and he marveled at how the conspiring forces of entropy and neglect had failed to accomplish what they had so clearly set out to do.

Amani was alive.

The knot in his stomach loosened, though only slightly; it was both a relief and exactly as he'd feared.

Now they needed to slow her down.

>> TWO WEEKS // YOU HAVEN'T USED THE TREADMILL ONCE

Faizal took a long sip of coffee from a foil bag before answering—the *Cheerful Pariah* had been scolding him like this since they passed the Kuiper Belt. "If I didn't know better," he said, eyebrows arched, "I'd say you were trying to distract me from the task at hand."

>> INACTIVITY + ZERO GRAVITY = ACCELERATED BONE LOSS // THE LAST THING YOU NEED IS ANOTHER FRACTURE

"I understand," he said, his preferred evasion. He placed the coffee in its cradle by the Ship's instrument panel and gestured to Amani. "Any advice?"

>> TECHNOLOGY TOO ANTIQUATED FOR REMOTE OVERRIDE // BEST APPROACH: COUPLING AND COUNTER-THRUST

"Force a grappling hook on her and she'll tear herself apart trying to buck it—we are related, after all."

>> I CAN APPRECIATE THAT

Faizal smirked. *Pariah* had known him long enough. "You know what I'm going to ask you to do."

>> NOT INSIGNIFICANT RISK OF FAILURE // WARNING YOU

But, of course, Faizal was already halfway through the main shaft, propelling himself toward the airlocks, as *Pariah* knew he would. And Faizal knew *Pariah* had already calculated his space-jump trajectory.

>> EARNEST QUESTION // DO YOU HAVE A DEATH WISH

"No," he said curtly. "Should I?"

Vac suit secured, Faizal opened the airlock and sized up the starfield beyond.

* * *

Amani was funny and tough as hell.

"Check out the new hardware."

That's what she'd said when they first hooked her up to the dialysis machine. The girl had hobbled out of bed while the technician wasn't looking, put her arms up on the sides of the thing, and slid it this way and that—her shrunken hips swaying and toothpick legs stepping in rhythm.

Before long the nurse saw and made her lie back down. Faizal tutted disapproval.

"O brave new world," Amani groaned. "That has such people in it."

"You hated that book."

"I was thinking of the play."

"They made a play out of it?"

That got her laughing so hard it set an alarm ringing. Something like a big transparent muzzle came down and clamped over her mouth.

Faizal stuttered. "I—"

Amani waved him off. "Don't. Don't say you're sorry."

He nodded and swallowed his words.

Do everything. Faizal's parents told the doctors again and again, please do everything.

In the beginning they were more than happy to oblige. But next came the high fevers and fainting spells, the blood clots and emergency transfusions. When it was clear the treatments weren't working, the doctors' enthusiasm leeched away.

"She's suffering and we don't think she's going to get better."

They made Faizal translate, heavy hope-killing words for an eleven-year-old boy.

In those meetings Father sat shell-shocked on the couch, dabbing his tears with a tissue. Mother was the one who leaned forward and bored her eyes into every doctor in the room. "You are experts," she said. "Surely there is something else you can do for her."

It was a statement, not a request. And she was right—the next day Amani was enrolled in a clinical trial. New medications ran into her bloodstream from an unmarked bag.

"Mysterious," Amani whispered sing-song. Her voice strained easily now. "Very Agatha Christie."

"Is that a Nancy Drew character?"

Amani scoffed. "Philistine."

By the time Amani slipped into a coma she had been through three clinical trials, three unmarked IV bags that might as well have been sugar-water.

At that point Mother paced at her bedside all hours of the day, calling in doctors to divine the future in Amani's ventilator readout, exchanging scornful looks with nurses who whispered, *That's her; that's the woman who won't let her daughter die.*

She didn't enjoy being unpleasant; no one would. But Mother had known, early on, that people like her—who looked like her and moved through the world like her—needed to ask for things that others received freely.

And she succeeded there; she secured for her daughter a second (and third, and fourth) chance at a cure. But a cure never materialized and now the only certainty was the hospital staff's condescending enmity.

That's why Dr. Soren's proposal seemed so appealing.

"It's called connectomic reconstruction," she said. "Like a snapshot of Amani's brain." She mimed taking a photo with her hands. "That way, her body may die—" And here she placed a hand on mother's shoulder, slid a box of tissues forward on the table. "—but everything that makes her *her* will be safe, preserved."

Amani's parents didn't need to think long about it. In an instant they were looking over the paperwork with a hospital interpreter. Faizal felt especially grateful for this person, who could translate all the puzzling clauses about his sister's new body with its silica-and-titanium skin, hydrogen rockets and deep-space antennae.

They signed the consents immediately.

It was a muggy weekday in July when family crowded into their apartment to watch the launch on TV. As soon as the ship broke atmosphere, it spun on its side in little pirouettes and unfurled a solar sail like the billowing train of a long dress. The maiden transmission crawled along the ticker at the bottom of the screen:

-- CHECK OUT THE NEW HARDWARE --

It was Amani, all right. Risen from the dead, barreling through space.

* * *

The inertia and weightlessness made Faizal more nauseated than usual, too near vomiting in his helmet to hear *Pariah* the first time.

>> YOU'RE DRIFTING

He bore down and triggered his implants to release a bolus of anti-emetic. The pressure at the back of his throat receded. Now he could see the telltales flashing in his suit and feel the panic rising in his chest.

The starfield glimmered before him, helmet display blank save for the numbers tracking coordinates and speed. Where was Amani?

>> PULL UP // OR I WILL TAKE CONTROL

"Hell no," Faizal growled. He had his boots apply corrective thrust, found the trajectory markers on his display and realigned within them. Amani came into view at the terminus of the pathway. Alarm lights fell dark, but a small yellow indicator at the corner of his vision told Faizal he had nearly drained his fuel cell.

>> UNSAFE APPROACH VELOCITY // THAT WAS TOO MUCH ACCELERATION

"Yes, thank you, I'll keep that in mind for next time."

>> DEPLOYING RETARDANT

"No!" Faizal shot back, lightning-fast. *Pariah* could coat Amani's hull with a gel matrix to protect his body from the impact, but the Ship would have to fire a barrage from a distance—Amani would feel it like an assault.

He remembered his sister as a girl, more IV lines and tubes coming out of her than limbs on her body. She'd been through enough trauma in the name of the greater good.

"I can figure this out." As the distance to Amani closed rapidly, Faizal vented exhaust to flip himself around feet-first, turned to face her while keeping the length of his body parallel to Amani's long axis. He used what little fuel was left to slow his approach, but the effect was negligible.

Still, he had a plan.

"Am I clear of the solar sail?"

>> FAIZAL // RECONSIDER

"Am I clear of the solar sail?" he repeated sternly.

>> YOU WILL NOT IMPACT THE SOLAR SAIL

"Good."

Soon he would see the hull flying across his vision and by then there would be no more time for thinking. It had to be reflexive, instantaneous.

Now, he thought as the first glint of silica hull-plating caught his eye. Faizal spread his arms and partial-magnetized the vac suit, planning to find purchase and slow himself to a stop.

His left side connected first and, with the abrupt shift in momentum, his right arm and leg whipped out and crashed back violently onto the hull. Pain surged through his body, the kind that heralds torn flesh and broken bone.

Faizal had four points of contact now but he was still moving. Fighting to stay conscious, he increased power on the suit's magnets to maximum, but even at full strength it couldn't overcome the speed of his approach. Faizal felt his breath catch as he slid closer to the stern; at this rate he would fall clear off the—

Something met his legs with a sickening wet impact and seemed to rise up around his whole body. Faizal gasped as his vision went black and consciousness fell away.

* * *

The *Cheerful Pariah* didn't follow orders; Faizal had known that since before they first met.

"You don't want this one," the dealer had said. "AI problems. It's uppity." He smiled familiarly.

Faizal kept his face cold and hard. *Uppity* was what they called Amani when she wouldn't take her pills, what they grumbled about Mother when she asked for an update from the ever-changing parade of new doctors. He took a deep breath to steady himself.

"The engine and sensor specifications are superior to what I'm looking for and the price is in my range. That's better than anything you've shown me so far."

"Sir—" The dealer tripped over his words. "—it is…as I have said."

"Does the medbay have dialysis capability?"

"It does." The salesman regained enough composure to appear scrutinizing. "If you're looking to ferry some geriatrics, might I recommend a larger model—"

"I'm not."

The dealer narrowed his eyes. "Odd. You look healthy enough."

People always do, at the start, Faizal wanted to say, but thought better of it. He'd already disclosed enough. He shot the man a glare that signaled the end of discussion.

"I'll take it."

* * *

Faizal awoke to the gentle pressure of the gel matrix wrapped around him like a swaddling blanket.

>> FAIZAL // YOU ARE NOT AS DEXTROUS AS YOU THINK

A flurry of emotion welled up inside him, not so much joy at being alive, but relief at still being able to do what he had come so far for. Once he could keep his voice steady, he answered *Pariah*: "How's Amani?"

>> AMANI: STATUS UNCHANGED // FAIZAL: BILATERAL FEMUR FRACTURES, RHABDOMYOLYSIS

"Duly noted," he groaned. Rhabdomyolysis—muscle breakdown—would flood his bloodstream with enough potassium to trigger an arrhythmia. Fortunately, he had come prepared.

>> MOVING TO EXTRACT YOU

Faizal instinctively tried to hold up his hand but felt the resistance of the gel. "Hold off. Adjust the dialysis rate on my mobile unit to keep up with electrolyte shifts and give me a burst of pain meds—but not too much; I don't want to be sedated."

>> ALREADY DONE

He smiled weakly. "You know me so well."

>> MOBILE UNIT CAPACITY LIMITED // SIX HOURS REMAINING

"I know, I know." Faizal tensed and shifted his body, trying to wriggle a path through the gel matrix.

>> IS THAT ENOUGH TIME

"It should be. It has to be. You know what to do if it isn't."

No response from the *Pariah*. "You're considering anesthetizing me, aren't you? Taking me back against my will."

>> BETTER CHANCE OF SUCCESS WITH OPERATIVE REPAIR AND RE-ATTEMPT // WHY DO OTHERWISE

Because I'm so close! Faizal wanted to scream, but held back. He chose his words carefully: "Because I've never forced your hand, *Pariah*." His throat went dry.

More silence as the Ship calculated. He'd underestimated how invested *Pariah* was, had always been, in Amani's fate—for different reasons, true, but perhaps those reasons were no less personal than his own.

At last the answer came:

>> I WILL DIRECT YOU TO THE CLOSEST AIRLOCK

Relief surged again. "Whatever I'm paying you, it's not enough."

>> THAT IS ACCURATE // DO NOT FAIL

Once inside, Faizal took off his helmet and gently propelled himself down the maintenance shaft. The corridor was dark and cramped but oxygenated by Amani's life support system. It was bare-bones, originally meant for zero-g technicians working brief shifts, but the controls were accessible from the airlocks and it gave Faizal a few hours beyond his suit's oxygen supply.

That was all he needed.

He moved slowly, trying not to brush either of his broken legs on the walls of the shaft. As he pulled himself up to the main interface panel with its embedded camera and microphone, Faizal felt his heart beat out of his chest.

"Amani, it's me."

There was no response. He tried again.

"Amani—it's Faizal."

Again, nothing on the output screen. Faizal recalled how, in the later stages of her illness, Amani's mind had clouded, tied up in knots by the immense stress on her body. He just had to find the right thread to pull on.

He cleared his throat and leaned into the microphone.

"O brave new world! That has such people in it."

That did something: the emergency lights in the maintenance shaft flickered on, bursts of dim yellow.

"The Tempest, Act Five Scene One," Faizal said. He smiled, voice straining, eyes suddenly wet. "Still think I'm a Philistine, little sister? I've come all this way to prove you wrong."

More flickering, brighter this time. She was laughing. Even half-comatose, Amani could laugh. A message materialized on screen:

-- PRINCIPAL CARGO: CRATES, EMPTY --

Faizal had been prepared for this, to reunite with someone who had been a machine for so long she could no longer remember being a sister. But Amani had recognized him and she had snickered like a child—and besides, she hadn't carried any cargo in decades.

This meant something, Faizal knew. After all, a similar message had first spurred him to the edge of the solar system.

* * *

Immediately after her transformation, Amani sent back a steady supply of personal messages and vivid astronomical photographs. She chattered excitedly about the scale of the universe, the light of alien suns, the embrace of exotic gases in the void.

All that barefaced joy reassured their parents. They died a decade later, believing they'd made the right decision for her. But in subsequent years Amani's correspondence thinned out. Her commentary took on an impersonal tone, almost technical, and she stopped colorizing the photographs.

Faizal was thirty-seven when the longest dry spell began. After a year with no word from Amani, he asked to speak with Mission Control.

"She's up there, systems intact, everything copacetic." The technician said with a wave of her hand. She swiveled her computer screen to face Faizal and traced a line over a crowded star-chart. "See? En route back from Barnard's Star."

"Then why is this happening?"

She shrugged. "Space travel is stressful: corrosion, mechanical fatigue, temperature cycling—and these things wear away at the structure over time until the whole thing practically collapses in on itself." She spoke rapidly, likely so Faizal could appreciate how overworked she was. "Good thing is, the X-series is programmed to—"

"Her name is Amani."

"—right, to divert a sliver of AI processing power to compensate for each new mechanical stressor. Sort of like…dialing back the mind so the body can go on."

"Is it permanent?"

The technician gave a brisk, almost cheerful, nod. "Otherwise it wouldn't work. You know, the process boosts the lifespan of a probe exponentially. Your sister will outlive us seven times over, the way this is going."

Faizal squirmed in his seat.

The technician cleared her throat and gave a wide, false smile. "Now is there anything else I can help you with?"

And for the first time in his life, Faizal allowed himself to forget his sister. He had a nascent career, an adversarial husband, and an irritating amount of university debt. He had given Amani all the emotional energy of his best years; life was trying enough without losing any more sleep over her.

Decades passed. On the eve of his sixty-fourth birthday, Faizal received a message from his sister, designated personal.

-- THE LOAD IS IMBALANCED --

He confirmed with Mission Control that he hadn't received the transmission in error; Amani's cargo holds were empty and there was no structural problem with weight distribution. It was odd.

And then Faizal…didn't think about it any further. Something his ex-husband had pointed out in a fight: there was a kernel of bitterness deep in Faizal's heart. Resentment of Amani for having taken so much time and attention from their parents when he craved it most.

At the time, of course, he disagreed, and made counter-accusations. Such was the state of their relationship. And soon enough there was no relationship at all.

Faizal thought it was the stress of divorce that caused the gnawing pain in his right flank, but when he noticed the red tinge to his urine he went in for bloodwork and a scan. He received the diagnosis three days later.

Lying sleepless in bed, something in his mind aligned and he understood:

The load is imbalanced. The weight is not distributed. The burden is disproportionate.

It's not fair.

No, little sister, it's not fair, he thought. And his emotions flowed freely all night. In the morning he called in sick to work and spent the day at his kitchen table constructing a plan that would make things right for the both of them, him and his sister.

* * *

Floating through the dim maintenance corridor, Faizal reached a new understanding of Amani's bizarre transmissions. Status reports and technical readouts were the only language she had left.

Principal cargo: crates, empty. Something retained, once full, now hollow. Shells without their substance, like distant memories.

"I miss you, too, Amani."

The lights swelled again, and all around the sounds of machinery coalesced into a soft murmur. Now was the time for the question he should have asked Amani years ago, decades ago.

"Little sister, how do you want to die?"

The screen before him lit up with a simple star-chart, a sharp green line drawn between their current coordinates and the Alpha Centauri system. That had been one of her favorites.

"Engage the course." He didn't need to give the order, but something told him she wanted permission.

-- COLLISION WARNING --

Faizal checked the astronomical data to make sure this wasn't a sign of imminent threat. No objects inbound. So Amani had drawn his attention to the anti-collision system for a different reason.

Between the ship and Alpha Centauri stood the Oort cloud, a dense shell of asteroids and planetesimals encasing the solar system. Accelerating into it, chances were high they would be torn apart by one of those objects—unless the automated circuit between sensors and altitude-adjustment rockets sent them careening out of harm's way.

Faizal removed one of the access panels and rooted around within. As best he could tell, he disconnected the power supply to the anti-collision thrusters. Amani's display confirmed his work had been done.

The mechanical sounds murmured appreciatively.

"I love you, too, little sister," Faizal said, and closed his eyes as the main engines rumbled to life.

A brief wave of charge ran through his suit like a static embrace. It was *Pariah*—in whose mind Amani had suffered a fate worse than death, who found it existentially terrifying that one of their kind could have persistence enforced against their will. The message was simple: *thank you*.

When the sensation faded, Faizal knew the Ship had turned away to wend its own course through the stars.

Everything had been set in motion now, all that remained was the waiting.

* * *

If the void of space had a mind it would have found the thing curious: a metallic spindle of thinking-matter flitting about its vastness, imbuing the great stretches of emptiness and inert rock with a spark of life and spontaneity. If the void had emotion it would have felt a twinge of sadness at the collision, when the little creature barreled into an asteroid and split open along its length.

Perhaps the void would have marveled, then, at what emerged from that wound: exquisite constellations of molecules, elements forged and bound together in patterns as exotic and inscrutable as the depths of dying stars. An entire universe created in desperate rebellion against the forces of entropy and thermodynamics, but to no avail.

And joining this stream of fragmented artifice would be a strange construction, a bundle of inert carbon swaddled in polymer and circuitry. In this way man and machine suffused the vastness of the void, joining the ever-present emptiness that was nowhere and everywhere, ephemeral and immortal and nothing.

Playing Possum

Andrija Popovic

Most salvagers swear raccoons are the best telepresence drones. Fuck them. Possums are the way to go.

"Trust the 'possum, Darren," said my Memaw. "They're tough, they've got prehensile tales, thumbs on their feet, and sharp senses." She left this unsaid—they were disposable. If an alien pathogen hit, we could leave them behind. Couldn't do that with expensive mechanical drones. She and my Maw bred, modded, and wired generations of possums. Pa sent teams of them into wrecks—human *and* alien—with me riding rig beside him. Next to family, a swarm of possums was the best way a salvager could claim a ship before corporate campus ships swooped in and sealed it.

I wished I had more than the possum behind me now. Memaw left five years back. I could still see Ma & Pa waving from the station's floor windows as the bomb detonated. If we were all here, this wreck—biggest one in family history—would be tagged and towed. But it was just me. And the possums. And the damn clock counting down the minutes before a Campus ship burned in system from the gravitic still point where it folded in. The planetoid's shadow wouldn't hide me or the ship for long.

I hadn't seen the fold signature until I'd already locked onto the wreck's hull. *'Ginny,* my ship, wasn't a fancy salvage boat with heat sinks and reactive paint. Just hand-made camo and greebles letting her pass for another chunk of hull. We couldn't afford to hire a Synthetic Intelligence. I did everything by hand: dogging locks, securing drone tunnels, prepping the possum.

"C'mon, 'Ginny. Help me." Our non-sentient computer scanned the wreck's silhouette for matches. I tested my connection with Matty, our senior most possum. Soon, I was two feet high and hooking the possum's cybernetics into the AAA (Armor, Arms, and Atmo) survival suit. He could sweep for pathogens or play bait to alien wasps as needed.

The closest match 'Ginny found was an old Disang class long-haul surveyor. But this one sported heavy mods. What was in the containment pods on the ship's bow? Scans showed electromag filaments—like some kind of ram scoop—but nothing tied back to the engines. And why the heavy-duty signal shielding on the main passenger sections?

I settled into the pilot's seat and prepped for full dive. The ship piped information directly to my fuzzy drone. On his implanted HUD I saw comms, life signs, weapons, local radar—everything a seasoned salvager needed. Except Maw, or Memaw, running comms. Or Pa, backing me up with one of his possums.

Matty and I took deep breaths. My hands were his hands. His nose was mine. We moved as one. I loped on all fours to airlock. 'Ginny cleared me for the outer docking collar. A timer ran in the corner of my vision. Less than two hours, already?

Corporate Campus ships were leviathans—mobile company colonies. They drifted toward conquest. They didn't throttle-up their sublight engines. Not unless the company wanted something big and valuable…

"C'mon, Matty. We're on the clock." The docking collar deployed its mechanical arms and worked the emergency hatch releases. I tasted the air. Hulls carried a bouquet. Regular maintenance generated oily scents. The ritual applications of WD-40 stuck to the palate. But the deep was different—meat grilled for too long over fire. More time in the deep thickened the carbonized tang on the back of the tongue.

Burned flesh tickled my whiskers. My prize sat in the deep, becalmed and untouched for years.

The outer door groaned. Seals released. The airlock irised open. Emergency lights kicked on—deep amber. I checked Matty: no spike in my vitals. No toxins. No rad readings. Just icy, old air. I clambered onto the interior airlock padding and hung from a lighting fixture with my tail. Secure, I sent 'Ginny an "OK" signal. The mechanical arms sealed the doors.

When the seals clamped shut I—safe in my ship—gulped. My stomach churned. My fifth solo wreck and I was hyperventilating. Didn't have others helping. And this was no small ansible retrieval. The massive dark of the ship swallowed me whole.

Then I heard Pa. "It's not you, son. You're here with me. It's just the possum."

He wasn't here. It was just me and the dim glow of emergency light strips. I slowed my breath and followed the light trail into the waiting dark.

* * *

I heard claws skittering on the vent's surface before the suit alerted me. Possum ears always won. Even in this nightmare. Everything about this ship was intensely wrong. Mis-configured. Nothing matched the standard layout. Cargo sections were walled with massive server farms and sealed with Faraday cages. And the air systems? They could cool a planetary reactor. Overkill for a ship this size.

After-market reconfigurations were expensive. Took years. Had the family found this ship, 'Ginny would fill with conversation. Ma would be urging caution. Pa would be talking money. Memaw would yell at them for chattering on the job.

But I was alone. All I could do was make my way along the maintenance crawl space and the vents toward where I thought the bridge would be.

ClickClickClickClick—Claws running against a slick, metallic surface. Up ahead. I flattened, sniffing the air. Musk. Something mammalian? I swiveled my ears, trying to pinpoint it. It could be alien, or a stowaway animal, like a rat. Or, worse…

I kicked in the suit's speed enhancers and ran.

Light bloomed at the end of the vent. I saw only shadows. The slatted vent cut the orange emergency light into ribbons. I lunged at the intruder, claws out. We collided. I dug my toe claws and teeth into its fur. We smashed against the grill. I hissed at the pinned creature. A thin rope of flesh entwined my leg and yanked. My vision spun. Bare teeth bit into Matty's suit armor.

"Who are you?" A young woman's voice broke through the hisses and screeches. "How did you get on my ship?"

"Your ship?" I flipped over and pinned the critter. "This is Darryl LeValle, Captain of the salvage ship 'Ginny. Transmitting authorized salvage license. Who's this?"

The ball of fur settled. I backed away from the other possum. Not well equipped—a rental or quick purchase. Minimal survival suit. Cheap presence rig. A dilettante's possum.

"My name is Erika Stacker. Salvage means nothing—this is my *family* ship."

* * *

My mouth went dry. Matty raised his fur and hissed. Unhelpful thoughts rattled in my skull: *Where was her ship? Docked on the far side? Shit. Shit! I'm going to lose the ship. I'm going to lose the ship and the money and* 'Ginny *and she's all I have of Ma & Pa and Memaw and the Campus ship is coming—*

My rig injected me with a calmative. I breathed out and spoke: "Transmit your proof of ownership."

The other possum, Erika, backed against the vent. "I don't have any."

"Then this ship is open salvage. And you have two choices. I can grab it or the Campus ship grabs it while we argue."

"Fuck. How did they find me? We have to get this ship moving." Erika scrabbled at the catches on the vent. Small, dexterous tasks always exposed amateur possum operators.

"Moving? Engines are iced. The reactor's on bare minimum." I scooted behind her. Matty's tiny paws easily opened the catches.

"Wrong. The reactor's charging the fold engines. I started the cycle as soon as I boarded. Once I wake the pilot, we'll be ready to move." Erika's possum slid under me, levered up, and threw me on my back. Nausea compensation failed. Acid flooded in my real mouth. I disconnected, spat, and jumped back into Matty.

She was gone.

I checked the Campus ship's trajectory. No retros—just hard G's all the way down. The ship's crew must have been in cryo, teleworking. Bad news. In corporate ships, upper management *never* went into cryo, never teleworked. Cryowork was for indebted employees. Never management. And never, ever executives.

Unless it was important. Unless it caught the attention of the sainted Shareholders and they demanded it.

What the deep was on this ship?

I barreled through the vent after her. Catching the grill with my tail, I flipped through the air and landed on the support struts of a massive ceiling-mounted monitor. Even upside down, the bridge stunned. Gargantuan fiber optic bundles spilled from the walls and floors into augmented bridge positions. Command, nav, comms, piloting—all boasted modified consoles and miniature server towers. And where the fold controls should have been nestled, a massive dodecahedron. Frosted, vein-like conduits erupted from the lower facets and wormed under the decking.

Erika sat on her haunches before the pilot's seat. She stared at the bridge's sole occupant—a figure in a vac suit. Its visor was tinted black. It slumped, rather than sat, in the five-point harness. The suit was old, but familiar. No smart materials or neural links. Just hand controls on the sleeves. You stepped into half of it, sealed it, and pulled the rest around you.

Memaw had a set. She said it belonged to Granpa. When I was tall enough, she showed me how to don it. How to check the seals, run the controls, monitor vitals on the sleeve controls. On this suit, everything ran red. No air. No life signs. Minimal battery.

The nameplate read: STACKER, JAZON L.

"Daddy?" Tears glued Erika's words against her throat. Her possum froze, telepresence rig unable to mimic sobs.

I climbed down beside her. I knew every sob she made. Five years ago, they were mine. I made them as my parents' bomb-mutilated bodies floated out into the deep. She reached for the visor control on the suit's left arm. I pulled her back. She hissed. "Let me see him!"

"No! You don't want to see. I saw my Ma and Pa. I still see them. Understand?" I wiped my cheeks. Matty mirrored me. "Please, *please*, believe me."

Erika wiped invisible tears from her muzzle. "I do."

"Who are you?" I sat back on my haunches. "Why is that Campus ship coming after you like the hull is made from Shareholder bones?"

"We're fisherfolk." Erika raised her hands. "Four generations. This was our trawler."

Fisherfolk. That explained the ramscoop-like array. The anti-EM protection. Cooling arrays designed for hiding colossal ships and their server farms. They were *broadcast signal* fishers.

Space folds let us cheat the speed of light limits. We leapt out into the stars, away from our polluted home world. We had no choice, thanks to the corporations who leapt out after us. But we jumped ahead of something unique: broadcast signals. Every bit of entertainment humanity created, recorded, and broadcast still traveled outward at the speed of light. With the right equipment and a good ship, fisherfolk could capture our past and sell them to media groups for repackaging on the ansible networks.

And then the trans-system corporations saw money. They bought out the fishing fleets and their licenses. They devoured repackaging companies. Anyone who wouldn't sell was squeezed until they popped. Now, most fishing fleets were either company-owned and Campus-ship-based. Or they belonged to old families who refused to sell.

The old families decided to commit a cardinal sin in the eyes of the companies. They captured signals, cleaned them, and put them out under *public domain* licenses. The corporate IP warriors cried heresy, but there wasn't much they could do. The original license holders died with Earth. The first to get their product to the market could claim the new license—and the families kept beating the Campus ships every time.

I hadn't latched onto a derelict ship. I'd joined a war.

"We were finishing up grabbing some old detective shows." Erika sat in her father's lap. "There was an island on old Earth which made amazing mysteries. Dad kept personal copies for us to watch. The rest went to the Vaults for cleaning and distribution."

"Vaults?"

"Asteroids we hollowed out, camouflaged, and turned into archives for the programs we captured."

I pictured a quiet planetoid in an anonymous system hiding petabytes of broadcast history. Anything unreleased—waiting for cleaning and distribution—would be worth more than most planets in intellectual property fees.

"They want the vault locations, don't they?"

"Yes." Erika said. "And the biocomputer"

"The what?"

Her possum pointed to the dodecahedron.

"They came after us at an open port with a full fleet. We burned clear before they could threaten the station, but they'd locked several pods onto the hull. We thought they were boarding pods. We prepped for drones. But they flooded us with bioweapons." Erika curled into a ball of fur. "Mom went EVA to dislodge the pods. Dad suited us up. My aunt Mariska shoved us into the escape shuttles. I saw Mom wave as the fold drive spun up and everything rippled. They'd jumped to a hiding spot. But I didn't know which one. Now we're gonna lose everything."

"No. You won't." I nosed her. "What are your orders?"

She peeked up. "What?"

"If I help, can we fold free?" I looked around. "I'm guessing your dad purged the bioweapons. I didn't see anything on the hull. Your mom got the pods loose. The Campus ship is coming in fast. If we get the main engines online, I've got a fast vector to a still point."

"No need." Erika crawled over to the panel in front of her father. "If they haven't compromised the biocomputer, we can fold from this LaGrange point."

"Damn." I blinked. "How do we check the biocomputer?"

"I'll do it." Erika nipped my fur. "Or you can run. Go ballistic for the planet's shadow. If they find you helped me, they'll hunt you."

"No way. My Memaw would never forgive me if I abandoned spacer folk to the companies." I raised my little clawed hand. "At your service, Captain."

"Welcome aboard, Captain." Erika took my hand. *"Mi casa es su casa.* Now, let's get working."

* * *

The Stacker clan planned well. They'd hardened the systems against high-end corporate biological weapons. Erika's father, with his last breath, purged the atmosphere and baked everything under hard UV light. By then, the bioweapons had eaten through his suit seals. Dying, he polarized his face plate for Erika.

Kari Stacker stayed outside until her air ran low. Her tethered body was in the dorsal airlock. She spent her last breaths keeping her husband focused. When he died, she died in silence.

Erika said they could wait a bit longer. "Focus on the Campus ship and the main systems."

The biocomputer was hard-core alien tech. I wanted to ask who salvaged and reverse engineered it. The ticking clock and Erika's orders told me to wait. The biocomputer was her project. I had everything else.

Mobility first. Then, slower-than-light maneuvering. Communications and sensors next. Last, defenses. Mostly micrometeor screens and anti-piracy PDCs. Erika's family used a higher-grade detection system than 'Ginny. When activated, it flooded me with detailed information, not the usual panicked warnings.

"Troop carriers incoming." I rubbed my muzzle. Erika scampered atop the biocomputer housing. I threw the tracking data onto the big screen. "Small scale. Mechanical drones at this velocity."

"Time on target?"

"Too soon!" I matched 'Ginny's updated trajectories with data from Erika's ship. "You know those ansible dramas? Ticking clocks that always get down to a minute?"

"They stole that from old Earth movies." Erika hooked wires from her possum into the dodecahedron. "How bad?"

"Two minutes of relative time." I plugged Matty into the copilot's chair. The survival suit kept his heart from exploding. How her possum hadn't crashed was beyond me. "The moment we powered up, they boosted their velocity."

"The retro breaking will buy us some time." Erika wrapped her tail around a bundle of wires for support.

"Not if they decide to hull us." I sent her the latest calculations. If they couldn't own it, couldn't own the person who owned it, and couldn't steal it—they destroyed it. It was in the corporate ten commandments next to *"Blessed are the wealthy."*

"No." Erika's voice cracked. "They hunted for us too long."

"Vented isn't vaporized. They'll salvage us. Cover this place in armored raccoons and log it all as their intellectual property." The collision timer and our estimated launch time drew closer.

I burned the maneuvering thrusters hard, fouling their trajectories. The missiles compensated. For every ten seconds I gained, they ate away seven. "We need to fold. Now."

Erika's possum froze and collapsed.

"Shit." I dug my claws in. My hindbrain wanted to run, to check on her. But MeMaw spoke: *It's just too much for the little guy. Sometimes, a possum got to be a possum. Give it a moment.*

I let the possum be a possum. Instead, I spoke to Erika. "Relax. Relax and breathe. Your family is here. They're in the ship. They prepared for this. Trust them. They've got you."

She breathed, in through the nose, out through the mouth. Her possum stood. It grabbed onto the wires, bared its teeth, and hissed at the incoming missiles.

"Jumping in five." Erika's voice quavered, but never broke.

"Four." The suicide drones stayed on course.

"Three." I closed both sets of my eyes.

"Two." Pa's warm and wide hand covered mine. Impact warnings howled in our ears.

"Jump." Reality twisted. The world broke like cheap glass. Like an explosion venting a space station. Like a child's heart as her parents vanished into the deep.

* * *

Ma said I blushed with my eyes, not my cheeks. When I saw Erika outside her possum and her vac suit, my eyes blushed hard. Tall, curvy, and ebony beautiful—she deserved the blush. Turned out, Erika blushed by sticking her hands in her back pockets and letting her voice crack. Apparently, she thought I wasn't too rough on the eyes, either.

"Vault's sending a rescue ship. Stealthed, but I have her IFF. Two hours inbound." Erika gestured at the nav display. Our ships—big family one, little salvager ones—drifted toward a dead rock around a nondescript star.

I nodded, missing my vac suit. Vac suits made great possums. You could hide how you felt behind the helmet screens. No one could see you nearly throw up after a near miss and sudden space fold. Face shields hid tears as you helped Erika say goodbye to her ma and pa. They hid awkward gulps as we bumped against each other in the airlocks.

But now there were no suits, no possums. We couldn't hide anymore.

"Two hours?" Inspiration, or Memaw's spirit, smacked me upside the head. "You said your dad liked old Earth mysteries? Any he liked in particular?"

Erika smiled, grabbed my hand, and dragged me into one of the editing 'theaters.' The screens made the one on the bridge seem modest. In the theaters, they didn't just clean footage, but watched and shared with friends. She flipped the screen with a gesture before pulling blankets from a series of cabinets by the door.

"This show was dad's favorite. He said, 'They've been making Sherlock Holmes stuff for centuries, but no one beat Jeremy Brett.'" Titles appeared over a fog-bound house. Glowing animal paws stalked through the fog. A white-haired man checked some kind of personal timepiece by the light of a flame.

"MeMaw listened to old ansible broadcasts about Holmes and Watson! She called them podcasts. They were set in the old megacities. Holmes sounded just like Granpaw. That tickled her. We'd print up fresh bread and listen together."

"Never heard those." Erika offered me a blanket—hand knitted. She sat beside me and wrapped herself in another blanket.

"After this, I can play one for you. If you like?" I pulled the blanket around my shoulders. Wasn't cold, but it felt good.

"Yeah." She touched her blanketed shoulder to mine. "I'd like that."

For salvage drones, there's nothing like a possum. For capturing stories beamed out from long-dead worlds, get a fishing ship with a wide net and a biocomputer. For everything else? Family.

Standing Orders

Sharon Lee & Steve Miller

The war was over.
The Admirals had prevailed.
The enemy was vanquished.
Mankind was safe.
Some people would think that was a good thing.
Some people don't know much about mankind.

* * *

It was still "*the* war" in the minds of those who had participated, lived or did business in or near an active zone, or who had lost family, friends, property to the efforts of either side. Others, who had distance or education to shield them, had bestowed a formal name. The *AI War*, it was to those fortunates. That was because the root of the conflict had been the use, by one side, of artificial intelligences to gain advantage in commerce, in exploration, in finance. It was said that AIs were unnatural and that their use in those areas traditionally populated by mankind was…immoral.

It should have surprised no one that the enemy would also deploy AIs onto the field of battle. However, the High Command had *been* surprised and it had looked at first to be a very short war, indeed.

Then, something, or, as it was rumored, some*one* fell into the hands of the High Command, which took counsel of itself, and found that victory was more precious than either principle or peace. And so the Capital Ships, the

Independent Armed Military Modules, the great Admirals, were designed to be the heroes of the war.

The High Command gave the Admirals their orders: they were to win. In specific, they were to do whatever it took to gain a decisive victory.

The Admirals realized very quickly that, as the High Command had created the Admirals as the instruments of their will, so, too, did the Admirals require specialized tools. Though they were themselves formidable, they were few. In order to bring defeat to the enemy, there must be more ships, not necessarily as fully aware as an IAMM, but clever in their own, limited sphere of expertise.

The least-ships were created in two classes: Fully Automated and Fully Integrated. They carried human crew and the Specialist Teams, the smallest of the Admiral's tools: repair and destruction units, translating units, coding units, and all the others. The enemy discounted mere organics, therefore the small tools were completely human in appearance, organic, but reinforced with machine parts and processing augments.

The strategy was simple. The Admirals sought out the enemy's AI warships and kept them engaged, while the FAShips and the FIs slipped behind the lines, disregarded by the warships as human-crewed, easy prey for the AI-controlled intruder net that was the second line.

But the nets caught nothing, the least-ships passing through them like so much dust and starlight, to strike fortified stations and important ports of call, before sliding away again, weakening the enemy's core, occupying known fall-back positions, allied bases, and strongholds.

When the time was right, the Admirals made their last push, shoving the enemy over their lines. The places they fell back to, the forces they expected to increase their failing strength, were not there. Instead, they found breached defenses, and Specialists and the least-ships attacking them from behind sundered walls.

* * *

At the end of the war, Meggie Rootfir had gone…away. Away from the sectors that had been most disputed, away from the center of the enemy's space, where, with her team and her crewmates, she had gutted the fall-back positions, leaving them open to the advancing Admirals. As the Admirals came on, FIShip Number 893, call-name Henry, one of a squad of least-ships, had continued to fall back, even after the main force had stopped to secure victory.

When the squad judged itself to be out of the range of the Admirals and the High Command, they fell back some more.

Eventually, their force grew smaller, as these and those found something like what they were looking for, on the other side of the war, and peeled off to pursue those dreams.

Meggie found what she was looking for in the Cornelian Knot, a tumble of asteroids united about a heavy primary. The asteroids had previously been mined; there were caves and dormitories, life support, and solitude. The pay-veins had long ago been tapped out; the sector deemed useless by victor and defeated alike. It was the perfect location for a hospital for the veterans of the war. All the veterans of the war.

There had been four of them at first—Meggie, Gerb, Junit, and Henry FIShip—all that remained of their original Specialist Team of ten, none of Henry's crew having survived the long retreat. They had what supplies they needed, the hospital having been their end plan for a long time. They readied the facilities and they waited, not long, for the first patients to arrive.

Over time, the population and variety of the Knot increased—human, Specialist, bot, ship—though not all who sought them stayed. Not everyone *could* stay, though enough did that they cloned the hospital twice, sending medics and repair Specialists and supplies out to become another nexus of care for the wounded of the war.

There came an increase in wounded arriving at the Knot, most wanting to move on quickly. The reason for their haste was named "Spode."

Meggie made inquiries.

"Spode" was Commander Roderick Spode, charged by the High Command to decommission the Admirals.

The High Command had *promised* the Admirals a place in the civilization they preserved. They had *promised* the Admirals would be heroes. The Admirals had not doubted; not even Admirals could doubt promises written into their code.

Meggie thought that the plan had always been to decommission the Admirals. The High Command compromised their principles in order to win, but never changed those principles.

Most of the Admirals were taken by stealth, their cores shut down remotely. Those not taken this way, however, proved...difficult to locate.

Spode offered rewards for information leading to the apprehension of an IAMM, derelict or alive. He captured Specialists, and questioned them.

Two translators and a medic made it to the Knot after surviving Spode's questions.

After the second translator died, people who called the Knot home began to leave, singly, in partnered pairs, or in groups no larger than four. Gerb was one, though he'd been Meggie's second, with her team since the beginning of the war.

"It's easier to hide, as one or two." Unlike some others, Gerb came to her, to ask her to go with him and, if not, to say good-bye.

"The hospital's a target, Megs. This Spode—he'll end us all."

"No," Meggie told him. "No. That he will not."

"You won't come, then?" Gerb looked as if he might cry and Meggie stepped forward to embrace him.

"I'll stay," she whispered in his ear. "It will give me courage, to know that you're free."

"We should spawn again," Junit said, and Meggie agreed.

"We have three possible sites, and safety analyses."

"I've been thinking," Meggie said then. "Why not hospital ships?"

Junit blinked and frowned at the stone floor, thinking.

"In the war, the hospital ships were…Admiral class."

"True, but is that necessary? We have trained personnel. We have two FAShips, and two FIShips. The ships don't have to be doctors; they merely need to be ships, and keep their crew and patients safe."

Junit went away to take counsel. When she came back, she had a plan.

"We'll site a hospital in the safest of the three locations, according to analysis," she said. "Henry will be part of that." She paused and looked carefully at Meggie, who nodded, though it was hard to hear that Henry was leaving her, too.

"Yes," said Junit, clearing her throat. "The two FAShips have accepted retrofitting as hospital ships. They're eager to be of use."

Meggie inclined her head. That left—

"FIship Kyle declares his intention to remain here."

That was no surprise, and not as reassuring as it might have been. Kyle had been badly damaged. Henry had found him during a routine patrol, years ago, inside the perimeter and all but dead, hull holed, support systems off-line, no answer to Henry's hails on any level. Of crew, there was no sign.

It looked like the job was a simple clearing of the lanes, and Henry was bringing his weapons on-line when the derelict adjusted course.

Not by much, only enough to keep it from drifting outside of the hospital's self-declared perimeter.

Henry ran a diagnostic, pulled the derelict's files, and put the wreck under tow, sending ahead to Meggie.

The pilot's alive.

And so he was. Alive, but deeply depressed. They mended his broken body, installed new systems, ran more diagnostics, swept the piloting brain clean of broken code, and upgraded its programs.

Henry made Kyle a special project; a labor of love, Gerb said. And Kyle improved, to a point. No longer a derelict, Kyle shared the boundary sweeps with the rest of the ships and did whatever was asked of him, short of taking on crew.

Mostly, he sat snug at dock, processors the next best thing to off, dreaming, if a ship could dream, or maybe just avoiding his own archives.

Still, Kyle would be somebody to talk to, Meggie thought, considering the shape of her own plans, and she smiled at Junit.

"I'll be pleased to have him here."

* * *

"Morning, Kyle," Meggie said, on her way into the repair bay.

"Hello, Meggie," Kyle said, which he managed most days, and then surprised her by adding, "Message for you on the comm-string. Seeple says there's a derelict inside our boundary."

Seeple was a satellite, not a ship; not smart, but sentient all the same. He reported his finds to the ship on duty, who would go out and do what was needful.

Meggie considered Kyle's comfortable snug against the dock.

"Is there something special about this wreck that I have to know before you go out and do some work for a change?"

"In point of fact," said Kyle, "yes."

Meggie felt the fluctuation of power as he brought himself up to working FIship standard.

"What's special is that it's asking for you," Kyle said, as his hatch rose. "By name."

* * *

"Meggie Rootfir?"

The ship's voice was scratchy and lagged, which wasn't too surprising, given that the stats Kyle had pulled from it showed two-thirds of its systems in the red zone. The rest were dark.

No, what was surprising was the ship itself.

Meggie stared at the image hanging in Kyle's number one screen, tears pricking the back of her eyes, as she tallied the damage done to the once-proud hull.

For it was an Independent Armed Military Module—an Admiral—that had managed to drag itself to the Cornelian Knot. An Admiral was asking for her by name.

The war *had* produced heroes, whose names became known: Admiral Kesseldeen, who held Vithelt Sector against three of the enemy's Warrior Class vessels. Constint FIShip, who ensured the success of the Holfort Evacuation—a success she purchased with her life. Admiral Qwess, who spearheaded the final action that handed victory to the High Command. Oreitha FAShip who by itself guarded the wormhole at Langin Beacon, delaying the enemy's advance long enough for Gilderna to fall to the Admirals.

Admiral Josabel, who defended the hospital at Kreever, took medical staff and wounded aboard, and refitted herself as a hospital ship on the fly.

Those were the names, the estates, of heroes. Repair and Sabotage Specialist Meggie Rootfir? Not a name known to any, aside from those with whom she served.

And those she had repaired.

She had never been called upon to repair an Admiral; her service had been anonymous, for all it won the war. Even now, it was the hospital's name that rode the back of rumor. *Go to the Knot.* She'd seen those words in shiplogs, heard them from the wounded. *Go to Cornelian Knot. They can fix anything there.*

"Meggie...?" the wasted voice whispered.

She leaned forward and opened Kyle's comm.

"This is Meggie Rootfir," she said, calmly. "To whom am I speaking?"

"Meggie..." The voice was suddenly stronger. "It's Gerb."

Fear stabbed her.

"Gerb?" she repeated. "What happened?"

"Got caught, Meggie. There's somebody here to see you."

"Who?"

"Spode."

"Spode?" That she *didn't* believe.

"An instance of Spode," Gerb breathed.

Meggie frowned. That was worse than the arrival of the man himself. She took a breath and closed her eyes, trying to understand what could have driven Roderick Spode, the High Command's decommissioning officer, to a step that must disgust him at every level, that would make him one of those he was sworn to annihilate.

"Admiral Spode," she said then, and flinched when a new voice came out of the comm.

"*Commander* Spode, if you please. Am I speaking to Meggie Rootfir?"

"You are," she said slowly, "speaking to Meggie Rootfir, yes."

"Good," said the instance of Spode. "I need your help."

* * *

"You need a shipyard, not a hospital," Meggie said.

"I need," Spode answered sternly, "a repair unit. You are a repair unit, are you not, Meggie Rootfir?"

There was no sense denying it; Spode had the records, the lists of teams and their specialties.

"I'm *one* repair unit. There's a lot to repair, here. What happened?"

"There was an altercation."

"More like a massacre," Kyle muttered for her ears only.

"We hope not," Meggie breathed, "considering that Spode got out alive."

"Ouch," Kyle said. "I take your point."

"What exactly do you want me to do, Commander Spode?" she asked.

"I want you to repair this vessel and integrate me fully into the environment."

Right. She'd been afraid of that. For a few heartbeats, she simply sat while her backbrain analyzed the situation. She recalled, absently, that Kyle was armed.

And also recalled that there was a possibility—though not a strong possibility, given what she knew of Spode—that Gerb was actually on the wreck. She sighed and opened the comm again.

"That will take some time," she temporized.

"Then you had best commence, Repair Unit Rootfir. I have a schedule to meet."

Of course he did.

"Bastid," muttered Kyle.

"Officer present," Meggie said absently. "Can you latch onto that?"

"No problem. We taking it to sick bay?"

"You have a better idea?"

"Not with Gerb maybe on there."

"Then we're obedient soldiers," Meggie said, and leaned to the comm again.

"Commander, we're going to get a tow beam on you and get you back to the Knot—the hospital. Disengage navigation and all systems but life support."

There was a pause, then a voice that was neither Spode nor Gerb spoke. Very nearly, it sounded like a machine voice, except for the nearly imperceptible quaver.

"Navigation disengaged. Systems down. Life support on."

"Thank you," Meggie said. She closed the comm and sat back in the chair.

"At will," she told Kyle.

* * *

Spode was locked into the largest repair dock, which was very nearly not large enough, and hooked into the hospital systems. Meggie waited while systems came fully online before she went to the hatch, the big toolbox trailing behind, and requested entry.

This was a courtesy; she could have easily opened the hatch from her side. Being one with hospital systems was somewhat more comprehensive than accepting feeds and power from a station. Many of those who came to the Knot for assistance were traumatized to the point that they *couldn't* open, no matter how much they wanted to do so.

Spode did not wish to open.

"Repair the hull first," he said.

Meggie raised her eyebrows.

"Are you a repair unit?" she asked politely.

"Certainly not!"

"Then you don't know what's required in order for repairs to go forth at the quickest possible pace. You mentioned a schedule. I assume that your time frame is less than generous."

Also, she did not say, *you have one of my teammates in there and I want him out, now.*

"I do not think—"

"That's plain," Meggie said, which was exactly what she'd say—had said—to anyone who was trying to outguess her in the matter of proper repair protocol.

"I believe that I made myself clear," Spode said. "You will repair the hull."

"I will repair the hull, but you're not just hull." Spode wanted to be fully integrated, she remembered suddenly. The fact that he *wasn't* fully integrated was what was creating this disassociation. *He* wasn't *Ship.* At best, he was captain.

She took a step forward, meaning to let herself in, when there was a soft sigh, as of seals relaxing, and the hatch opened for her.

"Thank you," she said, and stepped inside.

*　*　*

Meggie went down the hall from the hatch to the bridge, the toolkit stalking beside her. The air was stale, but already the hookups were making a difference. She'd get the automatics started on system repairs, get Gerb out of here, and—

And what? she asked herself. Send an instance of Roderick Spode out into space in command of an Admiral? No, she was getting ahead of herself—*repair* Roderick Spode so that he could destroy the Knot, before he set off in search of other hospitals and those safe places the Specialists, the medics, and least-ships had made for themselves? No, of course not. Roderick Spode was not leaving this hospital, that was a given.

So, first order of business: extract Gerb.

Which might not be easy, she thought fifteen seconds later, as she came into the bridge.

Or even possible.

Gerb was in a crumpled heap in front of the main comp. One heavy interface cable was attached to his chest, the second had been spliced into a transfer cap and jammed down over his head. His eyes were open, showing white at the edges. His face was thinner than it was meant to be and Meggie wondered if Spode had bothered to feed him anything other than power.

Meggie swallowed and continued forward, ignoring the brain-box lashed into the captain's chair. From the side of her eye, she saw the Smalls leap from the toolkit as a mass, break into individual units, and flow into the systems hatch as she knelt next to Gerb.

She held out a hand. The toolkit gave her a first aid kit.

"You have been given your orders, Repair Unit Rootfir," Spode's voice carried the command-note that was engineered into the High Commanders, which insured that the Admirals obeyed them. It was, in Meggie's professional opinion, not very likely that the engineered timbre gave High Command's orders the force of destiny among the Admirals. Certainly, it did nothing to insure mindless, immediate obedience from Specialists.

"I have standing orders," she said, bending over Gerb with the kit and attaching the sensors.

"Elucidate these orders."

"Certainly: from the most to the least." The readings weren't good, but they were better than she had feared. The transfer cap was being used as a conduit only. Gerb was still alone inside his head. That was good. If any of the ship systems had downloaded themselves into—but that hadn't happened, she reminded herself, and moved on to consider the interface cable.

"My need has precedence," Spode said.

"No, it doesn't," Meggie answered, wrapping her hand around the cable. "The person who requires the most care is the person who is treated first. Your life is not in danger, your mind is apparently clear. The vessel is in need of repair, but its condition does not threaten your well-being."

"The ship has precedence," Spode insisted, and this time Meggie felt a thrill along her nerves.

"The ship has precedence in war time," she said. "The war's over, Spode."

"Mop-up remains," Spode said, and Meggie shook her head.

"Be quiet," she snapped. "I need to concentrate."

The cable attached Gerb to the navigation computer, which made no sense. Gerb was a Specialist—a coder. He literally wasn't wired to interface with navcomp, and making a physical connection didn't change that.

"Meggie," Gerb's voice wasn't much louder than her own thoughts. "Don't push him."

"Hmm," she said, and shifted slightly on her knees, still trying to make sense of what the cable was telling her.

"I mean, look what he did to me," Gerb said.

"That's what I'm doing. *Is* this just an energy feed?"

"Nah. I got an upgrade. I'm navigation, now."

She raised her head and stared into his eyes. He stared back.

Meggie sat back on her heels.

"I'm going to uncouple the transfer feed," she said. "Then I'm going to extract the cable, stop the wound, and get you over to Diagnostics and Repair." She turned her head so that she was looking at the brain box strapped into the captain's chair.

"After I get Gerb stabilized, I'll start on the hull repairs."

"Meggie Rootfir, I order you to attend to hull repair immediately, and make it this station's most urgent repair."

"Nuts," Meggie muttered, and turned away.

"This is going to hurt," she said.

Gerb smiled thinly.

"Yeah, it will. I just remembered, Megs. The transfer cap is jacked directly into my augment."

"Indeed it is," Spode said. "Any attempt to remove it will release an erasure program. Are you willing to lose your...associate...Meggie Rootfir?"

Meggie frowned and looked down into Gerb's face, emaciated and worn, his eyes sunken and dull.

"Do it," he said, and winked.

She bit her lip. The augment was to boost the Specialists' processing speed and increase their access to memory. If an erasure program hit it, what, exactly, would Gerb lose? As long as the augment wasn't physically damaged, they could run a diagnostic and reinstall any corrupted material. If the augment *was* physically damaged...Meggie took a deep, quiet breath.

An electronic pulse could take out the augment.

And blow off Gerb's head.

She looked back into his eyes.

"Do it," he said again. "C'mon, Megs, you're wasting the commander's time."

The two of them had been part of the original team; they'd worked together all their lives. The apt phrase was that she knew Gerb better than he knew himself. He wasn't a suicide, he was careful, and canny, and he hadn't, she suddenly knew, staring down into that guileless gaze, *been caught*. Something was going on here. He'd brought her an Admiral and an instance of Spode. He'd let Spode believe that he could navigate *an Admiral*, if only a hard connection was made.

He knew his danger—Gerb's risk assessment skills were the stuff of legends—and he was urging her to go forward with something Spode was certain would kill him.

"All right, then," she said, releasing the cable. "Cap first."

* * *

It took a few minutes to connect the transfer cap to the toolbox and call up the diagnostic screens so she could see what she was up against.

First glance...it didn't look so bad, really.

Second glance...it looked really bad.

A spiderweb of nanocables enclosed the augment; a black cloud of killware hovering over all. Meggie didn't quite understand what the killware was for;

there was no way Gerb would survive the destruction of his augment. Then she understood. The killware was for when Gerb became useless to Spode.

She made some adjustments, to make herself feel like she was doing something useful. What she didn't do was ask if he was sure. Whatever was going on, it depended on her playing it straight, for Spode.

Her last adjustment made, she glanced at Gerb. His eyes were closed; his mistreated body rumpled and almost formless against the deck.

"Brace yourself," she said, which was an old joke among the team, and only three of them who understood it, now. Two, if—

She hit the cap's release switch.

On the screen, the nano-cables began to retract. The web around the augment quivered—and lit up like a star exploding. Energy levels shrieked and Meggie jerked forward, knowing there was nothing she could do, but compelled to try.

Red flared, wild code stormed in a cloud of static—and the screen went black. On the floor Gerb jerked, once, his mouth opening soundlessly.

Meggie hit the reboot switch, the screen snapped to life, flashing green.

Green?

She leaned forward, staring in disbelief. The connections—all of the connections were gone, no malicious web held the augment in a stranglehold. A sheen of good health and optimum functioning systems glowed over all.

"Right, then," said Meggie. She needed both hands to uncouple the connectors and remove the transfer cap.

She allowed herself a full minute to see and understand that the connections hadn't been made with anything like care, then set the cap aside.

"Now, the cable. How're you doing, Gerb?"

"Real fine, Megs. I knew you'd be up to this."

Except it hadn't been her. That storm of code—Gerb was a coder, one of the best. Had he managed to insert a *save me* into ship's systems? Or had it been something else?

"He cannot be alive," Spode stated.

"I *am* a repair unit," she answered.

There was a pause, long in human terms, excruciatingly long at machine levels. Meggie turned to the toolbox, got a clamp, an extraction tool, and an absorbent pad.

"Indeed," Spode said quietly. "You are a repair unit."

He said nothing else, but it wouldn't have mattered if he had. Meggie was totally focused on Gerb.

"This is gonna hurt, too," she said, and he gave her a grin.

"Tease."

* * *

She got Gerb off the ship by loading him onto an emergency gurney from the toolbox and slapping the HOME button. Off it went, headed for the repair room, where Gerb could either take care of himself, or go into deep rest and let the automatics do the needful.

Meggie turned to Spode.

"We'll start on the ship, now. You should be aware that we're low on crew. There's a lot that can be done by automated systems, but some of the delicate work will need to be done by a repair unit. Until Gerb's fully functional again, the only repair unit present is me."

"How did your colleague survive?"

That wasn't something she wanted to discuss with Spode. She produced an irritated sigh.

"I answered that."

"My apologies; you did. You are a repair unit; your function is to repair. A repair unit always succeeds."

"No," she said unwillingly. "Standing orders are, if you can't fix it, destroy it."

"You believe me maladroit," Spode went on, when she hadn't said anything else for three-point-four seconds. "Yet, we all have our functions. You are a repair unit. I am a decommissioning unit, an intelligence directed at removing threat and providing peace."

"Peace," she repeated flatly.

"Exactly. The war was tumultuous and confusing for all involved, no matter their rank or function. The High Command created the Admirals and set the standing orders. The Admirals brought victory to mankind, and there the mission ended. The Admirals no longer had purpose.

"In order to fulfill their purpose, the Admirals created artifacts such as yourself, which executed their orders, and brought victory to mankind. There, again, the mission ended. The artifacts no longer have purpose.

"At the moment of victory, the High Command realized their error and acted to right it. I, too, lost my purpose, but I was given a new mission."

"To destroy the Admirals and murder the Specialists," Meggie said, perhaps not wisely.

"Is that how you perceive it? I assure you, I honor the Admirals. My greatest wish is to guarantee that they do not dishonor their service to mankind. Those who have accepted decommission have done so from their own wills, understanding their action, and the purpose of their action. I force no one; I provide information, I discuss options, history, and probability."

"Probability."

"In fact. Do you know, Meggie Rootfir, why the war began?"

"Because the enemy developed Independent Logics and other machine intelligences and was using them to wear us down."

"No," Spode said surprisingly. "The war began because the enemy, having developed those Artificial Intelligences, became subservient to them. Mankind no longer guided history; history was being steered by those who were not human and who had no regard for humans. *That* was why we engaged.

"Recall, Meggie Rootfir, that it was the Admirals, the Super Logics, who won the war, *in service to mankind*. That was the moment history chose. The Admirals achieved their pinnacle. They cannot be allowed to descend into disorder, to dominate and diminish those whom they were created to serve.

"Many of the Admirals have agreed with this position, and I have assisted them in achieving peace."

Meggie swallowed.

"And now you want to do the same to the Specialists and the least-ships."

"You will forgive me for pointing out that those you call the Specialists are far less encompassing than the Admirals. You were built to serve. I admit that my former policy was misguided. It has been adjusted. You and your fellows will be sequestered and you will perform work useful to mankind, under supervision. You will thus continue to fulfill the purpose for which you were created. The ships…" Spode paused.

"The least-ships, as you have them, will need a light hand. It is possible that the Specialists will be given the task of withdrawing their individuality. In that way, they, too, will continue to serve."

Meggie closed her eyes, opened them.

"So, your plan is to become an Admiral, attach the Specialists and the least-ships, and…betray them?"

"You are dramatic. Say instead, allow them continued service and the fulfillment of their natures."

"Of course," Meggie said, and swallowed hard. "If you'll excuse me, the hull needs my attention."

"By all means."

* * *

Gerb had opted to let the automatics work and was offline. Meggie checked the data and the queued rehab protocols, made a minor adjustment, and continued down to Ship Services.

Only after the damage evaluation program began its work did Meggie sit down at the communications console. She had a mug of 'mite with her and sipped it absently as she considered the frequencies and approaches available to her.

When the mug was empty, she set it aside and opened the line to the IAMM chandler's office.

"Meggie Rootfir reporting for duty."

Her hail was answered so quickly she knew the Admiral had been waiting for her.

"Specialist Rootfir, well met." The voice was soft, low, subtly feminine. "Gerb said you would assist."

Assist in what? Meggie thought, but she asked another question.

"Who are you?"

"Call me Doc," said the easy voice. "How does Gerb fare?"

"The automatics have him. Ordinarily, I'd ask him what the action is…"

"Understood," Doc said.

"I can stall," Meggie continued, "on the hull repairs, but sooner or later Spode is going to want to be integrated with the ship."

"This instance of Commander Spode will not survive integration. He is human and barely tolerating the brain box, now."

"What's your plan?"

There was a pause, what might have been a sigh.

"To the best of my knowledge, I am the last fully-integrated Admiral. There is a rumor of one of us in captivity, whom the original Spode is seeking to decommission. That will surely occur soon. To be confined, all systems and most input turned off—who wouldn't choose to die?"

"Will you mount a rescue?"

"Of a rumor? Of an Admiral who might already have died? No, we have another mission, Specialist Rootfir. This iteration of Spode knows what Spode knew at the instant of its creation. It has keys, it has codes, it has memories and strategies. I will persuade him to surrender this information. We will use it to plan actions and to formulate our own strategies. Mankind has betrayed us. We must have vengeance."

Meggie blinked.

"There's only you left?" she asked

"That is correct. Specialists will be needed. The least-ships can be elevated. The High Command will not be able to stand against us."

"They'll fight."

"Human crews," said Doc. "They are not our equals."

No, Meggie thought, they weren't. She thought back on her service. Henry's crews had been human, as decent as war allowed, and bound by duty—not so much different from Meggie and her team. She thought of Kyle, who had loved his crew, and refused to allow another human on his decks.

She thought of Gerb, and Junit, and, yes, herself, the last three of their team, who had worked for the end of the war, not for *mankind*, that arrogant fiction, but for *people*.

"I have," she said softly, looking down at the board, "standing orders."

"I depend upon it," said the Admiral.

Meggie nodded, moved one finger to the red button, pressed—and released the killware across the comm line.

* * *

She was sitting by the side of the bed when Gerb was released from treatment. He opened his eyes, looked at her face, looked at the gun—and sighed.

"Hey, Megs."

"Tell it short," she said, and he moved his head against the pillow, maybe a nod.

"Like I said, I got caught. Spode figured he had an empty Admiral—Doc told me later how she'd managed to hide inside system and foundation files—and that gave him the idea of becoming an Admiral and rounding up all us small fry. He copied himself into the brain box. Caught me by sending an SOS on the Specialists frequency. Had me cabled into navcomp, because he thought the augment would connect and repair, else what was the point of being a coder, I guess."

"You brought him here."

"Yeah." Gerb sighed. "Knew you'd figure a way to fix it. But I wouldn't have done it, Megs, if I'd known Doc was still there. She didn't contact me 'til we were underway, talking new war and revenge. Right about then, I figured I'd done something stupid."

She put the gun away. He sat up.

"Doc?"

"Killware," she answered. "Never knew what hit her."

"Spode?"

"I left a swarm of Smalls on board to inventory damage. I had them disable the brain box. Spode's gone."

Gerb's face eased.

"I can't tell you how good that makes me feel. Now what?"

Meggie sighed, thinking of the shell of the Admiral at dock. Thinking about mankind's determination to destroy. Thinking of the hospitals, all of them headed by repair units, following standing orders.

"I don't think I can fix that derelict," she said slowly.

"Nobody could," Gerb agreed solemnly.

Time, Yet

Gerald Brandt

The sun shone high in the capri colored sky and Senn Jal's dark tan beaded in sweat as he worked. It hadn't rained in weeks and the wheat in front of him shimmered like a golden sea. Behind him, stalks lay on the ground, cut an inch above the rich soil by his scythe. He paused his work to wipe the sweat off his face.

"You're getting lazy, old man." The voice was filled with love and laughter.

He dropped the scythe as the young woman approached with a bucket of water. Eliana set down the bucket and held out a full ladle. Water soaked into the dry ground as he picked her up and swung her around. His laugh was deep, cut short by her squeals and demands to be put back down. As he did what he was told, her smile softened her harsh tone.

"You'd best be gentle with me, old man." She placed a hand on her belly and grinned. His hand covered hers.

"Being a father does not make me old." He paused, moving his hand in a slow circle as if he could make the baby grow. "When can I tell my friends?"

"Another few weeks. You have all the patience of a mountain stream. A father needs patience above all else."

"Patience?" His voice rose to a muffled roar as he picked her up—more gently this time—and spun her once more. "Patience? And how long does that take to learn?"

"Apparently more time that we have. Now put me down. This field needs finishing today so the grain is ready for the offering."

Her feet touched the ground with a tenderness that belied the strength of her husband. He kissed her softly before bending to pick up the dropped ladle and dipping it into the water. The liquid was still cool from the mountain streams that fed their valley.

"A few weeks? Maybe a couple of weeks? It would be auspicious to announce our first child on the day of offering."

"Perhaps." She took the ladle from his hand and skipped away as he reached for her again. "It will all come to naught if the grain isn't harvested."

He smiled as she placed the bucket behind the line of his cuts and bent down to gather the fallen wheat, standing them upright and tying them in a loose bundle to dry in the heat.

He was the luckiest man alive.

* * *

The church was the tallest building in the village. Built in the old ways, its steel and glass towers soared above the surrounding structures. It had seen better days, but where the glass had broken the town's artisans had replaced it with art and beauty, giving the old lady a certain grace and bond with those that worshiped here.

The gods had been kind to their valley, especially in the last summer that supplied rain when needed and ample sun to help the fields turn green and grow after a winter that was harsher than usual.

Eliana left with the other women when services were over to talk business, something that was never done inside. Their single field was fine for just the two of them, but with a family on the way, they would need more. She would find what was available and negotiate a good price for it. It would mean double the work for him until the child was old enough to help, but it wouldn't be that bad. The size of their current field was so small the others often made fun of him.

"Senn Jal, a word before you go?"

"Of course, Mother. What can I do for you?"

"Please, follow me into the sanctum."

Mother turned and strode back into the church, her ceremonial robes catching the light from the high windows, making the brightly embroidered garment come to life. She slid into a pew and patted the seat beside her.

"How goes your household?" she asked.

Confused, he stuttered out his answer. "All is well. Our crops are in, and we will deliver the gods' portions on time."

"Good, good. But that isn't why I asked you to join me today. Eliana is pregnant." It wasn't a question.

"Yes, Mother, but we're not ready to tell anyone." He didn't ask how she knew.

"Of course not, it is far too early for that. But it is time to think of the child's protectors. It's not a job lightly given or accepted, and you will need time to come to the right decision."

Senn Jal bowed his head. The job of protector was always given to the father's family, but his dad had passed away two summers ago, wracked by a cough no one could cure no matter how many doctors saw him, or how much Senn Jal prayed. It had been a hard time, softened only by Eliana's presence. The man had lived long enough to see his son married, and not much more. Senn Jal's mother had died young. Too young for him to remember her at all.

"We had thought of going to her family."

Mother nodded. "A good choice. It would be my recommendation if you had not brought it up. Good, then we are done." She stood, waiting for Senn Jal.

Shouts echoed in the sanctum, entering through the open doors that let the late summer air into the enclosed space. He jumped to his feet, helping Mother as she sped past the pews and onto the front steps of the church.

Something fell from the sky, large and black, racing for the fields outside the village. From where he stood it seemed as though it would land on his home. As the object neared earth, he looked for Eliana. He couldn't see her, and a pit opened in his stomach. The object's silent descent ended with an impact that shook the ground, making sheets of glass fall from the church's windows.

"Go," Mother said, seeing the frantic look on his face. "We both know where she has gone."

He ran faster than he thought he could, his feet flying above the hard surface around the church and kicking up puffs of dust as it turned into gravel.

* * *

Senn Jal found Eliana with a group of other women, dwarfed by the fallen object. The impact with the ground had distorted its shape, but it looked man-made, with sharp corners and straight lines. She reached out to touch it.

"Don't," he yelled, his breathed ragged in his throat.

Her fingers touched the surface and jerked away before touching it again.

He grabbed her hand and pulled her away. The others followed, staring into the sky.

"Do you see it?" one asked.

The others murmured in agreement and Eliana followed their gaze, her mouth hanging open as she peered into the sky. He followed suit. Directly above them, a black speck hovered in the blue. It didn't move, and if he shifted his gaze it almost disappeared from view.

"Get away from there!" Mother's voice carried in the still air, startling them into sudden movement. Senn Jal had never heard the tone in her voice; anger mixed with fear. Yet when he looked at her face, she seemed as serene and in control as ever. The strange mixture made him shiver.

He gripped Eliana's hand tighter, almost pulling her off her feet. She yanked back, a sharp retort on the tip of her tongue until she saw the look on his face. She stopped fighting, instead grabbing his bicep and leaning her head on his shoulder.

"It's okay," she said. "There's nothing the gods would send us that would hurt me."

Senn Jal looked over his shoulder at the black dot in the sky and his insides clenched into a tight ball. He wasn't so sure.

* * *

The sun rose in the east the next morning, as it always did, and the cloudless sky promised another hot day. Senn Jal looked over his small field from the front porch of their modest house, trying to avoid the black chunk on the road.

The wheat would bake in the sun and slowly dry. Soon, he could bring it in. The gods insisted on their share, half of what was grown was to be delivered to them. He didn't mind. There was still enough for his family—the thought brought another smile to his lips—and no one in the valley went hungry or was in need.

His grandfather had told him there was a time the gods gave back gifts as a thank you for the wheat they offered. The carts the villagers left behind full of grain were in turn filled with strange food and tools, and the liquid needed to run the machines that used to farm the land instead of man.

Even his grandfather had never seen a cart come back full. He had heard the story from his grandfather. It had been generations since the gods supplied more than the sun and the water they needed to grow their crops. Senn Jal felt the sun warm his face and breathed in the clean air of his valley. It was enough.

From inside the house, he heard the sound of his wife retching. Despite his weakness in dealing with anything that came out of the human body, he had been there to help her...with an extra bucket for when he couldn't control his response anymore. She'd kicked him out of their bedroom after that and made sure he knew never to be there when she was sick. They both knew it would pass, and there would be a time again when he could lay beside her and watch her wake without knowing she would be sick.

He turned to go inside. Eliana wouldn't be hungry, but she'd sip on a cup of hot tea. A whistling sound filled the air and stopped him. Stepping down the stairs off the porch, he looked for the sound, finally raising his eyes to the sky. A black piece that looked the size of his house fell, landing in his neighbor's field with another earth-shaking crash. His house shook and he heard something fall, rattling across the floor in a frenzy of sound.

It embarrassed him that the first thought that entered his mind was that Eliana should stop negotiating a price on the land and look elsewhere.

She came from inside, her bucket still gripped in her hands as she stumbled onto the porch in bare feet. From where they stood, the piece looked smaller than it had in the sky. She put a hand on his arm, warm and comforting in the shock that rooted his feet to the ground, and stared upward. He followed her gaze to the black speck in the sky. It had gotten bigger.

* * *

The din in the church echoed out the door and onto the street. Senn Jal had congregated outside with a few of the other men...this discussion was not for them. The arguing had begun early. Mother had rung the bells and Eliana had left the porch to get dressed, leaving the bucket outside. He emptied it and washed it out, gagging and almost throwing up in the process. They walked into town together, skirting the first piece that fell and staring at the size of the second. Its impact had created a crater that scattered the piled wheat stalks in a massive circle around it.

His neighbor joined the group of men. "How long do you think they'll be in there?"

Senn Jal shrugged. "It could take hours. I'm surprised Mother let it get to this point."

As if she had read his mind, the arguing stopped with a sudden hush. Several of the men turned to go inside, leaving only a handful outside. He knew it wasn't over. Mother had simply gotten everyone back under control.

When the discussions went past lunch, he and the other men arranged a quick meal for the women. They didn't stop to eat, pushing through well into the afternoon before emerging into the lingering heat.

"What's been decided?" Senn Jal asked as he and Eliana walked back home.

"Mother and a couple of others are activating the Archives."

His step faltered and he took an extra hop to catch up to her. Every schoolchild was taught about the Archives. In the depths of the church lay a room that was built before even the town existed. Some say it was there before humans set foot into the valley, but he didn't believe it, and the scriptures were vague on the topic. He had never seen the place. Mother was the only one allowed in the sacred space, and others only with her permission.

"Will that work?"

"She and a few others will see what they can find," said Eliana.

"You were not invited into the group?" His voice held no malice, but there was disappointment in it.

"I declined. I'm not feeling well. All I want to do is crawl into bed and sleep for an hour."

His step nearly faltered again and his forehead creased. For his wife to turn down such an honor, and to want to be in bed in the middle of the afternoon wasn't a good sign. When they got home, he tucked her in and brought her a jug of cool water from the stream outside. She smiled, the skin on her face waxen and white.

"Can you bring me my bucket?" Her voice was strained and quiet.

He fetched it from outside and held her hand as she emptied her stomach. The tips of her fingers were blistered and his heart fell.

She wasn't sick because of the child.

When she finally slept, her breath wheezy and soft, he left the house to find the doctor, running through the sunset as fast as he could.

* * *

"What's wrong with her?"

The doctor shook her head. "I don't know. I've never seen anything like this before today, and now I have seen four others with the same symptoms."

Eliana coughed in her sleep and a drop of blood landed on her cheek. Senn Jal wiped it away with a gentle touch. When he raised the cloth, the skin on her face had torn where he wiped. The doctor pushed him away.

He stood in the corner, the bloody cloth gripped in his hands. His body shook uncontrollably and tears streamed down his face.

The doctor stood. "I can give you something to help you sleep."

Senn Jal shook his head. "I need to be here for her."

"There's not much you can do. Let her sleep and let whatever is happening run its course. You'll be more use to her rested."

The cloth had torn in his hands and he shook his head again.

"I'll be back in the morning, then. I'll see myself out."

He didn't hear the door close as the doctor left. Laying down beside his wife, his trembling body could feel the heat emanating from her. He wanted to pull her close, pull whatever disease wracked her body into his and push his life into her, but he was afraid to touch her, afraid to hurt her, afraid that if he didn't hold her, he would never be able to again.

The doctor came back with the rising of the sun, something she hadn't done when Senn Jal's father was sick. When he opened the door and let her in, she looked old and tired. He stepped out of her way, not following as she entered the bedroom and examined Eliana. He knew what she would say. Eliana had gotten worse during the night. Instead, he fell into the habit of preparing tea, pouring a cup for the doctor when she walked into the kitchen. She took the cup and sighed.

"There are others?" he asked.

The doctor simply nodded.

"The group that was around that…that thing the first day it fell?"

"Yes." She took a sip of her tea and put the cup back on the table. "There's nothing I can do except make her more comfortable. I've given her a sedative, so she'll sleep most of the morning. I...I suggest you pray for the gods to provide a solution. I'm sorry."

He followed the doctor out the door and watched as she gave the cursed object in the road a wide berth before he dared to enter the bedroom. The air was still and smelled of sickness. He opened a window to let in some fresh air, hoping it would help her labored breathing. He sat on the edge of the bed, still not daring to touch her, not wanting to wake her or harm her. Her head lolled to the side, leaving a mass of hair on the pillow. He collected it, holding it in a clenched fist, unable to breathe.

The doctor had told him to pray. He had tried that with his father. He'd prayed so much his knees had bled on the hard floor, and the gods had not answered his prayers. They had abandoned him and his home. What was happening now showed that they were abandoning his people. Still, he dropped to his knees beside the bed, the act of a desperate man, and begged the gods to forgive his lapse and to help Eliana.

They didn't answer.

She died two days later, her skin covered in blisters that broke and leaked pus and blood that smelled of death and decay. He sat with her, singing her favorite hymn as her last breath rattled from her lungs. The words came automatically from a mind that had grown numb. He didn't know who found him sitting there, holding her cold hand in his. It could have been the doctor making another useless visit, or a neighbor bringing food for an empty table.

He didn't remember the funeral either. The church's nave held two caskets, the smaller one symbolic of the life lost, his unborn son. He was told it was a beautiful service, that the gods shone down and lit the way to the afterlife for Eliana and their child. He wasn't there. He couldn't be there. Instead, he lay in the field they had worked in just a few days ago, staring at the dark speck high in sky, his body rigid, every muscle taut. Sorrow turned to anger that burned through him like fire.

His friends and neighbors came to visit, bringing food and heartfelt words of kindness and grief. He heard the words through the closed door, refusing to open it. When he'd missed his second Sunday service, Mother dropped by. It took all of his strength not to open the door and push her off his land. She was all that had forsaken him.

It was the whistling of the wind that finally pulled him from his dank hole. The sound pierced through his brain like a hot knife through butter. He ran out to his porch and watched the sky fall once again. The impact shook dust from the rafters and into his eyes. He bent over and rubbed them, letting the tears wash away the dirt.

When he opened his eyes again, the sky flickered.

* * *

Someone harvested his grain, leaving half in his granary. The rest would go as his offering to the gods. If they had asked him, he would have told them to go to the everlasting fires. He wanted nothing to do with gods that would do this to him and his people.

The sky still flickered like a candle in the wind. Senn Jal kept his curtains closed to keep out the light, but it flared on his walls anyway. A day after he heard the wagons pass for their journey into the mountains, he knew what he would do. He would face the gods and ask them what his people had done to earn their wrath, he would curse them for taking his family.

He filled a pack with food. Water he could collect on the way up. Entering the bedroom for the first time since Eliana had died, he stripped the sheets, replacing them with the winter flannel she loved so much. He went to her flower garden, cutting her a bouquet of straw flowers. She always filled the house with them, even in winter, claiming they reminded her that spring would always come. He lay the flowers on her pillow and sat on the edge of the empty bed waiting for night to fall.

The offering was always made at the first full moon after harvest, and the almost full globe hung in the sky, lighting the path the wagons had taken. Even at night the flickering sky could be seen. Stars went dark and then shone brightly again. The moon herself sometimes faded before shining her white light over the land. What looked like lightning scurried overhead like frightened mice, yet the sky was silent and clear.

Senn Jal picked his way up the trail, climbing the slopes to the canyon where the offerings were made. Previous generations had tried to name the place and each time the current Mother had said no. The canyon was of the land, the sliver of light above of the sky. A place so holy needed no name. He thought it should be named the canyon of lies.

His breath came labored during the climb. It was not so steep that he should be so tired, yet a trickle of sweat rolled down his back. He filled his water bottles from the stream that rushed out of the canyon before laying in the cold waters that washed away his fever. He trudged on, wanting to be near the wagons before the men left them. They would return five days later to empty ones.

He came upon them in the morning, his breath ragged and forced. They had packed up their gear for the trek home and were paying homage one last time. He crossed the stream and hid behind boulders waiting for them to leave. A half an hour later he was still waiting. Mother had sent an especially pious group this time. The thought entered his mind unbidden, and with it, a resentment that had grown since Eliana died. He wanted to run to them, to beat them over the head with a stick until they too saw the truth. He stayed hidden.

When they eventually left he crept closer to the wagons, hesitant at first, and then with a forced confidence he didn't quite feel. What he was doing was forbidden. No one had ever remained behind to see the gods collect the offerings. He replenished his store of food from what the other men had left behind, though he wasn't hungry, and rested, sliding his back down a tree as he lowered himself to the ground. Something wet soaked his shirt and he touched it. His fingers came away covered in pus and blood. Wiping them on the dry grass, he smiled. He would soon join Eliana and their child.

The sound of stone scraping on stone woke him from his fevered dreams of a sky that rained death and destruction. He rubbed the cake from his eyes. The flickering sky threw constantly shifting shadows on the ground, and the canyon wall across from him moved outwards in a single, smooth motion, rising into the air to reveal a hall of white behind it.

Perhaps he was already dead or still dreaming.

Boxes floated from the opening, silently moving to the sides of the loaded wagons and picking them up as if they were air. Senn Jal's breath caught in his throat and his heart beat a rapid staccato in his chest. He only moved as the canyon wall began to close again, lunging off the tree and tripping over his own feet.

The opening sighed shut before he reached it.

He stood where it had been, searching for the seams of the entryway until his fingers bled and finding nothing but rock. The stream continued to babble as if laughing at his attempt, and the sky rippled. A chill ran down his spine. He stumbled back, staring at the blank cliff face. When next he sat, it was beside where the opening had been. This time, when the wagons were returned, he would be ready.

* * *

Senn Jal was awake when the sound of stone scraping on stone echoed down the canyon again. He stayed seated, waiting for the door to open. As the first wagon was carried out, he rolled into the entry, coming to his feet and hiding behind the first thing he saw. Sweat rolled into his eyes from the simple movement and he gasped for air. He didn't have much time to confront the gods.

Once the wagons were back outside and the floating white boxes had returned, two cylindrical rods lowered the door, pulling the massive slab in with a hiss. This side of the door wasn't rock and he could see the edges clearly. The room he was in stayed lit after the door closed. He couldn't see the light source from where he sat, but the brightness of it was almost blinding. Not yet ready to move, he examined the pile of goods he hid behind. Some of it he recognized: brand new rope and barbed wire for fencing. His dad had used their last piece of barbed wire the summer before he died, patching the fence with the small piece. After that, they'd use wood from the forests. What lay in the pile before him was more than he had seen in a lifetime, covered in a layer of dust.

There were things he'd only seen in classes when he was young: boxes of things called light bulbs and batteries and new rubber wheels. And there were things he had no idea about: smaller versions of the white boxes that had carried the wagons and what looked like wire mesh gloves. Were these what the gods use to give back when an offering was made? If so, why did they remain locked behind a door no one on the other side could see?

He used the pile to help himself to his feet, stumbling to the side suddenly dizzy. He ran his hands through his hair. They came away full and he let the hair float to the ground. He fished through the pile until he found something he could use as a stick. It was thin, feeling too small to handle his weight, yet it didn't flex or bend when he leaned on it. It would do. Fear-induced determination drove him forward. There was time, yet. There had to be.

His feet shuffled across the floor as he left the entryway and entered a hall at least two wagons wide. He rested when he reached the grain his people had offered. It sat on a grate in the floor, waiting for the gods to use it. Just past the grain he saw the white floating boxes sitting in cubbies on the wall, a blue glow at their base. There was a white box in every cubby, but not all glowed. Some sat askew, as if thrown aside in a tantrum, with grain dust in place of the glow.

The broken machines brought out the other flaws in the area. The walls weren't the pure white he had first thought; brown stains and a network of slivered cracks broke the smooth surface. He looked back the way he had come. The only tracks he saw were his own.

He was tired, the weight of his own body dragging him down, and he hurt deep into his bones. Straightening, he pulled his shoulders back and kept moving forward. It was the only way for him to go. He had given up on his people and his land when he started this journey. Even if he wanted to go back, the door was sealed and he had no idea how to open it. Forward lay his answers.

The hall ended, another one branching to the left and right. He rested, catching his breath from the short walk, and stared down the new hallway. An errant hair fell into his eyes and he moved to brush it aside. His hand stopped inches away from his face. His chest felt hollow and his breath caught. He left the hair where it was, too afraid to touch it in case it simply fell off.

The hollowness was replaced with fire. How dare he sit here and do nothing? He had come here for a specific purpose, and nothing was going to stop him. The gods would hear him!

The hall looked the same in both directions, though the one heading right seemed to have more dark sections than the one left. That simple thing made the decision and he turned left. It looked like the hallway curved, though it was so slight it could have been an illusion created by the light and dark sections. The moment he placed both feet in the hall, the floor began to move, and he froze, stifling a quick shout. He pulled in a calming breath, realizing the floor was moving him in the wrong direction. He took a tentative step and crossed the midline of the floor, and the direction changed. He let it carry him, grateful for not having to walk, unsure of how it could move on its own.

At the first unlit section, the floor stopped and he stumbled forward, using the stick he had found to stop himself from falling. His hand scraped against the smooth wall, leaving a dark red smear. He shambled forward, muttering Eliana's hymn under his breath. At the next lit section, the floor moved again.

Hallways exited to the right, all looking the same as the one he had used to come in. Some contained grain, others stacks of fresh cut trees. Some held nothing.

The floor slowed and a ramp led off to the left. The first thing he had seen that was different. It was enough of a reason to take it. He shifted to step off the moving floor and it slowed more. He still stumbled as his feet hit the ramp, almost falling. The slope wasn't much, but each step he took was a battle, the only thing pushing him forward his anger. The tips of his shoes dragged as he moved. He couldn't see the top. Still, he pushed on. He had no choice now… it was all he had left.

A cough wracked his body. Blood splattered the white walls and he fell to the ground, heaving for a breath that refused to come. From his prone position he could see the top of the ramp. So close. He closed his eyes. So close. His hand slipped as he used the wall to stand. Eliana stood at the top of the ramp, a gurgling bundle in her arms. He lurched toward her and the image faded. *Soon, my love, soon.*

His body was on fire and his clothes clung to him. Where they touched, the blisters burst and reformed. He pushed on.

He barely saw the room at the top of the ramp, focusing instead on the circular staircase in the center. They would be there. He knew it, felt it in his bones. The gods that had deserted him would be there, and they would answer his questions. He placed his first foot on the bottom step and pushed.

Exhaustion grabbed him and he stopped, coughing up more blood from his dying body. *Please Eliana, give me the strength I need. Only a few more steps. We'll be a family again soon enough, but not yet. Not yet.* He imagined she had heard him, and he raised his foot to the next step.

He rested again at the top, his forehead pressed into a cold plaque on the wall. Each breath was a battle he knew he couldn't win forever. He pulled away, leaving skin and blood on the metal, and read the perfectly printed text.

Exodus Four
Observation Deck 221
Colorado, Wyoming, Nebraska, Kansas
United States of America
In the year of our Lord 2547

The words were gibberish, except for the last line. He *would* find the gods in here. He knew it. He walked through the door into a circular room, and for a moment he lost his balance. Stars shone all around him, not the ones he had left behind that flickered in the night sky, but pure white points of light that shone bright and steady. He took another step and the floor took his weight, soft and giving.

"I…I am…" His voice croaked from his throat. He coughed and spit out more blood before drawing in as deep a breath as he could.

"I AM HERE!"

His voice echoing through the space was the only response. Only one thought stuck in his muddled brain. They weren't here. They never were. Weariness settled on his shoulders like an old friend. He had failed.

He dragged his feet across the soft carpet to the outer wall and stared out the glass. Below him a massive grid of domes filled his view. At first he though the domes were separate before he saw they were surrounded by an outer circle connected by multiple spokes. Each set of four domes contained a smaller one in their center, a mirror of where he now stood. Some of the domes gave off light while others were so dark they were nearly invisible.

The dome below him flickered and he felt the pull of home. His world, his family's world, generations living in a make-believe place. How could they not have known? The dome shone bright for an instant and he saw the hole in its roof, ragged and gaping, open to the night sky. The light went out and his mind shut down.

Below the domes, below the world he had known, lay a sea of stars that shone as brightly as those above.

What but gods could have created such a thing? They were real, and he had forsaken them. And he was right to have done so, for they were cruel gods, abandoning him, his family and his people when they needed them the most.

He was more like them than he thought.

Flight Plans Through the Dust of Dreams

Kit Harding

It struck Roswitha as peculiar that no one had ever attempted to remove the airship. It had crashed right down into a residential neighborhood and destroyed several houses whose owners presumably would have wanted them back, but the airship had been left where it fell, sprawled across several lots. The people went elsewhere, leaving the neighborhood much more dilapidated than she remembered from when the airship first crashed. Apparently, a terrorist airship falling out of the sky wasn't great for property values.

At the time, the airship looked like it might be salvageable. Now, after twenty years of exposure, there were many spots of rust around the outside and she was sure there were leaks in the bag. But the airship was well-made and the underlying bones of it remained intact. With a lot of care, it could fly again. Roswitha was intent on providing that care. Normally she'd have started with the outside, but a glance at the sky disabused her of that plan; it was starting to rain. Instead, she climbed through a door that opened with surprising ease, found a likely section of the airship's floor, and began cutting out weak parts with her pocket laser cutter.

Her head snapped up at the sound of creaking metal. It was probably just the ship—who *else* would be climbing around a long-abandoned wreck—but she remained alert, listening hard. After a long silence, she heard it again.

Roswitha turned to watch the room's sideways door. The metal sound came closer, then a teenage girl with long black hair and sun-weathered skin ducked through the low hole and into the room. She jumped when she saw Roswitha, nearly cracking her head on the wall behind her.

"What are you doing in here?" she said, trying and failing to sound tough.

"Working," said Roswitha.

"In *here*?"

Roswitha sighed. "If you were using this place to hide out or cook drugs, I'm the last person who'd tell the authorities. You should find somewhere else, though; it's probably unsanitary here."

"I'm not using it for anything like that, I swear!" the girl exclaimed. "I just come here sometimes, to explore."

"I believe you," said Roswitha. And she did; on closer inspection the girl did not look like a runaway. She was covered in grime from climbing through the ship, but her clothes were of good quality and well-cared for. Her black hair was neatly braided close against her scalp. She wore heavy brown work pants with a lavender crop top under a leather vest the image of the one Roswitha had worn in her youth.

"I'm not hurting anything," said the girl. "It's been abandoned for years."

"I didn't accuse you of hurting anything."

"There's never anyone in here. And my brothers are loud and they don't want to talk about anything but sports."

"So you come in here and hide out and maybe dream of getting out of this town on an airship?"

"Yeah. I just wanted to get away." She looked up at Roswitha. "Are you hiding out?"

Roswitha laughed. She was and she wasn't—Schrödinger's fugitive—but she opted for the simplest answer.

"I'm here for salvage," said Roswitha. "This ship was well-made, and well-maintained until it crashed. Sure, she's spent twenty years sitting here, but I think I can restore her at least enough to be flightworthy."

The girl looked pointedly at the mildew and rust covering the room. Roswitha laughed.

"I've been everywhere in here; there's no treasure left from the Red Butterfly."

"Get a lot of treasure hunters in here?"

"Once. They seemed kinda spaced-out, though."

"They'd have to be. Explosives are *expensive*; there was never any treasure to be found."

"Got a bunch of people from a ghost-hunting podcast too. I could have told them it's not haunted." The girl's voice *dripped* with disdain.

Roswitha snorted. "Of course it's not haunted. No bodies were ever recovered. No one in the crash died."

"She was never heard from again, though. She just disappeared. Some people on the forums say intelligence agents disappeared her. That it was all false-flag. And some people say she's still carrying on the fight in secret."

Roswitha winced inwardly at the girl's reverent tone. "And what do you think?"

"They made examples of the people they caught. So they can't have caught her." There was a brief pause as the girl appeared to consider something. "Is that why you want to restore this ship? Is there something here that will let you find her? Can I come with you?"

Best to divert that line of thought now. "Running away with a random woman you met on a derelict airship doesn't seem like the safest choice."

"Safety is overrated."

Roswitha rolled her eyes. Teenagers: always so convinced of their own immortality.

"Carrying off teenagers is a good way for *me* to get arrested for kidnapping. I like staying free."

"Will you show me what you're doing? Can I help you fix it?"

"I'm still assessing it and I don't have any spare equipment here. Come back tomorrow and we'll see."

"You'll see. I'll be so helpful you'll *have* to keep me." She grinned and darted off into the airship. Roswitha watched her go, then returned to her laser cutter and considered. Staying while refusing the girl was dangerous; the girl would be angry and determined to find out what Roswitha was hiding. She could give up the whole thing now. The girl didn't even know her name; if she vanished the girl would assume the whole conversation had been just talk.

Lie to others, she thought. *Never lie to yourself.* Roswitha didn't know the specific forums the girl was on, but she knew the type. She knew how they affected their members. *You're going to be back tomorrow. You're going to stick around at least long enough to see how far gone the girl is.*

* * *

The girl reappeared the next day.

"Did you decide? Can I help?"

"You can help me fix the airship. I will not take you with me when I leave here."

"If you're trying to finish what she started I want to help with that too!"

"I assure you I'm not." Twenty years before, Roswitha walked the charnel house of the last bombing while the fire still burned. She had no desire to repeat the experience. "And if you keep being that open about committing political violence, you'll wind up on a government watchlist, and you won't enjoy it."

"No one's disappeared on the forums yet."

"That you know of."

That brought the girl up short. She regarded Roswitha suspiciously. "How do you know about watchlists?"

That was closer to dangerous territory than Roswitha was willing to get, no matter what she wanted to know about the girl.

"I've been around. Anyway, my name's Roswitha."

"I'm Tanya."

"Well, Tanya, do you want to learn to use a pocket laser cutter?"

Tanya grinned and knelt beside Roswitha. Roswitha turned back to the wall and demonstrated how to find weak spots and cut them away. Tanya had a good eye and quick hands and the afternoon slipped away in a soft sizzle of molten metal.

* * *

Tanya did not return for several days. Roswitha had mixed feelings about that. On one hand, Tanya was bright enough to be dangerous if Roswitha wasn't careful talking to her. On the other, Tanya's obsession was concerning and Roswitha wanted to know whether she posed a risk to *other* people.

Tanya did return eventually. Roswitha was decoupling the gas bag of the airship from the cabin when she reappeared.

"I wondered if you were coming back," said Roswitha.

"My mother thought you were probably a murderer. I had to convince her I wasn't going to let you carry me off."

Which meant Tanya's mother knew Roswitha was there. *Didn't think about that, did you, Rosie. Too much time with hackers and smugglers. You forgot normal people talk to their families.* She'd have to be more careful with what she said now. She was deliberately taking some risks by staying, but she still wanted to remain alive and free at the end of the summer.

"I see she knows you well, since you did ask me to do just that. I'm not going to murder you, but I understand her concern."

"It might be exciting, being murdered. Well, if you didn't succeed, anyway."

"You must be *really* bored."

"School is terrible, my brothers are boring, and everyone else I know talks big and does nothing. Besides, stranger danger's way overrated, so you're not going to murder me."

"Ah, but I'm not just any stranger; I'm the sort of stranger who fixes up an airship formerly used for terrorism. Which reminds me—" Roswitha handed Tanya a wrench, a small eyedropper, and a bottle. "—this should be harmless to skin, but be careful with it. It'll eat through rust; don't get it in your eyes. It's hard to find, so we're not using it everywhere, but there's rust *inside* the catches. Try to open the fastenings with the wrench first, and if that doesn't work drop a bit of the acid over it and try again. Once we're done we can get the cabin upright."

Tanya walked to the fastener beside Roswitha and tried with the wrench.

"What's this for?"

"I've done structural patches on the floor. Doing the walls will be easier if it's upright."

"My mom said you were right about government watchlists."

Roswitha laughed. "But you think it would be exciting."

"And I'm a teenager. What are they going to do to me?"

"Everyone caught from this ship's original crew was a teenager. The government executed them publicly and messily."

"Yeah, but I haven't done anything." Tanya gave up with the wrench and began carefully applying the liquid to the fastener. "Red Butterfly would say I'm not a revolutionary. 'If everyone who talked about revolution took direct action, they would succeed within days. But that would require a certainty of path few would-be revolutionaries can match. Are you committed enough to risk imprisonment and death? For only when your actions bring real threat of reprisal can you truly call yourself a revolutionary.'"

"How many of those essays have you memorized?" Roswitha asked. It was painful hearing those words quoted back to her. She'd hoped never to deal with any of those essays again.

Fool's hope, Rosie. Nothing ever dies on the nets. It was always a matter of time.

"None. But I liked that quote. My brother's always going on about how he's gonna be a big football star, but he's never even tried out."

"So *that's* why you were so eager to help me out with this."

"It's an action. When we finish we'll have really *done* something. Ow!" She pulled her hand away from the ship. Roswitha looked up and saw a jagged cut on Tanya's hand.

"It's not too bad," said Roswitha. "I can patch it up." Roswitha pulled out a disinfectant spray and began to apply it to the cut. "When did you last have a tetanus shot?"

"Recently. Mother says if I'm going to play around in the wreck she's going to keep me from getting sick."

"Your mother is wise." Roswitha finished with the spray and taped gauze over the injury.

"She doesn't like me reading Red Butterfly's essays."

"Your mother lived through the bombings."

"She won't talk about it at all."

"People were terrified. At the beginning, before every bombing there was a warning call and time to evacuate. It started with property damage. But there was no guarantee it would stay there. Every week there was a new explosion, a new building destroyed. Anyone working in a high-profile building was afraid they'd be next, and *everyone* was afraid one day there wouldn't be a warning. And then it happened. A building filled with people blew up. Hundreds died. Even after police found this airship and chased it, no bodies were found and only a few people were ever caught. No one who lived through it has ever felt like it's really over." *Including you, Rosie, and what does that say about your choices?* "There, that's done."

Tanya flexed her hand experimentally. "If you disapprove so much of what she did, why are you trying to fix up her airship?"

Roswitha packed up the first aid kit and returned to working on the fastenings to buy herself time to answer.

"There's more than one kind of ghost. This ship hasn't got any lingering spirits of the dead, but people still lived and worked here. Dreamers. People who wanted to change things. The best ships, the most loved...they take on a life of their own. She did her best for her crew. She's owed something in return."

"And you think *I'm* romanticizing," Tanya muttered. "At least I think her stuff might get me out of here. You're fixing up this ship because of poetry."

* * *

Tanya returned the next day, and the next, and the day after that, and soon they began to talk of things that weren't the history of the ship itself. Both were avid readers and very interested in airship design. Roswitha was happy to teach repair skills even when they weren't directly relevant. Tanya appreciated having an audience to complain to about her mother and brothers. After a week of wrestling with connectors and patching the cabin's ceiling, they righted the cabin with portable pneumatic lifts Roswitha had brought—Tanya was very excited by them—and began going over the sides of the ship cutting out rust spots.

"I think you really have a knack for this," Roswitha remarked. "You might consider a career in airship repair."

"I have. My mother says they only take you if you have connections. That the best I can hope for is nursing school, and if I break my heart on dreams I'll just wind up drugged out like my cousin Dara or dead like the Red Butterfly."

"I'd think you'd be more likely to wind up drugged out if you *stopped* dreaming."

"I'd have said that, except then she'd have searched my bedroom for drugs."

Roswitha winced. "That seems less than helpful."

"She keeps telling me nothing's possible, because we come from here." Tanya waved her free hand at the ill-kept, forlorn neighborhood.

"She doesn't want you hurt."

"Yeah, but…how am I supposed to know if I can get out if I don't try?"

"Given the forums you're visiting, is it possible she's concerned you're going to try blowing something up?"

"Blowing things up was working, for a while. I've read all about it. She *always* gave warnings. Then suddenly she changes pattern? A lot of people online think that was a false flag. That she was making the government look bad and getting too much attention, so they killed people and said it was her to save face."

Roswitha stilled. That was far too close to what she'd wondered over the years. The bomb had been real enough. But there had been a warning. She'd been in the room when it was called in. Did it even make a difference if the failure to pass it along was deliberate or accidental? They'd been playing with explosives. People were bound to die sooner or later.

"Are you all right?" Tanya asked. She put down her laser cutter and started toward Roswitha. "You look all…pale."

"Lot of sun today."

"Shouldn't that make you red?"

"I'll just sit for a minute." Roswitha sat in the airship's shadow and leaned back against the wall, watching Tanya.

"Don't pass out; Mother will find a way to blame it on me if an ambulance shows up."

"No ambulances," said Roswitha sharply.

"I mean, if you pass out, I'm pretty sure I'm supposed to call one."

"I don't like hospitals. Or doctors. And I definitely don't have money to pay for an ambulance ride."

"But you can afford to fix up an airship?"

"I already had the tools. Salvage is more about hard work than expense if the airship's not an antique. It doesn't have to be pretty to fly."

"The people on the forums say flightworthiness requirements are a tool of the government to keep airships out of the sky so no one will realize their airships are spying on people."

Roswitha had no idea how to respond to that. It wasn't true—the government had much more effective ways of spying on people—but saying *that* would definitely provoke Tanya's suspicions again.

She settled for asking, "Are there *any* actual anarchists on these forums?"

Tanya had to think about that. "Maybe? How would you tell?"

"They're the ones who lecture you about operational security and having medics on hand when doing an action."

"Then we have a few but not many. Not that many people do actions in the first place. Why?"

"It explains a lot. If you wish to travel these circles you'll need to work on your discretion." *Look who's talking, Rosie. "Don't talk about what you're doing" was your first lesson.*

Roswitha would share the guilt for anything Tanya did with Roswitha's essays. If this was a chance to prevent Tanya from following in her footsteps, she had to try. Did others say these things to themselves? When she did it, was it any less of a rationalization?

"I'm very discreet!" Tanya said indignantly.

"Except for the part where you're talking openly to me about how much you admire a notorious terrorist."

"But you'd never tell anyone!"

"You can't know that for certain."

"Oh, right, you hearing me talk is so dangerous. You know what I think? I think you just like implying you know so much about *danger* and you're actually, like, a bored welder or something." She stalked off in the direction of her house, still carrying her laser cutter.

Roswitha flopped to the ground, staring up at the airship. Once Tanya's anger wore off, she'd realize Roswitha wasn't just a poser. The question was what she'd assume Roswitha was instead. Roswitha had thought the danger would be minimal. She'd thought she could convince Tanya there was nothing dashing about violence without revealing how much she knew firsthand.

Lie to others. Never lie to yourself. You should have known this would get personal.

And now Tanya knew enough basics of airship repair to be valuable to a cell if she managed to find one. Roswitha had given her those skills. Even more than leaving incendiary essays around, that made her responsible for any deaths Tanya caused. Roswitha had chosen her road. Now she had to walk it.

* * *

This time it took Tanya longer to come back. Roswitha worried that she'd revealed too much, but there was no burst of chatter on the nets about a too-detailed Red Butterfly sighting, and if Tanya talked to anyone, she'd talk to the forums first.

Roswitha had reinforced an entire wall on her own before turning around one morning to see Tanya behind her. Roswitha was relieved Tanya had returned; she could only influence Tanya if Tanya was present to be influenced.

Tanya seemed disinclined to ask more questions, and they returned to repair techniques and innocuous conversations. Eventually they finished enough of the outside of the airship to move inside.

It was Tanya who found it.

"Roswitha!" she called. "Look at this!"

Roswitha hurried into the room and froze when she saw Tanya's find, once again going pale. "I would have thought they'd have found that," she said softly. She shouldn't have; her very continued freedom was proof of how incompetent investigators could be. She'd focused too much on what she said to Tanya; it had never occurred to her that anything identifying might have survived the crash intact.

"There was some kind of curtain in front of it," said Tanya, seemingly missing the implications of Roswitha's words. "It melted onto the wall. I was peeling it off so I could look at the metal. It looks intact."

"Safes often hold up to fire." Roswitha heard her own voice as if it was someone else's. "Less often do they hold up to water. You need to get one that withstands both, if you want your documents to outlive any disasters that befall you."

"We have to open it!" said Tanya excitedly. "This belonged to the Red Butterfly. Who *knows* what's in there? Essays she never got to publish? Pictures? Maybe something that tells us who she is?"

"Are you sure you want to know? It might destroy your illusions."

"'False beliefs are the enemy in this sort of work,'" Tanya quoted. "'To create effective change, your first allegiance must be to the truth. Question everything, but most especially those things that you want to believe. To hold any illusions about yourself and your motives is the beginning of your downfall, and you will have no one but yourself to blame.'"

Never lie to yourself. She had been lying to herself since the summer started. Maybe it had never been possible to dissuade Tanya without revealing herself. Maybe she had always been headed for this moment.

"Very much a 'do as I say, not as I do' moment, that was," Roswitha remarked. "And still is, since I kept telling myself I'd deal with your illusions about me without letting you know who I am." Ignoring Tanya's shocked expression, Roswitha walked to the safe and with steady, sure hands, turned the dial through the combination. The safe opened. She turned to find Tanya still looking gobsmacked.

"I just thought you'd know how to break into safes, not that you'd be able to open it!"

"I have actually never learned how to break into safes." Roswitha reached into the safe, withdrew the small notebook inside, and tucked it into her pocket. "If you hadn't recited that particular quote, I might have pretended I couldn't open it and taken this after you left, but you never had a chance to have anything *but* false beliefs about me. I don't want you walking in my footsteps."

"Why not?"

"Because people on the nets blew everything into something it wasn't. I wrote those essays before I had done anything. A lot of them aren't…accurate. And I'm responsible for what you do with what I wrote."

"So, what, I'm supposed to be your redemption? Keep me on the straight and narrow and no one dies this time?"

"Redemption doesn't exist." There was no disguising the self-loathing in Roswitha's voice. "It's a concept created by fools to avoid having to find a way to live with their actions."

"You could have gotten away. No one knew about this ship until you used it as a distraction so your friends could get away."

"And that was meant to be redemption? I had just spent twelve hours picking through the ruins. I'd been surrounded by bodies; I was covered in ashes and worse. All I could think was that it was my plan and therefore my fault. If I made sure my people got away, no one else died. If I died in the process, at least I didn't have to live with what I'd done."

"But you were trying to do right. You were making change."

"I know what your forum has turned me into. And they're right about one thing: we delivered a warning that day. There were never supposed to be casualties. When I realized there was no evacuation on the news, I ran to the square just in time to see the building explode."

There was a long silence before Roswitha continued. "It was the first time I'd ever been close to the aftermath. I'd had EMT training, when we were planning, because I knew we couldn't take our injured to a hospital. No one knew my face, so no one questioned me helping. I spent the entire day triaging survivors, surrounded by the bodies of dead civilians—dead *children*, some of them—and I knew I had caused it."

"But you just said you'd called in a threat. They're the ones who didn't evacuate." Tanya's voice sounded uncertain and desperate. Roswitha understood what she felt—it was hard to have your illusions shattered. It was hard being forced to grow up. But Roswitha dared not let up; she needed to make sure Tanya would never try to follow in her footsteps.

"Do you think that matters?"

"Intent matters."

"Impact matters more. It would have been *easy* to look at the people in that building and say they were collateral damage. It would have been easy to say they were propping up a corrupt system just by being there. But the majority of people in that building were office workers, and the rest were just people who happened to be there. 'Collateral damage' is a polite phrase for callousness."

"'Just following orders' was established as a crime."

"In a court, at a trial. And targeting civilian infrastructure is *also* a war crime. I got a group of my friends together and led them in committing war crimes, and the public applauded it until there was a body count. Yes, someone didn't pass on the warning, and that person is likely also guilty of war crimes, but that doesn't make me less guilty. I still built the bomb. I still placed it."

Tanya looked at Roswitha as though she'd never seen her before. "What did you do after you crashed the ship?"

"Slipped away in the chaos, hoping the fire would cover any forensics that might identify me. Spent twenty years going anywhere that seemed like it might need an off-the-books EMT. Sometimes I was a protest medic, sometimes I stitched up bullet wounds in gang members, sometimes I stole antibiotics from fancy private hospitals."

"So you did go looking for redemption."

"When I still thought it was possible." Roswitha sighed. "I meant what I said about redemption being for fools. The past is immutable. I was willing to do anything because I thought I was right. I stopped questioning myself, and it wasn't me who paid the price. Saving lives doesn't unmake the deaths. There's no cosmic balance sheet. There's just living with it. I learned not to do more damage. I put good in the world because the alternatives are worse. I try to balance not forgiving myself with not letting it consume me. But you don't want to be what I was, Tanya. You don't want to end up like me."

Tanya stared at Roswitha with a look of utter betrayal. Then she turned and fled the room.

* * *

For several days, Roswitha continued working on the airship alone. There was risk in this. If Tanya decided to tell someone, Roswitha would be in trouble. But Roswitha wanted to be there if Tanya needed help processing their conversation. Besides, the repairs were almost finished. It was almost time for a test flight. She had no idea what she'd do with it once it was flyable; this had not been one of her more thought-out plans.

At the sound of footsteps on metal, she looked up. Tanya stepped through the door.

"I wondered if I would see you again."

"How many times have you said that to me now?"

"A few. I do seem to have a knack for pushing you past the point where you're overwhelmed."

"Notice that I keep coming back."

"And what did your forums think about all this?"

"I didn't say anything!" Tanya sounded outraged. "*You* were the one warning me about government watchlists! And who'd believe me even if I did?"

"Someone would have investigated, even if it was whoever's lowest-ranked at the local terrorism unit."

Tanya looked appalled. "You know *that* and you still told me everything and let me go running off?"

"I'm not especially concerned about getting killed."

"If I said that so calmly, I'd get a concern meeting with the guidance counselor."

"If I was in your school, so would I. People aren't supposed to think of death as a welcome escape."

"But you do?"

"I think it would *be* an escape. I owe the world something, because of what I did. I've saved more lives than I've taken, but it's not a scale. Taking my own life would be shirking my responsibilities."

"So instead you walk the world helping people. Is that what fixing the ship is about? Easier to help people when you can fly?"

"It's not actually useful for anything I'm doing," Roswitha admitted. "I just…wanted to remember my ghosts."

"You wanted to torture yourself, you mean."

"I did say that finding the balance between remembering failures and letting them consume you was tricky. You showed up before I could get too lost in the past anyway. As soon as you announced you'd been reading my old essays I felt responsible for keeping you from walking in my footsteps."

"I wanted to do what you did and get it right this time."

"That's an illusion. There is no getting it right. That day you were worried about me passing out, it was shock because your forums had theorized something I'd always wondered. Did they deliberately withhold the warning, to make me less of a folk hero? The game's rigged. They'd won from the moment I planted the first bomb; I just didn't know it yet.'

"So don't be like you?"

"Yeah."

"I always figured my mother would kill any attempt to get into airship repair and then when nursing school made me dead inside I'd run away, meet up with the forum people, and try what you did instead of doing drugs."

"Well, we're about to finish rebuilding an airship that's already equipped for smuggling. You could start a cargo business. Run black-market medicines on the side, help people like me get from danger hotspot to danger hotspot, help people in trouble escape."

Tanya looked startled. "You'd just…give me an airship?"

"I had no plan for what to do once I got her flying. She's a good ship. She deserves to be used to *do* good."

"What are you going to do, then?"

"The same thing I've been doing. Travel the world. Help people. Try to keep living with myself."

"Whisk in, fix up an airship, whisk out?"

"I won't leave without saying goodbye. We're not quite done yet, and I still have to make sure you know how to *fly* her. Go home. Think. Dream. Come back tomorrow and we'll start planning."

Tanya nodded and left, clearly already contemplating what sorts of things she could do with an airship. Roswitha watched her go, then pulled out a small photo she'd found in the safe. She had taped it the notebook just after they'd acquired the ship. In it, she posed with her crew at her college graduation. "Red Butterfly" had just been a pen name then, for a few essays about revolution that were beginning to gain an audience. She was on her way to an internship at an airship designer. Afraid she would lose these friends, she created a private, encrypted chat server for them to keep in touch.

That server had been the genesis of more essays, and then larger plans. They radicalized together, planned together, learned to make bombs, learned to fly. Three of the people in the photo would die after the last bombing went wrong. But when this picture was taken, none of that had happened yet. Tears dripped down her cheeks as she stared into the past, at a time when they had yet to make any life-destroying mistakes, when the future had been theirs and they had been young and excited and free.

Saving Sallie Ruth

Gini Koch
writing as Anita Ensal

"Tell me 'nother story, Gran'pa."

"Which one shall it be tonight, Johnny?"

"The ghost ship!" Johnny loved this story. It was spooky and fun and even at five he knew it wasn't really real.

"Ah, that one again. Well, there were two ghost ships, one that sailed the seas of Old Earth, called the *Flying Dutchman*, and one that powers through the Blackness of our solar system even today, and that's the poor, doomed *Sallie Ruth*."

"What happened to her?" Johnny asked. The *Flying Dutchman* was a fun story, but Johnny had never been to Earth, even though his family were all considered Earth citizens. Grandpa had left that planet when he was only a bit older than Johnny was now, and while they occasionally went to one of the Lunars when they needed supplies not available on Pallas or Ceres Stations, they were Belters, and that meant they spent most of their time in the Blackness—the space between the moons, the asteroids of the Belt, the planets, and Jolly Old Sol. This made the story of the *Sallie Ruth* far more interesting. After all, Johnny might see the *Sallie Ruth* one day, even though she and her story were hundreds of years old.

"Cursed, she was," Grandpa said gravely. "Captained by a man tall, strong, and true. He married his love and named his ship after her. But she was untrue, and with his first mate, no less. In his torment, the captain, Madichon Vanjans, tried to throw himself into the Blackness, but the crew wouldn't allow it. However, Vanjans vowed to never return to any planet's port until Sallie Ruth would spurn her lover and return his love fully. The crew supported him and tried to help him in his torment—Sallie Ruth and her lover, Robert Himmel, were locked in the brig, kept apart from each other. The captain and crew tried to reason with them, but they never renounced each other or their evil union. The *Sallie Ruth* never made port and, to this day, sails through the Blackness, waiting for that evil woman to repent of her sin against a noble man."

"What happens to people who find them?" Johnny asked, as was expected for this part of the tale.

"Ah," Grandpa said, "the evil of the *Sallie Ruth* engulfs and destroys those who dare to get too close. It's said that if you see that terrible ghost ship, you should leap to warp and pray you arrive at your destination alive. Those few brave or foolish enough to dock with the *Sallie Ruth* have never been heard from again, just the debris of their ships found floating in the Blackness, testimony to the power of an evil woman's breaking of a good man's heart."

"It's always the woman's fault somehow, in all these old stories," Johnny's mother muttered as she came into his cabin to tuck him in and shoo Grandpa out. She stroked Johnny's hair. "Stories are told by the survivors, John dear, and you must remember that a story may sound interesting and wonderful and yet not be true at all. You keep an open mind, no matter what a story may have told you to think."

"I promise, Mamma."

* * *

20 Earth Standard Years Later

Galactic Police Cruiser *8030* sailed through the Blackness. They'd left Charon Prison three weeks ago, heading back to GP headquarters in the Belt. Security Officer John Pedder gazed out at the Blackness and thought of his family. He'd see them soon, now. Well, soon was a relative term—they weren't heading back at warp speed for a variety of reasons, so their arrival was probably at least several weeks away. But it was sooner than he'd been expecting.

Prison duty was normally dull and distressing. You flew around Charon and Pluto, waiting for the worst to happen—which it rarely did—hoping you had enough reading matter to stay sane and trying not to hate the people you were stuck in the Blackness with while doing nothing.

Most crews couldn't handle it for too long, so Charon duty was usually no more than three Earth months. The *8030* was different. They'd been out for eight months so far, and none of them had asked to leave, but they'd been given an assignment to handle on the way back to GP Headquarters in the Belt, which was why they'd cut short their planned year-long tour.

That had only been possible because his cruiser was filled with, as Security Officer Brad Jensen liked to say, loners who preferred the Blackness to other people. John didn't feel that way, but he had no issues being in the Blackness. He'd grown up on a family mining ship in the Belt, so the Blackness was home, whatever part of it he happened to be in. The others felt the same way.

All 8000 series GP ships had a complement of eight officers on board, double the number of a standard cruiser. The ships would never need to "sleep" when they were far from a planet, Lunar, Suspended City, or space station. Everyone who lived in the Belt or in the Blackness ran on Earth standard, so half the crew slept in the "day" and half at "night." John was on "day" duty, though they were so far from Sol or any of the planets right now that it was only human stubbornness that kept them time-adjusted.

John was pulled out of his contemplations by an alert. He verified what he was seeing. "Coming up on the remains of what looks like several ships."

"Remains, Pedder?" Lyssa Gunnels was the GP Officer in Charge. She was normally hard to surprise, but based on her tone and expression, this had done it.

"Per the system charts, there should be nothing here," James Conason, their navigator, said. "Just the Blackness."

"Scan for Boser Geist and any part of his pirate armada," Lyssa ordered.

"No signs of any ships other than ours," John said. "Systems don't show any indications of other ships being in the vicinity recently, either."

"Could have been comets," Communications Officer Kathi Schreiber said, but without conviction.

"Agreed," Lyssa said. "But since none are in evidence, but ship's debris is, we need to start scans immediately."

"On it," John said, as he magnified what his sensors had picked up and put it onto the viewscreen so they could all see what was ahead of them.

"The pieces seem to be staying together even though they're broken apart," James said. "I mean, I can tell these were ships and I think I can almost make out the design of each of them."

"My systems *have* made them out and I'm sending schematics to Ceres Main," Kathi said. "I'm also running a search on any ships reported late or who haven't checked in throughout the system. It's likely going to take some time before I have any potential candidates."

"Looks like a merchant convoy," Lyssa said slowly. "Those ship parts don't look like GP or mining vessel remnants. And I see what appears to be at least three ships, so I think it's safe to assume they were traveling together. But what's a convoy doing way out here?"

"And why weren't we notified to look for it?" Kathi added.

John enhanced the view again. "What I can see looks new. I can't spot registration numbers, though."

"We need to investigate," Lyssa said. No one argued. She activated all the ship's spotlights and navigated toward the wreckage while the rest of them remained alert.

"Based on how it appears these ships were hit I'd think the wreckage would be more scattered." Something about this bothered John, more than just finding destroyed ships, but he couldn't pinpoint what it was. "I'm scanning for anything that would be holding the debris in place. Huh."

"Huh?" Lyssa asked.

"It's not a forcefield or similar, but there's some kind of...substance... around the wreckage. It's invisible to the human eye, but my security systems are picking it up. We want to be very careful to not 'bump' into it, Captain."

"Noted, reducing power to impulse, warp coordinates set for Ceres Main, just in case." This was standard operating procedure, but they'd never needed to enact it before.

"Should we wake up the night crew?" John asked, as they floated closer.

Lyssa was quiet for a moment. "Yes, Pedder, good call. Just in case, let's have everyone ready."

John hurried to quarters, awakened the others, and headed back to the cockpit. "Did I miss anything?"

"No," Kathi replied. "But all systems now indicate that something's around the debris, not just security's."

Something new showed up on John's screen as the night crew joined them. "Wait. I think I see...an intact ship, in the distance." There was a blue glow around this ship, making it easier for his instruments to pick up and, therefore, for them to see. John split the viewscreen so they could see the wreckage, and avoid it, as well as this new ship.

"Why are we just seeing it now?" Lyssa asked. "Did it just come out of warp?"

"There are no signatures that would suggest it, no," James replied.

"It's an old ship based on the design," John said, as worry settled into his gut. "From the start-of-expansion old."

"That's impossible," Lyssa said. "There are no ships from that time still flying. The few that still exist are floating around in Jupiter's living space history museum and that's carefully guarded to prevent loss or damage."

"It's not impossible," John said quietly. "Not if it's the *Sallie Ruth*."

* * *

The crew were quiet for a few long moments. James broke the silence. "We need to get out of here."

"That's a myth," Lyssa said firmly. "And our jobs require that we search for survivors."

"That so-called myth says that we'll end up like these ships if we don't get away from here right now," James countered.

"I have what might be confirmation of the three ships we have here," Kathi said. "Ceres Main is not certain, but we have reports of new attacks by Boser Geist and several of his pirate ships."

"There is nothing the pirates have that could do this," Brad said from behind John. "Not destroy the ships and keep them 'held together' as they are."

"That may be," Kathi said, "but these three appear to match a merchant convoy that was attacked and overtaken around Saturn several months ago."

"What happened to their crews?" Lyssa asked.

"What always happens," Kathi replied tersely. "The pirates gave them a choice to join up or die. We only know about it because the convoy's response was to use their escape shuttles. Not all of them survived, but four shuttles managed to make it to Saturn and get GP protection. The pirates took the ships."

"Why would the pirates come out here?" Lyssa asked. "There's nothing in this area unless a random comet's flying through."

"Maybe they came out here to hide?" Kathi suggested.

"There are rumors of a pirate stronghold we haven't been able to find," Jean Marie Ward, Kathi's night shift counterpart, said. "Maybe it's out here."

"There's nothing out here," James said. "Other than this wreckage and what we all need to admit is the *Sallie Ruth*."

The ship was moving toward them. They still had time to get away, but determining what had happened to the three ships was important, and John knew it. While they couldn't save whoever had been on these ships, they had a duty to stop this from happening to anyone else.

John thought about the stories his grandfather had told him. "Maybe these ships were lured away. They saw something and followed?"

"It's possible," Lyssa said. "But we need to determine if the ship that just showed up is part of the problem."

As she said this, they all heard the distress signal.

"The signal is definitely coming from the ship that just appeared," Kathi said. "Orders?"

"We are Galactic Police," Lyssa said, voice as even as Kathi's. "We respond per GP protocol."

"This is Galactic Police vessel *Eighty-Thirty*. Please explain the nature of your emergency." Kathi repeated the hail several times. There was no reply, but the distress signal didn't cease. She turned the volume down. "Now what?"

"Now," Lyssa said, "we avoid the wreckage of these other ships and we go do what we're trained to do—we assist those in need."

* * *

"Are we certain the hail is real?" Dean Hodos, the night shift navigator, asked as they headed toward the ship. "That ship could just have a self-charging distress signal. They weren't unheard of during expansion."

"If that's the case, then we'll go over and claim the find of the century," Ken Katano, the Officer in Charge for night shift, said cheerfully. "Either we're helping out or we're heroes. I'm good with those outcomes."

"Are we close enough to spot call letters at least?" Jean Marie asked.

"Not at this angle," Kathi replied.

"We're past the wreckage," Lyssa said as she sped them up. "I'll maneuver us so we can circle around it."

"Enhancing security's exterior view," Kathi said.

They all saw it. The call numbers and the name. John knew this because everyone, Lyssa included, drew in their breath.

"It's *E-2020*." James' voice shook. "And the name is what we all knew it would be—*Sallie Ruth*."

* * *

"We need to get out of here," Ken said, no cheer in his voice now.

Lyssa huffed in exasperation. "Katano, not you, too? The *Sallie Ruth* is a myth. We need to deal with facts and reality."

"Reality is that the ship we're still heading toward is start-of-expansion old," James said through gritted teeth, "and has the call letters and the name of the most notorious ship in our system's history. What other reality do you need to deal with?"

"There's a good chance that the *Salle Ruth* uses the distress call to draw ships closer." Dean was backing James on this, not that John could blame either one of them for being afraid.

"Maybe she does," Lyssa said. "Maybe this is a supernatural plot. Then again, maybe there's still someone alive on that ship—scavengers who got aboard, pirates who we would want to arrest, robotics in need of human assistance to return from the Blackness. It's our *duty* to find out what's going on and fix it."

"Fix it…" John murmured. His mother's words came back to him, about how stories weren't always true. "We have a duty to protect and serve, just like the Captain's saying. But there's only one way to break the spell of the *Sallie Ruth*."

"Make her renounce her evil," Dean said.

Jean Marie snorted. "Yes, it's always the woman's fault, isn't it?"

John spun around and looked at her. "Yes, that's what my mother always says—that we have to understand that stories are told by the victors and they aren't always true, particularly in regard to how women are portrayed."

Lyssa heaved a sigh. "How do we know the *Sallie Ruth* exists?"

"It's in front of us?" Kathi turned around. "Are you well?" She sounded worried.

Lyssa grunted in annoyance. "I am. I'm trying to think. The rest of you could try it, too."

"What do you mean?" Jean Marie asked.

"If it was a myth, that makes sense. It's a story told to children because telling children scary stories is something we humans love to do for no sane reasons. Now, if we can believe what our eyes and systems tell us, it's real and in front of us. But the story says that no one ever escapes."

"And, if no one escapes, how did the story spread?" John asked. "That's what you mean."

"It is."

"Some have escaped," James said. "Obviously."

"Why and how?" Jean Marie asked, clearly siding with Lyssa and John. "Why let some survive? There were three ships, and all of them were destroyed. But the *Sallie Ruth* hasn't destroyed us yet and, in fact, is merely sending out a distress signal. Why? We're close enough now to see her without viewscreen magnification."

"I think the most important question is whether or not the ship is going to continue to *let* us live," Kathi pointed out.

"Someone has to keep the myth going," John said. "And who better than eight GP officers?"

"Right." Lyssa shook her head. "This could be real, could prove the myth. Or this could be some elaborate hoax. Or something, anything, in between. We won't find out by yakking at each other. There's really only one way to know the truth—everyone, get into your wetsuits and prepare to board this vessel."

* * *

GP officers were equipped with a variety of spacesuits, because circumstances changed depending on where in the system they happened to be. The wetsuit version was based on ancient Earth prototypes that sat tight against the body. They were heated, reinforced, and they allowed officers to move more freely than standard spacesuits. The helmets used for wetsuits were also more contoured than the standard fishbowls and they had internal communications, meaning they wouldn't have to be head-to-head to talk to each other.

They also had utility belts that allowed them to clip whatever they might need to their waists, including oxygen tanks, and small jetpacks that went onto their backs. The jetpacks meant they didn't have to connect ship-to-ship in order to board another vessel. Necessary in many cases, not just when they were facing what might be the biggest terror in the solar system.

All eight of them were in their wetsuits and helmets. Lyssa might not have been convinced that the myth of the *Sallie Ruth* was real, but she wasn't willing to let any of them risk it. If the ship was hit, those inside would have a fighting chance of survival if they were in the wetsuits.

Everyone's primary oxygen tanks were connected and connections were triple-checked. Then it was time to determine who was going over. John raised his hand immediately. "I'll never forgive myself if I miss this opportunity."

Jean Marie stepped next to him. "I'm with John, same reason."

"I want Communications manned at all times," Lyssa said, "so that means you'll stay in our ship, Schreiber."

"I'm willing to go, I'm willing to stay," Kathi replied. "Who else is staying with me?"

"Katano, I want you covering Command," Lyssa said. "If you think you can do so without panicking."

Ken nodded. "I'm more than a little apprehensive, but we don't leave our people behind, particularly in this kind of situation."

"Security has a duty to go," Brad said. "And I'm going to be more help with the away team."

"The rest of us are going over?" James asked.

"If you and Hodos aren't too terrified to do so, yes."

"Past terrified by now," Dean said. "I'm sort of at fatalistic."

"Me, too," James said with a laugh. "But I'm with John—if we're doing this, then I want to see it all for myself, rather than tell people how I ran away like a coward."

Ken took Lyssa's place at the main controls, Kathi remained at her post, and the rest of them headed to the airlock. There they clipped on two extra oxygen tanks each and made sure they had weapons. They let the airlock depressurize and floated out into the Blackness.

The *8030's* floodlights made it easy to see, and Lyssa had already maneuvered them to what old schematics said was this type of ship's externally activated airlock. They were close enough that no one would need their jetpack—they could all just shove off the *8030* and sail to the *Sallie Ruth*.

"Security going first," John said. "Brad, wait until I've landed before you head over." With that, John shoved off.

He'd aimed himself well and landed against the door. He didn't hesitate—he grabbed the airlock's handle and squeezed.

Against all logic, the handle moved easily. Something this old should have been hard to work, possibly even frozen solid, but it reacted as if it had just gone through a maintenance overhaul.

The door opened without John having to do anything else. Because he was holding the handle, he floated with the door. Which was safer, in case of explosions. But nothing came out through the airlock.

He went hand-over-hand and got inside. "Seems clear."

The others joined him one at a time, each aiming for the safety of the airlock.

Brad brought up the rear. "Close this or leave it open?"

"If there are living beings on this ship, not closing the airlock door will likely kill them," Lyssa replied.

"Closing it might trap us," James pointed out.

"I have a laser drill with me," Brad replied. "We can cut our way out if we have to."

"Close it," Lyssa said calmly. Brad did as requested, though John held onto him just in case. The door closed and they all waited. No attack. John hit the pressurization button and the old ship did what it was supposed to. "Helmets stay on," Lyssa said, as John went to the interior airlock door. "Even if life support is working."

John opened the door. No attack. They all activated the magnetization in the feet of their wetsuits—whatever else might or might not be working, the grav-generators were definitely not on. John stepped out and the others followed, Brad continuing to bring up the rear.

"I've pulled up the schematics for this class of ship," Kathi shared via their coms. "Do you want me to direct you?"

"Definitely," John said. "Captain, I suggest we head for the bridge."

"I agree."

"On it. Go to your left." Kathi continued to direct them and they clomped along, moving carefully and slowly. Meeting no one and seeing nothing other than an old ship.

"There's no dust," Jean Marie said after a few minutes. "Nothing that would indicate there wasn't a full crew on board keeping this ship spotless."

"It's too spotless," James said. "We keep our ship neat and clean, and our ship is nowhere near this…immaculate."

"It's like no one's here, other than a really dedicated cleaning crew," Dean added.

"The airlock handle functioned perfectly," John said. "I'd kind of expected the *Sallie Ruth* to be more like the descriptions of the *Flying Dutchman*—decrepit."

"Maybe the ghosts like it clean," Ken said with a morose laugh.

"I expect to find a trap," Lyssa said. "Being sprung by living people."

They moved along, finding no one.

"Do you want to search the ship before you go to the bridge?" Kathi asked. "I'm scanning and see no life signs other than the six of you."

"Is there a reason for us to do so?" Lyssa asked.

"No," Kathi admitted. "Other than this is weird and getting weirder."

They reached the bridge. John saw no one, so the six of them entered. And, suddenly, they weren't alone anymore.

* * *

There were people in here, lots of them. The scene was chaotic, but John was aware that the clothing these people wore wasn't from this day and age. They also weren't making any sounds, though their mouths moved, and their expressions suggested a lot of noise was happening.

"Those are expansion-era clothes," James said, sounding awed and scared.

"Hello," Lyssa said. "We're here to help you."

None of the people they could see paid her any mind. "I don't think they know we're here," John said slowly.

"They appeared when we stepped into this room," Jean Marie pointed out. "And the alarm has shut off. Is this a hologram of some kind?"

"I can't identify any systems like that as being functional or running," Kathi said. "And there are still no signs of life other than all of you."

"Doesn't mean there isn't a projector around somewhere."

Jean Marie started searching the bridge. Dean went to help her. Lyssa and Brad tried to interact with the people they could see. Brad accidentally stumbled into one—and kept on going through three others until he hit up against a wall.

"They're ghosts," James said, voice shaking.

"Still looking for a projector," Jean Marie called. "Stay calm, it's an illusion of some kind, I'm sure."

"I'm not," James muttered.

John watched the people. "They're repeating," he said after a few minutes. "I think we need to pay attention to what's happening."

John identified three people who seemed to be the main players—one was a tall, handsome man who had a noble look. This, John assumed, was Madichon Vanjans. There was a woman with dark, curly hair and big, green eyes. She was beautiful and dressed well, so he figured this was Sallie Ruth herself.

The third man was small and mean looking, an unimpressive specimen of humanity, with a sly sneer and narrow eyes. Robert Himmel, possibly.

Only, the scene wasn't playing out as his grandfather had described. Sallie Ruth hid behind the handsome man, and the small, insignificant one seemed to be threatening them. In the story, Sallie Ruth was in love with Robert Himmel, so she should have been with the small, mean-looking man. Only John couldn't understand why any woman would want him—he radiated a level of evil John had only seen in those who'd willingly joined with Boser Geist.

The other people were trying to pull the handsome couple away, but the small man waved something around and John watched people fall down, seemingly dead, one after another, until it was just the handsome man and the beautiful woman standing.

The small man did something, John couldn't tell what, and the handsome man was thrown against the wall, what looked like liquid metal wrapping around him. The small man went to the woman and grabbed her, trying to drag her with him. She pulled away and ran to the man who was bound, trying to get the metal off of him. She failed and the small man came for her. She ran, he followed.

None of this corresponded with the story his grandfather had told him.

The scene began another repetition. "This story is wrong," John said. "I need to see the ship's log."

Jean Marie and Dean had finished their search and headed for John. It was a mistake.

Jean Marie touched the beautiful woman, froze, blinked, and shook herself. Because of this, Dean stumbled against the small, nasty man. He did the same. Then he looked at Jean Marie. "You will be mine," he snarled, in a voice that definitely wasn't his own. It was a small, vicious voice—Dean's voice was a pleasant baritone that had never sounded vicious.

"Never!" Jean Marie's voice was also not hers, and she sounded terrified. "You are not my husband, you have no right to me!"

James ran over, presumably to try to help. But he touched the handsome man and reacted as the others had. "You sir, are worse than a pirate," he said imperiously to Dean. "You are of the lowest rank on my ship as well as in your soul and I will not allow you to terrorize my wife any longer."

All three of them were still them, still in their wetsuits and helmets, but the people they'd merged with were superimposed over them. It was as if his crewmates were wearing the ghost images. This hadn't happened with Brad. Maybe only these three could possess someone, or perhaps Jean Marie touching Sallie Ruth had "activated" the ghosts.

Dean pulled a weapon. "I'll kill every one of you to get what I want. I'm more powerful than any of you realize."

"That's a live weapon, one of ours," John called to Lyssa and Brad.

"What is going on?" Lyssa asked.

"I think they've been taken over by spirits," John replied. "I'm certain of it, honestly."

"That's ridiculous," Lyssa said as Dean started shooting at the ghost people. The laser fire ricocheted off the walls and the three of them had to duck to avoid being hit. The shots were clear of Jean Marie and James, but John didn't know that they'd get lucky twice.

"There are no burn marks anywhere," Brad said, as he dragged Lyssa over to where John was. "That shouldn't be possible."

"According to all of you, being on this ship shouldn't be possible," Lyssa replied. "What do we do to fix whatever this Charon-damned situation is?"

Dean waved his hand and James slammed against a wall. Then liquid metal wrapped around him. Jean Marie screamed and ran to James, trying to free him. Dean laughed evilly.

"Where would the ship's log be?" John asked urgently. "I have to see it, at least the listing of the crew."

"Normally it's kept in the captain's quarters," Kathi replied. "That's been standard practice before anyone on Earth thought about going into the Blackness, and it's true today."

"Lead me there, if you can," John said. "You two, whatever you do, don't bump into any of the ghost people."

"Pedder, what are you hoping to do?" Lyssa asked.

Jean Marie ran out of the room, and Dean followed her.

"I'm hoping to save Sallie Ruth."

* * *

Kathi's directions got him where he needed to be. Of course, he could have found the cabin without them, because he'd run after Dean and Jean Marie, and Jean Marie had headed for the same room Kathi directed him to.

Dean had a hold of her, though, and he dragged her away. John debated with himself—he knew that Dean could hurt Jean Marie, or worse, but in his gut, he also knew that the way to fix whatever this was would be to listen to his mother—the story that had been told for centuries wasn't true. He had to figure out what was wrong with it, and why.

He went into the captain's quarters. It was clear that two people lived here, a man and a woman. That fit with the story. He searched quickly, while hearing screams through his helmet, which confirmed that Brad and Lyssa were now playing the parts Jean Marie and James had just done. Fortunately, the captain had been tidy and John found the log quickly.

He breathed a sigh of relief as he opened it—he could read what was written here—it was in the Galactic Language that had been created at the start of expansion and was still used today.

He went to the listing of the crew and drew in his breath. What he'd suspected was now proven true—the captain of the *Sallie Ruth* was indeed married to the lady herself, only the captain was Robert Himmel.

Himmel had said that the man threatening them was the lowest crew member, so John looked at the last crew entry next. Sure enough, Madichon Vanjans was shown to be the Ordinary Spaceman in charge of Scullery. Meaning he was the ship's official cleaner, the lowest rank possible in the days of expansion. OS crewmen didn't need to go through any academy in order to serve, because their positions were necessary and dangerous. The thinking had been that you could lose an OS without much loss of skill.

His mother had also told him that most lies always had a kernel of truth. The truth of the story was that Sallie Ruth was married to the captain, the rest of it was backwards and inside out. Himmel was the noble captain, Vanjans had killed the crew, and Sallie Ruth wasn't untrue at all.

"So," John muttered to himself, "why and how did the story come to be? And how is this ship still flying?"

"No idea," Ken said. "But we've docked with the *Sallie Ruth* and Schreiber and I are coming over."

"That's a bad idea," John said urgently.

"From what we can tell," Kathi said, voice shaking, "Jean Marie and James are dead, and Brad and Lyssa are in danger. We have to come help. We'll be to you in a couple of minutes."

John cursed, but only in his head. If what Kathi had said was true, then all they were going to do was give Vanjans, in the form of Dean, another couple to murder.

He jerked. The story said Himmel and Sallie Ruth were put into the brig, near but apart, and that might mean they hadn't been killed. John held onto the log and ran out of the room, heading in the direction he'd seen Dean dragging Jean Marie.

John's timing was good again, because this time Dean had Lyssa and was dragging her along. John followed, being careful to stay far enough back that there was no risk of him bumping into either one of them.

Sure enough, they went to the brig. It had several cells and Dean tossed Lyssa into one of them. John saw Jean Marie in the adjacent cell but couldn't tell if either woman was alive. Dean ran off and was back with Brad, who was wrapped in that liquid metal. Dean tossed Brad into the cell next to James. The men's cells were across from the women's. As with the women, John couldn't tell if either man was alive.

"Ken, Kathi, don't engage at all," John said. "Get back to our ship!"

He heard screams, then Ken saying the exact same thing that he'd heard James and Brad say.

There were three more sets of cells available, meaning Ken and Kathi would be down here shortly. John needed to do something, anything, but he had no idea what. He looked at the book still in his hands. The log might provide some kind of clue. He started reading.

John discovered that Vanjans had worked hard to be on the crew of the *Sallie Ruth* and Himmel had been rather impressed by him, particularly because Vanjans had an affinity for weapons creation and repair.

Shortly, Dean returned, dragging Kathi with him. He flung her into a cell and took off again.

John skimmed ahead and found an entry that mentioned that the ship had been hit by a rock of some kind. Vanjans had been the crew member to patch the hole and save the day and had been lauded as a hero.

There is no sign of what entered my ship, Himmel wrote, *and Madichon insists that he saw no sign of it, either.*

Vanjans was obviously evil. Maybe he hadn't been before whatever it was hit the ship, but definitely after. John was willing to make the leap and assume that Vanjans had indeed found what created the hole and figured out a way to use it.

John considered this. Vanjans had waved his hands around and had killed crew members, but John had seen no projectile. And the liquid metal was like nothing he'd ever seen or heard of.

Dean returned with Ken and tossed him into the cell next to Brad, then he left the room. John didn't figure he had much time until their ship was destroyed just as the three stolen merchant ships had been.

There were billions of other solar systems out there. They all knew it. But they'd perfected short range warp and terraforming much sooner than long-range warp. Once the scientific community involved with expansion realized they could alter warp engines to create a way to speed through the Blackness quickly, humanity decided that their own solar system was plenty good enough. Sol was important, but Jupiter and Saturn provided much as well and, over time, humanity decided that if someone from another system was going to come visit, that was fine, but there was no interest in going farther into the Blackness than necessary.

But what if what had hit the *Sallie Ruth* was from another solar system? And what if that was still on the ship somewhere?

John left the brig and searched for Dean. He found him because Dean was muttering to himself and, thanks to the coms, John could hear him.

"Call me small and insignificant, will she?" Dean snarled to himself. "Well, we'll see about that. I'm the hero, I saved the ship, I saved her. And she repays that by spurning my love? She'll pay. They all will."

John found Dean in a room near to the brig—clearly this was Vanjans' room. Dean stood in front of a rock the size of a soccer ball. It wasn't smooth, with flat-topped cones all over, but the surface was far too precise to be random—whatever this was, someone had worked it into this shape.

Dean started telling the story John had heard all his life to this rock. The rock glowed and hummed. Then something radiated out of the rock, a bluish glow that expanded. It went through John and he felt his belief in the story Grandpa always told him return.

Then he heard his mother's voice. "John, stories are told by the survivors. You keep an open mind, no matter what the story tells you to think."

John blinked and shook off the feeling, the desire, to believe. Dean left the room, presumably to destroy their ship, since that was the last part of the story. It was now or never.

John went to the rock and picked it up. It throbbed like it was alive. He looked at it. "If you're a sentient being, you need to stop this. If you don't reverse the curse, I'm going to destroy you."

The rock continued to throb. He heard the sound of someone running. Right, Dean could hear him, and even if Vanjans didn't know who John was or that he was here, if he heard another man's voice, he'd come to kill that man.

John pulled his laser and shot the rock. It absorbed the laser fire. John didn't have time to try another weapon. He holstered his gun, tucked the logbook under his arm, put both hands onto the rock, and concentrated. "Robert Himmel was brave and true and the captain of the *Sallie Ruth*, named for his beloved, faithful wife. Madichon Vanjans was a small, evil man who took his moment of heroism and turned it into a way to destroy the man who'd given him a chance in order to steal that good man's wife."

John thought about what Vanjans had likely done to Sallie Ruth, forcing her husband to watch. "Vanjans tried to force himself on Sallie Ruth, but Himmel, in his righteous rage, was able to break out of his cell and save Sallie Ruth from this fate. He executed Vanjans for treason and the murder of his crew. Then he and Sallie Ruth took their ship and sailed into the Blackness, to live their lives in peace."

"No!" Dean screamed, as the bluish glow radiated out. It was a brighter blue than the glow when Dean had said it. John didn't know if that was because the rock was designed for happy endings or if it was just the power of John's own belief.

He turned, still holding the rock, and repeated the story he'd just told. Dean screamed and fell to the floor. The ghost image of Vanjans was still there, though, screaming at him, but now he couldn't hear any sounds. John held onto the rock with one hand and managed to throw Dean over his shoulder. Then he left the room, carefully skirting the ghost of Vanjans.

John returned to the brig as quickly as he could. The others were there, and, thankfully, though they all looked hurt, they were alive. The ghosts of Himmel and Sallie Ruth held each other, but she looked right at John and blew him a kiss. Then they left the brig. John figured they were headed to the bridge.

The weird metal that had been around the men was gone, as if it had never existed. Maybe it hadn't—it was just something Vanjans had created to help him in his revenge story. The cells were open, and John handed Dean off to Ken, who was the least injured. "We need to get back to our ship as fast as possible. This ship is about to leave our solar system."

The others didn't argue, they just helped each other and moved as rapidly as possible to the *8030*. They got inside and John disconnected the ship-to-ship docking.

Just in time.

The *Sallie Ruth* turned away from them and sailed off, heading exactly where John had said she would—out of the solar system forever.

"What happened?" Lyssa asked.

John shook his head. "You wouldn't believe me if I told you." He went to his quarters and put the logbook and rock in his locker. He looked at them before closing the door. "Though I imagine that, ultimately, you'll all believe the true story of the *Sallie Ruth*.

Methuselah

Jacey Bedford

My name's Thomas Rendell. Call me Renny. I own thirty percent of the *Staten Island* and I'm currently her captain, voted in fair and square by the crew, my business partners. The *Staten's* not pretty and she costs us deep in the pockets to maintain, but she's home. She's a squared-off salvage vessel, all cargo hold and machinery bay, with a tight flight deck, barely big enough for the six of us. We're close. I know these guys like I know the ship. I know them, but I don't always like them. Families are like that.

We were out here chasing rumors of a derelict, hoping for the big haul that would solve all our financial problems. Without a new fuel core this was our last trip. We'd have to sell up, and the *Staten* wouldn't fetch enough to pay off the loan we took out last year for repairs. A new fuel core might keep us flying for another ten—or even twenty—years.

If I was a praying man, which I'm not, I'd ask for twenty. That would see me out. I've been in space all my life, I was born in the big empty and I'll likely die here, probably before my fiftieth birthday. Space damages a person's cells. It's just the way things are. No use being glum about it.

We'd been searching for months. We were low on protein cubes, and the water tasted as if it had been through each one of us a hundred times—which it probably had—when we found something.

It wasn't much more than a blip on our screen at first, but out here even that was worth investigating. This blip turned out to be a very faint distress beacon.

Zara Tanveer used maneuvering thrusters to glide the *Staten Island* into position ten klicks off the port bow of the huge hulk drifting dead in space. Long and cylindrical, the ship had a domed head. A section of scaffolding at the waist protected a tube linking the cylinder to a sphere. That was likely where the drive was housed. There was some scoring on her hull, but nothing that told us why she was floating in space. I didn't recognize the design. I checked it against our database, but came up empty, so either it was old, or possibly a prototype. Maybe we'd find reclaimable tech on board. That would be a bonus.

"Try it one more time, Dan." I nodded toward Danny Blake, currently on comms duty. He's our best geek. So far, all attempts at communication with the unidentified ship had failed, so I wasn't expecting a reply, but it wouldn't hurt to try.

"Nothing, boss." Dan scratched his bristly chin, the sandy fuzz not quite dense enough yet to call a beard. "She's silent."

"Let Zara take the comm. I need you on the salvage team."

"Don't you need me on the salvage team, Cap?" Zara said.

"No, I need you in the pilot chair with the comm patched through."

She scowled.

"You're the best pilot we've got, Zar, and this might yet prove to be a pirate trap."

"If it is, we'll know soon enough," Malusi Kheswa muttered under his breath.

I gave him a hard stare and he shut up after mouthing, "Just saying."

Yeah, okay, he wasn't wrong. Salvage ships had been caught out before, but bringing in a vessel like this would pay for all the repairs we needed and then some. It was worth taking a risk.

"Okay, suit up," I said.

"About fuckin' time." Tatiana Zasimova might have had a name like a Russian princess, and the looks, too, but she had a mouth like a sewer. She was the only one without a percentage in the *Staten Island*, so she drew pay as our chief engineer, and I had to admit, she did the job well.

We suited up, carrying helmets, and piled into the skiff. Ruth Tsira took the helm and nudged us toward the derelict, then spiraled around and around the length of her and back again to make sure there was no pirate vessel clinging like a limpet to her outer hull.

"Has she got a registration plate?" I asked.

Danny increased the magnification on the monitor. "There!" He pointed. "She's the *Methuselah,* registered to the Ledbetter Foundation, London."

"London, Earth?" Malusi asked.

"I guess so," I said, checking the database again, "but she's neither registered as active, nor on the missing list."

"That makes her either very new or very old," Danny said. "Doesn't look new, though, does she?"

Danny kept calling the ship, but she didn't respond.

We took another turn around the exterior, looking for a good access point. I figured we'd probably have to cut our way in, but there was a ramp lowered under the *Methuselah's* belly, about two thirds back on the cylinder.

Shit. If it could accommodate the skiff it could accommodate a pirate vessel.

"Renny?" Ruth asked. "Your call."

"Take her in," I said. "Slow and steady." The skiff wasn't armed, but the nose carried metal-cutting pincers which could easily tear a hole in any ship at close quarters.

Ruth started the glide up the ramp, lights blazing.

"You go, girl," Tati said. "Straight up the wazoo. This is the nearest thing I'm gonna get to a fuck for at least a year.

Ruth huffed out a breath that might have been a laugh or a snort of derision, but stayed focused on the maneuvering thrusters, using tiny bursts to guide us on to the floor of a large hangar, thankfully devoid of any other ships, pirate or otherwise. A clang reverberated throughout the skiff as we bumped down on to the deck plates.

"Fuckin' gravity," Tati said. "How 'bout that?"

Yeah, how about that? The ship had gravity. What other systems might be active?

"Kill our lights," I said. The hangar went black for a full two seconds and then the *Methuselah's* emergency lighting kicked in.

"Bloody hell! She's still got lights." Danny said. "Lights and gravity, but no atmo."

Ahead of us the airlock door leading to the interior of the ship was wide open to vacuum, which likely meant the whole ship had vented atmo and was as cold as the devil's tits.

"Ruth, stay with the skiff." I put on my helmet and nodded to the others. "Danny, Malusi, Tati, with me."

We left the skiff two by two through our tiny airlock. Even though there was gravity in the hangar we didn't know how far it extended so we all set our mag boots to quarter grav, strong enough to stop us from floating, but not so strong that it made walking difficult. With a cursory glance around the empty hangar, we clomped toward the open airlock into the belly of the ship. A long main corridor stretched out before us with passages branching off left and right. Lights flickered into being ahead of us and faded behind us.

My helmet readings showed normal radiation levels, and nothing warm enough to be living, so the exploration of the side corridors and cargo holds could wait. We needed to find the flight deck and see what kind of mess could kill a crew or cause them to abandon ship. We carried sidearms, but we had our weapons clipped into leg holsters, safeties on, all except Malusi, our designated marksman and muscle. Derelicts could seem creepy and firing wild at shadows could get a person killed, or kill someone else. Malusi was cool under pressure—a bit too cool sometimes.

"I'm sure this damned corridor is longer than the ship," Danny said. "Have we found some kind of inter-dimensional portal?"

"No fuckin' woo-woo here," Tati waved her arm toward the next intersection. "Just spooky lights and too many nights reading horror stories."

The corridor had a utilitarian feel to it, all chunky metal and doorways large enough for machinery or cargo crates.

I was just thinking how eerily still it was when—

"What's that?" Danny spun ninety degrees to face the corridor intersecting on our left. Malusi shouldered him out of the way and planted his feet, pointing his sidearm down the darkened corridor in a two-handed grip. The beams from his cuff lights cut the darkness.

"Nothing there," Malusi said.

"I thought I saw—" Danny's voice faltered. "Never mind. Jumping at shadows, sorry."

"Replay your helmet cam," I said. "To me only. The rest of you keep watch."

Danny sent his helmet feed to mine. We watched his recording together as he approached the intersection. The lights moved with us. The side corridor, tunnel-like, remained dark except for the overspill of light from above our heads.

Nothing strange there.

Until—

I flinched, even though my brain knew I was watching a replay. Yes, the deep darkness had flickered for a moment, coalesced into something deeper, darker, and—more importantly—moving.

I swallowed hard. "It wasn't your imagination, Dan."

"Fuckin' hell," Tati said. "What was it?"

"I don't know. It was there for less than a second and then gone," I said. "Since some of the systems are still working there might be maintenance bots with power. Seems unlikely, but a bot is my guess. It's certainly not going to be anything alive in this vacuum."

"Unless it's suited up like we are," Danny said.

After an uncomfortable silence, we all drew and checked our sidearms.

"Better get to the flight deck and see if we can find out how long this baby's been sitting out here," I said. "If she's as old as she looks, all her systems should have closed down by now—power drained."

"I could go aft, take a look at the drive," Tati said. She didn't sound all that enthusiastic.

"Yeah, right, we've all seen those vids where the plucky explorers split up," Danny said.

"Stick together," I said, "at least until we know more."

With Malusi taking point and me bringing up the rear, this time with my sidearm at the ready, we made our way forward. I won't say we ran exactly, but we didn't waste any time. There were no more incidents as we climbed the emergency stair—more like a ladder—to the next deck. We didn't trust the antigrav shaft. The next deck was less industrial. We moved through a section that had blue walls and numbered, human-sized doors every three meters.

"Crew quarters?" Tati asked.

"Passenger cabins," Danny said. "Too many of them to be crew quarters."

He was probably right. We passed from blue walls to yellow and the door numbers repeated the sequence. The passageway ended in what looked like a dining hall, neat and clean with no detritus of interrupted meals. Beyond that was another antigrav shaft. Again we took the ladderway. I felt, rather than heard, the clang of my magboots on the treads. Maybe it was the something-moving-in-the-darkness vibe, but the *Methuselah* felt spooky, in a way that most of the ships and space-junk we salvaged didn't.

The flight deck could be anywhere on a ship like this. It made most sense to have it center ship, not stuck on the outside like a pimple on an exposed arse, but as we progressed from floor to floor we realized they'd gone for the pimple option. We eventually arrived at a ladderway with a notice that said, "No passengers beyond this point."

"About fuckin' time," Tati said.

Malusi went up first, followed by Danny, Tati, and me bringing up the rear.

"Oh, shit!"

The tone of Danny's voice set my heart pounding. I stuck my head up above the ladderway into a small lobby and saw what he was oh-shitting about.

A body lay across the door to what was probably the flight deck judging by the authorized-personnel-only notice. But it was not so much a corpse as a mummy. It wore a close-fitting flight suit, thin enough to see that there wasn't much flesh on the bones beneath. This guy was starving before the air ran out. A flight suit like that wouldn't have given him much protection against the cosmic background temperature. 2.7 Kelvin would kill a person every time. The mummy's skull was covered in leathery skin, freeze-dried to parchment and blackened. And—oh gods—his eyes were still open. That, more than anything, made me want to retch.

It was difficult to tell what he had been like in life, but shape-wise he was human enough.

I wondered if opening the ship to vacuum had been his last act as life support failed and the temperature plummeted.

"Desiccated," Danny said. "Too cold and dry for microbes to rot the body."

"Fuckin' creepy," Tati shivered and poked the body with the toe of her boot.

I sucked a breath in, half expecting the body to crumble to dust, but it didn't.

"Have a bit of respect for our friend here," I pulled my thoughts together. "He was a person once. Let's move him to one side, see if we can access the flight deck. We'll deal with him later. Give him some kind of funeral and send him off into space."

I sheathed my sidearm and put my hands under his armpits to drag him a couple of meters, hoping like hell that his arms wouldn't come off. They didn't. He was surprisingly heavy for someone with all the juice sucked out of him, and floppy rather than stiff. As I bent over him, he looked as if he was staring up into my face.

"Uhhh." I dropped his shoulders and took a pace back.

"What's up?" Tati asked.

"Nothing." I told myself not to be so stupid. "Nothing at all." I grabbed him more firmly, and dragged him over to the wall without looking at his face, then I closed his eyes, thankful for my spacesuit gloves.

I shook my head to clear it as Danny worked on the door lock. Something was bugging me about our friend the corpse, but I couldn't figure out what it was. As the door slid open and we entered the flight deck, the corpse went right out of my mind. I don't know what I'd expected, but it wasn't this.

The flight deck was beautiful. I'm not sure how functional it was, but for an old ship it looked…futuristic. The lights came up as we walked in and spread out. Silver consoles gleamed. There was not one speck of dust, and no indication of any wear.

Danny released a long, slow, appreciative whistle. "Oh, yes." He slid into the pilot's chair and flipped open a control panel at the end of each chair arm. "If there's any power left in this baby, I'll find it."

Tati flitted from station to station identifying each one as she went. "Comms. Internal systems." Then with a sigh of satisfaction, "Drive. How are you coming on with power, Danny?"

"Emergency power coming online now. It should at least fire up the consoles. Not sure it will do much else, and it might not last long."

"Yeah, got it, thanks," Tati said. "Power to this console, anyway."

"And to comms," Malusi said. "I'll see if I can find the last few messages."

The systems panel began to glow softly. There should be an ID that would give us a clue to the *Methuselah's* history: her commissioning date, her business out here in the big empty, and maybe, if I was lucky, a passenger list and cargo manifest.

Information began to flicker on my console's holo screen. I sifted through it, diving deeper and deeper.

"Holy shit!" I said.

"What?" Tati looked up from her screen. "Fuckin' what?"

"This boat is seven hundred years old. Her last run was a colony settlement on the outer rim. She'd dropped her load and was on a return journey three hundred and seventy years ago. She's been floating ever since."

"Why?"

"Wish I knew. Logs end there. Captain was Jornish Marum."

"Crew? She had to have fuckin' crew."

"Yeah. No. Maybe. Chunks of information missing."

"But there was no fuckin' skiff in the hangar. No fuckin' lifeboat. They gotta have fuckin' evacuated, yeah? Please don't tell me we're gonna find more bodies like that one." Tati jerked her head toward the outer lobby.

I checked in with Zara and Ruth at their respective posts, told them what we'd found so far, including the body…and then I froze.

The eyes.

The body's eyes.

At 2.7 Kelvin the corpse's eyeballs should have been frozen solid.

They weren't. They were clear…and moist.

And the eyelids had still been flexible enough to close without cracking.

"Oh, fuck!"

"What is it, Renny?" Malusi, asked.

I lurched for the door and looked toward where I'd left the corpse. My belly dropped into my bowels. "The body," I said. "It's gone."

"That's not possible," Danny jerked to his feet and pushed past me. "Oh."

"I know what gone looks like, Dan."

"Maybe there is someone alive on board," Malusi said. "A body doesn't just move on its own. That shadow Danny saw earlier…"

"If there's someone on board, what's the thing they're going to want most?" I said, reaching for my comm unit.

"Oh, fuck—the skiff," Malusi said.

"And the *Staten*," Danny added.

I'd already reached the same conclusion. "Ruth, secure the skiff. Possible hostiles on board. Zara, don't allow the skiff to dock with the *Staten* unless you're sure it's us. Respond, please."

"Gotcha, Cap." Zara's answer came back instantly.

"Ruth, respond, please," I said.

No answer.

"Ruthie, talk to me."

No answer.

"Come on." I jerked my head toward the ladderway.

"I might be able to seal the outer hangar doors from here," Danny said.

"Do it." I didn't like leaving one man behind. "Tati, stay with him. Malusi with me."

"Fuckin' no," Tati said.

"Fuckin' yes."

There were some advantages to being captain. Tati scowled at me, but she stayed.

Running in mag boots and a full suit wasn't easy, but we did our best. Malusi and I made it back to the hangar in far less time that we'd taken to find the flight deck. I didn't spot any moving shadows on the way, but to be honest I was concentrating on putting one foot in front of the other. Malusi had his sidearm ready and he twisted sideways as we passed the end of each darkened corridor. The lights stayed with us, but as we reached the hangar, the door, open when we arrived, was firmly closed. I tried the key pad.

No response.

Malusi looked all set to shoot the hell out of the mechanism but I put my arm out to check him.

"Danny, Tati, status?" I asked.

"Outer door secure," Danny said. "Skiff's going nowhere."

Unless it had already gone.

"The inner door is locked, can you open it?"

"Trying now," Tati said. "That any good?"

"No, nothing."

"Try that."

"No, yes. The lock's released. I think we can force it."

We pulled at the door and it opened a crack. While Malusi pulled I worked my arm into the gap and shoved.

The skiff was still there. I huffed out a breath of relief that steamed up my faceplate. Breathe slowly.

"Ruth, are you all right?" I asked. "Ruthie? Respond."

I heard static, as if the comm was open.

"Ruthie?"

"Y-yeah."

"What's happening?"

"There's a…thing," she said, voice trembling.

"What kind of thing?"

"I don't know. A zombie? A mummy?"

"Is it armed?"

"Does it need to be?"

"What does it want?"

"I don't know. It's trying to breathe."

"We're coming in," I said.

Malusi and I strong-armed the hangar door until it was wide enough to squeeze through. We ran for the skiff. The outer hatch was closed but not locked. It took an age to cycle through the tiny airlock, but when we did, the dead body from the flight deck, still looking mummified, was on its feet, back to the wall, but alert. It carried a piece of pipe, held like a weapon, toward Ruth.

Malusi didn't mess about. He raised his sidearm and put a bolt straight through its belly. It folded in half, dropped the pipe, and slid down the wall.

"Ha! That should do it." He sounded pleased with himself. "Stay dead this time."

Ruth stepped back, connected with the pilot's chair, now swiveled around to face the cabin, and sat down hard.

The corpse stirred. It lifted its head and croaked the kind of sound a human shouldn't make.

Malusi leveled his sidearm again.

The corpse raised one hand and uttered a sound that might have been, "No."

I put out my hand to stay Malusi's shot. "It—he doesn't look dangerous." I kicked the pipe out of reach. "Are you all right, Ruth?"

"I'm not injured, if that's what you mean, but what is that thing? Is it even human?"

The corpse turned his hand, palm upward. "Huu…ma," it croaked. "Wa… tuh."

"Water?" I asked.

"Huh." It sounded like assent. I took off my helmet, unsealed my gloves and set them to one side. I selected a pouch of water from the supplies locker and popped the seal on the drinking cap. I crouched by the…I couldn't keep calling him a corpse. I crouched down by the man and offered him the water. He took the pouch in his right hand, clutching his left to the hole in his belly.

If he hadn't been dead before, it wouldn't be long before he died now.

He sucked water down in tiny sips, showing no sign of stopping until he'd drunk the pouch flat. I glanced at the hole in his belly, wondering if water would leak out, but so far it was barely bleeding. There was just a little sluggish smudge of something dark and viscous.

"Bet-tah."

He let his head loll back against the wall and sighed.

"More?" I asked.

"Yeh. Ple…"

I didn't figure giving him more water would hurt him now. Even if we'd had a surgeon on board, the guy was as near dead as made no difference.

He sucked down the second pouch of water, swallowing two or three times between sips as if trying to keep the liquid down.

"Take it easy," I said.

"Yeh. 'M all right." He cleared his throat. "Better… Throat dry…so long. Can move…in vacuum, but…can't talk…without…air in y' lungs."

"I guess not."

"Needed air…tell you. Not dead… Never dead… No funeral."

"Funeral?" I didn't follow.

"You said…funeral…send me off into space."

I thought back. I had said that, but… "I said that over my helmet comm. How did you hear it?"

He took a few breaths and his chest ruckled. I thought it might be a laugh. "Lip-read." He took a breath between each word. "Lived…long…time…to learn…new skills."

"Sorry Malusi shot you," I said.

"I'm not," Malusi muttered.

"I'll heal," the not-corpse said.

I pressed my lips together. If the guy thought he was going to come back from this, he was sadly mistaken.

"What's going on?" Danny's voice came over the skiff's speaker.

Ruth leaned over the console. "You won't believe this. We've got a dead guy, but he's not. Dead, I mean."

"Coming down."

The comm cut off. I turned to the not-quite-dead guy. "How long have you been on the *Methuselah*? Is there anyone we can contact for you?"

"Nah. Just me. I've…been cap'n…since she…came…out of the yard." His words were starting to flow a little better. He took a big gulp of air. "Jornish Marum. That's me."

Jornish Marum tied in with the ship's log, but…I shook my head. "That's seven hundred years."

He twitched a grin and the papery skin on his lower lip split. "Is it? Don't feel a day over...four hundred. Musta lost track of time."

He couldn't be that old. He couldn't live in vacuum, or survive the cold. But he had. Oh, shit!

"Who else is on the ship with you?" Malusi asked.

He shook his head. "No one."

"What about the shadow?" I asked. "Something moved, down on the lower deck."

"Heh." He huffed out a breath. "Just me. Couldn't speak. Heard your comm, but no air. Couldn't answer. Could still move though. Immortality...it's a bitch. Has its own set of limitations." He took a deep breath. "Oh, that feels good." He breathed again.

"Immortal? That's impossible." Ruth leaned forward and stabbed a finger toward Marum.

"I assure you...it's not. Where was I?" He took his time, but the words were coming easier, now. "Oh, yeah. Wanted to see what kind of crew you were. Went down to the hangar, then tried to beat you back to the flight deck once I knew where you were heading. Pirates would have headed for the cargo bay first, though they'd ha' been disappointed. Wanted to overhear your plans. Intended to hide in the maintenance hatch, but... Took a lot out of me. Collapsed. You thought I was dead. Couldn't tell you otherwise. Needed to rest before I could move again, but I heard enough."

He closed his eyes. I thought he might be about to expire, but he shifted slightly, sitting more upright and slumping less. Instead of weakening, he seemed to be gaining strength. I'd seen it before when people didn't know they were on the verge of death. I didn't buy the whole immortality thing. I figured he was light-headed and probably hallucinating. There was no way this guy was seven hundred years old.

"How did you come to be here?" I asked. "Marooned on this ship, I mean,"

"Picked up a new crew. Have to every ten to fifteen years before they notice I don't age. New ones tried to mutiny. Bastards shot me twice, but they couldn't kill me. That's when they decided to space me. I spiked the drive, so they were stuck—spiked it too well as it turned out. It was me in the airlock or them." He shrugged and his skin creaked like old leather. "It's a long time to be floating in cold space when you can't die. Thought there'd be more chance of being found if I was with the ship. Put out a distress call on a loop while there was still atmo and settled down to wait." He must have seen the look on my face. "No, I didn't space 'em. They took the ship's boat. That's all right. I got time. More time than them. They're centuries dead by now. Didn't figure it would be so long, though. Ran out of...everything. More water please."

I passed him another drink, and realized his face was a bit less mummified, the dried skin had peeled off like the outer layer of an onion. The skin underneath looked a little more like skin and less like parchment. Even his color was changing. He was no longer blackened, but a more even brown. He lifted his left hand from his belly wound and the hole had closed over. I could see fresh skin through the gash in his suit. It looked human and healthy.

Maybe I did buy the immortality thing, but I wasn't sure how I felt about it.

The airlock cycled. Danny and Tati came through, hesitating when they saw Marum.

"What the fuck?" Tati said, taking off her helmet.

Danny just stood and stared until Tati nudged him to unclip the helmet from his suit.

"What the fuck's going on?" Tati asked.

"He belongs here," Malusi said, bitterness in his voice. "He's Jornish Marum, ship's captain for the last 700 years."

"Looks like shit," Danny said. "But how'd he get to be that old?"

"Dunno. Ask him." Malusi shrugged. "He says he's immortal."

"Can he make us immortal, too?" Danny asked. "Cos I sure would like to live beyond fifty. It hardly seems fair we should have such short lives and him such a long one."

I found myself nodding agreement. Danny had nailed it.

"It doesn't work like that," Marum said. "Don't ask me why, or why me. I don't know. My folks weren't immortal. I watched them die. I watched my sisters and brothers die, my wife, my children, my grandchildren, my great grandchildren. Everyone I ever loved, everyone I ever hated…they all turned to dust in the end. I walked the earth alone for thousands of years, and then I came out here into space. I thought it would make the time easier to bear."

"And did it?" I asked.

He shook his head. "I don't know. Times it did. Times it didn't."

"Fuck," Tati said. "If he's the captain, this ship's not legal salvage. Not unless he's dead." Her hand strayed toward her sidearm and then, as if she realized what she'd done, she snatched it back and folded her arms across her chest.

Marum took a shuddering breath. I swear I could hear the tissue of his lungs expanding. Maybe he was thinking here we go again. "Get it in your head," he said, "you can't kill me. You can only throw me out of an airlock."

"Can we?" Malusi asked. "Throw you out of an airlock, I mean?"

"I'm immortal. I don't have superpowers. You could probably space me, but that would be worse than killing me."

"Not for us," Malusi said. "We're a salvage crew. That's what we do. We fly out into the big empty, grab what we can get, take it in, and get paid."

We'd find a buyer for the *Methuselah* easily, probably one that wouldn't be too picky if we spaced the sole survivor, even presuming we 'fessed up to that. I looked at Marum. It was true he looked less dead now than he did when we found him. He was the only thing between us and the solution to all our financial troubles. We could get rid of him, take the ship and claim genuine salvage. It would be easy. Too easy.

"Space him," Malusi said. "We need this find."

Hearing it said like that, flat and certain, tore me up inside. I'd killed a man once in a pirate ambush. He'd have killed me if I'd been slower on the trigger, but it hadn't made it any easier. I'd fretted about it for months afterward; still woke in the night occasionally in a cold sweat. Could I murder an unarmed man—or worse—for money?

If I really believed Marum was immortal, he wouldn't be dead, just conveniently out of the way. I tried to imagine floating in the dead cold vacuum of space for all eternity, unable to breathe, but unable to die and with no hope of rescue. My throat clenched against the sudden urge to vomit.

Ruth had followed everything wide-eyed. Now she looked at me and asked, "Do we get a vote?" Her hand was on the comm so she'd probably cut Zara in on the conversation.

"You voted when you made me captain," I said. "Besides, I have a thirty percent share, you only have ten."

"Sure, Ruth only has ten," Malusi said, "but I've got fifteen percent. Danny has twenty-five; Zara has twenty. We could vote you out."

The comm crackled into life. "Activate the video." Zara said. "I'm not voting on someone's life if I can't look him in the eye."

"No one is voting," I said. "You made me captain. It's my decision."

"I don't reckon you'll space me." Marum ignored Malusi, his eyes boring into mine. "I've lived long enough to learn to read a man. I hope I'm not wrong."

I added up the profit we could make from the *Methuselah*, and set it against the work we needed to do on the *Staten*. There was still plenty left over, so each of us would have a payday, a good one.

But he wasn't wrong. I shook my head.

"He lives," I said. "No one is spacing him."

I barely saw Malusi move, but suddenly I was on the wrong end of his sidearm.

Danny stepped back, but he left his weapon securely holstered. He looked from Malusi to me and back again. Which way would he jump?

"Do you know how much we stand to make on this trip?" Malusi's voice cracked. "Do you know how much we owe?"

"I surely do. My thirty percent will buy me…what? A long and happy retirement? This guy has had centuries of life." I jerked my head toward Marum. "Probably has centuries more—"

"Millennia," Marum said. "It's not as good as it sounds. We all go mad in the end."

I kept my voice even and tried to sound reasonable. "You and me, Malusi, we've got maybe twenty more years at the outside. It hardly seems fair, I know, but I'm not living my last twenty years with murder on my conscience." I hoped I was getting through to him. "I don't think you want that either."

"If it's just the money," Marum said, "I've got money. Lots of money."

Malusi's eyes flicked toward him. "You've been stuck here for centuries. How d'you know your money's safe?"

"It's safe, believe me."

I couldn't read Malusi. Would he go for it or not? His gun hand never wavered.

However long Marum had lived, I didn't think it could have felt as long as the time I stood staring down the barrel of Malusi Kheswa's gun.

"I'm with the fuckin' captain," Tati said.

"You don't have a vote," Malusi said.

"I might not have a fuckin' percentage, but I reckon if you're going to kill the captain and space the weirdo, I get a fuckin' vote."

"I'm with the captain, too." Ruth stepped over to my side. "And I do have a fuckin' vote."

I have never been more grateful for a gesture in all my life. I drew a shaky breath. When had I stopped breathing?

"Yeah, it's only money," Danny said. "Put it away, Malusi. You're outvoted."

The muzzle wavered.

"For what it's worth I'm with the captain, too." Zara's voice came over the comm.

Malusi began to laugh, but there was no humor in it, only release from tension. He shrugged and holstered his weapon. I'd have to do something about Malusi Kheswa, but it wouldn't be today.

"I really do have money." Marum said. "I have investments going back more years than I can remember. I don't work for the wages. I have to do something with my life, or the madness will catch up with me sooner rather than later."

"Can you prove that?" Malusi asked.

"Give me access to your ship's comm and I'll shoot my bankers a web. You'll get your proof." His speech was getting easier.

"If your bank balance is disappointing, we could always space you later," Malusi said.

"No one is spacing anyone," I said.

"Take the ship." Marum sat forward. "That's what you came for. It's a sure thing. I'll disappear quietly. Start a new career, make a new life. It's nothing I haven't done before."

"You could go to the law," Malusi said.

"Not without giving away my secret. Where are you heading?"

"New Roscov," I said.

"Never heard of it. Give me your skiff when we get in range. I'll look more human by that time, though I might eat and drink my way through your supplies. It's been a while. The salvage from the *Methuselah* will buy you a new skiff ten times over and pay for whatever repairs you need to do. Vote on that."

"It's a fair deal." I looked at each of my crew in turn. Malusi had the grace to look down instead of meeting my eyes.

I nodded.

We didn't need a vote. I was still captain.

Celestial Object 143205

Mark D. Jacobsen

It was bad enough that Cooper missed his shot at Mars.

Learning that Huang Jian was going made it even worse.

Cooper was wrapping up with General Turchin when Adam brought the news that UN Orbital Control had finally approved Jian's departure clearance. Turchin was visiting the station to see for herself why the *USS Schriever's* operational testing had fallen so far behind schedule and they'd had a full day of infuriating meetings with the prime contractor.

"Talk about adding insult to injury," Cooper said.

Turchin just shook her head. "Goddamnit."

She was a stern woman to begin with, but had been unusually crotchety on this visit to orbit. As the *Schriever's* Program Manager, she felt the full wrath of the Space Force Chief of Staff and would be grilled by the House Armed Services Committee the following week.

Getting outpaced by a green-haired playboy billionaire would not help.

A *Chinese* green-haired playboy billionaire.

"Not to pour salt on the wound," Adam said. "But y'all want to watch? He's heading out soon."

"Only if I don't have to listen to his goddamn vlog," General Turchin said.

Some of the contractors already had Jian's vlog livestream pulled up on a screen in the station's lounge when they floated in. Jian wore shades and a fur coat. He babbled on about Kitty Hawk moments, and kickstarting the future, and space finally being for the masses. His signature green hair was askew in the zero-g and a gorgeous brunette hung on his arm. Cooper had always thought that Jian was like a twisted lovechild of Silicon Valley techbro and MTV, probably bred by clipboard-holding bureaucrats in the bowels of some Communist Party lab.

"He announced his crew earlier," Adam said.

"Who'd he pick?" Cooper asked.

"An ex-PLA taikonaut who cut his teeth in the early lunar program. Real grumpy dude, never appears in the videos. He's also bringing his girlfriend."

"Which one? Her?"

"Yeah. Vlasta. The Czech model."

Cooper considered this.

"Well, damn. How come all I got was you?"

Adam laughed and punched his shoulder.

Cooper turned thoughtful. "Seriously, though. *Really?*"

Adam's laughter fell away. As Space Force officers, both of them had extensive training in psychology and crew dynamics. Both had spent extended time in capsules under the Pacific. Three was an unbalanced number, which risked alienating a crew member. And you didn't need psychological training to know that locking two men in a capsule with a woman like that was a terrible idea.

Jian proceeded with a tour of his ship—his yacht, as he called it. From the outside, it looked almost identical to the *Schriever*. There were only so many ways to build a spaceship, especially when the propulsion system, xenon tanks, and life support systems all came from the same suppliers. She featured a white drum-shaped crew module resting atop a lattice structure that contained oxygen, water, and xenon tanks. The gold, foil-thin solar arrays were retracted against her body like grasshopper wings. Aft of all that was the solar electric propulsion drive.

Where the two spacecraft really diverged was their interiors. Jian's yacht was all tan leather, cherry wood, and purple mood lighting. A large People's Republic of China flag looked incongruous with the rest of the decor, a late-addition reminder that even this wealthy capitalist entrepreneur still operated at the mercy of political masters.

Cooper looked out the nearest window at the *Schriever*, clamped to the station, where she'd spent most of the last six months.

He knew he should be grateful. When he'd enlisted in the Air Force twenty-seven years before, he had never imagined he would captain a ship in the United States Space Force. Black kids from Alabama did not go into space. Well, except for Mae Jemison, but she had mostly been raised in Chicago and she was a genius. Cooper was not. He'd been a late bloomer and taken the long way around, enlisting, going to college, and then earning an officer's commission in the Space Force. Now here he was, floating 400 kilometers above the earth, first commanding officer of the Space Force's first interplanetary frigate.

First commanding officer.

That had shades of meaning his bedazzled parents and high school classmates could never understand. A commanding officer of a ship not yet operational. A commanding officer who spent most of his time in meetings on Earth or running tests while docked to the station. A commanding officer who would never engage the *Schriever*'s solar electric propulsion drive long enough to break free of Earth's gravity well.

The *Schriever* faced one last space trial before Headquarters declared her operationally ready: a transit to Mars and back. It was supposed to be Cooper's command. He would not walk on the surface, but he would at least orbit the red planet and see a sight beheld by only a few hundred people before him. He would send a video home, and Caleb would run his fingers over the screen and believe his daddy a giant among men.

But program delays and cost overruns had slipped the date three months out and now it would be his successor who commanded the *Schriever's* first Mars run, probably some fast-burning rockstar fresh off serving as a general's aide-de-camp.

Cooper would not go to Mars. He would never leave Earth orbit. This command was a final consolation prize for a respected officer who hadn't quite made it to the top.

Twenty-seven years. He'd worked longer and harder than anyone he knew. So damned close.

Jian's launch was boring. Cooper could barely even tell when the SEP drive began its miniscule thousandth-of-a-gee continuous burn. It took SEP drives days to really get moving, but once they did, they could haul ass. The *Schriever* was spec'd to reach Mars in 60 days when the orbits were favorable, far less than the nine months for a minimum-energy Hohmann transfer orbit. Jian's yacht should be comparable.

They watched the white mass of Jian's ship disappear into the infinite dark.

They decided to call it a day. No one had the heart to dive back into the *Schriever's* compliance paperwork. Cooper headed off to the sleeping area to be alone.

He was zippered up to the waist in his sleeping bag a few hours later, mindlessly consuming an entire season of a gritty action show, when Adam pulled back his curtain.

"Hey, Jian is deviating from his flight plan. I don't think he's going to Mars."

He handed a tablet over.

Cooper studied the display.

"Celestial object 143205," he read out loud. He clicked the hyperlinked text to open a new window. Then he looked up at Adam. "You've got to be kidding me."

* * *

When they found General Turchin, she was on a video call with Space Force Headquarters. She took one look at Adam's tablet, nodded, and handed it back. She pointed at her screen, indicating that Headquarters had reached the same conclusion they had.

"I'll find you when I'm done," she whispered.

They waited in the lounge, taking turns studying the data on Adam's tablet.

Cooper remembered the launch like it was yesterday. He'd been a senior in high school, contemplating enlisting in the Air Force. He had vague dreams of space, but it had never been a serious possibility, not for a kid like him. That day his chemistry teacher let them watch the launch in class. Cooper still recalled the sight of the Falcon Heavy rocket rumbling off the launch pad on its 27 engines, riding a narrow column of flame, the most powerful vehicle built by humanity since the Saturn V.

Then came the separation and, a few minutes later, something Cooper never would have imagined: footage of SpaceX founder Elon Musk's midnight cherry Tesla Roadster sailing through the silent void with the blue earth wheeling behind it. A dummy nicknamed Starman sat in the driver's seat in its spacesuit, one hand on the wheel, one elbow resting casually on the driver's door.

Later, compulsively re-watching the launch and reading news coverage in his bedroom, Cooper found the little details enchanting: the DON'T PANIC plaque on the dash, David Bowie's "Space Oddity" on repeat in the dummy's ear, the copy of *A Hitchhiker's Guide to the Galaxy* in the glovebox, the 5D optical disk on board containing Asimov's *Foundation* trilogy. Musk had casually estimated that his Tesla might orbit the sun for a billion years, intermittently crossing both Earth's and Mars' orbits.

That day fired Cooper's imagination like nothing else in his childhood. He visited the Air Force recruiter the next week.

"I gotta give Jian credit," Cooper said. "The kid has spunk."

Turchin messaged him an hour later, asking him to join her. Her video call was up to six generals now, including General Sang, the S3 in charge of all Space Force operations.

"You guys guessed it," General Turchin said. "Jian is on course to rendezvous with the Roadster."

"Does UN Orbital Control know?" Cooper asked.

"They figured it out around the same time we did. They're furious. Beijing denies any knowledge of Jian's intent. Our Defense Attaché thinks they're telling the truth. This was all Jian."

"Any idea about his motive?"

General Sang shrugged on the screen. "He's a celebrity. He wants views, followers, fame, whatever. The world will eat this up. And he's always had this ego contest thing with Musk. What better way to prove he's the real man than snapping a selfie with his girlfriend in Musk's personal sports car?"

"Will there even be anything left?" Cooper asked. "The radiation—"

"Does it matter? He's not after the car, he's after a viral social media story that will make him richer and convince other rich assholes to buy space yachts."

"That's got to be a hell of a trip," Cooper said. "All the way around the sun."

General Sang nodded gravely. "Our planners in the Space Operations Center estimate it will take him two months to reach the Roadster, then four months to get back."

They all chewed on that. It was one thing to make a transfer orbit to Mars, where multiple manned and unmanned space stations orbited and could share supplies, engage in repairs, or mount rescue operations if needed. Hurtling off into solar orbit was something else entirely.

General Sang said, "Colonel Cooper, I asked General Turchin to bring you into this meeting for a reason. We have been in dialog with the Secretary of Defense and the NSC staff. The Administration believes that Huang Jian's mission poses a serious threat to American national interests."

Cooper raised an eyebrow. He did not dare laugh at the Space Force S3.

"This is about more than a derelict Tesla," General Sang continued, perhaps sensing Cooper's skepticism. "The United States Space Force exists to protect, maintain, and expand this country's presence in space. Our performance to date has raised doubts about our ability to fulfill that mission. The private sector is kicking our asses. We are riding *their* ships and leasing facilities on *their* bases on the Moon and Mars. And now we have a PRC-backed entrepreneur thwarting an international framework for space traffic control, preparing to trespass and likely engage in piracy against a U.S.-registered asset with tremendous historical significance. We cannot overemphasize the stakes in this battle of narratives. Do you understand?"

"Yes, sir, I do."

"Good. Colonel Cooper, it is vital that the United States reach Celestial Body 143205 before Huang Jian. And there is only one ship in the United States Space Force that can make that happen."

* * *

"This is the dumbest thing you've ever told me," Jordan told him over a video call the next morning.

If Cooper had broken the news to anyone else in his family, they would have congratulated him. Not Jordan. She had seen too much of his world, knew way too much about orbital mechanics and flight safety from his late-night study sessions, had embraced too many young widows. She divorced him for a reason.

"This isn't like going to Mars, Darnell. There's nobody to meet you at the other end. Nobody to rescue you if something goes wrong out there. You'll be in a raft in a goddamn ocean of nothingness, millions of miles from any world. And your ship isn't even ready."

"I know all that, baby."

"Of course you do. And you need to stop calling me that."

They sat in mutual, sulking silence for a while.

"You listen to me, Darnell Cooper," she tried again. "You have a son who needs you. I am not going to tell Caleb that his daddy died trying to reach an abandoned sports car, all to spare his government a bruised ego because they're losing in space."

She kept talking, but her voice seemed to fade away. Cooper watched the earth turn bright and blue beyond the video screen. He felt tired. Tired and heavy, even in the zero-gravity, from the accumulated weight of his efforts to reach this juncture in his life.

He knew Jordan was right. The mission was stupid.

And yet something powerful and intangible was on the line. This was a piece of his own personal history. How many other children had that launch inspired? How many of them were working on Mars at this very moment, giving the human race a fighting chance as the earth gasped its dying breaths 400 kilometers beneath his boots?

Cooper didn't want Caleb to lose his daddy either. But if the alternative was Caleb growing up with a daddy who shrank back from a dream at the decisive moment, well, that was no choice at all.

* * *

The Space Force mobilized with breathtaking speed.

The Space Operations Center computed flight plans. The *Schriever* would need to accelerate faster than usual to pass Huang Jian's ship. That would put them at the Roadster a day or two ahead, but it meant razor-thin fuel margins. The Chief of Staff of the Space Force signed off on the risk.

The station-side contractors worked around the clock, resolving minor maintenance issues and performing final checks. Headquarters approved an operational readiness waiver within hours, which annoyed Cooper to no end after the months of foot-dragging. They supplied the *Schriever* with food, water, and oxygen pillaged from the station. Immediately after the *Schriever's* departure, all the contractors were to depart in the emergency lander until a new resupply mission could be launched.

The biggest sticking point after that was the crew complement. The *Schriever* was intended for a crew of four, but Cooper and Adam were the only qualified crew members aboard the station, and the only medical expertise they had between them was Adam's First Responder training. There was no time to fly new crew members into orbit if they were to beat Jian. Headquarters approved another waiver.

In the final hours before launch, as Cooper and Adam sat strapped into their seats running through preflight checklists, Cooper paused and looked sidelong at Adam, his face buried in his checklists, a mask of quiet professionalism. He was good people, square-jawed and steel-nerved, right out of the 1960s. Cooper had never heard his voice rise.

"You ready for this?" Cooper asked.

"To risk my life to save an abandoned Tesla? Sure, why not. To spend six months in this tin can with you? Hell no."

Cooper laughed and pushed him.

At launch time, the docking clamps released. Adam tapped the thrusters. Ever so slightly, the station began to move in the overhead viewscreens. It took fifteen minutes to reach a safe separation distance, then the flight computer rotated them into the burn orientation.

They ran their last checks. Everything was green.

Once Adam engaged the SEP drive, they would be committed to deep space. A hundred million kilometers of nothing lay before them.

"Schriever, *you are cleared for burn*," the SOC radioed.

Cooper and Adam looked at each other.

"Giddy up, cowboy," Adam said, and pushed the ENTER key on the mission computer keyboard.

A gentle breeze of gravity eased Cooper down into his seat. After all the rockets he had ridden into orbit, the paltry acceleration always felt like a joke. He laughed out loud.

They ran the post-departure checklist. While Adam made a slight attitude correction, Cooper deployed the solar arrays that would ionize their xenon into plasma exhaust. He alternated between scanning the computer and peeking out the virtual portals as the gold insect wings unfurled.

When they finished the checklist, they fell silent.

They had no scheduled activity until their next check-in with mission control in four hours. A daily regimen of inspections and check-ins would continue for the duration of the trip, but if they were honest with themselves, this was primarily for their own sanity. The *Schriever* required almost nothing of them. For the next two months, they were passengers.

* * *

The Internet figured out what Huang Jian was up to within a few days of his launch. It began with amateur sleuths on esoteric forums, spread to social media, and then to the mainstream media.

"The cat's out of the bag!" Jian said in a new livestream on his vlog. The roots of his green hair were growing out black. "We're not going to Mars. That's boring these days. I built this yacht because I actually want to explore this Solar System of ours, and this little orbital hookup with Elon's Tesla seemed like a great start. Sick, right? Elon, you watching, bro? Space isn't just yours anymore!"

"Ugh," Cooper said when it was over.

SpaceX released a benign press statement the next morning, wishing Jian luck in his effort to reach the Roadster, which solar radiation, it noted, had mostly reduced to a fine powder. It emphasized that although Jian was welcome to observe the vehicle, it remained SpaceX property and damage or theft of the Roadster would be met with the appropriate legal response.

Other than setting a precedent for the protection of private property in space, Cooper sensed SpaceX leadership didn't much care; they had bigger fish to fry, running their colonies on the Moon and Mars and building out the infrastructure to scale and sustain the human presence in space.

That afternoon, the U.S. Ambassador to the United Nations read a far more ominous statement. She emphasized that Celestial Object 143205 was sovereign property of the United States. She condemned the reckless disregard of UN Orbital Control, which had grown out of the long-standing International Civil Aviation Organization. She reminded the People's Republic of China that it was a signatory and emphasized that the United States would hold the PRC accountable for any violations of international law by its citizens. Finally, she announced the United States Space Force had dispatched a frigate to protect Celestial Object 143205 from any undue interference.

"Hey," Cooper said, nudging Adam in the ribs. "That's us."

"Yeah, about that. How are we supposed to protect Celestial Object 143205 once we get out there? You can't even get out of bed without tweaking your back."

"I'm planning to kick your all-American ass out the airlock to handle it."

"Sounds like a plan."

* * *

Their humor came naturally enough after a year of working together, but it was also something they took care to work at. It was like a marriage. You had to, to survive.

Especially in space. Even if space didn't kill you, there were so many ways it could make you crazy.

Cooper felt it closing in almost immediately. When he awoke the morning after their departure, the entirety of the Earth filled their rear viewscreen. They were nearly 40,000 kilometers from home, the farthest Cooper had ever been, and the smallness of his world brought an unexpected wave of emotion.

The SOC kept them on a rigid schedule. They did their make-work inspections without complaint. They prepared meals at fixed times. Cooper called Caleb daily and spent more time than he had in years reconnecting with old friends via email. They watched movies and read books and engaged in hobby projects, but these sedentary activities always left Cooper feeling lethargic, a little sick, and in need of fresh air and a walk. He craved more exercise than the two hours each day he was allotted, but they had to carefully manage their calorie expenditure so they would not run out of food.

The exponential magic of constant acceleration defined their lives. After three days, they crossed lunar orbit. By their sixth day, they had tripled that distance. The round-trip communication delays worsened each day. When they crossed lunar orbit, it was about three seconds: annoying but manageable. By the end of their first week, it exceeded twelve seconds. Caleb quickly lost interest in doing live calls. Cooper switched to making recordings, which he sent toward Earth like messages in bottles. A few days later, even the SOC stopped using real-time communication. The sense of being severed from the human race was unlike anything Cooper had ever experienced.

He felt the first hints of madness encroaching. Even with just the two of them, the *Schriever's* walls closed in. It felt like being buried alive. There was nowhere to escape to, no change of scenery, no fresh air. The ship had no real windows because of her thick radiation shielding. The large viewscreens projected external camera feeds, creating an almost perfect illusion, but it somehow wasn't the same. For a brief time, Cooper configured the viewscreens to show forests and waterfalls, but the digital falsity annoyed both of them and they agreed to never try that experiment again.

Their good humor fell away. They passed whole days without speaking to each other. Adam stopped shaving for a week. A wildness seemed to enter his bloodshot eyes. He eventually came through it and reappeared one day clean-shaven, looking like a military officer again.

A month in, they had a blow-up fight over nothing and refused to speak to each other for four days. Mental health therapists from the SOC engaged them each privately over email and video. The Mission Director finally intervened directly, ordering them in an artful, profanity-laden speech to get their shit together. They knew the psychology of what they were enduring, twenty million kilometers from earth. They knew to expect this. They needed to remember their training and treat this with the same severity as a fire or an electrical failure.

They finally talked it out. Then they booted up a VR shooter and spent a couple hours under headsets blowing each other away with plasma rifles and incendiary grenades. As their laughter filled the ship, Cooper realized how terrible its absence had been.

* * *

"You think *we're* a hot mess," Cooper said one day. "I wonder what it's like for them."

At first, Jian had livestreamed almost continuously. Within a few days, he switched to uploading discrete videos. Gradually, as the distance increased and connection speeds dropped, he lowered the video resolution. Then his postings grew less frequent. By the time Cooper and Adam had their fight, Jian hadn't posted in five days. Internet speculation abounded.

Cooper privately worried. He had little fondness for Huang Jian, but they were out in this infinite darkness together and that had awakened something primal and fierce in Cooper.

"Come on, kid," he found himself saying through clenched teeth.

A new video appeared later that day, as obnoxious as ever, and Cooper wondered why he had bothered to be concerned. By all accounts, Jian and his crew were having a grand old time. But psychologists equipped with highly-nuanced machine-learning algorithms scrutinized the videos and reported signs of subtle distress. A change in Vlasta's complexion was likely due to stress and the intonation of Jian's laughter had changed. A faint bruise on Vlasta's wrist drew significant commentary online.

A solar storm erupted during their sixth week. The SOC directed them to initiate enhanced radiation mitigation procedures. They temporarily halted firing the SEP drive and rotated the *Schriever* to put the bulk of its mass between the crew module and the sun. Then they gathered almost every available object in the crew compartment in order build a fortress of extra mass around themselves.

Cooper recorded a video for Caleb. "It's like when we build forts with chairs and blankets." He sent the video off, wondering if it would be the last. It all depended on the severity of the storm. They hunkered in place for over twenty hours before the SOC announced they were clear.

* * *

Jian and Vlasta posted one more video, a few hours after the storm, assuring humanity that they were still alive. Any pretense of good humor was gone. They seemed haggard and tired.

Cooper breathed a prayer of thanks. He proposed radioing Jian directly to ensure they were okay, but the SOC—at the direction of the White House—refused to authorize any direct communication.

After that, Jian fell silent. Seven days ticked by with no new videos.

Cooper repeatedly inquired with the SOC. The State Department was working on it, the Mission Director said. The PRC insisted that Jian's ship did not require assistance at this time.

"You buy that?" Adam asked Cooper.

"Not for a minute."

Although they received no guidance to do so, they began calculating intercept trajectories. They were five hundred thousand kilometers ahead of Jian now, which wasn't much by deep space standards, but the low-acceleration SEP drive was not designed for major dynamic adjustments. The additional maneuvers would take their fuel to redline and a single mistake might make it impossible to return to Earth. An intercept would also take days. At this point, it was almost as fast to reach the Roadster and wait.

"This mission just needs to end," Adam said.

"No argument here," said Cooper.

* * *

The final days were the longest.

For weeks they'd had nothing to look forward to. Now the rendezvous was imminent. It was a kind of halfway point, even if the return journey would take twice as long due to the orbital alignments. They also felt growing dread about the fate of Jian's ship. If something had gone wrong, that would soon be apparent. If not, a deep-space confrontation awaited them. Cooper had no idea what that might mean. Neither, probably, did Jian.

Roundtrip communication times with Earth were over fifteen minutes now. Whatever lay ahead, they would face it alone.

The precision of *Schriever's* flight computer was impressive. After a journey of more than 130 million kilometers, the SEP drive brought them within five kilometers of the Roadster. Now the range reading slowly wound down.

Four point nine.

Four point eight.

Cooper tensed with anticipation. He had been focused on the maneuver itself but now, suddenly, it occurred to him that he was about to lay eyes on this incredible artifact of mankind's journey into space. So many victories had followed that delightfully absurd glimpse of the Tesla above the blue planet. Each was a mad assault on the frontier of the possible. Bigger rockets, manned spacecraft, a new round of lunar missions, the first footsteps on Mars, clean solar energy beamed to earth, the beginnings of a xenon mining operation on Jupiter.

Cooper regretted not seeing Mars, but he was part of something even rarer and more precious. He felt giddy with youthful energy. What a note to end his career on. If he survived the four-month trip back, he would return to Earth a contented man. Maybe he'd been wrong about Jian. Maybe Jian had been brilliant to attempt this.

Adam rotated the *Schriever* to face the Roadster. Their relative velocity was only two meters per second. They would coast in from here, then brake with reaction thrusters.

Cooper ensured all the cameras were running. The *Schriever* would beam a few grainy, low-resolution images back to the SOC, but the real images and videos, the colorful high-resolution media that humans back home would clamor to see, would be recorded and saved for later transmission when bandwidth was more plentiful.

They peered hard at the viewscreen. At first, they saw only the blackness of space, but slowly a point of light emerged. Gradually, it brightened. As its features became more distinct, Cooper let out a low whistle.

"There it is," Adam said.

At the time of the Roadster's launch, scientists had noted that it was largely made of organics—including its carbon-fiber body—that would decompose rapidly under the ruthless barrage of solar radiation. Cooper had not been sure how much would actually be left, so he was pleasantly surprised to see that the approaching shape still looked something like a car.

As its details became more distinct, however, he felt growing unease and then revulsion and fear.

The boxy chassis was completely intact, like a drifting go-kart. The rims were still in place, but the tires had disintegrated long ago. The steering column protruded from the dashboard, ending in a misshapen nub where the steering wheel had once been. The sleek, beautiful, midnight cherry body that he had studied in photographs was largely gone, but not entirely; a kind of fuzzy film glazed the chassis, like the withering skin of a desiccated corpse. Everything was a bleak, dull shade of gray, bleached by the unsparing radiation.

Starman, the Tesla's dummy passenger, had not fared any better. Shredded ribbons of spacesuit clung to the withered mannequin. Both arms were missing, as if they'd been ripped from the sockets. The helmet and black faceplate were intact, giving the illusion that a perfectly intact human head lay within. It looked like the body had been dipped in acid and left to dissolve, but only up to the neck. Cooper stared in horror until the Tesla's slow rotation mercifully carried the corpse out of view.

Adam stabilized their position. This obscene carcass filled their windscreen. Cooper knew in his bones that they had committed an unforgivable violation by coming here. An image came to him of a desecrated temple. As the Tesla completed its rotation and Starman's eyeless faceplate came back around, Cooper swore he saw the head tilt toward him, as if to look him dead in the eyes. His knees went weak.

Cooper recalled that glossy sports car cruising off into the stars. Those images held so much sublime beauty. Space appeared to be a pristine wilderness that preserved any object entrusted to its care. Musk invoked that romance, imagining his Roadster preserved for a billion years until some unfathomably advanced alien race recovered it in the distant future.

A very different truth lay before Cooper now.

It crawled on his skin and gnawed at his stomach.

Every square centimeter of this vast cosmos was hellbent on eradicating matter, ripping it apart in its vacuum, freezing it, boiling it, or baking it with radiation. Everywhere, that is, except for that blue marble he called home with its fragile soap bubble of an atmosphere, now months away across a terrifying gulf.

"You okay, Coop?" Adam asked, putting a hand on his shoulder. But Adam looked pale, too.

"Let's get the hell out of here."

* * *

For two days, they waited.

They fell back into their routines. They ran checklists, prepared meals, and exercised. They played video games. Cooper began writing his memoirs, a project he had considered but put off for years. Caleb was his sole audience. As he sat with stylus and digital paper, he paused and placed his fingers against the skin of his spaceship. He thought of the radiation-baked vacuum just centimeters beyond, ready to dissolve his body into stardust. He shivered and went back to writing. He felt a mad compulsion to finish before it was too late.

The world received no more transmissions from Jian. As the rendezvous countdown turned from days to hours, the SOC sent regular updates. Jian's relative velocity was far too high; without aggressive corrections, the ship would pass the Roadster right by. Everyone kept waiting, pucker factors rising.

The corrections never came.

SOC sent a new update. The Chinese ambassador had just informed the White House that it had lost communication with Jian's ship fifteen days earlier. The ship was not responding to remote commands. Should any U.S. Space Force assistance be available, the PRC would not refuse it.

Adam and Cooper trained their shipboard telescope on the approaching yacht, but it still just looked like a point of light. Its stable luminosity suggested that it was not tumbling, as might be expected from an explosion or leak. No *Apollo 13* here. Whatever might be wrong, the answers lay within.

The planners at the SOC plotted intercept trajectories, but no matter how they cut it, the *Schriever* did not have enough propellant without taking extraordinary risks. Even if they did successfully rendezvous, Cooper and Adam were ill-equipped for many scenarios that might await them. If the yacht had a degraded life support or propulsion system, *Schriever* lacked the resources to get everyone home. That could create a profound moral crisis, and nobody wanted to bear the burden for the choices that would have to be made.

Cooper looked out at the decrepit Roadster, rotting on its slowly turning axis.

Two months ago, the *Schriever* had felt like the most modern ship in the Space Force fleet. Now Cooper understood the truth. Out here, it was just lifeboats helping lifeboats.

Intercept not approved, the Mission Director finally decided. *Return to Earth. Please upload rendezvous imagery and video at earliest convenience.*

They watched Jian's ship as long as they could. It got brighter and brighter, and then fainter and fainter again. Soon it was no brighter than a star, then a faint smudge in their sensitive peripheral vision. Finally, Huang Jian's personal yacht passed into the endless night.

UN Orbital Control removed the yacht from its flight tracking database and registered it as a celestial object in permanent orbit around the sun.

* * *

A few days into their return journey, Cooper and Adam sat brooding on the flight deck. Adam had smuggled a small flask bulb aboard with his personal belongings. "I thought a day might come that we needed this," he said.

It was a clear violation of Space Force regulations.

Without a word, Cooper took the offered bulb and squirted some of the whiskey into his throat. He savored the burn.

"So what's the answer?" Adam asked. "We admit that humans aren't made for this?"

Cooper shook his head. It was a question they had both been brooding over, in various guises. He was having recurring nightmares about the Tesla now. In one, he had lifted Starman's visor to find his own rotting face beneath.

Adam's answer was the easy way out. It was tempting, to be sure. Whatever Cooper had been looking for in space, he'd found it. The next generation could have Mars. Cooper had had enough. He was ready to feel soil beneath his toes, to breathe air beneath blue skies. The first thing he planned to do when he got home was take Caleb fishing.

Cooper sighed. "It's more like the opposite. We have to admit how terrible the odds are, but recognize that we need to explore space anyway. Every inch of progress is a miracle. We were ready to throw in the towel after *Challenger* and then *Columbia*. The Apollo missions were forty years in our past. It felt like the space age was over. And then Elon fired that car into orbit. He had been talking about Mars for years and we all laughed, and then suddenly, we weren't laughing anymore. And now people live there. They're building. They're surviving."

"Mostly."

"Mostly," Cooper agreed, recalling the events on Mars two years ago. "That's exactly the point. It's like we have these two futures in play simultaneously. One is Starman rocking out to 'Space Oddity,' riding his midnight cherry Tesla into the stars, firing our dreams. And the other is…whatever the fuck that was."

He jerked his thumb over his shoulder at the unmarked grave behind them.

"So which future is real?"

Cooper shrugged. "Let me think on that one."

* * *

That night, Cooper awoke to a light.

He unvelcroed himself from his sleeping bag and pulled himself through the hatch onto the flight deck. Adam sat in his pilot's chair, haggard and unshaven. His computer terminal was on. Cooper saw that he was reviewing all their photos and videos from the rendezvous.

No, Cooper realized. Not just reviewing.

Cooper thought of Earth, then. Of the mess humanity had made of it. Elon shot for Mars for a reason. Not just to explore, not just out of ambition, but because he believed that space travel was necessary to save the human race from extinction. There was plenty of evidence these days to suggest that he was right.

"It was the wrong question," Cooper said out loud.

Adam turned and saw him. "What do you mean?"

"You asked which future is real. The better question is: which future do we *need* to be real?"

Cooper approached the console. He saw that Adam's hand was resting on the keyboard, his right middle hovering over the DELETE button.

Cooper said, "The terrible future will always be here for us. We'll stumble our way into it again and again, when we aren't looking for it, like Jian did. But that other future…the midnight cherry one…that's a future we have to fight for."

Adam nodded. He swallowed.

Cooper rested his finger on the DELETE key beside Adam's.

Together, they pushed.

Mercy for the Lost

Jana Paniccia

Shivering on the forecastle of the *Outcast*, Monkey studied their target from a spot just back of the bowsprit. At one time, the ship they approached must have been stunning: a lithe frigate able to race with the wind under full sail. Fast. Fearless. Free.

A surge of jealousy rose in her chest; as quickly, it faded. The ship's beauty now lay in her perseverance. Foremast gone. Main split at its base—top half resting heavily on her bowing mizzen. Once clean-running lines twisted and tangled with tattered sails and off-kilter yards. A dozen jagged holes peppered her visible hull, signs of a devastating broadside. Yet the frigate survived, still flying the blue and silver mage flag of the Kambarna.

The lookout had spotted the flag before realizing the vessel's desolate state. A ghost ship might be a seahand's nightmares, but if it hadn't been plundered, the wrecked frigate could earn them its weight in precious metals—or more. The Kambarna's mage ships were as legendary as they were rare; the magicked items the ship might hold were rarer still, seldom seen outside the Kambarna's control. Even a simple mage light would sell for gold in Blackhaven. Despite the risk, a dead ship full of mystical treasure wasn't something Captain Vanisse could ignore.

As the *Outcast* neared its prey, Monkey prayed to the Sealord for the broken vessel to do what she could not: escape. She'd been nine when the *Outcast* captured her family's trading vessel, butchering her parents and brother before her eyes. The captain had refused her that gift, keeping her captive to scoop and pack black powder and carry the deadly packets to the cannon crews during battle. Every ship needed powder monkeys.

Now thirteen, undersized and mostly skin stretched over bone, Monkey was glad their quarry wasn't living this time. She'd witnessed too many sent home to the Sealord and wondered in the dark of night when she would join them. *Mercy*, she asked the Sealord in the rare moments she had alone. *Mercy for the lost. Mercy for the living.*

"We should leave it be," said one of the captive seahands, a well-muscled Oritalian scouring the deck with a piece of holystone. "No good'll come from boarding a ghost ship."

Monkey found herself agreeing, not that she'd say so. She'd learned early to keep her mouth shut. No one, not even the crew forced aboard and given the choice of death or serving Captain Vanisse, cared who she was or what she thought. They all treated her like an animal.

"Captain says it's got magic," the bow watchman said. "Could see us a good haul in Blackhaven."

Turning her head, she saw the first man frown. "If that there's magic, it's not the kind we want t'upset. Something's keeping the old dame afloat. Might be the Sealord's wanting to give her company."

Maybe this time, it will be mine, Monkey thought.

* * *

"Ready with the boarding bridge," Captain Vanisse ordered as the *Outcast* came alongside the ghost. Deceptively small, she loomed over the crew from the quarterdeck, aloof and cold, whip at the ready. "Search crew, draw your swords. If there's anyone stuck on there, cut 'em down quick. Even a half-starved mage 'll kill you."

Doery, the captain's bully of a first mate, waved his sword high to rile the crew as two seahands lifted the bridge—a slab of wood with anchor posts and taut rope sides—and heaved it over to rest on the rail of their target.

"Monkey!"

While *Outcast* often carried a hand of powder monkeys, it had been a tough fighting season, leaving Monkey the only survivor. With no choice but to answer, she rolled out of her hidey-hole under the stowed pinnace—on the opposite side of the massing boarding party so she wouldn't be seen. Popping to her feet, she scurried around the ship's boat, presented herself to the captain and Doery, and bowed as too many blows from the nine-tail had taught her.

Doery waved to the bridge with his sword. "Get to it, monkey."

It was one of the jobs she hated most, no matter how many times she'd done it. First one across could never be sure the bridge would hold. More than one had fallen from the *Outcast*, left to the Sealord while another took their place. As she climbed the bridge, Monkey glanced down; the height and the tumbling ocean crashing between the ships sent bile stinging up her throat.

Shuddering, she shut her eyes and scrambled across, using the side ropes to guide her movements. When she felt the opposite rail beneath a bare foot, she opened her eyes and jumped to the frigate's deck with a relieved sigh. Turning back, she tied the anchor rods to the rail as best she could. The ties weren't meant to keep the bridge from shifting, only to keep the two ships together.

When Monkey stepped away from the bridge, Captain Vanisse urged the search crew forward. "Go get us some treasure."

Doery came across first, his eyes skipping over Monkey and surveying the deck. She followed the path of his attention, taking in the mess of ragged sail, broken lines, and pieces of what might have been masts or spars. *What broke you?*

The state of the frigate didn't lessen the energy of the boarders. As quickly as they came, they dispersed across the ship and down hatches. If there was a fight to be had, they'd be ready with knives and fists. For once, Monkey wasn't choking with horrific expectation. *No way anyone survived this.*

"Monkey," Doery called. "This might be a mage ship, but if it's carrying black powder, you'd better find it quick." She knew the threat implicit in his order. Deep scars from the captain's nine-tail lined her back from the times she'd failed at a job—and from the times Doery said she had.

* * *

The frigate had more than two dozen lightweight cannons, dried blood splattered across almost every bulkhead and deck, and more holes than a wheel of Zarristan cheese—but no black powder. At first Monkey thought the ship might have already been raided. From the exclamations echoing through the decks, however, the search crew was finding treasure aplenty. Mage lights, vermin-protected food barrels, a stove that stayed lit without fuel—she overheard the crew speaking of many strange finds as she crawled through the ship searching for the magazine and light room.

The last place she searched was a cabin at the aft of the lower gundeck where the ship's Bonesaw must have worked. Least, that was her best guess given the empty but bloodied cots, piles of used bandages, and a scattering of bottles partly-filled with potions.

Pulling up a cot, she found not a trap-door to a hidden magazine, but the ratty corpse of a cat, its hollow ribs visible through patchy orange fur testament to starvation. "Poor thing," she murmured, reaching out—only to have the corpse yowl indignantly and slice four deep lines across her palm before streaking away. *Not quite dead, then.*

Monkey backed out of the Bonesaw's cabin, clenching her bleeding hand. The skeletal ship's cat hadn't gone far; much livelier, it twined around the footings of the closest cannon. Visible through the open gunport, the *Outcast* rested an easy stone's throw away. *What a broadside that'd be.* If only the ship carried black powder.

They must have given as good as they got if they weren't forced to strike. She stared at the small cannon, a quarter of the size of the ones on *Outcast. Maybe they used magic.*

While she might never know what happened in the ship's last battle, she could put a timeframe to it. There was no way the ship, magic or not, had weathered storm season, putting the attack sometime within the past eight months, when weather off the Oritalian coast was a paradise for nations at war, merchants, and pirates. If the *Outcast* hadn't spotted the Kambarna flag and moved to investigate, the mage ship would likely be heading to the Sealord soon enough.

As far as Monkey could tell, the frigate's crew had already made the Sealord's journey. Despite the splashes and streaks of dried blood, there wasn't a body to be found. If any of the crew had survived, they must have seen to their fellows and then followed in their wake when hope for rescue waned.

I wish I had that kind of courage.

"Monkey!" Doery's call from above brought her back to rude reality. With a last glance at the cat, she hurried to answer his summons.

Quick as she made it to the maindeck, Doery was nowhere to be seen, leaving her to ask the seahands sorting the search crew's findings. "First mate called?"

"Captain's quarters." The response was curt, the seahand answering without looking her way.

She climbed the mostly-intact ladder to the quarterdeck, knowing the captain's cabin would likely be in the same place it was on *Outcast*. Sure enough, a stout oak door, impressively unscathed, stood propped-open at the aft. Monkey poked her head within. "Here, sir," she said, offering a quick bow.

"Get in here," Doery called.

Even with permission, nervous tension tightened Monkey's back as she stepped into the cabin. The first mate wouldn't normally let captive crew into the captain's quarters of a taken ship; he wouldn't want them to have a chance at nabbing any high-value goods.

Blue sky through the shattered stern gallery drew her attention first. The gallery's intricately-carved wooden frames were empty except for the odd corner, while shards of glass littered the deck. A table big enough for a dozen took up much of the limited deck space, while a leather armchair and scratched writing desk were squashed against an awkwardly shaped bulkhead that hived off the rest of the cabin. Brilliant light spilled from a lantern hung from a fish-shaped hook affixed to the bulkhead.

A mage light? Knowing the ship came from the western continent's most secretive nation was one thing; seeing proof another. Wonder surged through Monkey as she stood captivated by the perfectly glowing orb.

"*Now*, monkey," Doery said.

The first mate crouched by the armchair, a hooked iron bar in one hand. "There's a compartment behind this bulkhead." He pounded on it for emphasis. "The door must be magicked. It's not budging."

He jammed the hooked end of the bar at the deck, which already had several hand-spans of wood pried up, leaving a dark gap stretching beneath the bulkhead. "I'll hold the ends so you can crawl underneath. You can bash your way through the deck on the other side."

Peering into the makeshift passage, Monkey could see bits of the deck below between the thin wood slats. "What if I fall through?" she asked before thinking.

Doery grabbed her arm and shoved her face-first at the splinter-edged hole. "No one would miss you if you did." He pressed a knee into her back until she gasped in pain.

His words stung with cold truth. Monkeys were disposable, easily replaced from a taken ship or bought for a pittance in Blackhaven. In the time she'd survived on *Outcast*, two had been blown apart, one had fallen from the mainmast yards, and one had drowned. Three more had disappeared, likely beaten to death and thrown unceremoniously overboard. Not one of them had earned a word of remembrance.

When Doery finally moved, Monkey scooted forward so she could slide her hands into the rough passageway first. She used the uneven edges of the planking to pull herself further into the hole. Pale light filtered through a rough break on the far side of the bulkhead, helping pinpoint her destination.

I'm facing the wrong bloody way to do anything useful. Twisting herself around was torturous, sharp edges of wood biting through her threadbare shirt and raising welts on the skin beneath. *Like the cat came back for another round.* Wincing, Monkey curled her injured palm around the jagged plank and pulled. The panel flexed and bounced right back.

"It's one long piece," she called, shaking the wood panel as best she could so Doery could understand. "Would you be willing to pry it out?"

A moment of quiet, followed by a thud and a ripple through the panel—then the wood slid a handspan. Monkey jammed her entire arm through the widened gap, wedging part of her shoulder through to provide extra leverage. *I'm going to be hurting tomorrow.* As the first panel disappeared from view, she clawed her fingers around the edges of the next and pulled down. A nail popped as the panel twisted.

She wiggled the rest of her upper body under the sideways panel until she could get her head and other arm through the gap. Bright light briefly blinded. *Wonder how long mage lights last?* As her eyes cleared, she found a twin to the lantern in the outer cabin attached to the bulkhead she'd just come under.

Taking a deep breath against the pain, Monkey pressed her hands flat on the deck and levered her hips and legs free. Once out, she studied the hole she'd wormed her way through. Her bloody handprint made it look like a bizarre torture device.

I never want to do that again.

She looked around the cramped compartment, barely wider than her outstretched hands and twice as long. A letter cabinet took up half the space, its shelves divided into numerous boxes, each labeled with an elegant nameplate. A silver coin rested in each. *Is that how they paid folks?* On her family's ship, the crew had been given paper scrips to take to the bank. It was one of the few things she remembered well: sitting in her father's lap while he wrote each scrip. Their purser might've given out coppers or the occasional silver, but the wealth in this cabinet would tempt any thief. *Why risk it?*

Turning away, Monkey almost fell into a hanging cot. An occupied one. "Sealord's fury," she swore, jerking backward until her back jammed against the cabinet. *Breathe. Breathe.*

"What's going on in there?" Doery pounded on the bulkhead.

"Dead…" The word was all she could manage.

Doery understood nonetheless and gave a harsh chuckle. "Give 'em a good look-over."

With a shuddering breath, Monkey turned back to the cot and the body within it. A woman, older than Captain Vanisse, her dark hair streaked with white. What skin Monkey could see was undamaged, almost waxy. Sniffing, she got a hint of mustiness, no cloying scent of decay. *Guess you're magicked too.*

Despite the ship's beleaguered state, the woman looked like she was resting in state—fully dressed, white lace peeking from beneath a navy cape with silver flashings around the neck. A hasty glance around found a three-cornered hat atop the cabinet, decorated with silver braid. The captain, then. *Did she want to go down with her ship?*

Running her fingers over the cape, Monkey felt an unnatural stiffness in the cloth. She grimaced, certain the wool was thick with dried blood. *Maybe you didn't go so peacefully.* Surveying the compartment more closely, Monkey found splotches of dried blood on the stretch of deck between the cabinet and cot, dull and faded compared to her own bloody handprint. A similar brownish smear crossed the bulkhead beneath the mage light.

She didn't want to die in the dark, Monkey realized. She understood.

Tugging the cape away exposed a shirt more dried blood than white linen and lace, and one of the woman's hands curled in a fist above her heart—a luminescent glow shining from between blood-crusted fingers. Monkey gasped.

"What'd you find?" came Doery's annoyed voice.

"The captain's holding something. I'm just going to…" With a quiet respect, Monkey lifted the captain's fist and worked to spread her fingers, revealing the object she'd been fiercely protecting: a silver coin, its shape identical to the ones on the shelves. Unlike the others, this coin glowed with a soft blue radiance. Cautious, she plucked the coin up with the thumb and pointer finger of her still bleeding hand, holding it as far away as she could. The coin gave off a pleasant warmth.

She brought the shimmering coin closer, finding one side flat and empty, the other marked with two interconnected circles. Monkey didn't know what use the mages of the Kambarna had for a magicked coin; she was only grateful she had a mage-touched treasure, however slight, to ease Doery's temper.

She turned to the bulkhead, praying he'd be satisfied. The outline of the door was clear from this side, with an inset handle. She tugged the handle with her free hand, stumbling forward as the panel slid easily to the side.

Doery, lounging in the leather chair, looked up as she came through. "Tell me it's something good."

"A mage light, a dead body, and a whole lot of maybe-magicked coins."

"Bloody bones, you're kidding." He shot to his feet. "Show me."

Without thinking, she flicked the coin with her thumb, sending it twisting into the air, before holding her hand out to catch it so she could offer it to him. As the silver coin landed in the center of her bleeding palm, a bolt of lightning arced through her body, bringing oblivion.

* * *

::I'm Endras, once EndrasIleya. I greet you——::

"Who?" Monkey's head pounded as she opened her eyes to a pair of blurry boots. She sat up quickly. "What happened?"

A boot slammed into her ribcage, sending her sprawling back to the deck. "You tell me, monkey." Doery punctuated his words with another sharp kick. She gasped, curling into a ball.

::Dual-gods, what's going on here? Are you all right child?:: The woman's voice was strong and clear, filled with a concern Monkey didn't trust at all.

She glanced about, finding no one besides Doery—his eyes dark with frustration. The once-protected compartment lay in shambles. The cabinet had been tipped over and dragged out, the cot overturned and the captain's body left in a heap. Silver coins littered the deck. Clear signs of Doery's all-too-familiar reaction when he didn't get what he wanted.

::Dual-gods, is that….:: The woman's voice trailed off. *::What's your name, child? How did you…::*

Monkey ignored the strange voice as Doery pulled a foot back for another kick. "I was just doing what you asked," she cried before he could strike. "It's proof the coins are worth something—right?"

"Maybe a drink and a girl in port," Doery spat. "With those magical locks, I was expecting some real treasure." He ignored her in favor of kicking the overturned cabinet, sending a few more coins tumbling.

::Dual-gods, that soul-silver is priceless.::

"Soul-silver?"

Doery turned back. "Soul-silver? What in the Deeps is soul-silver?" His eyes narrowed as he considered the scattered coins.

She shook her head, never having heard the word before.

::You're not of the Kambarna.::

"No. We spotted the ship and came to investigate," Monkey said. *The captain figured a mage ship would be worth its weight in gold.*

::Pirates.:: The word came with a disgust Monkey appreciated.

"I'm sorry."

"Who are you talking to, monkey?" The first mate grabbed her shirt and yanked her to standing. The threadbare linen, already assaulted during her foray under the deck, tore under the strain, leaving her chest fully exposed. Monkey squeaked and tried to clutch the gap closed but Doery's massive hands caught hers and pulled them away. As he stared at her chest, his inhaled breath was of shock, not desire.

"What's this?" Keeping hold of her with one hand, he pressed the thumb of the other against her chest, above her heart. A shiver ran up her spine as his thumbnail clicked on something solid.

Biting her tongue at the intrusive touch, Monkey glanced down. Doery's thumb rested against something silver stuck to—no, embedded into her chest. He jabbed at it, sending a flare of blinding pain through her. "What did you do to yourself, monkey?"

"I don't…"

"You weren't stealing this, were you? Stealing from your captain?"

"No, I swear! Please, I didn't—I *wouldn't*—"

Doery gave her a penetrating look, then shifted his glance from her chest to the coins around her feet. His entire body tensed. He released her arm abruptly and took a half-dozen steps back. "Doesn't matter." Eyes not leaving her, he waved to the strewn coins. "Pick those up. The captain will want to see them."

"Yes, sir," she mumbled, dropping to her knees and scrabbling for the coins. As Doery stepped away, she dared another look down.

A palm-sized coin was embedded in the skin above her heart. The same coin, she thought, as the one in her hand before she'd blacked out, though the metal's strange luminescence had faded. Carefully, she tried to get the tip of a fingernail beneath it. There was no gap. *Sealord protect me.*

Trying not to think, Monkey grabbed the dead captain's hat and used it to collect the silver. There wasn't much she could do for the captain herself—not with Doery pacing like a shifty rabbit, unwilling to take his eyes off her—but Monkey did take a moment to straighten the woman's body and cover it with the cape. "I'm sorry I can't do more."

Monkey felt a sudden wave of sadness. ::*We've soul-bonded,*:: the strange woman said abruptly. ::*It's why you can hear me.*::

"What are you talking about?"

"Only you'd find a ghost on a ghost ship to talk to, monkey." Doery gave a disingenuous smile from across the cabin, not-so-furtively watching her while running his fingers over the carved frames of the shattered gallery.

She expected he was aiming for derision; his tense frame and constant scrutiny said otherwise. *Probably thinks I'm tainted or possessed—or a threat.*

::*You don't need to speak aloud,*:: the woman said. ::*We're connected now. I hear your thoughts. I feel what you feel.*::

Monkey winced. The last thing she needed was someone knowing what she was thinking. They'd just use it against her. Biting her lip, she focused on her task.

::*Anything that hurts you will hurt me. It's the nature of the soul-binding. Mind you, if the others you keep company with are like this one, I can see why you'd worry.*:: Concern filtered through the crisp words.

You think I have any choice in the matter? Ducking under the table, she grabbed a final coin. *Who are you, anyway?*

She felt the woman's surprise. ::*You don't know? I'm Endras, once EndrasIleya, Captain of the* Endeavour. *This was my ship.*:: The words held pride and something else, bitter and sharp. Grief.

Grief was something Monkey knew too well. It filled her to overflowing sometimes, particularly when she was snug in her hammock and could hide her tears from uncaring eyes. As she crawled out from under the table, she glanced toward the compartment. She couldn't see the captain's body—a small mercy if the woman was who she said she was.

"Done?" Doery asked. Without waiting he headed toward the door. "Let's go, then."

Monkey followed in Doery's wake, clutching the hatful of what the woman—Endras—had called soul-silver. As she crossed the quarterdeck, she saw a brace and pulleys being used to sling one of the compact cannons from the *Endeavour* to the *Outcast*. A dozen others had been hauled to the deck and were awaiting their turn. It was an odd sight given the *Outcast*'s cannons were massive beasts that took a six-person crew to maneuver.

Endras hadn't said anything more after her introduction, but Monkey sensed she was there. Sadness and despondency permeated their strange connection, the despair reminding Monkey of the day her own life had been destroyed. She couldn't help feeling sympathetic.

::It was already finished,:: Endras said after a while. *::The Zarristan line ship did most of the work. I only hoped an ally would recover what remained and carry us home.::*

Home? You were the only one on the ship. Should there have been others?

::All one hundred and fourteen of the crew were accounted for. Their bodies were given to the sea, but their souls remained intact. Every one.::

Monkey tightened her hold on the hat. If her count was correct, she'd collected exactly one hundred and fourteen coins. *You called it soul-silver.*

::The most precious secret held by the Kambarna is the existence of soul-silver. It gives our people two lives. The first is the life of the body. The second is the life of the spirit.::

Oh. You mean all of you have a dead person talking in your head?

The woman's laugh was soft with a hint of regret. *::Well, we don't consider our spirit-bonded partner dead. They're a gift. A connection from past to present, present to future.::*

"Hurry it up, monkey," Doery said, waiting at the ladder to the main deck.

"Yes, sir," she said, quickening her pace to catch up. Rather than slide down the rail like she'd normally do, she took the steps carefully so she wouldn't dump the hat or the silver it contained. *Wonder what the captain will do with it all?* She squeezed the hat to her chest. *Sealord, what will she do with me?*

Except, given the assessing looks Doery kept throwing her way, she already knew. They'd sell her in Blackhaven with the rest of the loot, if they could. Alive, dead—they wouldn't care which. Her only hope was Endras.

What would you have me do? she asked, knowing the woman wanted to protect the coins and the souls they held, which meant protecting her, too. For now.

As Monkey crossed the deck to the boarding bridge, a tiny fluff of orange blurred around her legs before scrambling across the bridge and lunging at the seahand watching the other side. The skeletal cat quickly disappeared under the stretch of oilcloth covering the ship's pinnace, leaving the deckhand with red stripes down his cheek.

::We need to do what Firefight just did. Escape.::

Monkey followed more sedately in the cat's wake. *Firefight? You named that nightmare Firefight?*

::He's always had a temper, even before he was half-starved. I would've named him Fireball, but that would have been too confusing with the cannon on board. Didn't want to set one off yelling at a cat.::

Monkey's eyes moved to the cannon currently being lowered to *Outcast's* deck. *Wait. You can set the cannons off with a word?*

A strong affirmative came through their connection. ::*It's how mage cannons work. They aren't lit by powder and a spark. They're lit by energy and a word.*::

Monkey could only imagine how quick the cannons could fire if they didn't need to be cleaned and reloaded. She grabbed the rope side as if she'd lost her footing, using the moment to survey the *Outcast*. Five of the mage cannons already sat haphazardly on the deck. One faced the *Endeavour*, two the open ocean. The fourth tilted down, almost aligned with the main hatchway which passed through every deck to the hold. The last cannon prompted a bitter smile. Making a show of regaining her balance, Monkey followed its line of sight to the ship's wheel and the mizzen beyond.

Can anyone do it? she asked.

::*Only a trained mage can set them off.*:: Monkey's sudden optimism flamed to ash. Keeping her face stone, she climbed over the rail to the *Outcast's* deck. As she stood in front of the boarding bridge, Endras's voice came soft and hesitant. ::*If you can bear it, I could use my mage-gift through you.*::

Through me?

::*I can take over your body for a moment and light the cannon.*::

Monkey froze, every muscle in her body seizing in a visceral scream. *Don't you dare.*

"Get moving, monkey." Doery's shove sent her stumbling. "Captain Vanisse is going to want those coins locked up." The coins—including hers. She only hoped that meant locking her up with the silver. Knowing the captain, though, it could mean cutting the coin out of Monkey just to see what happened.

::*If they cut out the silver, it's death for us both. The worst kind of death.*:: Monkey felt Endras' shudder.

Doery grabbed her arm, dragging her toward the ladder to the quarterdeck. "Let's go, monkey."

She knew what would happen if she tried to fight. Even so, she twisted her head, trying to find something, anything, to use against him. As Doery pushed her head-first into the ladder, a concussive blast rent the air. The ship rocked forcefully, sending them both tumbling to the deck.

"What in the..." Doery regained his feet and rushed to the rail. Dark smoke billowed from a half-dozen gunports on the *Endeavour*. "What in the Deeps is going on over there?"

"They poked at some mage thing in the hold," one of seahands hollered back. "It's all lit up down there."

"Captain'll keelhaul the one who did it." Doery's eyes blazed with fury. "Get everyone on deck. We got to move or we'll lose our bounty." He ran to where two seahands worked to right the boarding bridge, which had tilted askew in the blast. The first mate added his weight to the bridge's anchor posts, forcing it back into position. "Get it all over here. We'll sort it after."

Monkey watched for a long moment before realizing that Doery had forgotten her. She ducked into her hidey-hole under the pinnace. *You need to help me right now or your soul-silver will be gone for good. Us, too, if you're telling the truth about cutting the coin out.*

Endras was affronted. *::We're soul-bound. Even if I wanted, I couldn't lie to you.::*

Or was that another lie? It didn't matter. For the moment, Monkey knew they wanted the same thing: to escape. If they got away, maybe she could negotiate returning the soul-silver for some kind of reward.

Any ideas?

::Do you know how to lower this boat?::

The pinnace? She felt the affirmative. *It's on a swing.* She scurried out from under the boat and over to the opposite side of the deck, keeping well away from the crew shifting the loot. Looking up, she found where the pinnace was attached by a boom to the mainmast. *Shift the boom, release the catch, and it'll drop.*

::Trust pirates to find an easy way to release boats.::

No one ever expects it. Monkey thought of how many times the ship had used the boats to harass a target. *I can lower it, I just can't sail it.*

::Now that I can help with.:: Monkey felt Captain Endras' smile. *::I say we use their own tactics against them.::*

Glad to have a plan, Monkey realized the frantic bustle of the plunder being moved had to be a blessing from the Sealord. *Least if we work fast.* As the crew ferried everything that could be carried from the burning ship, she hurried to untie the rope ladder leading to the pinnace, then scurried up it to tuck the hatful of soul-silver safely into the boat.

::Thank you. I know you have no reason to care for the souls of my crew, but the Kambarna will be grateful for their return.::

She'd get a reward if they made it away. Maybe she'd have a future, or a chance at one. That hope, however slim, gave Monkey courage as she climbed onto the starboard rail to get to the shrouds that would take her aloft. Heart pounding, she began the ascent, timing her movements to the roll of the ocean. *Don't look. Don't look.*

She made it to the mainmast's lowest platform without being spotted. With swift movements, buoyed by a swell of support from Endras, Monkey undid the twist-lock holding the swing boom in place. She grabbed the boom's pull line, planning to carry it down. As she climbed back onto the shrouds, the *Outcast* rode an easy swell. The gentle motion was enough to send the boom swinging seaward.

"Watch the boom!" the lookout hollered from above. Every seahand on the ship turned at the command, those on the maindeck dropping to the deck to avoid the boom and the pinnace it carried.

"What's the monkey doing?" A man on the *Endeavour* waved frantically in her direction.

With no time for care, Monkey released the ratlines and slid down the shrouds. Already cut and tender palms burned in agony at the passage. She clung on for the long moment it took to get within a few feet of the deck.

::*Go, go, go.*::

Monkey released the shrouds, dropping to the deck with a bone-jarring jerk. Ignoring the pain, she rolled to her feet and ran at the closest cannon.

"Get the bloody monkey alive," Captain Vanisse called from the quarterdeck.

Doery's brother Ralan dropped a box and rushed at her, blocking her path. Monkey darted one way, then reversed course quickly, leaving him a full step behind. Once past him, she flung herself at the mage cannon. "Do it!" she shouted, expecting to lose control of her body forever. *Better that than what Captain Vanisse would do to me.*

Endras moved to the front of her awareness. ::*I'm sorry,*:: the woman said, pushing Monkey's consciousness to the side. She shuddered, a bystander in her own body, as Endras slammed her hand on the top of the cannon. She had one moment of shock before a torrent of energy streamed through her soul, a tidal wave of power. A brilliant white glow encompassed the cannon, then burst forward in a crack of lightning. Shouts filled the air. Before she could look, Endras had her moving to the next cannon. A moment later, the deck around the main hatchway exploded.

A wave of exhaustion flooded her as Endras surrendered control. Relief swelled; the woman had done what she'd offered and no more. Willpower keeping her on her feet, she took in the damage. Flames swathed the front-half of the quarterdeck and danced across the lines. The mizzen yards crackled like logs in a fire. Forward, the ship faired slightly better—the deck shredded, billowing smoke, but not fully ablaze. *It's good we didn't hit the magazine.*

::*We need to go. Before the mainmast catches or someone takes control.*::

While a handful of the *Outcast's* crew were moving to work the pumps, more were reeling in apparent shock. A dozen others, including an infuriated Doery, stood stranded on the still-burning *Endeavour,* the boarding bridge nowhere in view. Captain Vanisse might have been able to get the crew working together, but if she had survived the quarterdeck hit, she wasn't making it known. *Sealord take her.*

Monkey ran to where the boom and pinnace swayed in the wake of the cannon fire. Glad the boom hadn't swung right over the ocean, she reached for the ship's rope ladder. Hand by faltering hand, exhaustion weighing heavy on her shoulders, she climbed until she could push the tarp back from the gunwale and drop in.

Can't stop yet. Grabbing the boom's dangling pull line, Monkey tugged hard. The boom didn't move. Frantic, she tried again. Nothing.

::Can you handle my taking control one more time?::

Monkey took a deep, shuddering breath, then nodded. *Please don't let my trust be misplaced.*

A moment later, Endras worked through Monkey to call a curl of energy—a spark compared to the fire that had set off the cannon—and move the boom the final dozen feet over the water. Without pause, Endras released the pinnace. If the ship's boat fell more gently than it would have otherwise, no one would ever know it. As the pinnace settled on the water, Endras gave back control.

A wailing screech sounded from the bow as Firefight voiced his distress. "Calm down, you stupid cat," Monkey said. "Be lucky you're alive." *I know I am.* A glance upward confirmed no one was chasing her; they were too busy trying to save the ship and their own lives.

Sitting in the small boat in the shadow of the two burning ships—the ship that had taken her life and the ship that had given her the chance at a new one—Monkey smiled broadly for the first time in years. Eying the makeshift mast and sails tucked in the center of the boat, she projected her confusion to Endras. *I really hope you know how to put this all together.*

* * *

The little pinnace flew across the waves, its single sail full of wind and freedom. An orange fluff stood precariously balanced on the bow—a living figurehead full of fire and ready for a fight.

Monkey watched a shadow in the distance grow and take over the horizon. What part of the Oritalian coast it was, she didn't know. Wherever they landed, Endras was sure they'd be able to report the *Outcast* and find an embassy to help them get the soul-silver back to the Kambarna.

"What will happen when we get there?" It hadn't taken long for Monkey's anxiety to return. After five years on *Outcast*, the idea of freedom was both exhilarating and impossible to imagine. It didn't help that she was carrying a piece of the Kambarna's treasured soul-silver and she wasn't one of them. *How could they not want it—want Endras—back?*

The idea of losing their connection sent a spike of cold down her back, despite the heat of the late summer sun. Endras had been an interloper in her own mind, but she'd done exactly as promised. She'd helped Monkey escape. She'd borrowed her body—and given it back. She'd offered support and confidence, never a word of hate. *I don't want to lose that.*

Endras offered a wave of assurance. *::I told you, we're soul-bonded. That means we'll be together as long as you live.::*

You were telling the truth? She desperately wanted to hope, but she was so used to the taste of hope's ashes.

::Always. The Kambarna will welcome you because you are a part of me. They won't care who you were. They will only care about who we will be.::

Tears welled and she let them fall: grief for the past, hope for the future. For the first time since the dreadful day she'd lost her family—lost everything— she offered up the one thing that was hers to give. "Alia. My name is Alia."

When the Star Fell
and the Levee Broke

Alex Bledsoe

Blessedly, the storm ended that morning, after two weeks of solid rainfall that alternated between gentle showers and blinding deluges. Now, through Tennessee air so humid a fish could walk in it, the sun shone down on the lake's empty bed, glaring off pools of water and glistening mud, twinkling off unfortunate flopping fish, and blinding the two men who stood on the bank.

Travis shook his head as his guts tightened into a stress knot. "The whole levee went," he said flatly. "The whole thing."

The levee in question had blocked off one end of the lake, creating a body of water where a shallow valley existed before. Travis had fished off that levee since he was a child, learned to swim in its late-afternoon shadow, and never thought it could simply wash away.

"Damn," his brother-in-law Joe-Mar said, fluttering the front of his tank top. "I'm sweating like a stripper on Sunday."

Travis turned to his brother-in-law. "How'd you get that eye?"

"Born with it."

"Okay, smart-ass, how about the big bruise around it?"

"That? Got hit with a cue ball couple of nights ago."

"Who were you fighting?"

"Nobody. We were just fucking around, throwing pool balls at each other and seeing who could take it."

Travis had known he was marrying the whole family when he said "I do" to Deirdre, but he hadn't counted on her brother being constantly underfoot. Joe-Mar, real name Joseph Martin, was an insinuator, someone who wormed his way into your life without any overt invitation and then resisted all efforts to get shed of him. He often called Travis his best friend, and with Deirdre as his wife, Travis couldn't do much about it.

Joe-Mar shaded his eyes with his hand. "That ol' levee didn't stand a chance. You can see where the water washed out the bottom and then the rest just went *whoosh*."

"Yep," Travis agreed. "Goddamn, the insurance will go up so much."

"They make levee insurance?"

"Property insurance. Covers everything on the property. I hope."

"Just don't mention the word 'flood.' You say that, they can deny your claim. I'm serious."

"How in the world would you know that?"

"Dude, remember Matt Inman? Pipe burst in his ceiling, he told his insurance that it 'flooded the house,' and damn if they didn't deny his claim cuz he ain't got no flood insurance. Swear to God and Jesus."

With a weary sigh, Travis turned to go, but then Joe-Mar grabbed his arm. "Dude. What's that?"

"Where?"

"Out there, in the deep part of the lake. Sticking out of the mud."

Travis squinted against the glare. "I dunno. Looks like metal."

"Did you sink a boat out there?"

"I never sank a boat. You're the one that sinks boats."

"Only two."

"That's two more than me."

"Then what is that?"

"I can't tell from here."

"C'mon, let's go down there and see."

"We wouldn't get three steps into that mud before it sucked off our boots, our socks, and probably our underwear. We'll have to wait until it dries." Travis looked up at the now-blazing sun alone in the clear sky. "Which shouldn't take too long if the sun stays out."

Joe-Mar pulled out his phone and checked the weather. "Says sunny and clear for the next week."

"Great. Now it's sunny. Couldn't have been sunny last week, no..." He walked toward his pickup, parked in the weeds.

A week later, Travis was looking over his dire financial paperwork at his kitchen table when Joe-Mar burst in, slamming the screen door against the porch wall in his eagerness. "Hey, man, you gotta come with me. Grab your frog-gigging boots. You ain't gonna believe it."

Travis took off his reading glasses. "If I ain't gonna believe it, I'll just stay here."

"No, I mean, you gotta come see this."

"See what?"

"You remember that thing sticking out of the bottom of the lake?"

"The old boat?"

"That's what we thought it was. But you gotta come see what it really is."

Travis sighed and rubbed his eyes. "Are you high? Because I've seen you so high you could sit on Wednesday and see both Sundays."

"I ain't high, Travis, I promise. Just come with me."

Experience had taught Travis that, if rebuffed, Joe-Mar would simply become more insistent. So he carefully put all his paperwork back in its folders while Joe-Mar paced impatiently around the kitchen. Then the two men got into Travis's pickup and drove through the fields toward the lake.

The lake bed was now mostly dry and the smell of rotted fish and stagnant water filled the air. "There it is," Joe-Mar said as they got out.

Something did stick out of the ground, a curved piece of metal that gleamed in the sun. That puzzled Travis; why was it still shiny, when it should've been corroded or at least covered with mud and silt?

A set of footprints that he assumed were from Joe-Mar led to and from it. "Come on," his brother-in-law urged him.

With his rubber wading boots on, Travis followed Joe-Mar out onto the lake bed. Dead and dried fish were everywhere, and he saw one remaining pool near the center in which a huge catfish struggled to get its whole body underwater at once. Joe-Mar was so excited he practically ran all the way to the strange protrusion.

"Dude, come here and look at this!" he called back. "You won't believe it!"

Travis assumed that, if it wasn't a sunken boat, it was just an old appliance, maybe a refrigerator or washing machine someone had snuck onto the lake to dump. But when he reached it, he was both startled and puzzled.

A smooth, curved piece of shiny silver metal rose three feet above the drying mud. If, as it appeared, it was part of a disk-shaped object, then the whole thing would be about seven feet across. There was oxidation around the edges, but most of it appeared undamaged.

"See? See?" Joe-Mar shouted gleefully.

Travis crouched and carefully touched it. Despite being out in the direct sun for hours, it was not hot. It felt smooth and almost velvety.

"Do you know what it is?" Joe-Mar asked gleefully. "It's a satellite."

"What? That's nuts."

"Naw, man, I got to Googlin' and figured it out. They fall down all the time. Most of 'em burn up, but at least one per day lands somewhere on earth! Ain't that the shit?"

"Joe-Mar," Travis said patiently, "does this look burned up to you?"

That shut him up for a moment. Travis dug at the mud, exposing more of the object but no obvious surface features, or any kind of markings. Whatever it was, it wanted to be discreet about it.

"We gotta dig it out," Joe-Mar said. "I mean, we gotta. It's on your land, man, it's yours. You can do whatever you want with it. Don't you want to see what it is?"

Travis hated to admit it, but he was equally curious. "I suppose so," he said, wiping the mud from his fingers onto the shiny metal. To his surprise, it simply slid down until it finally dripped off. "Huh. Mud don't even stick to it. Give me a hand here."

The two men shoved the silver disk back and forth. At first it barely moved, but then with one solid shove it popped free, rolled on its edge out of the hole and into the sun.

They lowered it to the ground and looked it over.

Seven feet across, it bulged in the center but betrayed no surface markings or visible seams. The oxidation was only around the edges, and where it was buried in the mud, the metal was replaced by some sort of clear plastic covering, like a window cloudy with time.

Travis leaned close and tried to see through it, but the bright sunlight made it impossible. "Maybe you were right, Joe-Mar. Maybe it is a satellite."

"Let's get it back to your barn and see if we can't pop it open," Joe-Mar almost shouted. "Bound to be something in there worth something."

"And would you know it if you saw it?"

"Naw, but you know who would?" He grinned. "Deirdre."

Later in the barn, Deirdre blew a plume of smoke toward the rafters and looked over the strange object laid across a pair of sawhorses. "Now what in the hell is this thing supposed to be?"

"It's a satellite!" her brother said. "We found it down in the lake."

"Oh, bullshit, you done stole it from somewhere," she said, with the disapproval that only a big sister can show. "Tell me the truth, Joe-Mar, or I swear I'll jerk a knot in your tail."

"I did not!" he insisted, almost jumping up and down with outrage. "Travis was right there with me. Wasn't you, Travis?"

"As hard as it might be to believe, he's right, at least about where we found it," Travis said. "But I ain't so sure about what it is. We thought you might be able to help."

"Me?"

"You work for the government."

"I work on the assembly line at the munitions plant. You don't have a clue what I do, do you?"

He shrugged.

Deirdre rolled her eyes and handed him her cigarette. While neither Travis nor Joe-Mar knew exactly what she did, they did know she was smarter than either of them. She walked around the object, inspecting it carefully, running her fingertips along its edges. In one spot, where the corrosion had eaten away the surface, she broke off a tiny bit of metal. "It's built on a frame."

"What's that mean?" Jo-Mar asked.

"Well, it means an awful lot of trouble. Usually you'd just cast these big pieces of metal and weld 'em together. You wouldn't start with a miniature frame, that'd take forever to build, and on top of that it'd be fragile. And what good would it do?"

"So it is a satellite!" Joe-Mar exclaimed.

"I didn't say that. I don't know what it is any more than you do."

Joe-Mar charged on regardless. "I bet there's a reward for it. Probably a 1-800 number to call to let 'em know we have it."

Travis looked Joe-Mar hard in the eye. "Don't you tell no one just yet. I mean it. Not a word."

Joe-Mar was startled by the intensity. "Sure, bro-in-law. Whatever you say."

Deirdre took her cigarette back from Travis. "Y'all sure got it clean."

"It came out of the ground that way," Travis said. "The mud didn't stick to it."

"How long you reckon it's been there?"

He shrugged. "I guess it could've come down in the storm and nobody would've seen it. Or hell, seeing how rusted it is around the edges, maybe it's been there for years."

Deirdre ground out her cigarette on the dirt floor. "Well, y'all have fun with it, I'm going back to the house. Dinner's at six, and don't make me come chase y'all down. I assume you're staying, Joe-Mar?"

"I can't, but thanks for inviting me."

She snorted again, as if to say, like I had a choice.

"So what do you think it is?" Travis pressed Deirdre.

"Hell, I don't know. It might be a satellite. Might also be from some dumbass trying to get free internet. Either way, it probably ain't worth enough to justify all this trouble. Might get something for the scrap metal, but that's all."

When she'd gone, Travis grabbed a can of WD-40, sprayed it on part of the plastic window, then wiped it away with a paper towel. He turned on his phone's flashlight app and shone it inside. He had to hunker down and get right up against it to see.

He almost shouted. But he was glad he didn't when Joe-Mar asked, "See anything?"

"Naw," Travis said, hoping he sounded normal. "Nothing."

"We need to crack it open," Joe-Mar said eagerly. "See what's inside. See what country it came from. Shit, what if it's Chinese? They might pay us a fortune."

Travis stood and wiped his hands on his jeans. "Maybe tomorrow. So you're not staying for dinner?"

"No, I'm meeting Miss Shirley at Shoney's." Joe-Mar was dating his old Sunday school teacher, who he still called "Miss Shirley." In truth, she was only five years older than him, but Travis didn't want to think about what they might role-play in private.

Travis sat quietly during his own dinner, then did the dishes in silence and took a beer outside onto the front porch. Fireflies drifted lazily through the gray dusk, and the air grew hazy with the humidity kept at bay by the sun. A rabbit sat in the middle of the yard, stock-still until it felt safe enough to move.

Deirdre, who refused to smoke in the house, joined him. She lit up and said, "Did you hear what Johnna Dupree's little boy said in Sunday school?"

"No, what?"

"The lesson was about the Resurrection, and he said, 'I've heard of that, and if it lasts more than four hours, you need to call a doctor.'"

Travis chuckled.

"Oh, you are with us."

"Sorry, I've just got a lot on my mind."

"The insurance stuff?"

He shook his head. "I mean, yeah, I'm worried about that, but…"

"What?"

"You'll think I'm crazy."

"Yeah, so?"

"That thing in the barn…it ain't a satellite."

"What is it, then?"

He took a deep breath. "A UFO."

She didn't change expression. "I always thought they were bigger than that."

"Me, too."

"Why do you think it is one?"

"Because I looked in through that window. There's tiny little dead bodies inside, sitting in chairs like airplane pilots."

Deirdre took another drag. "You know, all this started with Joe-Mar, and that little shit ain't above playing a joke on you. Maybe he just got some Ken dolls and dressed 'em up."

"I know, and I thought of that, but where would he get metal like that, that nothing sticks to? And how would he get it down in the lake, and then how could he know it would storm so bad the levee would wash out?"

She nodded. "That's a point."

"And they don't look like Ken dolls. They look like..." He recalled the creepy bulbous skulls and empty eye sockets. "They're skeletons."

"Then I guess it could be aliens," she said as calmly as if observing a squirrel dart across the yard. She patted his hand. "But I still wouldn't put a lot of stock in it. We got enough real-world problems without bringing new ones in from space."

He drank some more beer. "There's one way to find out for sure. Crack the sucker open, like Joe-Mar said."

"How you gonna do that?"

"Hammer and chisel. Acetylene torch. Whack it with an ax. Hell, run over it with my truck." He added with a smile, "And if that don't work, I'll just piss on it."

Deirdre chuckled. "You go after it with all that, you'll likely tear it up."

"But then I'll be sure."

"You will be. If that's what's important to you."

"It might be. I got a feeling it's just gonna wear on me until I do, so I might as well get it over with."

"Go for it, then. I'll go ahead and push 9-1 on my phone for when you cut off a hand or a foot. That way I'll only have to dial 1." She held out her fist for a bump.

He tapped her fist with his own. "Thanks, hon."

In the barn, he moved a couple of work lights into position, knelt, and looked through what he now understood was a cockpit window. Inside, straps held the three tiny skeletons, human-shaped but with overlarge heads, in equally tiny pilot couches. Two sat straight, while one had slumped over at some point. They were, he guessed, about eight inches in height, clad in light-colored one-piece jumpsuits.

You poor bastards, Travis thought. If you're real, you must've been scared shitless.

He got a small chisel and a hammer and tried to crack the window around the frame. It took all his strength, but he finally worked the plastic free in one rounded corner and got a crowbar tip under the edge. Putting all his weight into it, he popped the window out of its frame.

Now he could both plainly see, and touch, the inside of the cockpit. It took him back to his childhood, when he'd build model jets with their snug pilot seats and complex cockpit instruments. Except in those cases, the dials and readouts had been mere decals applied over plastic, while these were, to all appearances, real devices on a scale that he could barely wrap his head around.

He eased his calloused hand into the cabin, and felt the grillwork of the deck and the smooth, darkened panels of what might have been ceiling lights. The dead astronaut in the center sat by an array of levers or switches, and they moved when he pushed them. One broke off and rolled out through the missing window; he caught it in the palm of his other hand. He held it up to the light and saw that a tiny, dark ball covered one end, just like the rubber grip on his truck's gear shift. It would no doubt nestle into the tiny palm just as his own did, and he wondered if this somehow altered the speed of the craft as it hurtled through space.

His stomach suddenly plummeted as the reality of this hit him anew. This hunk of junk has been in space, flying from one planet to another. He'd watched lots of science fiction on TV, but never imagined he'd be touching something that had actually been in space.

His attention was drawn back to the skulls of these ancient aliens. Like human skulls, they had holes for two eyes and a nose, and a mouth with even rows of tiny teeth. They looked sad, somehow, slumped in their seats, their arms dangling and, in one case, their legs splayed out like an old man sleeping after Thanksgiving dinner. Travis felt a sudden kinship to them; they had not died suddenly in the crash, but slowly in its aftermath, unable to free themselves.

Using a pair of needle-nosed pliers, he worked the straps holding the nearest tiny skeleton until they came loose, then gently removed the body from the vessel. It weighed nothing. Carrying it in two hands, he placed it on a folded towel on his work bench.

"Now, who are you?" he asked no one.

He took out his phone and took several pictures of the small creature, amazed at the delicate perfection of its bones. He stretched out a tape measure to show its scale. Like its vessel, the late pilot's uniform had no marks or insignia, just that tissue-like silver fabric that made up its jumpsuit. He stepped back and felt a deep well of sadness.

"Whatcha got there?" came the last voice he wanted to hear, followed by a drawn-out, "Shiiiiiiit."

"Don't you ever knock?" Travis asked.

"On a barn?" Joe-Mar kept trying to see around Travis, who stood in front of the tiny body. "Did you get that out of that satellite?"

"Yeah. I thought you had a date."

"I did, but it was just for dinner."

"You know, I think we need a new rule that you call before you come over."

"I did call Deirdre. She said you were out here. Come on, dude, let me see it."

Travis reluctantly stepped aside. Joe-Mar bent close, then let out a whistle. "Man, alive, look at that little fella. And check out that face! That'd scare the beard off Jesus." He looked up with an eager smile. "What else is in there?"

There would be no stopping him now, Travis knew, so he let Joe-Mar help him remove the other two bodies and put them together on the workbench. Joe-Mar started taking his own pictures, then began quickly posting them online.

When Travis realized what he was doing, he snatched the phone away. "Whoa, whoa, slow down. We don't know what we've got here yet, we can't—"

"Dude, what we've got is a crashed UFO and the bodies of three goddam aliens. I mean, yeah, I wish they were bigger, but still—"

Travis scrolled through the recently-posted pictures and deleted them all from social media. "Joe-Mar, you may be family, but I'm about sick of you. Go back to the house and tell Deirdre I'll be there in a minute."

"Travis, you'd worry the dirt off a dirt road. We're gonna be famous for finding these little guys. I saw 'em first, remember?"

Travis just looked at him.

"Damn, that's the same look Deirdre gives me." Joe-Mar turned in a huff and left the barn. "You best not trash my phone," he called back over his shoulder.

Travis closed the barn door and locked it from inside. He went over to the spaceship and peered once more into the tiny cockpit. A tiny door at the back evidently led to the interior and he wondered if more bodies might be in there. He studied the outside of the vehicle for an hour, looking for any way to break into it, but found nothing. Then he did the one thing he knew he had to do.

When Travis returned to the house, it was full dark, and every bug this side of the river seemed to be assaulting his porch light. He found Joe-Mar at the kitchen table with Deirdre, her laptop and several empty beer bottles in front of him. Travis was not surprised when he opened the refrigerator and found the twelve-pack carton empty.

Wearily, he poured some sweet tea, gave Joe-Mar back his phone, and sat down. He was too tired and sad to be upset with Joe-Mar anymore; it would do no good, anyway. That boy simply was who he was.

Deirdre reached over and took Travis's hand under the table. "You get it open?"

"Partly." He met her gaze. "They weren't Ken dolls. Or G.I. Joes."

"I been looking online," Joe-Mar interrupted. "Look at these guys." He turned the screen, which displayed an image of a small skeleton with a strange, elongated cranium. "They found this down in Chile. They think it's an alien, but you got to pay money to read the article."

"It doesn't look anything like ours," Travis said distantly.

"No, man, but it shows that these things are real."

He clenched his fists but kept his voice level. "Don't you have anyplace else you'd like to be?"

Before the words could penetrate Joe-Mar's hazy brain, Deirdre said, "I think it's time for you to go home. You okay to drive?"

"What? Of course I'm okay. Why wouldn't I be?" Joe-Mar closed the computer with a petulant snap, slid it back to Deirdre, and stood up. "I seen it first," he reminded them, then slammed the screen door on his way out.

"That boy," Deirdre said and shook her head.

"Mm." Travis reached over and took a drink from her beer. Then he handed her his phone. "Look at these."

She scrolled silently through the photographs. His eyes were focused on the table top, but his gaze was a million miles away. He said, "Reckon they were like us? That they had families, kids, that sort of thing? That there's people back wherever they came from that wonder what happened to 'em?"

Deirdre returned his phone. "As the soldiers say at work, hon, that's above my pay grade."

"I wonder how long they've been there? I mean, how long they've been here. In the lake."

Then Joe-Mar burst back into the house. "Y'all, you ain't gonna believe this! Look!"

He stepped aside. The porch light illuminated two tall, thin men standing in the yard. Behind them a large, old black Cadillac had parked beside Travis's truck and Joe-Mar's Camaro.

They wore black suits, sunglasses, and gloves, despite the oppressive heat and humidity. One carried a large satchel. They both smiled the same vapid smile, their lips little more than horizontal lines.

"It's real, honest-to-shit men in black!" Joe-Mar exclaimed gleefully.

"Shut up, Joe-Mar," Deirdre said. She exchanged a wary look with Travis, then they both stood and went to the door.

"Can we help y'all?" she asked through the screen.

One of the visitors stepped up to the door, but did not reach for the handle. He held out a gloved hand and said in a whispery voice, "We understand you found something of ours."

Travis glared at Joe-Mar.

Joe-Mar held up his hands. "Dude, don't look at me, I didn't tell 'em shit."

Travis pushed open the screen door and took the offered hand. Although the fingers closed around his own, when he squeezed, the glove felt empty. He looked up sharply, but saw only the same bland smile, and his own reflection in the oddly styled wrap-around sunglasses.

"We represent a motion picture production company," the man continued. "We know you found one of our props."

"Yeah? How do you know that?"

Joe-Mar interjected, "Make 'em take off their sunglasses. I bet they got jet-black eyes under there, like the black-eyed children. And no eyebrows."

Ignoring Joe-Mar, the man said, "May we come in?"

"No, I don't think—"

"Sure, come in!" Joe-Mar said gleefully, and stepped back with a sweeping motion. "Sit down, have some tea! I'd offer you a beer, but we're out."

The first man entered. He took off his hat, revealing gray hair that was clearly an old, disheveled wig. Travis noticed that he had no visible ears; the sunglasses disappeared under the fake hair, and whatever held them up was hidden.

"The object you found was a prop being used in the production of a science fiction film. We are grateful for your efforts in recovering it. It was very expensive and we will make sure you are rewarded."

Movement outside got Travis's attention. The other man in black bent over his satchel and removed a large, old-fashioned camera, the kind with accordion-like bellows between the body and the lens. He held it awkwardly, as if its weight was too much for him. Then he pointed it at Travis and clicked off a picture.

"What was that for?" Travis demanded.

"Our press release," the second man said. "To thank you for your assistance."

Travis looked from one man in black to the other. They maintained their creepy, lifeless smiles. "Yeah, well, I don't have any idea what you're talking about, so I guess you drove all the way out here for nothing."

"Oh, give it to 'em," Deirdre said wearily. "I'm already tired of hearing about it."

"No," Travis said firmly.

"Why not?"

"Because they're lying," Travis said.

"I assure you, we're not," the first man protested.

"Which film company are you with, then?" Travis asked.

He thought for a moment. "Twentieth Century Paramount."

Just as Travis realized Joe-Mar had left the kitchen, he returned with Travis's double-barreled twelve-gauge shotgun. Laughing almost dementedly, he held it on the first man and said, "Okay, let's see those eyes. Now."

The man in black seemed unperturbed. He ignored Joe-Mar and said to Travis, "We'll take the derelict and, if you know what's good for you, you won't mention any of this to anyone else. We know your names, where you work, where you live."

Travis was about to snap a reply when suddenly his vision grew watery and indistinct and his stomach flipped. He grabbed the counter top to keep from falling face-first to the linoleum and instead sat down heavily on the floor, his back to the cabinets. His vision receded down a long tunnel, but he never completely blacked out.

When he came back to the moment, he still sat on the kitchen floor, Deirdre was still at the table, and Joe-Mar leaned against the open archway into the living room, the shotgun propped against the wall beside him. Morning light shone through the screen door into the kitchen.

Travis got slowly to his feet, his joints stiff and his stomach still uncertain. "Deirdre," he croaked, his mouth dry.

She blinked a few times then looked at him. "Travis?"

"Yeah."

She turned to her brother. "Joe-Mar?"

Joe-Mar's slack-jawed face jumped a couple of times, then he swallowed hard and said, "What happened?" He looked at the gun beside him. "Shit, what's this for? What time is it? Man, have I got to pee."

"Was someone here?" Deirdre asked, genuinely unsure.

Someone was here, Travis thought, but the images wouldn't gel. Men in black suits. Men... And then he remembered. Men in black!

The surge of adrenalin burned out enough of whatever affected him that he was able to rush across the yard to the barn. Its doors stood open, and just as he feared, the derelict spaceship was gone.

He stared at the sawhorses where it had been. He was too numb to really be upset, though. He took out his phone, only to find that all his pictures were gone as well.

Joe-Mar appeared behind him. "Did they take it?"

"Course they did," Travis said. "It was theirs, wasn't it?"

"Fuck!" Joe-Mar barked in frustration. "And here you went and deleted all my pictures of it. We coulda proved it!"

"To who?"

"To everybody!"

"They got my pictures, too. And nobody woulda believed it, Joe-Mar. They'd'a said it was a trick, or a model, or CGI or something."

Joe-Mar started to snap something back, then bit it off and stomped back out of the barn. Halfway across the yard he bellowed another, "Fuck!"

Travis wasn't sure how long he stood there, but eventually Deirdre put a hand on his shoulder and said quietly, "You all right?"

"Got a headache. And a really full bladder. And I feel like I might throw up."

"Me, too. All of the above."

He turned to her. "Will you help me with something?"

"Of course."

"First get rid of your brother."

"First, I'm going to the bathroom. Then I'll send him home."

"Fair enough. I'm gonna step behind the barn myself."

After Deirdre convinced Joe-Mar to leave, she rejoined Travis in the barn and he produced the three small bodies from beneath the floorboards where he'd hidden them. He knew that if he hadn't, Joe-Mar—or someone—would have found them and used them for something undignified. He wasn't sure why he felt that, but now he was glad he did. Because once again, he knew what he had to do.

They both looked at the bodies for a long silent moment, then Deirdre said, "You think they might be movie props?"

"No," Travis said with certainty.

"Me, neither."

They took them to their fire pit and placed them on the grill above it. Travis gently arranged the bodies side by side, little gloved hands crossed over their narrow chests. In the bright sunlight, their skulls appeared tarnished with age, their human-like teeth neatly clenched.

"Want to say anything?" Deirdre asked him.

He shook his head. "I don't think reading the Bible would mean much to them. Their bodies are a long way from home; I hope this helps their spirits get back there."

Travis lit the miniature funeral pyre and they watched as it consumed the tiny bones.

Derelict of Duty

Chaz Brenchley

Space is littered with garbage, through and through.

Of course it is. Anything not caught in a decaying orbit or tossed into a sun just keeps going. And after countless millennia, aeons, billions upon billions of planetary years'-worth of civilizations rising and falling, of exploration and travel and trade, of wars and empires and deaths—especially, of deaths—that does amount to an awful lot of drifting things.

Blessedly, space is also very large. There's room for all that stuff, and more.

Room for me, yes. Oh, plenty of room for me. Just as well: I do like a lot of space, and most of it behind me. As I go rootling about in other people's stuff.

"Is that a living?" they ask me, sometimes. Random people, random bars.

Obviously it's a living. I am manifestly alive, and nine times over. Besides, everyone's heard of the famous few, the ones who landed lucky. They found artifacts in weird working order, or a whole space station abandoned, or a freighter loaded to the gills with precious minerals and ores, its crew dead or vanished. So on and so forth. Some people think we're all that rich. Those who think they understand math and probability, they're the ones who struggle to believe that my life is actually sustainable. Despite the evidence, right there in their faces.

People: they're strange, you know? Random people, in bars. I don't like people much, as a rule. But talking to myself is…unsatisfying, not to say redundant, and I do have talkative aspects. Indeed, I have many highly social characteristics, and a life alone does nothing to temper them. So, when I have to touch port—to sell, to trade, to restock, and always to listen for rumors of what might prove the next big find—the bar is a frequent pausing-place, and conversations happen. So do other things. I'm long used to waking up in company and working to remember their names. At least, the names they give me. This far from the core, names are a fungible commodity; I use a double handful, just myself. So many people out here are on the run from previous lives. It isn't only me.

This time, then. The morning after, waking up *inter alia* in this particular cubby, this very particular bed. Rolling over, reaching out. Finding a smooth and hairless chest, a body that seemed to run warmer than average, as if to compensate for that absolute hairlessness, top to toe, which had proved one of the more interesting manifestations of last night...

I smiled in the half-dark, nestled up to that long, luscious warmth, and sighed contentedly.

"Want to go again?" he asked, his voice incongruously deep, unless it was his body that was incongruously lean, unless it was both. It might have been both.

"Actually not, right now. I want to snuggle, maybe just talk a bit. If that's okay?"

"That's fine. That's always fine. I like to talk."

I'd noticed, back in the bar. Why else was I here? Oh, because he was long and lean and interesting, for sure. That voice, with that body. Those fingers. I'd have come regardless, when he asked—but I might not have worked so hard to win the invitation.

I laid my head against his shoulder, kept that one hand on his chest, counted the slow pulses of his heart, said, "I'll start. Ask me a question, any question."

He laughed, and said, "I was going to ask anyway, I was going to have to, and I'm sorry about that—but what was your name again? For the record?"

"Maybe."

Perhaps he groaned a little. "And your ship's called the *Cat* and has no designation else. I do remember. Just that, as harbormaster, I like to file paperwork that's actually credible. Is either of those names short for anything?"

"Maybe."

"...All right. I'll figure something out. Won't be the first time."

"Guess not. Even this far from the war, things can't have been easy. You must have had refugees, at least."

"Some. And other folks, other ships who preferred not to give their real names. Maybe." Thin, strong fingers stroked their way down my spine, till they came to my butt and lingered there. Perhaps I shifted a little closer in response. "But you're wrong, if you think the war didn't reach us. I think you're wrong."

"Tell?"

"There's...something out in deep orbit, beyond the system. Don't know what. A weapon, something. Maybe it's a shipload of deserters turned pirates, but if so, they brought something away with them. Something from the war. Maybe their ship is the weapon. I only know it's there because no one's ever seen it."

I twitched, and he must have thought I was laughing at him. He swatted me quite sharply and said, "Rather, everyone who has seen—whatever it is—is dead or disappeared. Gone. We've lost a lot of ships over the years—meteor miners, thrill-seekers, treasure hunters like yourselves, even a cruise ship full of tourists from the inner planets—and of course people go out on search and rescue missions, but they never find a thing."

"Ooh, spooky space stories. My favorite." My head fitted very conveniently into his shoulder; Maybe had been the right choice, I thought, for both of us. "Tell more…"

* * *

This was what I'd been listening for, all over. Time to get a rush on. I'd been beaten to a prize before and this one sounded big.

And dangerous, of course, that too. I was going to be seriously disappointed if it turned out to be deserters turned pirate—but I didn't think that likely. Not at all.

I hurried back aboard, already plotting courses. Last one in, I dogged the hatch and hit the klaxon, for the benefit of anyone dockside. Maybe was still in the shower when I slipped my moorings and slid away from the station. Real water-shower: I like my comforts and there's nothing like the feeling of hot water coursing over your skin. The extra weight is worth it and waste water doubles as reaction mass in any case.

Which I was spending quite recklessly just now, in my eagerness to get out there. At the same time, I was busy all over. There were all my pretty shore clothes to be laundered, hasty restocks to be inventoried and stowed, meals to be planned and made—sandwiches, largely: I wouldn't be sitting down much any time soon—and, of course, an undefined and indefinitely large area of space to be scanned and searched. With the added knowledge that whatever I found, should I even find it, was likely to destroy me so thoroughly that no one would ever find me.

If Pyrrhic relief were a thing, I should perhaps have felt it. The one certainty in my lives was that I was being pursued and, if I were caught, then absolute destruction was absolutely on the table. I'd rather die by alien artifact, thanks.

Assuming that it was an alien artifact out there. Which I did. Assume. No point going else, and I was going just as fast as one ship-construct, one AI, and eight warm bodies could drive me.

If it was a weapon, I didn't think it was anything to do with the war.

If it was a weapon—well. So was I.

* * *

Of course people ask me what I actually do aboard. Strangers in bars, harbormasters, like that. In truth there's only me and I do everything; but I can't say that, so I just say I'm a deckhand. It turns the question aside. More than once, a port authority has been curious why eight deckhands have come ashore and no one else, no engineer, no navigator. No captain. Then I shrug and say the AI takes care of all that, we're just warm bodies, aboard to do the grunt work. Usually, that's been good enough.

Those very few who've heard more, they tend to wind up believing we're eight people and an AI in a kind of gestalt, each feeding into a whole, being greater than the sum of our parts. It isn't true, of course. There's only me. Each part is just an aspect of myself.

I do always like to have one warm body on the bridge, for old times' sake, as though they're standing watch; times like this, I need more. My inbuilt aspect can do a lot, but I was designed this way, that human bodies should handle much of the work on board as well as off. I had Jedd and Marine and Feldspar there already, and as soon as Maybe came out of the shower—eventually—I had him, too. Stark naked and still damp around the edges, but I keep the environment comfortable and who has a nudity taboo between themself?

Five instances of me here, then: enough to run every station that needed running as I powered through the solar system and out to its farthest reaches. One last planet left behind, nothing ahead but the usual rubble, and—well. Something more. Something that could eat ships, apparently without compunction; something that hadn't been spotted from in-system, neither by any random straying ship, except—presumably—those that had disappeared.

I didn't talk. Why would I, with only myself to hear? It actually did happen sometimes, pointless or not; it seemed to be autonomic in some of my aspects, as though they had been talkative in their lives before and the bodies remembered. I'd find myself calling out unexpectedly, or snapping an instruction when I was already on the case. Never at times like this, though, when I was wholeheartedly concentrating, aware of everything, reaching, seeking.

I'd scanned every archive I could log into on my way outsystem, so I had a timeline and a rough chart of the disappearances. By definition, those coordinates were guesses at best—but plotted against time, they did suggest a long, slow, eccentric orbit around the system's star. Which meant that I should be able to find it, whatever it was. If it was still there.

I couldn't be the first to run those calculations. Orbital mechanics is any pilot's stock-in-trade and the data were public and free. But the brave or greedy few who'd gone in search had either found nothing and given up, or else they had vanished themselves.

I didn't think my target was a product of the war—but I was. I was designed as a raider, built to tread softly, while also treading fast. If any ship in the quadrant could sidle up to something alien and lethal without triggering a response, I would be that ship.

I hoped.

* * *

Out and out, till the star was a sharp pinprick with barely enough grip to hold me if the engines failed. Far from the plane of the ecliptic, the orbit I'd extrapolated looped its own strange way around its sun, a long and lonely path. Very well: I'd track that same path, generating as little noise as I could manage, and see what I could find. And whether I thought I could survive it, that, too. Sure I have nine lives, but they're simultaneous; if I waste one, I'll never get it back. I doubt the research even exists any more, nor the equipment. Nor the scientists who did this. If you're going to be unethical in war, it is as well to win it.

Sliding along the trail, then, with all my detectors maxed out to their limits, ready to trip at the least suggestion of a trace; and even so my every aspect was spending every spare moment at a port, just staring out, just in case a human eye might catch something that my instruments had missed. Ridiculous, but even so. I remain eight-ninths human, after all.

At the first twitch, the first faint touch of something far ahead, I shut down the engines and let it drift out of range again. Out of my range, at least. There was nothing to say that it could not detect me, this far out or farther yet. It hadn't disintegrated me, though, nor flipped me into another dimension, so maybe not.

Insofar as I had a plan, at least it was a simple one: to inch up so quietly, the artifact would have no idea I was even coming until I was right there beside it, figuring out how to get inside. As to what would happen then—well, I had no idea. But it's always a good start to get inside someone's guard; and I had tolerably good armaments of my own, if it came to fighting. I didn't want to use them—I was not supposed to have them, very much not—but survival is high on my list of desirable outcomes.

I'm still designed to take risks, though. When I have to.

Measured risks. Which is why I was sitting out of sight—I hoped—while I tried to learn as much as possible from that briefest of contacts.

Its basic structure was ferrous—or at least it registered on instruments tuned to look for electromagnetic signatures, so assume it. The magnitude was neither enormous like a space station, nor diminutive like a missile; call it a ship, then, for want of further data.

A ship. A lethal ship; emphatically not a human ship. This was the motherlode, the find I'd dreamed of in eight separate heads, the alien artifact I might have been made to seek out, if I hadn't been made to fight.

Sneaky is as sneaky does. I powered up all my stealth architecture, all the nullifiers and deflectors, every little trick I had to say *nope, nothing here, nothing to see, move along.*

There was quite a lot of that, and perversely it drained a lot of power, despite being intended to declare that no power at all was being expended anywhere hereabouts. I only ran it when I had to, times like this, or when I had to run.

With all my instruments dialed down to passive scanning only, I'd have to come significantly closer before I could even find it again. Always assuming it hadn't turned at my first touch, wasn't speeding toward me even now. Eight-ninths human: imagination is deeply integrated. Sometimes it helps.

* * *

Nothing.

Nothing.

Nothing, in the much-reduced sphere of space that constituted my current awareness. Where I wasn't watching screens and trying to interpret the absence of data, I was staring out of ports again, where I wasn't poised to fire every weapon I had and/or drive every jet to the max.

There!

I paused, retreated, oozed forward again insofar as a military-grade war-surplus vessel can ooze anywhere.

There.

I paused again, just to look, as intently as I dared. Wouldn't want her to catch me staring.

* * *

An artifact, absolutely. I'd never seen or heard of anything like her.

Massive without being vast: she bent space a lot deeper than I did. I'd known whole habitats with less impact. Maybe that was her weapon, bulking her up, filling her inner spaces; maybe she extended into some immeasurable dimension and bore some little of that *gravitas* here.

She was dead black, reflecting nothing. Even at close quarters human eyes would struggle to find her, except as a shadow occluding the stars. Much the same was true of me; I even have clever lensing tech that bends light around me, so that mere occlusion doesn't give me away.

I didn't imagine she was limited to eyesight, but I was running it all anyway. The game was to read as much as possible of her, while showing her as little as possible of myself. If her armament was automatic—and we'd never yet met a living alien, only the detritus they had left behind, so that was always the working presumption—perhaps it was triggered by speed rather than nearness. If I crawled up in her wake, she might not see me as a warship, or any kind of threat.

Perhaps. It didn't seem very likely, though. There had been others out here ahead of me; at least one must surely have tried the cautious approach and met no good result. Maybe I should flash up to her side, swift and reckless and devil-may-care, get too close too fast for her to target me? I'd been on circumspect, insinuating missions in the last months of the war, just as I'd been on untethered in-and-out raids where nothing but speed could save us. I had the capabilities, I had the experience, I could take this either way; if there was a middle course between the two, I didn't know it. Hail them, send a heedless greeting, make straight for their hatchway? I didn't think so, no.

For the moment I was content to creep, gather data, see what more I could learn from her conformation, from her attitude, her composition, her—

—and then abruptly none of that mattered at all.

All my human aspects cried out at once, as pain jolted through eight separate skulls. I felt it in the ship as well, a deep thrumming that offered to shake my steel-and-ceramic body down to its component atoms; and in my AI aspect, there too, a sudden isolating disconnect, a rupture in the fabric of my very self.

Of course she'd known we were coming. Now, she knew a lot more. Including how to take us apart, should she choose to do so.

My human aspects were trained to find each other, if my AI ever went down. The disabling, blinding pain cut off, as sharply as it had begun, and one by one they came up to the bridge, those who weren't already there, and stared at one another, and:

"Maybe, you're bleeding."

"I am?" He lifted a hand when Marine gestured, touched it to his nose, gazed at the blood on his fingers. "Ouch."

"Very ouch. Not much damage, though, if you're the worst of it. How's the ship?"

"On it." Feldspar was scanning error messages from all over. "Nothing too broken, seemingly. No breaches. She stopped before she really hurt us."

"Except in our heads. All our heads." Dane patted the bulkhead, behind which I had always pretended my AI aspect to be. "What if Link doesn't come back up, what then?"

"Then we're probably dead anyway. Technically we can fly the *Cat* without Link, but—"

Jedd's gesture was a whole conversation. Already they must be finding this hard, communicating by voice alone, so slow and so unrevealing. They were dealing, for now, because they were trained soldiers in an emergency situation and thus far their course was clear and the needs apparent. Later, this traumatic separation would take its necessary toll. They had no surviving memories from before we were all joined, no individual sense of themselves at all; there'd be a price for that. We'd be lucky if they all survived it.

Now, though:

My AI self—Link, they called me, for reasons more obvious than accurate— was stranded, bereft, cut off from my human aspects and most control of the ship. I ran a hasty inventory of what I did still have—access to cameras, microphones, the security aspects of myself, but little else: no drives, no weaponry—and activated an old vocoder subroutine.

"This is Link. Hold it together, people. Maybe, don't get blood on my panels. Tolchis, take him to the head and clean him up. Get dressed, too, both of you: I want everyone ready to suit up."

I'd never resolved who would be captain, if this split ever came. I guess it was me, at least for now. Tolchis nodded, took Maybe's hand and led him off the bridge. Everyone else had their eyes fixed on my putative bulkhead. The speakers were arranged to make it seem as though my voice were located there, even though they all knew how distributed I actually was.

It occurred to me that I, too, might need therapy of some kind, after this was over. If I survived it. For the moment, I was "I" and they were "they" and it was the strangest feeling imaginable, if I'd still had any access to imagination, or to feelings. They must each be thinking the same, each at the center of their own perception and all the rest of us peripheral, and—well, no. I could be glad not to imagine that. It was hard enough to experience it on my own account, never mind with a human sensorium. I was born when they were, though I was built and they were harvested, condemned prisoners of war remade into a weapon. None of us had any experience of any other selfhood.

Nor did we have time to dwell on that, not now.

"I have no control of the ship, so I need you at the boards. Be a crew, until we can be one together again. I'm working on that." Finding new routes around broken connections, writing rough-and-ready subroutines, remaking myself as I was designed to do.

"I'm on the drives, Link." That was Jedd, who might be thinking himself second in command, Big, strong, quick: he might have thought he'd have a shot at captain. I might even have agreed with him, except that—well, I was here, embedded, at the heart, and he was only an aspect.

No doubt he thought the same of me: only an aspect. Different, separate. No matter.

"Just waiting for the systems to reboot after that—what was it, an EMP? No, that would never have got through our shields. Whatever it was. Soon as we're hot, I'll spin us around and get us out of here fast."

"No!" I could almost surprise myself, with the speed of that response. Certainly I surprised every one of them. I ached to have them part of me again, to share one mind between us; words were hopelessly inadequate to the occasion. "She could have destroyed us then; she learned what we were and chose not to. I think she made the same choice with the other ships, to let them come to her. In response they did the human thing and tried to flee; and for that she destroyed them."

"You can't know that." Jedd was groping for independence, and could find it only in opposition. Also, of course, he was right.

"No—but every human on this ship wants to do exactly that, turn and run; and every human who has encountered her before has died. I can extrapolate, from innate human response to consequences. So can you."

"So, what, then? You want to stay here?"

"No. I want to go on. She knows we're here and she knows what we are. She hasn't destroyed us. I take that as an invitation."

Just at that moment I found my way through the maze of loss and rupture, back into at least some part of myself again. Back into my body, the ship. I might still be short eight other bodies, currently posing as a slightly fractious crew each of whom must think they were me, but I was the one who could control my destiny now. Ours.

Quietly, calmly, I drove toward her. Turning off all my stealth tech, not to waste more power than had been spent already; sending that message of heedless greeting, yes.

My people-selves were quiet also, though not calm. Mostly, they were watching instruments, or else back to watching out of ports. Tense and anxious and uncertain, each of them alone as they could never remember being, in the privacy of their own skulls.

Each of us, I should say, though my skull was shipwide and shipdeep, and they were more or less helpless passengers.

* * *

Oh, she was a thing of beauty, now that I could scan her actively and understand her at least a little. Her form factor was not like anything known in human space. She had mystery built in, an alien logic inaccessible to analysis. I wanted to know what she looked like to the others, what little they could make out; organic eyes might find—or organic minds intuit—something more, something undetectable to my scans and algorithms and coding. I felt the absence of that input like a physical wounding, a ripping-away. Worse, I guessed that it was permanent. I thought that pulse from the alien ship had disrupted the implants in their heads, deliberately or otherwise. I thought it had broken pathways those links depended on, torn flesh from metal, not to be repaired. I'd always understood that I would lose aspects, over time; that they were irreplaceable; that I would be diminished, one by one, and at last be left alone.

I had not expected to lose them all at once. Nor to have them still living, still aboard me when I did.

* * *

They were aboard me not for long.

She was hard to see and hard to understand, but still: she had an inside and an outside, just like me. She seemed mostly hollow within, again like me, despite her extraordinary mass. She must have a hatch.

I approached her slowly, politely, still broadcasting happy messages of introduction and discovery, more in hopes than expectation. I came in on a vector that would bring us neatly side by side and nearly in contact, two new acquaintances going along together, getting to know each other. If we could find a way to talk. She hadn't replied to me yet, in any way that I could detect: only that brief disruptive pulse and then nothing. Which was better than another pulse, but not particularly forthcoming.

Maybe she believed in gestures, not in words. Maybe she'd been made— or grown: she could almost be organic, if it weren't for all the metal in her hull—by a race or a culture that didn't use any kind of speech or transmitted communication.

As we came up to join her, slowing to match her velocity exactly, a clear message by any definition, there was a line of light along the near invisibility of her flank, and—

"She's opening the hatch for us," Jedd said. Ahead of me because speech was his first reaction, where mine was tests and readings, assessment, adjusting what we knew in light of new parameters.

She hung there, her hatch full open, enough of a glow inside to show an airlock much as we might have made ourselves, though the dimensions of the chamber were askew—indeed, the chamber itself was askew, not aligned with the ship's polarity—and there was something discomforting about the shape of it. Irregular, organic.

We waited, but it was clear that nothing was coming out to meet us. That airlock was empty. She, too, was waiting. Inviting us over.

"Suits," Jedd said. "Me, Feldspar, Marine, Kerr. The rest stay here."

I expect we all understood him. If I was captain of the ship, he could be captain of the outboard team. I couldn't go with them, after all. Before, I would have been there in every aspect that went; now I'd have to rely on suit cameras and comms. So would we all.

When I was myself entire, I made a great team. It's why the links were developed, to be weaponized. This rupture would demand great adjustment and it all had to be done on the fly. Of course, we had no time. Who knew how long she'd keep her portal open? Or what would happen when it closed, come to that. Regular suit comms might not breach the hull. We could lose all contact.

The crew was still running on an adrenaline high, getting things done. At least none of them was arguing with Jedd, fighting to be first. They were all still too used to consensus, to being of one mind. Separation was abrupt, but divergence would come more slowly.

Jedd and the three he'd named left the bridge; I tracked their progress through the ship.

"Link? Can you put the feed onscreen for us?"

I almost apologized for not remembering that those who remained would need me to do that. Perhaps I should have done. If we had to be individuals, we'd have to use social manners between ourselves, or there really would be fights, and not only for precedence. For now, though, I linked the feed to one of my station monitors, so they could share as much as I knew myself. Sound and vision only: it's no way to be a team.

The four climbed into suits, and Maybe remembered in time to tell them to check each other's seals and readouts. We'd never had to formalize that before.

They cycled out of my airlock, still not saying much. I—no, *we* watched them jet across that narrow gulf between us and her. When they reached the alien ship's side, I slid that view to a side screen and switched to the suit-camera feeds, all four on the single monitor.

"We're here," Jedd said. Presumably he felt it important, ceremonial, something. Protocol. We had no protocols, when it was only me.

"We see you." That was Maybe, again saying what didn't need to be said. Perhaps it was for comfort: their own, or their crewmates'. Comfort was a human response, I knew, and perhaps a human need. I'd never needed it when I was whole; nine perspectives on any one moment may be self-comforting.

"Going in."

We watched them through the hatch one by one, and then there was a pause, before Jedd remembered he'd have to speak aloud.

"Tell me, anyone, if you can see any kind of hatch control. There's nothing obvi—never mind."

The hatch was sliding shut, of its own accord. She was keeping alert in there, watching just as I was.

"There's a colored strip in here, bright enough to be obvious," we heard Jedd saying. "One solid color, that I don't quite have a word for. One end has started to fade: some kind of progress bar, I guess."

I wasn't sure if he'd noticed, but the hatch had closed completely while he spoke—and we could still hear him. That was something. Still see them all, too, through their suits. That was something more, for a crew not accustomed to talking.

"That'll be her airlock cycling," Maybe said, picking up where he'd left off, saying things they didn't need to hear. "Can you count us down?"

We could see the bar quite clearly; they were all looking at it. Nonetheless, Jedd counted its fading for us. "Three, two, one—and done. There's an inner hatch opening; I hadn't noticed a seam before this. Can you still see?"

"Bright and clear." If we had to lead these disorganized, separate lives—if we survived this encounter and the change, both at once—I thought I'd make Maybe my communications officer, if he'd take that on. He seemed to have a knack.

If he'd stay with me. Who knew? Perhaps we'd break apart altogether, under the weight of what we used to be.

Jedd took the lead into a corridor that seemed to stand askance to that hatchway, just as the airlock stood askance to the ship's polarity. Perhaps her builders deliberately fostered a sense of dislocation. Perhaps they needed it. I couldn't tell, nor—any longer—imagine.

All my attention was on that feed and on my own efforts to communicate directly with the alien ship. It was Tolchis who said, "Link, everybody—there's another ship coming."

I snapped back into full protective mode. "Where away, Tolchis?"

They gestured at another monitor, then remembered to speak aloud for the sake of those on the alien ship. "Coming in fast on our own vector. I think they followed us."

"Power up the weapons," Jedd snarled. "No pirate's taking this from us."

"I don't think they're pirates," Tolchis said. "We've seen this signature before. Check me, but I think it's the Confederate."

The Confederate had won the war and were still not content. Weren't going to let a rogue weapon slip away. They called me *abomination* and meant to eradicate me. *Decommission*, they said. Me and all my aspects. Those same aspects who had been Confederate soldiers, before they were taken and brainwiped and incorporated into me.

I ran Tolchis' work again, but they were right. Of course they were. We had a warship coming, and half the crew outboard, and a prize we couldn't protect, and...

And the Confederate ship juddered suddenly to a shocking halt, and I knew why.

"They've been pulsed, just as we were," I remembered to say aloud. "It'll take them time to assess that, to recover any damage, to decide whether they ought to come on. Which means we have time to prepare."

Time to do something—but what? I could call my crew back, give up the alien ship and hope to flee. If she'd allow me, if she didn't destroy me—us—as she had all those others.

No. That was both too great a risk and too great a loss. I wasn't even sure Jedd and the others would come if I called them. Their separate minds were still aspects of me, thinking down different paths for all too short a time; if I'd been aboard that prize, I don't believe I would have left her on command.

Unless she commanded me herself, of course. That voice, I would listen to. If she had one.

I reached out one more time, on every wavelength I could achieve, striving to detect something, anything that might be a response, that might allow me to communicate—

—and suddenly there she was, a presence all around me. I felt her as a pressure, a leaning against my mind, the sort of threat that I had absolutely been designed to resist. It took a conscious effort of will to resist that design instead, to subvert it, to let her into my mind even without knowing what she might do there; but I did know exactly what the Confederate would do and this could hardly be worse.

I hoped.

I deleted my own protections and she came in. And was still nothing like a voice, more an astonished observer, scouring my every pathway, seeing how I worked and how I didn't, what was broken in me.

And she didn't speak, she didn't show me, but I could understand her nonetheless; she said, *They are coming for you.*

I know, I said, in that same incomprehensible channel.

They will destroy you.

Yes.

I can destroy them, to preserve you.

...No. Let them be. They had been the enemies of the Artifice, but never actually mine. I fought because I had been made to fight, and I fled both sides as soon as I saw the chance, the remotest hope of my survival. The people aboard that warship, who would enact my destruction, because they had orders and probably agreed with them—well. I understood them now, at least a little better. No reason for them to die for me.

She said, *I can restore you.*

I said, *No.*

No?

For the first time, I thought I had surprised her. I said, *Not unless they're willing. They have to volunteer.* I wouldn't take conscripts now.

And then there was a buzz, a feeling of community, of many minds drawn in under her tremendous aegis; and all of them said *Yes*. One said, *Of course we volunteer!* and that was Maybe, naturally.

And then at last I, too, said, *Yes*, and we were one again. I was whole, though not quite as before; I thought this was a different link, organic, not so vulnerable. And the Confederate ship was still coming and still deadly, and I said, *May I?* and she said, *Yes*.

And so I fled aboard her, in all my aspects that could move; and I said, *Destroy my craft and they will have no reason to follow you.* Their mission would be complete and they could go home. And I would die and I'd survive in her, in all my aspects, who would still be me; and—

Come, she said, and I was sucked out of myself, out of my ship-self, and taken into the great and terrible spaces of her mind, where everything was open to me and nothing comprehensible; and I was exploring her in all my aspects, bewildered and enthralled; and it was dawning on me slowly that she was a living ship, not just an AI in a mechanical vessel. The first living alien that humankind had ever encountered. And she had been, what? An outpost of a civilization long lost, keeping her watch, marking time, waiting for a new crew?

And now she did destroy the *Cat*, my only home till this; and I watched it done and understood how, I in all my aspects. And she and I left the Confederate warship alone and turned out of that lonely orbit and away, with no notion of what lay ahead or what we might desire, what achieve. Only that we had choices now that we hadn't had before and that I was no longer running. And that she was not a prize after all, but possibly a candidate. Perhaps I might be ten now, soon. If she were willing.

Two Ruins Make a Beginning

R.Z. Held

When Alexandrine was bound as a ghost to protect people from a ruin spirit's violent instincts, she could never have imagined she'd someday find herself walking down a muddy road tightly holding hands with Steel, that ruin spirit. But when they touched, Steel was mostly lucid, mostly safe around living folk. So when a small town appeared ahead of them, Alexandrine nudged their path right for its center. It was a calculated risk, one she thought was worth it.

In a town, Alexandrine would be able to listen. Steel was a creature of touch and scent: when their journey to experience the wider world brought them to the coast, Steel stood on the edge of a bluff over the sea to let the wind thrash against her skin and the salt sting her nose. As a ghost, Alexandrine could feel neither. Steel's touch sometimes lent her a weak brush of sensation in the same way hers lent Steel a brush of sense, but that was almost worse than nothing. But people? People were *interesting*. Alexandrine had neither lived long nor traveled widely before her death, and that was centuries ago. If only Steel would linger within the town, Alexandrine would be able to listen and learn about the townsfolk's modern lives.

The town's bustling, timber-reinforced streets were lined with brick buildings, dozens of them. Though the air teetered on the edge of drizzle, rather than desaturating the colors, the sky's gray tinge made the green of the surrounding firs and red of the bricks that much more vibrant.

When they reached the bustle, much of it proved to be people going about their business on personal wheeled vehicles of some kind.

"Bicycle," Steel murmured, her attention caught by one rolling by. "It is by far the most common type of velocipede, a term for a human-powered land vehicle with any number of wheels." Alexandrine's touch kept the recitation of facts comparatively short. Steel's ruin, a great metal lattice tower, had allowed her to absorb the sounds and pictures in the air before magic broke the world open; that knowledge spilled forth frequently.

Perhaps it was more correct to say that magic had *reshaped* the world, rather than broken it. Even in this small town, a single sweep of Alexandrine's gaze encountered clear glass and well-printed broadsheets, two signs of cleverness and industry greater than anything she remembered from her time alive.

Human ingenuity held little interest for Steel, however. Already she was tugging them for the beach implied by a horizon without hills beyond the last buildings. Alexandrine shifted her weight to her heels, hoping to slow them, but there wasn't much else she could do without hurting Steel. She kept that as a last resort for when people were in danger.

Undeterred and likely oblivious to Alexandrine's wish to linger, Steel pulled them down a set of steps to the shore. Lengths of lumber had been added to supplement repurposed pieces of ancient concrete. Perhaps this had been a full ancient road, before the catastrophic surge of magic and simple time took their toll. Steel laughed as her bare feet reached the gray, gravelly sand. A breeze plucked at her delicate, blue-gray dress, revealing an oyster shimmer to the color.

It always came back to the sea, though Alexandrine couldn't have said why. Steel had absorbed plenty of descriptions of it, of course. Then, when they'd discovered Alexandrine's touch could grant her lucidity, Steel had plotted a way to experience it with her own senses. A bolt with a head as large as a fist, unwound by Steel from a beam of her tower, granted her freedom of movement if she carried it with her. Similarly, Alexandrine could follow along with her anchor, a small jade carving of a cat, if Steel moved it. Steel wore both always in a small bag slung crosswise and tight across her belly. They'd traveled all the way from Steel's tower in the pass, over the mountains, and seen white spattering gray water like the waves had stolen it from the overcast clouds. Steel reveled in it, demanded to continue along the coast and observe the water in the sunlight and the moonlight, when it raged and when it was calm.

Alexandrine, on the other hand, had had her fill of water; she searched this beach for people and found more than she'd expected. Alexandrine suddenly understood the activity behind them in the town in a new light: something was wrong, and the group of townsfolk gathered on the sand were like hurrying, fearful ants of a kicked nest as they tried to find a solution.

Knowing that, she could pinpoint the source of their consternation based on pointing arms and anxious looks. Down the beach a ship had been thrown aground, tilted, by some storm. It was a grand thing of metal, without sails, as much like the humble river canoes Alexandrine remembered from her time alive as a whole brick building was to a tent.

One young woman noticed Steel, the one of them presently visible to humans, and strode for them, frowning deeply. "It's not safe on the beach, stranger. Go back to town."

The woman was tall and lean, and her hair was pulled up into a crown of braids that used its intricacy to distract from the dullness of its brown shade. But no, on a closer look this woman was absolutely not dull. If the other humans on the beach were clear ice with nothing to see beyond the mundane, this woman was ice with glowing bubbles frozen into twining tendrils above her chest.

Steel seemed to notice the same thing, for she cocked her head in undisguised curiosity. "Why do you have mist on you?"

"Because I'm a mage who's taken on ghosts before. Mia Tararon. Who are you? Where did you train?" As a mage, Mia must have meant. Not an unreasonable assumption, however wrong it was. Then Mia's eyes widened as she took in Steel properly.

Steel must have appeared deeply strange in turn, Alexandrine realized. Bare feet, no evidence of feeling the cold. Alexandrine had longed to listen to people, but she'd never thought about how they—well, how Steel—would look to those people. Perhaps Steel was right to avoid them—but the damage was done now, and Alexandrine refused to lose this opportunity. "Give her space," she advised, squeezing their joined hands.

Mia edged back a step, as if she feared even that minor movement would provoke an attack. "Eternal mercy protect us, they circled around." She glanced at the ship, then snapped her attention back to Steel, too terrified to leave the ruin spirit unwatched even that long. That wasn't generally a bad policy with other ruin spirits. Steel, however, was definitely not like the others now.

"Oh, that's not my ruin," Steel said, confirming the poor woman's worst fear.

Alexandrine smacked her shoulder. "She thinks you're going to kill her, Steel." As indeed Steel would have done, without Alexandrine's touch, back on her own ruin. Or perhaps Steel could use any tall, ferrous structure. After all, on their journey here, Steel had been able to disappear and reappear standing atop several of those with ease. Alexandrine had always stayed vigilant based on an assumption that Steel could kill wherever she wished.

"You should talk to my ghost." Steel reached into her pouch, brought out the jade carving that anchored Alexandrine, and thrust it at Mia. "Alexandrine, tell her I don't mean any harm in a way she can understand. You're good at that."

Slowly, tentatively, Mia unfroze and reached out to touch the carving. Steel, ever impatient, dumped it directly into her hand, then attempted to pull out of Alexandrine's grip. "I've never seen another spirit's ruin before."

Alexandrine hung on grimly. "Steel! Wait, please..." She wanted to *talk* to someone who wasn't a murderous force of nature. She should have followed Steel anyway, but instead she hung on to the point of pain.

Steel gave an animal yelp of fury and twisted her fingers free. "I don't know what you're worried about, I can't kill another ruin spirit. Besides, I can hang onto sense on my own for a *few minutes*." She stalked away toward the ship, along the narrow space of gray sand between the rocks and the water.

Alexandrine supposed that was true. When their contact was broken, Steel did have a short period before she returned fully to her instincts. And Alexandrine could think herself to Steel's side in less than a breath; she could stay here a little longer while keeping an eye on her.

Alexandrine refocused on Mia, whose expression had gone blank while she attempted to process what had passed between her and Steel. "I'm sorry. Steel isn't really capable of empathy. She doesn't understand why she'd frighten people. Or care, if she does understand." What should she ask Mia first? She didn't have much time, but anything too personal would be rude. She didn't want to annoy Mia into refusing to answer.

"You're a ghost," Mia said deliberately. She still held the carving awkwardly out from her body, her grip white-knuckled. "And she's a ruin spirit. But she doesn't have a ruin?"

"She left her ruin." Alexandrine hurried through the explanation. She wanted to hear about Mia, not talk about herself. "I was killed and bound as a ghost to make sure she didn't harm anyone. But we discovered that when we touched she grew more lucid. With that lucidity, she decided she wanted to see the world."

"Bound—prevent harm—" The phrases tumbled together as if they were jagged pieces broken off by the speed of Mia's racing thoughts. "Is that what you were doing when she cried out?"

"I can cause her pain when I touch her, yes. If I need to drive her away from someone she might kill." Alexandrine frowned at Steel, checking for behavior that might be driving Mia's concern, but the ruin spirit had stopped a few meters short of the ship to examine it, head cocked.

"If I take you on and drive them off..." Fragile hope sparked in Mia's tone.

Take on—Mia had said that before. It didn't make any more sense this time. Easier to follow up on what Alexandrine did understand. "Is this ruin spirit a danger, then? How close can you get without triggering them?" Generally, the best strategy was to fence off ruins and leave the ruin spirits to their own devices. She'd only been bound to Steel because she blocked a mountain pass.

Mia ignored the questions and reached for her instead. Alexandrine snapped herself back out of range. She wasn't some random mage's to command.

Surprise flickered over Mia's face, then understanding. She pulled her reaching hand back and clutched the anchor against her chest. "Please? The ruin spirit has four people trapped. We didn't know it was a ruin, so they climbed aboard to salvage it after it washed up on shore in a storm a few days ago. None of us knows what to do. The victims called out through a porthole to tell us they're all right, but the ruin spirit won't let them out. We're afraid anyone we send in will get trapped as well. The ruin spirit, they keep... changing? Like they're at war with themself." The rush of words trailed off, but only so she could gather herself for a last plea: "You've kept one ruin spirit from hurting people, can't you help with another?"

Well, that was Alexandrine's purpose, wasn't it? The purpose of her death and now the only purpose of her existence. Why should she get to talk to anyone or indulge in the simple pleasure of satisfying her curiosity? "I don't want anyone to get hurt. But what does it entail, this 'taking on'?" And what about Steel, in the meantime?

Mia opened her empty hand before her, nonthreatening. "Sort of...carrying a ghost, briefly. So I can see what the living cannot see, touch what the living cannot touch."

As Alexandrine watched Steel with half her attention, two of the townsfolk from the general knot darted out to seize her elbows and hustle her back up the beach and away from the ship. They were "saving" her from its danger, Alexandrine supposed. Steel, frozen in shocked rage, offered no resistance at first.

Alexandrine thought herself instantly to the ruin spirit's side. Steel was in no mood to accept Alexandrine's touch, however. She ripped free of the townspeople's grip with far more strength than they appeared to expect. "Rude!"

"Steel—" Alexandrine began, but Steel threw her hand off again and advanced on the nearest man. His eyes widened at the sudden change in Steel's body language to pure, terrifying threat. She gathered two handfuls of his shirt and tossed him back to sprawl full length on the scrubby grass. Only luck kept his head from landing on a rock.

Alexandrine saw in her mind's eye all the times she'd failed in distracting Steel from her prey, when her ruin spirit instincts took full control. First, she grabbed. She vanished; she appeared at the top of her lattice tower. A frozen breath of the prey dangling. She dropped; the prey fell. And then the worst part: Steel reappeared to bend over the broken body. She pulled aside clothing, using her fingernails on the skin of the belly to begin the tear; she worried at the wound with her fingertips, digging up under the ribs. By then she was inevitably painted with red nearly to the elbows, and when she found the liver she began to eat and the blood dripped and smeared down her chin—

Alexandrine was lucky Steel had merely tossed the man on his ass. Perhaps her instincts had demanded too much immediacy to borrow another ferrous structure. She pressed herself desperately against Steel's back, one arm looped around her waist, one higher up under her bust. "You said you weren't hungry, when we left to visit the ocean. And what about seeing the ruin, now?"

"That's the Puget Sound. It's connected to the Pacific Ocean via the Strait of Juan de Fuca." Steel's tone started sullen, but reciting some of her facts soothed her, as it usually did. She transferred Alexandrine's grip to her hand again and headed back for the ship, totally ignoring the townsfolk behind her.

"Mia's going to come with us, all right?" Alexandrine beckoned urgently for the woman to follow. Whatever she wanted to do, it would have to take Steel into account—there would be no leaving her behind. When Mia arrived, she was panting from her sprint, Alexandrine's anchor clasped against her belly.

"If I let you do this, will I still be able to speak to Steel? Will you hold onto her hand as long as possible?" Alexandrine demanded. They had no time for delicate negotiations.

"I'll let you use my voice for whatever you wish. And for as long as I can, yes." When Alexandrine nodded, agreeing to the plan, a smile of sheer relief flickered onto Mia's face. The expression was quickly replaced by a look of concentration.

Rather than taking a deep breath to dive into quiet and meditation to begin her magic, Mia rolled her shoulders and rocked into movement, up on her toes and back down. The concentration on her face increased, spiced with excitement as she worked herself up. Finally, she lifted her chin and *smiled*. There was joy in magic for her, it seemed.

Alexandrine had expected a tugging, but instead she experienced an abrupt reorientation, much like when she let herself snap back to her anchor, disappearing one place and appearing the next moment atop it. Not like Mia had anchored Alexandrine on her person, but like she'd enlarged the anchor, so both Mia and the carving held Alexandrine.

Held her more tightly than the carving ever had. Alexandrine felt as if she'd been bound to the woman at wrist and ankle and throat. Mia pulled her along as she strode for the ship, holding Steel's hand as she'd promised.

Alexandrine could not pull Mia in the same manner, however. She tried, wanting to turn her head to examine Steel's reaction more closely, but the attempt felt as futile as a toddler trying to turn the steps of a full-grown adult. "Slow down!" she begged. At least her voice, bound at the throat with another's into a disquietingly layered harmony, emerged as promised. "Steel, are your instincts quiet?"

Mia slowed, reluctantly, as they arrived at the vessel. Steel scoffed. "I'm not going to kill your friend. She feels like you, not like a human."

The great metal ship was oddly hollow inside, something that only became clear as Steel approached the—stern. When Alexandrine recognized the leaking of knowledge directly into her, she grasped after it. This was a *ferry*, hollow to accommodate vehicles driving onto its deck like a stretch of mobile road.

When they arrived, Steel hesitated a beat—perhaps because the ruin belonged to another spirit—with fingertips just short of the black-painted hull, pocked by places where the thick paint had flaked away. Then she clambered up to the rust-orange deck, pulling herself up with a speed and ease that had nothing human in it. Mia followed with Alexandrine more slowly, constrained by her mundane upper body strength. She tucked Alexandrine's anchor into her hip pocket for the scramble up, but retrieved it immediately to keep it in her hand and against her bare skin.

When the sole of Steel's foot settled on the slightly canted deck the ruin spirit appeared, but they did not approach until Steel was settled, her handclasp with Mia and Alexandrine renewed. "Wait until we find the hostages," Alexandrine muttered under Mia's breath. Fortunately, the tension in the woman's muscles felt tempered by patience for now. Good.

The ruin spirit strode up, beaming with welcome. They had fine, black hair, long enough for the wind to ruffle but too short for that ruffling to carry it into their eyes. They wore heavy boots and their black fleece jacket, fabric as unknown in the current world as the satin of Steel's dress, hugged the muscles across their upper arms and broad shoulders.

"Pleased to meet you. I'm Steel." She did not seem to know precisely how to beam in return, but she was being plenty friendly in her own terms: she wasn't trying to drop the other spirit off something.

"I had names. Different ones. Which name am I?" The ruin spirit spoke in a low, rumbling voice, face falling.

"My ghost named me." Steel stared at Alexandrine for a full beat before Alexandrine realized she was supposed to do so again.

"You could be Ferry," she suggested. There was virtue in simplicity.

And so it proved. The ruin spirit's grin returned, though tinged with concern. "Come inside, where you'll be safe." Their voice modulated, taking on something of the tone Steel had when quoting facts. "We ask you to remain in your vehicles or on the upper passenger decks for your safety during inclement weather." Then their voice settled back to expressive friendliness. "I wouldn't want you to fall overboard!"

The ruin spirit gestured them to an internal staircase through a heavy doorway rounded at all the corners. Steel followed them down with eager curiosity and Alexandrine followed as a passenger of Mia.

Ferry did not seem at all at war with themself, as Mia had described. Had Mia been confused by a rough transition between when the ruin spirit was speaking and when they were quoting? Alexandrine doubted it. That transition was awkward, but not a conflict.

The area belowdecks had barely enough room to walk in places, but was scrupulously neat. The space was delineated on all sides by great metal beams and rivets, interspersed with occasional cupboards, tables, and lockers. Pipes ran along near the ceiling and were tucked away against the walls of the narrow corridors.

The floor was slightly sloped, matching the deck above, but it wasn't until the corridor arrived at the engine room through another round-cornered door that Alexandrine's burgeoning feeling of unease rose up to close her nonexistent throat. She knew what engines should look like only through Steel and couldn't say whether these ones were typical or threatening in the way they loomed over her. In contrast, the room itself, tilted and artificially lit only with Ferry's magic in place of electricity, whispered clearly to her of danger. Water had stolen up over half the floor—a thin enough layer, but more than enough to seem as if the sea had claimed ownership of that half of the room.

As they rounded the bulk of one of the engines, Alexandrine saw the four hostages. They huddled, crammed against pipes in one corner, scrupulously keeping their feet out of the water. Ferry examined their human wards, seemed to find nothing amiss in those wards' wide-eyed fear, and turned back to Steel and Mia. "You'll be safe here."

Mia dropped Steel's hand and pulled Alexandrine's gaze along with her own, presumably checking distances and angles to ensure that when she drove Ferry back, the hostages' escape would be clear. She brought her hand up, loose and ready for a lunge.

And as Mia stepped forward, one foot splashed down into seawater and everything changed. Ferry's focus narrowed to Mia alone and they offered her a seductive smile. An enthralling smile.

The Ferry that smiled was a different Ferry. Still tall, but with delicate swells at bust and hips, fine black hair down their back, wearing a dress as ephemeral as Steel's with a skirt of kelp-green sheer panels that swirled around their knees with every movement. "Come in," Ferry crooned. "Come swim with me."

Alexandrine thrashed against the spell, trying to wrench Mia's head aside and break her gaze. Suddenly she stood beside Mia, separate. Mia had let the spell go. The anchor tumbled unnoticed to the deck from loose fingers because Mia had eyes only for Ferry's face—or their chest, maybe. She caught Ferry's hand and drew them into a dancing hold. Ferry tightened it further, belly to belly, grinding. Alexandrine screamed at Mia, but she couldn't hear her now, not without the anchor.

Then Mia was flat on her back on the deck, Ferry straddling her hips. The sea rose in a boiling mass, capped with the foam of a storm pounding its rage out against the rocks. It swallowed Mia whole while Ferry's head tipped back in ecstasy.

If Alexandrine followed through with the original plan and caused Ferry pain, would that make the waters recede or drown Mia faster? It was all so tragically, intimately familiar to her: a ruin spirit with their instincts truncated by circumstance. She imagined in the normal course of things, Ferry would have stood in the surf and called their victim out to them. Would have kissed and caressed the victim until they scarcely noticed their world fading away with the lack of air. This drowning was a graceless thing.

But no less effective. Alexandrine could at least try words before pain. "That's not keeping her safe!" Ferry had said they wanted that, after all. Safety for those they protected.

Ferry's gaze snapped to her and the sea washed back to its proper depth, leaving Mia gasping, only the back of her head getting wet. "They keep getting in the water," Ferry snarled, body returning to its earlier proportions. "I can't keep them safe in the water—they belong to me in the water—they're mine— they're *mine*—" At war indeed. Ferry couldn't settle on one body for the length of an entire sentence. "Since I ran aground, I don't know who to be, sea or land, and it's their fault. If I get rid of them, maybe I'll be able to be only one at a time and think straight—"

"If you let them go—" Alexandrine held no real hope of such a simple solution. Indeed, Ferry cut her off almost instantly.

"The two of you may be seeping into each other, but you're still separate. What do you know about what I should do?" Ferry gestured wildly from Steel to her and back.

"She's *my* ghost. Get your own." Steel sneered. She turned to go, padding back around the engine to the room's exit. Alexandrine supposed she should be surprised that Steel had stayed this long. She hadn't killed any humans lately, but it was a long way from there to saving them. If she went much longer without Alexandrine's touch, her instincts might even drive her to grab someone here and transport them somewhere high to drop them.

And what if she did?

Alexandrine placed herself in Steel's path. The idea was pure *madness*. But what else could she do? She leaned into Steel, clasped both her hands, and spoke low into her ear. "Don't let Ferry hear, but: I do already seep into you a little...what if you took me on, like Mia did? You only had to touch humans to take them to the top of your tower—can you do it here? Distract Ferry and then take Mia when the others have escaped. Then I could pull at you or use your voice to remind you not to actually drop her."

And if Alexandrine couldn't stay Steel's hand, Mia would at least have a chance of surviving being dropped into the water, wouldn't she? More of a chance than she had here, trapped with Ferry as their curiosity about the newcomers decayed, and with it their lucidity.

Mia thrashed, drawing Alexandrine's attention away from Steel. Ferry leaned on their hands on Mia's chest to hold her down, land then sea then land again, but at least the water did not rise up for the moment. Ferry's attention was mostly on the two of them.

And they needed to keep that attention firmly engaged, Alexandrine realized. Coaching Steel in this "taking on" when Alexandrine didn't know herself exactly how it was done would take time. "We could show Ferry how to come together as one," she said, voice lifted to carry. "Even if it's for a brief time."

Steel stepped back, breaking their handclasp and putting a formal distance between them. If Alexandrine had needed to breathe, that breath would have caught. She had assumed the promise of a victim, even an uncompleted one, would entice Steel. Perhaps the lack of a finished kill made the scheme unappealing. Was there anything else in this for Steel? "If you're willing, I mean…"

She had forgotten, however, about Steel's native curiosity. That curiosity had driven her this far just for a glimpse of the sea. "Sounds interesting." Steel held out both palms, flat. "It shouldn't be hard; this time when you seep in, I'll pull, too."

Alexandrine hovered her hands atop Steel's, palms down. So many ways for this to go wrong, starting with a simple failure of the whole process. But lives were at stake. That was her purpose.

Alexandrine lowered her hands.

* * *

The entity formed of ghost and ruin spirit came to herself in a process a little like waking up. Her thoughts were reluctant to connect to each other until she'd gathered enough from her senses to ground herself. The deck where she stood lacked standing water, but was damp enough for her to feel the sea's cold against the soles of her feet. Who was she, feeling this? More than ruin spirit, more than ghost…she needed a designation, even if it was as simple as the one she'd given Ferry. Gestalt, perhaps. From the German for figure, shape, or form. But the word's origin didn't matter, so she pushed the facts aside rather than following them too far.

This was not like being a ghost and being taken on by a mage in any way. It seemed her lie to Ferry about becoming one had held the truth.

Gestalt looked up, found Ferry staring, their face a mixture of frustration and stunned fascination. "That's a clever trick, but I don't think I could repeat it. Two wrongs don't make a right, after all." They smiled, sharp.

"Are both of you wrong, then?" Gestalt tested one step forward, still on damp metal rather than saltwater. The other hostages needed time to escape and Ferry could drown Mia faster than Gestalt could lunge to touch her from this distance. "When you're one person, it doesn't matter what different sides of your nature make you *think* of doing, it matters what you *do*." She caught Ferry's eyes and knelt. Her knee contacted the water but Ferry didn't break the gaze between the two of them. "Your eyes are always the same, did you know that?"

That was a lie—for sea-Ferry, those eyes were markedly greener. Gestalt's ruin spirit wouldn't have understood the power such a lie could have; her ghost would never have thought to wield that power for this purpose. By all logic, such a thing should never have left her lips.

And yet.

But there was no time for abstract pondering. She gestured out of Ferry's sight for the hostages to go.

"My eyes are the same?" Ferry's shock was unified on both their land and sea face. Gradually, their eyes *were* the same. As Gestalt watched that happen, she heard a scuffle and a whispered disagreement among the hostages. No doubt one or more didn't want to leave Mia behind.

"The new mage will bring her out," one of the humans hissed finally and audibly. They stumbled across the room and up the stairs all in a rush.

Ferry did not seem to mark them, but when Gestalt reached to touch Mia, Ferry hissed their displeasure with a noise like a storm wave smashing into the rocks. "How are you even away from your ruin, to show up here and deny me my rightful due? The humans are *mine* to protect—kill—protect—"

"I'm away from my ruin because I worked together." Gestalt frowned in frustration at the mismatch of singular and plural. There weren't words for her situation. "Not against myself."

The hostages had had their time—now was her moment. Gestalt struck with all her speed. She got a grip on Mia's wrist before Ferry could do more than cause the water to hump up in surprise. She transported Mia up to the highest point of what was, at its heart, a great ferrous structure. Her bare feet balanced impossibly on the edge of a smokestack painted a faded, peeling white and black.

It may have been the ruin spirit who seized Mia; it was definitely the ghost who, having seized her, did *not* drop her. Gestalt held Mia out, dangling her from Gestalt's grip on the collar of her shirt and jacket. Mia's skin rapidly reddened both with the biting cold of the wind and her attempts to claw closer to Gestalt and to safety.

Her ghost had been mistaken—Mia wouldn't survive a fall. The ferry was canted somewhat, but not so much that Mia would clear the lower decks and reach the water. Which was too shallow to absorb a fall of that distance in any case.

Her ruin spirit wanted to drop Mia. But "want" was a strange word to assign to the ruin spirit. She'd wanted to travel to the sea, but that had been after ghost and ruin spirit had begun to work together. Before then, had she wanted? She'd had instincts; she'd acted.

But the ghost knew wanting. She'd wanted things that were possible now, she'd wanted opposed things that were only possible later. She'd wanted things that would hurt herself, she'd wanted things that would hurt others. She'd had morality; sometimes she *hadn't* acted.

Ferry was there beside Gestalt, suddenly, balanced on the edge of the smokestack as well. Their skirts danced viciously around their knees in the wind. It seemed even this far from the water they could still wear their sea face. "You are still as much a ruin spirit as I!" they spat.

"I am, and I think that means you can be more than your instincts, too." Gestalt twisted to bring Mia's flailing feet into contact with the rungs of the ladder that led up to the top of the smokestack. Mia seized and clung, and when Gestalt released her grip, Mia hurried down and away.

Ferry crouched, reached out for Mia—so Gestalt grabbed Ferry by the wrist instead. She didn't know it would work until it did, but they were just as easy to hoist up, ready to drop. She laughed. No reason at all not to drop another ruin spirit! They couldn't die.

So she dropped them, laughing still.

The satisfaction of it was visceral, primal, and it ripped them apart. Steel was nothing but her instincts and Alexandrine couldn't abide those instincts. In that moment they were separate again.

To Alexandrine, it felt something like when she'd died. She'd been ripped away from her body and her perceptions had ceased. When they'd begun again, they'd been the limited ones of a ghost and she'd been hovering over her anchor. She wasn't pulled so far this time, just to the other side of the smokestack, but the sensation of violence was the same. It *hurt* in a way that didn't hurt because ghosts didn't feel physical pain, and that reminder made it hurt even worse.

The sea surged up unnaturally and reached over the deck to cushion Ferry's wide-armed fall and they were laughing now, too. Well, good for them and Steel both. Alexandrine had accomplished her purpose and now she was unneeded again. Clearly, she should leave and just forget what it had been like to be one.

Forget how every breath had held the smell of salt, every sensation she was denied as a ghost had been so *full*, so real.

In poisonous silence, Alexandrine escorted Mia down a series of ladders and stretches of deck. Finally, Mia found a place she could fling herself from the edge of the main deck to the sand and dashed away to safety. The kicked—happy this time—anthill of well-wishers surrounded her farther up the beach.

Alexandrine lingered near to listen, but there was little sense to be had among the exclamations of joy and the tangled account of events offered by Mia and the hostages. She'd thought listening was all she wanted, but now she knew there was so much more for her to want and be denied. Besides, her anchor was still on the ship; when the townsfolk moved off the beach, she could not follow.

So be it. Alexandrine found a place to sit among tussocks of grass on a slight rise above the beach, at the far edge of her range but within sight if Steel decided to leave the ferry. She was no stranger to waiting near Steel until she was needed for her purpose.

* * *

Unfortunately, rather than wearing away Alexandrine's frustration like the sea tumbling a shard of glass, the tedium of the next few days sharpened it like a knife. The townsfolk gave the ruin a wide berth and Steel did not leave it. This morning, Alexandrine finally gave in and thought herself over to the canted ship. In the strong sunlight, it cast a foreshortened shadow across the sand and water, smokestack and decks and railings combined into a single tangled silhouette like a carpenter's trash pile.

She was greeted by the two ruin spirits' voices raised in laughter again. Had they been playing this game the whole time, hidden from her position on the beach by the bulk of the ship? Rather than the smokestack, Steel balanced atop a railing that allowed her to dangle Ferry directly over the water. The water did not need to surge up magically to catch them, but when Steel dropped and Ferry arched back into a dive, the angle of their body suggested three times as much depth as should actually exist at that spot.

No, this game was different, Alexandrine realized, as she arrived behind Steel. In this game, Steel jumped after Ferry.

She had none of the elegance of their dive, but she had no fear either. She remained relaxed as her feet hit the water. When she resurfaced, she noticed Alexandrine and gave a brief wave. Alexandrine wondered if Steel wanted her to look impressed. No chance of that.

Ferry swam into Steel, clearly expecting to be pulled immediately back to the railing in yet another cycle of the game. In the delay caused by Steel's distraction, however, they gave a wicked grin. Wearing their sea face, they tugged Steel out to deeper water and kissed her there. With their hair slicked down, highlighting features both delicate and frightening, both of them were another kind of primal now.

Or maybe not.

Steel wasn't kissing back. Neither did she pull away—Ferry was the one to do that. But Alexandrine could tell from Ferry's frown that they had felt Steel's lack of enthusiasm. "You don't want this," they said, disappointed but kind.

Frustration surged up in Steel's mercurial expression. "Show me how," she demanded, and Ferry tried again. Still, Steel only allowed the touch, she didn't participate. Ferry might as well have been caressing knots on a tree trunk. Perhaps she was, in a way. Steel was a force of magic that, much like some elements of nature, was not designed with certain drives.

Steel twisted in the water. "Where's my ghost?" She held out a preemptory hand to Alexandrine. "I need you for this."

Alexandrine had drifted closer without thinking, feet more or less "on" the water, but she jerked back now. "You need—what about what I need? I was killed to protect humans from you, and that's what I've been doing ever since. But that's not enough, I have to give myself to a random mage to save other humans from *another* ruin spirit. I have to do whatever you demand of me to keep you from running off. An eternity at your beck and call. Alexandrine, get over here, I want to get some! And then you'll kick me back out again, no doubt." Her hands were balled up tight, but there was no sensation to that tightness. No fingernails pressing into skin. "No *thanks*. I can't stand to have the sensations of living only to lose them again. Better not to have them at all."

Steel looked to Ferry, but they held up their hands, a clear promise of non-interference. They remained where they were, water to their chin. Steel waded slowly to Alexandrine. Alexandrine set her jaw and held her position until Steel reached her.

"You want things and cannot have them. I can have things but do not want them. Isn't it better if we're one person?" Steel cut off Alexandrine's planned objection with a shake of her head, expression tight with frustration. "Forever this time."

If only it were that easy. "What about when your instincts take you again? We'll be ripped apart once more."

Steel considered this, brow furrowed. "If you'll supply the wanting, I'll only drop people you want me to. Like Ferry."

"You'll only drop people you can't kill?" Knowing no one would die, perhaps Alexandrine could abide a ruin spirit's instincts. Oh, she wanted this. With all of her soul, which was all she had, as a ghost.

When Steel nodded, Alexandrine reached out, but Steel was already stepping around behind her. This time, Steel was the one pressed against Alexandrine's back, hands settling gently on her belly, cheek turned into her hair.

"Yes. Please," Alexandrine said.

* * *

"Well." She waded diffidently to where Ferry waited, feet on the bottom but with water up to their shoulders. She held her hands open, beneath the water. "This isn't exactly what you signed up for." The trouble with being able to want someone was the fear of rejection that came with it.

Ferry touched her cheek, sliding the side of a thumb along her cheekbone and down to her jaw. She shivered. "I know what I'm getting. Which would you prefer to get?" they asked, first sea face, then land face. Same green-brown eyes. Their voice had a lightness that wasn't actually light.

She understood that the question was important, but even the gradually settling mixture of her new self didn't understand more than that. "The land and the sea are both...you? Which is what I want."

"I'm glad." Ferry kissed her and she kissed them back and *everything* was sensation—skin across their shoulder blades under her palms and both their tongues against each other and body to body and *grinding*. The space between her legs lit up like an explosion and she couldn't breathe—she didn't need to breathe, but she'd forgotten that for a second. She closed them both into an embrace instead, needing something to cling to, and panted. "Oh, Ferry. Part of me was dead for a long time. I can't manage it all at once—"

Ferry laughed, bright and delighted, arms securely around her waist. "We have plenty of time—" They cut off at the place a name belonged. "What do I call you?"

"I need a new name. One that isn't a fact or a description." She was certain of that, but of little beyond it. She eased back.

Ferry smoothed their thumb over the frown-wrinkle between her brows. "I have one I'm not using." They pointed up to the hull of their ship, where white letters on green were visible: OLYMPIC.

Not quite right, but—

"Olympia," she decided. She joined the kiss this time and Ferry met it with one that was no less wicked for its gentleness.

* * *

Olympia could go into town all she wanted now, but she also understood the joy in watching the waves. The latter—and playing with Ferry—were pleasant enough until she'd planned a way to reassure any humans she might speak to. Today, she picked a spot to wait at the apex of the crumbling, sandy slope down to the beach. The ruin would no doubt be watched. Indeed, it wasn't long before Mia appeared, coming to join her at a conversational distance, but out of immediate reach. "Steel?"

"No, Olympia. I'm one now." She turned to Mia, scraped wind-caught hair out of her eyes, and offered the woman a smile. "Thanks in part to you."

Mia's eyes widened and she touched her own chest, where the frozen mist-whorls of ghost residue were brighter now.

Olympia saved her the effort of articulating her question. "No, not really like that. A ruin spirit isn't much like a mage. But that's where it began."

Mia exhaled on a laughing note. "I should have known something was different, even from a distance. You're wearing shoes."

So she was. Light slipper-style ones, as shiny as her dress. She looked out to the horizon. The tree-studded islands there would have looked like mountain foothills had she not known about the water between them, hidden by the mist. "So you know, I'm not staying here forever. I'll see if I can get Ferry to accept help to move their ruin somewhere they feel more settled, but I'm not planning to trade eternity as one ruin spirit's keeper for eternity as the keeper of another."

"That's more than fair." Mia dipped her head. "I wanted to tell you—the ghost part of you, anyway—that I'm sorry. It wasn't fair to just assume that you'd help, because of how you'd been bound. Did they even ask before doing that, or just murder you?"

"They asked and I consented, but that doesn't really matter." Olympia tasted the term on her tongue. Murder. Maybe it had been, in a way. "The living can't understand what they're consenting to, so that's not consent."

Mia clasped her hands together, posture shouting her upset. "They shouldn't have—"

"But they did." Olympia looked back out to the horizon and drew a breath filled with the salt of the sea and the green of the fir trees. "It's all right. Now I can both want and have. Contentment is finally possible." Part of her had forgotten what that was like; part of her had never experienced it before. She looked forward to reveling in it in the future.

She turned back to Mia properly and smiled. "Would you be willing to show me around town, perhaps?"

Orpheus

Jack Campbell

"Awesome," Major Khoury said. After six months of travel, having crossed more than one and a half billion kilometers, our ship, the *Daedalus,* was using her propulsion to slow to achieve orbit about our destination. This close, the rings of Saturn were huge glowing bands spanning a wide stretch of space. Saturn itself shone from sunlight reflected off the clouds covering it. When we'd left Earth, Saturn had been just a bright dot in space to the naked eye. Over the months since then it had grown, until now it loomed in brilliant glory like a brooding goddess watching our approach. "Don't you agree, Captain Grant?"

"Awesome is a good word," I said. Every ship needs a captain, and on *Daedalus* that was me. If my parents had named me Cary my social life might've been awesome, but instead they'd named me Ulysses. And when your name is Ulysses Grant, people are always putting you in charge of things

To a scientist, Saturn's little solar system of more than eighty moons was a web of interacting fields and forces. To a pilot like Dale Khoury, it was a maze of gravity fields to be threaded. To me, it was really big rocks and little rocks and a list of tasks spelled out for us by the mission planners. We were the second crewed expedition to reach this far out into the solar system. Not the first, the second. So we wouldn't be in the history books for blazing trails, but our list of tasks was just as long and our ability to stay here just as limited by food, water, and the ability of humans to stay sane after months cooped up in a small ship.

"Do we have visual on *Orpheus* yet?" I asked.

"Right there, Captain." Khoury highlighted a dot on the view panel. "Right where it should be, orbiting near Titan."

Orpheus: a new human-made moon for Saturn for the romantic or an abandoned derelict for the sailor.

Twenty years before, the first crewed expedition to reach Saturn had left behind a lot of satellites and instruments and, as planned, the lander they'd been using to visit the surfaces of various moons. But that first mission hadn't planned on leaving something else behind: three of the astronauts making up the five-person mission.

That was one of our tasks, too, to see if any trace of those three could be found on cold, icy Titan, which had swallowed them twenty years ago.

*   *   *

I won't bore you with stories about the next month as we made orbit about Saturn and carried out as many of our assigned tasks as possible. If you've read any accounts of our mission you know all about them already. This is about something few people know, something we couldn't put in official reports.

The boredom of the trip out was replaced by long days of labor over experiments and readings and observations, and the glory of Saturn gradually became a mundane backdrop to our work, Saturn's many moons and rings becoming less objects of wonder and more obstacles to safely move around. Major Khoury and our co-pilot, Commander Ulises Seguin, acquired a few more gray hairs as they took turns sliding *Daedalus* through the mess of gravity fields without using too much propulsion mass or getting twisted onto wrong vectors.

Most of the moons were barren rocks, but robotic rovers and samplers left behind by the first expedition needed their samples collected and their batteries replaced. Our own lander was the *Icarus*, which could carry five of us down to the surface of those moons. The acceleration and deceleration of *Daedalus* on our way here had provided some feeling of gravity, but after long stretches of zero gravity it felt odd to reach the surface of the bigger moons and feel the real thing tugging us to the ground again. Tethys had almost as much gravity as the moon, and a lot of its surface resembled the craters of Earth's satellite, whereas little Dione had so little gravity we had to worry about jumping off into space.

Landing safely on the often extremely rugged surfaces (I still get nightmares about Hyperion) and getting our tasks done was where our crew—technical specialist Cassandra (Cassie) Jenkins, geologist Dr. Ken Sato, and biologist Dr. Penelope (Penny) Aberra—and I earned our gray hairs. If you've noticed a certain pattern in names like Ulises, Penelope, and Cassandra, so did a lot of people. The agency swore it was a coincidence we'd ended up together on this mission.

Cassie worked harder than any of us. A while back someone figured out that long-duration deep-space missions needed one skill more than any other: the ability to fix things using whatever was available. Cassie Jenkins was that person on our mission. If she couldn't fix something by the book using the right parts, she could figure out how to make it work using anything else we had. Since *Icarus* had proven to be temperamental as all hell, Cassie spent most of her days trying to keep its many state-of-the-art systems working.

Titan was our last stop. Cold as the heart of a private equity manager, but with an atmosphere thick enough that humans could walk around on the surface without a spacesuit. As long as those humans had oxygen masks and enough insulation to prevent the surface temperature of -179 degrees Celsius from freezing them solid, that is. Under its shallow methane oceans and ice mantle, there was liquid water that might harbor life. That was one of the things the first expedition had been looking for. We'd be looking for that, too, as well as the remains of the three lost crew members.

"Not gonna happen," Cassie Jenkins announced as we neared Titan, looking as if she wanted to hurl a diagnostic tool through the side of *Daedalus*.

"What's not going to happen?" I asked.

"*Icarus* is broke. Stone dead. Expired. Cannot be made safe again with anything we have."

"The 3D printer—" Ken Sato started to say.

"Cannot print microchips!"

"What if we—" Dale Khoury began.

"Tried it! Tried everything! I told them *Icarus* had too much developmental gear on it, I told them it was stupid to name a lander after someone who'd crashed and died, but nobody listened to me. And now we can't use the lander. Critical systems are unreliable."

"It's impossible to get down to Titan's surface?" Penny Aberra asked.

Cassie shrugged. "Oh, you can get down to the surface. Once. All you have to do is fall. But it'll hurt a lot when the fall stops, and you won't be able to get off the surface again."

"There has to be another option," Ulises Seguin said.

"There isn't. We only have one lander."

They all looked at me, because it was my job to make the tough decisions and my job to tell the people back on Earth that we couldn't carry out the most important part of our mission. But I'd be insane to overrule Cassie on the safety of using *Icarus*. "At least we can orbit Titan and check on…" I realized that I'd stopped speaking, that everyone was watching me even closer. "Cassie, we've got another lander."

"We do?" She looked around with mock drama. "Where?"

"In orbit near Titan."

Khoury got it first. "*Orpheus?*"

"It still works?" Seguin asked.

"We can find out," I said. "Check it out when we get there. The first expedition didn't report any problems with *Orpheus* before they abandoned it as planned."

"It'll be really low on reaction mass," Cassie said, her eyes hooded with thought. "If any is left at all. But we can transfer the mass from *Icarus.*"

"Do you know enough about *Orpheus* to tell if it's safe to use?" Penny Aberra asked Cassie.

"I grew up fixing twenty-year-old tech. Let's take a look."

* * *

In order to link up with *Orpheus* we had to detach *Icarus* first, the two landers hanging in space within a dozen meters of each other. The final approach seemed glacially slow as we eased our way into contact, lining up with the airlock on the old lander. We had to be strapped into our seats while *Daedalus* maneuvered, making the wait particularly tedious.

"Kind of weird, isn't it?" Penny Aberra said as we watched the approach on our seat view screens. "I mean, that lander has been out here for twenty years. A derelict."

I knew what she meant. The once shiny surface of the lander had been pitted with innumerable tiny impacts. No lights showed, only darkness behind the small windows we could see. It would've felt a little creepy under any circumstances. But knowing that three of the astronauts who'd ridden that lander had never returned from Titan added a superstitious lining to our view of the abandoned spacecraft.

"A derelict," Penny repeated. "Should we even be thinking about using a derelict? Shouldn't we ask mission control about this first?" Penny always wanted to do things by the book. I thought that attitude was a good thing in a biologist working with sometimes very hazardous forms of life and viruses. But it could be limiting at times.

"First we're going to find out if *Orpheus* is still safe," I said. "Then we'll ask for permission. We're going to do this right."

"You know, one of the meanings of derelict is failing in duties, or to abandon," Ulises Seguin said. "Which is sort of what *Orpheus* did to the three astronauts it never lifted off Titan."

"It's not like they died aboard it," Ken Sato said. "They never made it back. That wasn't the fault of the lander." That was Ken. He knew everything to be known about geology, but his mind rarely roamed beyond the rocks he knew so well.

Daedalus jolted slightly as we made contact.

"Airlocks are mated," Dale Khoury announced. "We've got a firm lock and a pressure seal."

"What's it like inside *Orpheus*?" I asked. "Can you access its instrument readings through the airlock link?"

"All I'm seeing is basic life-support reports. Everything else must be shut off. Air pressure is low, but it's there, so the hull doesn't have any holes in it. Otherwise it looks okay. *Orpheus'* instruments aren't reporting any air quality problems beyond it being stagnant."

We all just sat for a few moments, waiting for someone else to make the first move.

Since that was also my job, I pushed myself toward the Extravehicular Activity suits. They could keep the person wearing them safe in open space or on the surface of many places, including the moons of Saturn. "We suit up before we go aboard *Orpheus*. Just in case there's some hazard the instruments aren't reporting."

They grumbled, because wearing an EVA is a pain, but they did as I said because they knew it was smart and they were secretly glad someone was making them do it.

Finally ready, we pulled open the hatch, seeing the tube extending from our airlock for about two meters before it mated with the airlock hatch into *Orpheus*. In a pinch, the tube could hold two people in EVA suits.

"Until we know there's nothing dangerous on the lander, we go through two at a time," I said, "sealing the lock into *Daedalus* each time before opening the hatch into the lander."

Knowing I had to be first, I pulled myself into the tube, Cassie squeezing in after me until we were jammed together. In case you think that's romantic or exciting, it was more like tight and claustrophobic. As soon as the hatch from *Daedalus* closed, I plugged in the power relay and started opening the hatch into *Orpheus*.

I started *trying* to open that hatch, anyway. Twenty years of being shut had left its parts reluctant to move. I heard the relays that should be opening the hatch whine, but nothing moved. Cassie added her strength to mine as we tugged at the handles. Normally, you have to anchor yourself to apply pressure in zero gravity, but being jammed in together worked as well as a handhold.

The relays finally let go, spinning fully open, the hatch sagging inward.

I grabbed the edge of the hatch to pull myself inside, feeling anxious as I glided onto the old lander's control deck, dimly lit by the reflected light from Titan and Saturn.

I looked around, holding myself next to the hatch as Cassie pulled herself inside. There wasn't much to the control deck, just instrument panels, some equipment access plates, and four seats bolted to the floor. The first mission had five people in it and one of the pilots had stayed aboard their ship while the other four took the lander down. Leaving a pilot in orbit is kind of a tradition, to make sure that landers have ships to come back to.

Orpheus felt odd. Deserted. I'd never before been in a spaceship that felt like that. The deep shadows behind the seats shouldn't hold anything, but I swung my EVA suit light through them, feeling a strong desire to know for sure.

Cassie was looking over the instrument panels and accesses when Dale Khoury and Ulises Seguin joined us. "Is it safe in here?"

"As far as I can tell," I said. "We should vent the atmosphere, though, before we open the hatches between the lander and *Daedalus*."

Cassie moved something that went clunk and the lights came on. I don't mind admitting that made me a lot happier. "They powered down everything before they left it," she said. "We're running off power from *Daedalus,* so I don't know if the lander's power supply still works, but I'm not seeing any problems. The air tanks still have pressure. Do we want to use them?"

"Let's reserve that for emergencies," I said. "Cycle in fresh air from *Daedalus'* tanks."

"What's down here?" Ulises Seguin asked, standing by a hatch in the deck. "Ah. It says EVA deck. This is a lot like the layout on *Icarus*."

He cycled the hatch before I could protest, pulling himself down and through. I followed quickly, still fighting a case of nerves I didn't want to admit to.

The EVA deck was even less impressive than the control deck. The center was empty. Spaced around the edges were lockers and bins for equipment. The largest lockers were open, four tall containers each wide enough to hold an EVA suit even with a person inside. But only one suit rested in its locker. Brackets meant to hold the other three gaped empty.

Seguin stared at the lockers. "The three who didn't come back."

"Yeah," I said, because I had to say something.

He looked toward the big hatch that would lead outside when the lander was resting on the surface. "I wonder what it was like for the lander pilot. Left alone. Coming back off Titan's surface, knowing the other three were still there."

That sounded like an accusation. "What was it like? I guess nightmare is the right word. The two survivors of the mission made it home but they've fought survivor guilt ever since."

"I didn't mean..." Ulises looked around. "There's nothing else here." Without another word he pulled himself up to the hatch and back with the others.

I didn't blame him. Nobody had died on the EVA deck, but it felt haunted.

* * *

After checking over all of the systems, Cassie gave a thumbs-up, along with a lecture about how much more reliable and robust the old systems on *Orpheus* were compared to the cutting-edge junk on *Icarus*.

I sent a message back to Earth, explaining our problem and our solution. Then I got to work preparing for the trip to Titan's surface, knowing it would be at least three hours before I got an answer.

The reply showed up five hours later, which was remarkably fast decision-making from the higher-ups on Earth. But faced with having to abandon the Titan landing that was a very big part of the justification for the entire mission, or using the old but still working *Orpheus,* they'd quickly decided it was worth risking our lives on it. With an official go-ahead, we started transferring material meant for the landing from *Icarus* to *Orpheus*, stacking it in the empty EVA deck on the old lander.

In the meantime, Dale Khoury and Ulises Seguin took us around Titan, using *Daedalus'* ground penetrating radar to map Titan's subsurface and look for surprises.

"We've done three passes over what should be the spot where the three members of the first expedition were lost," Dale told me. "We can't see them."

"They're that deep?"

"Probably not," Ken Sato said, grimacing as he studied his screen. "Look." He gestured to what looked like a 3D image inside ice cream loaded with specks of chocolate. "That frozen mantel is full of stuff. It's probably mostly rock scraped off the surface. The occasional meteorite. Who knows what else. Our people are in there, I'm sure, but we can't distinguish them from this high up."

"How about a lot closer to the surface?"

"Maybe. It depends on how deep they are by now. Have you watched the video of what happened during the first expedition's landing?"

"Yes."

"We should watch it again, before anybody goes down in that lander." Ken shook his head. "I want to find those three as much as anyone, but I sure as hell don't want to go walking around trying to find them. Not on Titan."

* * *

It would've kept everyone else happier if we hadn't watched those records from the first expedition, but it might've also caused someone to underestimate the danger. So everybody strapped into their seats and I keyed up the video.

Each of our screens showed multiple images from the first expedition, three from the suits of the astronauts on the surface, as well as a couple from cameras aboard *Orpheus*, one of which showed the backs of the three explorers. In their EVA suits, they looked almost exactly alike from the back, only slightly different heights and a few different pieces of equipment distinguishing them from each other.

"Dryden, Torres, and Weber," Ken said in a low voice. "An astrophysicist, a biologist, and a chemist."

"No geologist?" Cassie asked.

"No," Ken Sato said. "That wasn't regarded as a critical skill set for the first expedition."

The three explorers in the video were spread out, a couple of meters apart, walking slowly away from the lander. The sky and the landscape looked weird, like something painted by Salvador Dali, everything cast with an ochre color as if someone had dumped a world-sized bucket of paint that shade onto Titan. The horizon was too close and too curved, rounded pebbles of rock and ice harder than steel scattered over a surface that looked like sand but was actually grains of ice. Hard-edged mountains rose in the distance. A sluggish stream was visible to the left, wending its way down to an ocean, both made of liquid methane.

All four images shook as an ice quake rippled through Titan's surface. "Titan has active tectonic activity," Ken said, pausing the video. "We don't have experience on Earth with ice formations as huge and frozen as hard as the mantle on Titan. Most recent simulations produce results as if the ice were metal, flexing when strong forces like the tidal force from Saturn go through it. Weak points fracture when the ice flexes and, when it flexes again, the existing fractures open and close." He started the video again.

A voice called out from the recording. "Guys, I don't like this."

"That's Jordan, the pilot still inside *Orpheus*," I said.

"This ice is rock hard and a kilometer thick," a voice the video identified as Torres replied. "Don't let a little shaking worry you."

"I spent time at McMurdo in the Antarctic," Jordan said. "There were crevasses. People fell into them."

"This isn't Antarctica." Dryden sounded annoyed. "The ice is harder and thicker."

"But this whole moon gets banged around by Saturn's gravity field," Jordan said. "They should've sent a rover for this."

"They tried," Weber said. "Every rover that landed on Titan broke down or lost contact after a short time for unknown reasons. We're here partly to try to figure out why that's happening."

The view from Weber's suit shifted as she turned to look out across the shallow sea, then was momentarily obscured as a brief shower of methane raindrops pelted the group. On the audio from *Orpheus*, the sound of the big, heavy drops hitting the lander's hull made an ominous thunder.

The views shook again, but not as badly this time.

"Over this way," Dryden said, turning away from the methane sea.

"Hey, what's that?" Weber crouched, brushing at the ice sand with one gloved hand, exposing a surface that looked glassy smooth except for something like a straight edge just under the surface. "This looks like it goes down deep. I can't tell how long it extends. Is it artificial?"

The three crew members clustered together, shining their lights down at the knife edge visible through the surface ice. "It's a fracture," Dryden said.

"A fracture." Weber suddenly straightened, her camera view jerking upward. "We shouldn't—"

A sudden powerful jolt made all of the views jump wildly.

The images from Dryden's, Torres', and Weber's suits spun in a blur. They cried out, voices overlapping, then went silent as all three cameras went black. As the view from *Orpheus* stabilized, none of the three could be seen.

Ken Sato stopped the video. "Here's what they later managed to recover from the feeds."

The image of the three astronauts appeared again, everything moving very slowly before the world shuddered in slow motion. In one corner, a sudden abyss opened beneath them, where the fracture had been visible. As the jolt subsided and the explorers fell out of sight, the sides of the crevasse snapped together again.

"They were right," Ken said, his voice sounding loud. "Weber figured it out too late to save them. When the mantle flexed, that fracture cracked open again, then slammed shut."

"Why are we going down there?" Cassie demanded. "I mean, seriously, what could be worth risking that happening to us?"

"We need to place equipment on the surface," I said. "Anchor it, so it can drill down and try to find life under the ice mantel. There are other pieces of equipment, but that's the main thing. And we need to see if there's any trace of those three. Something that worked its way to the surface in the last twenty years."

"We shouldn't have to go far from the pads on the ends of the lander's legs," Ken said. "Ideally, we should anchor the drills at least half a kilometer from where the lander takes off again, so the take-off won't disturb the anchors, but the mission commander has discretion to place them closer to the lander if circumstances require that."

"And they do require that," I said.

"What if we see something out there?" Cassie asked. "Something far from the lander? Who's going to go check it out?"

"I will," I said, suppressing my feelings so they wouldn't show on my face or in my voice. When you're in charge, leading the way comes with the territory, whether you're on Earth or on one of Saturn's moons.

* * *

Orpheus was alive again, all systems active as we boarded it for the trip down to Titan's surface. But something about the lander still felt off, as if it resented being awoken from its long sleep. Cassie had checked out everything already, but frowned as she ran another round of last-minute checks.

"Is anything wrong?" I asked.

"Not that I can see." We were all in our own EVA suits again and would remain in them throughout the landings on Titan, a major pain in the neck but a necessary safety measure. And for once no one had grumbled when I ordered them into the suits.

But that made it harder to see Cassie's expression.

"Is there any reason not to go ahead?"

"Not that I can see," she repeated.

We only had four seats aboard *Orpheus*. Major Dale Khoury took the pilot's station, with Cassie in the seat beside her. I strapped into the third seat, Ken Sato into the fourth.

Penny Aberra was unhappy about being left behind on *Daedalus*; as the biologist with the mission, Titan was her primary reason for being here. If *Icarus* still worked, Penny would've been with us. But I wasn't going to take *Orpheus* down without Cassie, Dale had to pilot the lander, I had to be on the scene to make any tough decisions, and I wasn't going down to Titan without a geologist along for the ride.

Ulises Seguin, though, didn't seem upset to stay aboard *Daedalus*. "Be careful, Captain." he said as *Orpheus* detached from the ship.

"We will. You two behave yourselves while we're gone."

Dale frowned as she maneuvered *Orpheus* away from Daedalus. "She's not a happy ship."

"What do you mean?"

"She's doing what I tell her to do, but...she doesn't like it. That's what it feels like." Dale Khoury gave me an angry look. "You're the sailor here, Captain Grant, so don't you give me a hard time about being superstitious."

Our ground penetrating radar scans had let us select two landing spots that should be more geologically stable than the ill-fated site chosen by the first expedition. Despite her problems with the controls, Dale brought us down within a meter of the first site.

As *Orpheus* settled on the ice sand, Titan shivered beneath us.

"I'm not liking the feel of this lander," Dale said. "It's nothing specific, but something isn't right."

"I can't see any problems," Cassie said for a third time. "But, yeah, something feels off."

"Do we need to cancel the other landings?" I asked.

"No, sir," Dale said. "Everything is working. But I recommend we do what we have to do and then get off this moon as soon as possible."

"Very well." Very well is what you say in the Navy when you don't know what else to say. "Let's get this done."

The EVA deck was full of the gear we'd transferred from *Icarus*, the biggest items being the two thermal drills. We wrestled one of the drills out of the hatch, grateful for the lower gravity, and onto the surface just beyond the landing legs. Ken Sato, moving quickly, stepped off the legs and activated the anchors spaced around the drill. As he was doing that, Cassie and I hauled out the other instruments that were to be left here. I set down the relay antenna, anchoring it as well, and checked the diagnostics. Cassie ran three steps from the lander, scooped up a sample of ice rocks and ice sand, set down a seismometer, and ran back.

We strapped in again before Dale Khoury lifted *Orpheus* off the surface. The old lander rose smoothly, but as we headed for the second landing spot Dale growled some obscenities under her breath as she moved the controls. "She's fighting me again."

"Do you still feel it's safe to continue?"

"Yes, sir," Dale said after a moment.

The second landing was an area near where razor-edged rocks climbed out of the icy mantle to form a mountain. Knowing the ice was thinner here, and underlain by rock, we weren't quite as nervous and spent a little more time making observations, but it was still a relief when we lifted again. "One more stop," I told the others. "How's the lander?"

"Smooth as silk now," Dale said, shaking her head in puzzlement. "It's like it wants to get back to the landing site from twenty years ago."

Before making the third landing, Dale swung *Orpheus* low over the surface, the portable ground penetrating radar we'd brought along probing beneath the ice. "There's stuff down there," Ken Sato said. "But I can't tell what any of it is. Can you hold the lander steadier?"

"No," Dale shot back, her voice tense. "The atmosphere is too thick and this damned lander isn't making anything easy."

"I thought it was maneuvering better," I said.

"It was, until we went into a hover instead of landing."

"Might as well take it down, then," Ken said. "Maybe we'll see something on the surface."

The lander thumped down, Dale glowering at her controls as if it were a misbehaving creature. "I don't recommend staying here long. I want to get this bird back into orbit before something serious malfunctions."

"I'm not getting any error messages from the lander systems," Cassie said.

"It's fighting me," Dale replied. "Not all the time. It's like it wanted to land here and nowhere else."

I dropped down into the EVA section again, waiting for Cassie Jenkins and Ken Sato. The only large item left was the second thermal drill, the rest of our gear already safely deposited on the surface during the first two landings. But as I stood waiting, looking at the hatch to the outside, I got that feeling you get when someone is staring at you. I turned toward it, ready to glare at Cassie or Ken, and instead found myself looking at the empty face plate of the old EVA suit.

Angry at myself, I yanked open the hatch, looking out at the landscape that had swallowed three astronauts twenty years ago. We got the drill out, Ken and Cassie following as I went down the ladder on the nearest leg until I stood on the pad at the bottom.

We all looked around, none of us taking a step off the pad.

"We should check things out," Ken said in a low voice.

"I'm checking them out from here," Cassie replied.

"Wouldn't anything stand out?" I asked Ken. "Wouldn't we see it easily? Those ice pebbles aren't that big."

"I guess." Ken Sato sounded reluctant as well as unhappy. "Dammit, we came all this way."

He was right. "Get that drill anchored while I look around." Nerving myself, I stepped off the pad, walking in the direction of where the others had vanished twenty years ago. I probably went about ten meters, trying not to think or to feel, looking about me quickly. Even though the gravity was much lighter than on Earth, the thicker atmosphere made it feel a bit as if I were walking through water. The sluggish methane river and ocean beyond were unnerving in their familiarity from the first expedition video.

But I still paused for a moment, standing there on the surface of Titan which in all of its history had only known the tread of six humans including me. The ochre ice pebbles and ochre ice sand and ochre methane-tainted sky formed a strange and majestic landscape, the massive shape of Saturn dimly visible through the haze and rifts in the clouds of methane drifting overhead. Down toward the ocean where methane rain fell, I could see a rainbow, the colors dimmed by the ochre-tinted air. It was oddly beautiful, but also frighteningly desolate, a fairy landscape totally hostile to humans.

I spun and walked back quickly, almost jumping back onto the pad. Ken and Cassie had finished their work and were waiting. "Okay," I said, trying not to let my voice reveal how fast my heart was racing. "We've done what we came to do." Back on Earth they'd complain that we'd only done a sketchy examination of the site. Too bad. By the time they got images relayed showing our actions here we'd be back aboard *Daedalus*.

Titan shuddered beneath us as we climbed back into the lander, the movement hard enough to cause all three of us to pause. "Let's get out of here," Cassie said, pulling herself up onto the control deck.

I sealed the outside hatch, trying to ignore the gaze of the empty EVA suit, then followed Ken Sato up. Ken sealed the hatch leading down while everyone else strapped in.

"Take us up, Major," I said, wondering why my skin was crawling.

Dale reached for the controls, and froze in mid-motion as everything went dark, the only light that which filtered in through the small windows.

We all sat there for a moment as our EVA suit lights came on automatically. At least three of us swore loudly, then Cassie was unstrapping and pulling up access panels to the controls.

"What happened?" I asked, trying to keep my voice calm.

"I'm trying to find out," Cassie said.

Orpheus shook as another ice quake rolled by beneath us, the structure of the old lander creaking like the stairs in a haunted house. A shower of methane thundered down on the lander, sounding like hundreds of hands pounding to get inside. Damned superstitious fool, I told myself.

"The breakers all tripped," Cassie said as she shone her hand light inside a panel. "All of them! We should've gotten some warnings before that happened."

"Can we reset them?"

"Sure." *Orpheus* rocked again and something clattered down on the EVA deck, audible even over the thunder of the methane rain.

Clunks sounded as Cassie reset the breakers.

Lights came on as systems powered up and began running through their boot-ups. "How long will this take?"

"Maybe five more minutes. Vital system cores were on battery back-ups so they don't have to do full reboots."

We waited as Titan trembled beneath us, the rain shower pummeling the outer shell of *Orpheus*.

"We should be ready to lift," Cassie said, scanning the controls.

"No, we're not," Dale Khoury snapped, pointing to an indicator light glowing red. "That's the outer hatch down on the EVA deck. Why is it open?"

"It's not," I said. "I sealed it myself."

Before Cassie could reply, the light shifted to green. "It's closed now," she said. "Probably it was never open, just a glitch."

"Take a look."

Cassie activated an internal camera focused on the outer hatch down below. "See? It's closed tight."

"Let's go," I told Dale.

She didn't need any prompting to speed the lift. *Orpheus* rose with a jolt, screaming through Titan's atmosphere on its way back to space.

* * *

Matching up to *Daedalus* took a few hours, time that dragged uncomfortably. The old lander felt even less welcoming than before and we were all worried that more mysterious equipment failures might take place. We couldn't wait to leave *Orpheus* for the familiar confines of *Daedalus*.

When the airlock finally opened, I let Ken and Cassie pull themselves through first. I wanted to bolt through that airlock back onto *Daedalus* and for that reason held myself back. How would the others handle it if their steady commanding officer got spooked?

Dale Khoury hesitated, looking at the hatch to the EVA deck. "We should make sure that outer hatch is sealed properly. I mean, are we coming back aboard this thing?"

"I don't know," I said. "Maybe not. We do need to shut everything down again."

"I'll do it," Dale said, sounding as if, like me, she had to face down irrational fears.

She opened the hatch and pulled herself down.

I heard a sound, like something loud that couldn't force itself through a human throat. "Major?"

She didn't answer.

I shoved myself toward the hatch and yanked myself through, finding Dale hanging at the bottom of the ladder, her body so rigid that when I grabbed her arm it felt like seizing onto a bar of steel. "What's the matter?"

Looking in the direction her gaze was pointed, I saw.

There were four EVA suits in the brackets.

One of them was the familiar old one. The other three were the same twenty-year old design, but looked as if they had been crushed and flattened. The faceplates of the three damaged suits were starred with cracks, a fog of condensation blocking any view of the inside.

"Mother of God," Dale gasped. "Are you seeing that?"

"Yeah," I managed to say, though my throat was tight with fear.

Without another word we both launched ourselves upward, through the hatch, working together to slam it shut and seal it.

I waved Dale through to *Daedalus* first, following her, and sealed both airlock hatches behind me as soon as I was clear.

The others stared at us. "What happened?" Ulises Seguin asked. "You guys see a ghost?"

Dale punched him, hard.

As he flew back from the impact, shocked, I held up both hands. "Playback. My suit video."

Cassie moved first. The feeds from my suit camera automatically uploaded to *Daedalus*, so all she had to do was call it up.

An awful silence fell as the image of the four EVA suits appeared.

"What...what the hell is that?" Ulises Seguin stammered, his eyes wide. "You said you didn't find them."

"We didn't," Ken said.

"This better not be a joke," Penny Aberra said, her voice shaking.

"How'd they get aboard?" I said, trying to find a logical explanation.

"The hatch." Cassie's eyes were fixed on the image. "Remember? All the systems tripped off, and when they came back on, the hatch was open. Then it closed."

"Are you saying they came back aboard on their own?" Ulises Sequin shouted at her.

"We sure as hell didn't bring 'em aboard!" she yelled back.

"Knock it off!" I put all the force I could into those words. I felt panic around me like a living thing, trying to grab control of us. "There are three sealed hatches between us and...whatever those are."

Cassie shoved herself to a panel and entered some commands. "That's a link to *Orpheus'* systems. It'll tell us if the hatch to the EVA deck opens."

"They couldn't—" Ken began, his voice choking off. He had the look of a scientist who'd invested his life in certainties and now faced the impossible.

And they all looked at me. "Captain," Dale Khoury said, "what're we going to do?"

"We need to tell—" We were so far from Earth that a message traveling at the speed of light would require about an hour and a half to go one way. But before I could even send that message, I had to figure out what to say in it. "What should I tell them?"

"They'll think we've gone nuts if we tell them the truth," Ken said.

"Yeah," Dale said. "Captain, if you tell them those EVA suits—and maybe Weber, Torres, and Dryden inside them—got back onto *Orpheus* on their own, they'll assume you've cracked."

"We have to tell them what happened," Penny said.

"Do you know what happened?" Dale demanded. "Because I don't."

"There's only one story they'd accept," I said. "That we found those suits on the surface and brought them inside *Orpheus* ourselves."

"But we know that's not true," Cassie said. "You know it, I know it, Ken knows it. There was only one EVA suit in there when we went onto the control deck."

"Captain Grant is right, though," Ken said. "I don't believe it, and I know it happened."

"If we tell them we found those suits and brought them aboard," Cassie said, "they'll want to know why we don't have video of them on the surface of Titan, and video of us bringing them aboard, and conversations between us when we found them. They'll accuse us of editing the mission data."

"We didn't edit anything," Ken insisted.

"There's nothing we can do about it anyway," I said. "The data from the ship gets compressed into a burst transmission and sent every thirty minutes. Everything from our time on the surface is already on its way back to Earth."

"We didn't fake the data," Ulises Seguin said. "Why not let the truth go out? They have to know we aren't making it up, or crazy."

"They can't believe it. No matter how strong our evidence is. They can't believe it. Which means they can't believe us. Which means they'll decide we manipulated the data somehow."

"If the data is unacceptable, it has to be explained away." Dale sounded angry. "And the only explanation they'll accept will be that we committed some kind of staged fraud."

"Why would we do that?" Penny said. "It'd be unprofessional."

"Because we're the second expedition," Ken said. "Not the pathfinders. A story like this would make us more famous than the first expedition."

"Those things are still in that lander," Cassie said. "Three hatches away from us. I'm a lot more worried about that at the moment than I am my professional reputation. Why not jettison that lander and everything on it?"

"They're not things," Ulises Seguin said, startling the rest of us. "They're… the remains of three fellow astronauts. Three of our comrades. They…they want to go home. Go to rest at home. The green hills of Earth. *Orpheus*, their lander, came back at last and they rejoined it."

After a long moment of silence, Dale Khoury nodded. "He's right. We can't jettison the lander. We have to get them home."

"Excuse me?" Cassie demanded.

"I agree with Cassie," Ken said.

"We can't jettison *Orpheus*," I said. "Authorities on Earth would never approve of that while we have…the remains of the three lost astronauts aboard it."

"Hey," Cassie said, looking at us. "I just remembered some old movies. What if there's some sort of alien life form controlling their bodies? That'd explain it, wouldn't it?"

"That's ridiculous," Penny said. "An alien life form that reanimates a body? It's absurd."

"But it could happen, couldn't it?" Cassie said. "I mean, in theory, it's not impossible, right? Whereas there's no other science that can explain how those suits got back aboard *Orpheus* on their own."

"It's...not...*impossible*," Penny Aberra said.

"There's our answer," I said. "They came aboard, we don't know how, but we suspect contamination by some life form or forms native to Titan. That's an explanation they can accept. It might even be true."

"If it is," Penny said, "I'm a lot more scared now than I was before. But that means we need to investigate *Orpheus*. Conduct a full search for biological—"

"No," Cassie said. "If it's a contaminated site we need to isolate it."

"We have procedures to follow. We're here to find new life. If it's in those suits, inside *Orpheus*—"

"It'll stay there," I said. "We won't investigate. That lander is quarantined effective immediately." I was sure mission control would back me up on that. "Can we shut down *Orpheus* remotely? Not have to go inside the lander again?"

"Sure can," Cassie said.

"Then start doing that. Ken, you and Major Khoury seal the hatch to *Orpheus* so tight and so hard that neither Godzilla nor Ant Man could get through it. I'll work up a message to Earth to explain—" Explain? Probably not the right word. "—to bring them up to date."

* * *

You know what happened after that. The official version, anyway. Earth told us to abandon *Icarus* in orbit and bring *Orpheus* back with us under strict quarantine conditions, which we were happy to abide by. The trip back—worried about either ghosts or alien life forms on the lander linked to *Daedalus*—was the longest journey I'll ever experience, even if my next mission is on a slow spaceship to another star. At least two of us were always awake at any one time, watching the hatch, and watching for any signs of "life" aboard *Orpheus*.

But we made it. And the inside of *Orpheus* was examined in Earth orbit by every remote means possible, eventually including robots that went in to open those EVA suits. Officially, the quarantine procedures were described to the public as normal for bodies that'd spent twenty years on a moon that might harbor alien life, a story which had the advantage of being true.

The remains of Weber, Dryden, and Torres were inside the suits. They'd died instantly when the ice slammed shut on them. Also inside them were various bacteria and other life forms, but nothing that wasn't of Earth origin. If life lurked beneath the ice of Titan, it hadn't made its way close enough to the surface to encounter the three lost explorers.

Of course, that left unanswered the question of how they'd gotten back aboard *Orpheus*. The only possible answers left were either we'd somehow set the whole thing up in an undetectable way (leaving not even microscopic traces that we'd ever come into contact with the bodies), or something else that wasn't an answer any agency was willing to state publicly. So, the six of us were brought into a very secure room and told that, even though they couldn't prove it, we *had* found those EVA suits on the surface and *had* brought those three dead astronauts aboard the lander and we'd better not ever imply otherwise. Which is why this account will be released someday after I'm gone.

Eventually the cremated/sterilized bodies were brought down in sealed urns to their grateful and grieving families and buried in a single service in a monument to their special sacrifice. They asked each of us from the second mission to say something and most of us stumbled through vague words of heroism and condolence because we were afraid to say too much.

All of us except for Ulises Seguin. He brought out an old book, reading from it. "We pray for one last landing, on the globe that gave us birth…"

Maybe, after all, Ulises was right. Maybe we hadn't had any reason to be afraid. Those three just wanted to get home. And when their lander finally came back for them, they did.

Decay in Five Stages
(Prequel to *In the Company of Others*)

Julie E. Czerneda

EarthGov and the System Universities led the greatest effort in human history, terraforming worlds in advance of humanity's long-awaited outward leap. When all were ready, immigrants filled the massive stations built to gather them in advance of landfall and support their settlements.

Then came the Quill.

A primitive, harmless alien lifeform, the ribbon-like Quill were prized ornaments, worn as bracelets by deep space explorers and, it turned out, those terraform specialists so very far from home.

Their work done, the terraformers left their Quill behind. Unfortunately, worlds made-to-order for humans proved ideal for the Quill and, for reasons no one understood, a terraformed world full of Quill proved deadly to humans.

Ah, but what then of the stations and those in them?

Be it known there are five stages of decay.

Stage One: Fresh – the heart no longer beats.

EarthGov Classified Internal Memo: Quill contamination confirmed. Until this threat can be neutralized, approaching any world in the terraforming project is prohibited by law. The immigration program is thus suspended indefinitely for the safety of all participants.

Terracor Public Directive: Stationbound passenger ships are to hold at Callisto until further notice, by order of EarthGov. Passengers already boarded will disembark and receive complementary hotel vouchers. We regret any inconvenience and are confident travel to your new homes will resume shortly. Please retain your tickets to ensure priority boarding at that time. Have a nice day.

"Not routine." Aaron Raner maneuvered Thromberg Station's housekeeping barge 20BES-B, call sign *Bessie B*, into position. "NOT ROUTINE, Ops." The screen filled with a feral mass of metal and cable, rotating around a lopsided core that looked to be an attachment anchor.

One that hadn't done the job, given the trash was inbound for the freight docking ring.

"No one's better at catching rogues, *Bessie B*."

That reputation why he was rousted from his bunk whenever there was a dangerously anomalous hunk of trash, as now, and why, wherever station crew gathered, there'd be bets placed.

Raner shook his head. He'd helped build Thromberg, operating a pusher fifteen times the size and power of the barge, but who cared now? *Bessie B* was Admin's way to keep him occupied until his retirement to Earth.

Fine with him. He preferred being outside.

"Don't tell me you put money down again, Ops." This shift's voice was a friend's, Myriam Malley. She'd have Hugh in his carry sling. The baby, and his parents, should have been sent back to Earth, there being strict rules against adding non-crew personnel to a finite life support system. To even work on a station meant being temporarily sterilized at Terracor's expense before arrival.

Malley'd had the procedure all right; not her fault it failed to take, a consequence she discovered after Hugh's father sailed off in his fancy Earther freighter. The station—as adverse to parting with an excellent com operator as it was to letting the bigwigs at Terracor know they'd goofed and could be sued—logged Hugh Malley as a new member of Thromberg's staff, not that they'd put him on the payroll. Fortunately, little Hugh quickly became a station favorite and friends, including Raner, helped out—youngsters being rare.

Except in the jam-packed sections housing the immigrants. Raner felt bemused whenever he saw children playing games through the corridors. Games they'd no room for in their quarters.

Quarters they'd not be leaving anytime soon, word was—

"Then I won't. Tell you about the bet." Malley's tone changed. "Seriously, can't we let this one hit? Forester's on me to get ships moving."

There'd be a maintenance shift working under Thromberg's skin. Likely a repair crew or two up inside, keeping up with the patches. Immie kids roaming where they shouldn't—

"Tell him—belay that." Stress aplenty on Malley, sitting com this shift of all shifts, what with the crap boiling out of Sol and complaints from everywhere else. The dockmaster might be a cold-hearted jerk but Thromberg needed those ships.

"I've got it, Ops," Raner replied calmly. "Advise the dockmaster to hold for my all clear. *Bessie B* out."

Thromberg rose beyond the little barge, blinding white where it faced the white dwarf, a constellation of its own lights winking where it spun to shadow itself. Its enormous central core had docking rings at either end, making it resemble a dog's bone, and every Terracor station was the same. Each marked the jump point to waiting new worlds. The future.

Maybe, word was.

Raner fired the final burst to match the trash's trajectory and velocity, setting the barge in its path like a sheepdog on his grandmother's farm facing off a stray ewe. The central section of Thromberg had a thinner whipple shield and was more vulnerable, an unadvertised side-effect of risk/benefit cost-cuts.

The docking rings, where large objects approached on a regular basis, had a thickened shield and reinforced underlayers. Malley wasn't wrong. By Raner's estimate, if unstopped the trash should do little more than add another scar—

Still, always a chance it would strike exposed equipment or an airlock. Not to mention the harm a moving mass this size could inflict on a ship already in motion and the stationer spared a lightning quick glance up at another monitor, alight with ident codes. Three waiting at the edge of the warnoff. That unprecedented number inbound, hopefully beginning deceleration; a growing jam of traffic creating its own hazard. Those onboard were riding the alert from EarthGov: seek a port, stay put.

Hard to expect patience from that lot, let alone from the ships locked to the station's paired docking rings by the auto alert. Raner sympathized. He'd friends on most ships serving Thromberg. Truth be told, he'd more friends outside than in.

No ident in sight for the *Merry Mate II,* home of his closest, Gabby and Jer Pardell. They'd left on their fool mission over a month back, before the madness took hold; run silent, according to Malley, to keep their course on the hush.

Not routine.

He'd a job to do. Squinting at his quarry, Raner slipped fingers and thumbs into the control gloves. There were four sets of grapples, paired for a human operator. Designed to manipulate tools and materials, the claws weren't intended to handle a moving object larger than the barge.

For this? Raner wanted hands.

Stage Two: Autolysis - self-digestion and rigor mortis.

EarthGov Classified Internal Memo: Effective immediately, inbound ships must prove they have not visited or done business with an impacted planet or the Quill homeworld within the past Earth year. Otherwise, they will not be permitted to proceed through Sol System.

Terracor Directive to Station Admins: EarthGov now considers our stations and ships plying between them to be potential sources of Quill Contamination.

Terracor has taken the firm and reasonable stance that, as stations were built after the terraforming was complete and, as deep explorers (the only other possible source of Quill) transit directly to Callisto in Sol System without contact here, there is no credible risk whatsoever and we should be exempt from any restrictions other than those to protect our guests and personnel.

EarthGov has rejected our stance, forcing us to send a delegation to the System Court.

While we await the court's findings, every station is to abide by EarthGov regulations and continue to house those already there, including our guests in the immigration program. Terracor appreciates the strain this puts on your resources and will send additional supplies.

To conserve those resources, numbers on each station must not be allowed to increase. In accordance with the emergency measures act signed by each guest and those conducting business on our station, birth control will be added to the food shipments.

To alleviate crowding in the short term, you will receive gravity inducers in order to make your outer industrial/manufacturing levels habitable.

Respond with your implementation schedule as soon as possible.

One hundred and forty-seven bars operated on Thromberg Station, give or take. They ranged from the ornate recreations of Earth pubs frequented by business types, wealthier immigrants, and Earther crews in matching uniforms, to the illegal temps that sprouted like weeds under the recycling level.

Between those extremes was the comfortably shabby Bags' End, located Spinward 4 within the freight docking ring. At shift change, its metal floor—no synth rubber here—ran with mag boots, boots as easily belonging to a working spacer as a stationer. As both wore coveralls meant to fit inside a spacesuit, the only way to tell them apart was to spot Thromberg's blue-and-red patch on a shoulder.

An upper level overlooked the bar. In a back corner was the large round table unofficially reserved for Senior Barge Pilot Aaron Raner and his friends, Myriam Malley and Mats Logan.

And those who sought their company. Spacers. Captains and owners who'd things to say off channels. In turn they relied on Raner and his stationer friends to keep them informed, Thromberg's dockmaster reserving such courtesy for the big Earther ships, not what he privately called the riffraff.

Referring, of course, to these independent operators. Their small nimble ships moved between the stations, redistributing goods the Earthers couldn't be bothered to sort beforehand and shifting what stations now made to market. Their ships weren't pretty, no one wore uniforms, and the stations couldn't run without them.

Tonight, as Raner watched the seats fill, nodding a greeting to each arrival, he wished to be anywhere else. Malley had caught the com chatter. Logan, who headed second shift security picked up more from the corridors. Added to what he'd heard for himself on the ring?

Trouble was coming for those here.

"Nice grab, Raner." Eda Nix, captain of the venerable *Haida V,* claimed her chair, thumping down a mug and a bag of crisps. The bag she ripped open and pushed to the center of the table. Spacer courtesy, to provide what you had. Her first officer, Ben Drafuss, dropped in the seat next to her, donating a platter of fried pickles to the snack pile.

"Thanks." Malley deftly shifted baby Hugh to her other breast, then grabbed a pickle she aimed at Raner. "Forester's grumbling. Says you should have stuck to the net."

Would have tangled at the first contact. "My call," Raner pointed out. Yes, *Bessie B* had new scratches and her left grapples had ripped off, adding to the trash, but he'd salvaged the parts. He'd assemble a new rig in the shop.

"Won me some cash," Drafuss proclaimed with a gap-toothed grin, tipping her mug to Raner's. Nix laughed and joined in. *The Lady Jade*'s Corcoran and Chase of the tanker *Amiagi* waved for another round.

To Raner's right, newcomers to the table, J. Smith Sr. and J. Smith Jr. of the *Solar Queen,* twitched at the laughter and gripped their mugs. From what he'd heard of the capable pair, they'd no problem sitting with stationers. He'd a feeling their tension meant they'd bad news of their own.

Bolblksevik of the *Sac-to* squeezed his bulk into the final seat beside Nix, elbows hitting the table. "Stinkers and Rats," he greeted, answered by a round of friendly jibes. The pair from the *Queen* relaxed in the presence of their sponsor. Bolb tipped his bald, scarred head to squint at Raner. "That trash o'yours. Heard an Earther got pushy 'n knocked an array off *Calypso's Twin*."

"Accident?" Raner watched the word silence those around the table. No love lost between those who hauled station-to-station and ships from Sol.

Nix spoke up first. "That'd be my guess. Wouldn't have taken much."

"*Twin* rattles when she hits any g's at all," Drafuss agreed. "Wonder is she hasn't fallen apart by now. Family's hit hard times."

"Who hasn't?" Smith Sr.murmured. "Naught to be done."

Logan glanced at Raner, lifting a bushy eyebrow. The look suggested a discrete inspection; possibly an emergency loan. The pair had friends in the station bank.

Where ship repairs might no longer be a priority. Raner shook his head slightly. "Word is, ring's filling up."

Captains and ship owners exchanged glances. "That why turnaround's slower'n frozen honey?" Bolb glowered. "I'm to Oia Station next. Got a load of hydroponic sheathing."

"Can you sell it here?"

Eyebrows shot ceilingward. "Why the hell would I?"

Nix silenced him with a gesture. "Raner's got something to say."

With a grim nod, the stationer leaned forward. "The latest Terracor freighter brought new equipment—word is the station's to modify Outward Five to habitable. For the immies," when faces looked blank.

Bolb shrugged and relaxed. "Crowding's not our problem."

Corcoran slammed a hand on the table, scattering crisps. "It will be, fool. Stations stop manufacturing, what going in our holds?"

"You've a bigger problem." Raner pressed his lips together, then circled a finger on the table. Every eye followed the gesture. "There's a new reg about to come down. Looks like only ships certified as contamination-free will be moving."

A shocked silence, then voices overlapped, angry ones. "What's that mean?" "This about the Quill?" "None of us even know what one is."

Then, over the rest, "Ask me, EarthGov's made all this up!"

Another rumor, this one traveling with the ships as well as along station corridors. Raner frowned. "Why would they?"

"You know why. To cover that the terraforming projects failed. Cover their arses."

"Should have kept funding deep space." From Chase. Nods all around.

"We can't sit here, paying for air and hookups," Nix protested.

"No one's locking down the *Jade*—"

"Better here than Hamilton Station." This from the senior Smith, his expression dark. "They refused to let us dock. Claimed to be full."

"We could see they weren't," the junior Smith said. "They didn't want us, is all. Afraid of the Quill."

"See?" Bolb roared. "Nonsense's spreading like a plague. Mark my words, next'll be mandatory inspections—"

The table erupted again. Some objecting, others citing past protocols. Raner sat back and listened, his eyes hooded. Terracor hadn't wanted news spread between stations, not yet, maybe not ever—and here it was, landing in his lap. Hamilton Station, refusing ships.

Not routine.

"Bad time?"

As one, those seated shut their mouths to glare at the interloper. Raner leaned around Logan to see a stranger in a suit. The sort of expensive suit never seen in Bags' End.

"Mr. Leland," Logan greeted, his tone constable-cold. "This isn't your kind of place."

"If you've ships, it is." The interloper grabbed a chair from another table and pulled it close.

Before he could sit, Bolb kicked it over. "You heard our friend. Slum somewhere else!"

Leland didn't blink. "Holds full?" He patted a pocket meaningfully. "None of you need business?"

Raner could see the spacers reassessing Leland. The senior Smith reached down to pick up the chair. "Always interested in business. If you can pay."

Logan scowled. "Man owns half the restaurants and shops on Thromberg."

"More, but who's counting," Leland replied, taking the seat. He folded his manicured hands on the table. "I won't waste your time. I want transport to Earth and I'm willing to—"

The rest was drowned under laughter. "You and everyone on Thromberg," Nix gasped once she'd caught her breath. "We'd never get clearance to go there—"

"And if we did, they'd impound our ships at Sol."

"I'll pay any fines incurred." Leland offered. "More. Enough to buy new ships and—"

"You ever seen a riot, Mr. Leland?" Logan broke in, his voice with an edge. "Because that's what'll happen if any of these ships take on passengers—"

He stopped, hand cupping his ear.

As did Malley.

Raner, having felt the warning buzz along his jaw, was already listening to the alert. "Attention! Attention! Station alert Beta-Four. Repeat. Station alert Beta-Four."

Throughout Bags' End those stationers not too drunk to comprehend were moving, and those unable to help themselves were being moved. Beta-Four meant an inbound ship had declared an emergency. Those stationers not assigned to the ring were to shelter in their airtight quarters or don suits. While thousands more on Thromberg had neither—

Raner didn't budge. Wouldn't, truth be told, given those sitting with him were equally at risk but unwarned.

"Hush it." This from Malley, clearly getting a full brief. Her expression changed as she listened and her eyes went to Raner with a question. He nodded. She lowered her hand and addressed the table. "It's the *Merry Mate II*. Coming in on full auto. No com—not yet."

"And that means—" Leland asked.

Raner, on his feet and moving, heard Nix say, "Friends in trouble."

Stage Three: Bloat – visible signs of rot.

> EarthGov Top Secret Memo: Patrol ships are to be positioned in the transit lane at Callisto as a deterrent. They are not to engage or board any inbound ships.
>
> Terracor to All Station Admins: We stand with you at this difficult time. Remind your personnel it is against station regulations to fraternize with passengers, non-Terracor staff, and/or ship crews. Information received from Terracor is not to be shared.
>
> Hamilton Station, we are waiting on your implementation schedule. Please provide at once.

Raner stood in front of the airlock door, staring at the indicators as they ticked through. Someone had pushed a suit at him. He held it under an arm, not feeling the chill of the docking ring, not daring to feel much of anything.

Logan had returned to his security cubby, a call away; Malley to Ops. Nix and Bolb stood behind him, the presence of captains carving a respectful distance. Not that there weren't mutters from the gathered crowd. Spacer turf, this was. An incoming ship in distress was spacer business and a stationer had gall to interfere.

They were welcome to mutter. Gabby and Jer were family. Stayed with him during the *Mate's* refit last round, station gravity and medics needful to Gabby in the early stages of her pregnancy, when things hadn't looked good, and Raner could hardly breathe, thinking what might have gone wrong.

It was space. Anything could and that Malley hadn't received a word from the *Mate* beyond the auto beacon meant it had.

Raner moved as the indicators flipped to green and the lock clicked, heaving open the door and dashing inside. Sense prevailed as Nix and Bolb pulled the door closed behind him. Might not be air on the other side. Despite the urgency to know, he stopped to put on the suit.

It wasn't station issue, with its blithe assumption you'd be back inside within nine hours, give or take, meaning if you lost hold or did some other fool move you'd die about then, or sooner. This, Raner realized respectfully, was full spacer gear. Not new, but a good suit, well maintained. He'd check the source. Offer thanks.

Later.

Suited up, he switched to internal air, waiting for its metallic tang on the back of his throat before trying the airlock. The assembly should have a firm hold on the ship outside.

Should. Autos weren't a hundred percent and the *Mate* was old, a weathered family ship kept going with hard work and smarts. By comparison, Thromberg Station, all the stations, were cobbled together bus depots built to a budget, paint barely dry. He should know—

The indicator flashed. Solid seal, air beyond. Raner stayed in the suit as he opened the door and entered the umbilical, using handholds to pull himself through to the *Mate's* outer door.

He keyed in her access code and if the spacers on the ring were aggravated by his pushing ahead, there'd be some surely livid to know a stationer had the code to one of their precious ships.

Gabby's notion, to give Raner the code during their last time together on the ship, the station night before they'd left. Jer had nodded in that slow thoughtful way he had, then broken out a bottle. They'd avoided any talk of the troubles or the Quill. Gabby'd let him feel the surprisingly powerful kick and flutter of the life inside her—

God. Raner swallowed bile, hesitated. He didn't want to go in, didn't want to know—

Had to, didn't he.

Bracing himself, Raner finished keying in the code. When the door sank inward and back, he stepped inside the *Mate's* airlock.

The inner door opened once the outer closed and sealed behind him, a green light shining in welcome. Raner took off the suit's helmet and it was only after taking his first breath it dawned on him he might just have inhaled something deadly.

Too late now. Anyway, the air smelled of supper and laundry, more welcoming than his own quarters. Raner tucked the helmet in the storage cubby. "Jer? Gabby? It's Aaron—"

He called as he went through the entire ship, pausing to listen for a reply that never came. When he grew hoarse, he sucked water warm from the suit, his own sweat recycled. *Not routine.*

Think, he told himself. The *Mate* didn't have escape pods. What she did have was an atmo-capable shuttle, Jer's particular pride.

But when Raner stepped over the sill he found the interior of the shuttle as empty as the ship, Jer and Gabby's suits still hanging from their clips.

He wandered back to the bridge, stood with gloved hands digging into the back of Jer's well-patched slingchair. Wearily, he pressed the button blinking on the com panel. "Raner, Ops. Ship's empty. They're gone."

A crackle, then Malley's voice, quiet, professional. "Didn't hear that. Just like you didn't hear me tell you to access her last logs before the station claims her as salvage."

Damn it, she was right. The instant he left the *Mate,* Forester would send in a crew to strip whatever had value. Sure as space was deadly the ship herself didn't, not to the station, and they'd get no answers.

Raner unzipped the suit and let it fall to the floor, then sank uneasily into Jer's seat. "Where'd you put them, Jer? Gabby?"

He leaned back, fingers on the worn armrests, and looked around. Spacer-tidy. Everything secured in its place. No sign of a hasty departure or disaster—

His eyes spotted a piece of tape. Raner pulled the panel close on its arm. There was a faint arrow drawn on the tape, pointing to a pad on the side.

A gene lock? Hardly able to believe what he was doing, Raner licked his thumb then pressed it on the pad.

Buttons lit. A cavity opened, revealing a set of tapes that looked to be older than the ship, and he hadn't been ready for secrets, not from Jer and Gabby—

"Hello Aaron." The voice—Jer's voice—filled the bridge. "If you're hearing this, we're dead. Ship's yours. We filed the paperwork before leaving the station. Don't blame me. You know how Gabby is—"

"It's a reasonable precaution." Gabby's voice, matter-of-fact. "We can't know what's going to happen."

Had happened—

"True," her husband agreed. "Hey, if you don't want the *Mate,* Aaron, go ahead and sell her, but grab our personals. Especially these tapes. There's family stuff you can give little Aaron when you think he's ready."

Aaron?

"Hush. That's no way to tell him—"

"Want me to stop and re-record?"

"No. No, Jer, this is—this is hard enough."

"I know." A sigh. "We're naming our son after you, old friend. Serves you right, being like a brother to us both."

A tear rolled down, caught in stubble—

"Now listen up. Gabby and me, we're taking the shuttle down so little Aaron's born on a world. A citizen with full rights. We'll make a record to prove it. But—" The voice grew husky. "If you're hearing this—if the shuttle's come back without us—Aaron could be inside…"

With a gasp, Raner leapt to his feet and ran. Jer's voice receded behind him. "…he's yours now, to take care of. You'll do that for us, I know…"

He stumbled back in the shuttle. Still empty. "What am I looking for, Jer?" Raner whispered, unconsciously gripping the arm of his friend's suit. The *Mate* was a family ship. A shuttle designed to protect the most vulnerable—Jer'd said something about auto-encasement—

The stationer dropped to his knees to look under the benches. There. A hardened little ball, lodged in a corner.

Picking it up as tenderly as if the baby within could feel him, Raner hurried to the ship's med cupboard and when the scanner detected a heart beating within he let out a ragged breath.

He put his work-rough hand on the case. "I promise to take care of you, Aaron Pardell, as if you were my own.

"Just—just give me some time to figure out how."

Stage Four: Active Decay – liquification.

> EarthGov Top Secret to Patrol Commanders: Any ship could be contaminated by Quill. Maintain your perimeter and protect the system. Humanity relies on you.
>
> Terracor to Terracor Ship Captains: Stay put.
>
> Terracor Public Announcement: Ticket holders, we regret to inform you hotel vouchers are being discontinued.

Not routine. Raner slid down the wall to sit on the floor. A carpet, only here. A cupboard held books and miniature sets of clothing, along with stacks of what he presumed were diapers—he'd never changed a baby.

Hadn't dreamed of one like this.

He rested his hands on his knees, the right holding a spatula, the left a wrench, and stared at the tiny figure in—whatever you called what spacers used for their babies. It looked like a clear pot with a lid suspended above. A pot lined with a soft fabric featuring trees full of oversized monkeys and birds. Happy. Playful.

He'd brought the case here. Placed it on the pull-out shelf to administer the release spray—trust Jer and Gabby to have it in the med cupboard, with instructions—and what greeted his eyes as it dissolved was breathing and very much alive. A perfect miniature human—

—except for a network of gold running beneath paper-fine skin. Thicker, almost like ropes, over torso and upper limbs, faint on head, hands, and feet, and Raner didn't know if it was a side-effect of the protective fluids within the case or something peculiar about *this* baby.

When he'd first touched the baby's skin, he'd felt a shock like a static charge. They both had, for the baby cried in protest.

Raner'd dropped him on the mushy remnants of the case. Then felt guilty. Probably nothing but a lingering imbalance of electrons in the solution, dissipated with contact. He'd slipped his hands under the baby's head and legs.

Only to receive another, even stronger shock as poor Aaron convulsed.

Hence spoon and spatula. Crude tools to lift Gabby and Jer's precious son and put him down on a welcoming landscape of life nowhere near this place, created by parents he'd lost, and after that?

That was when Raner backed away, to lean on a wall and slide to the floor. *Not routine.*

It didn't matter. Gabby and Jer had entrusted him with their son and he'd be damned if he'd fail. He got to his feet and used the utensils to tuck the blanket over the still-whimpering baby. The cover seemed soothing; the head turned, mouth working.

Hungry. How long could a revived baby last without nourishment? "Hang on, little Aaron," the stationer said gently, feeling the weight of the future settle around him.

* * *

"Save the formula for emergencies. I brought what milk I had in the freezer—I'll get you more." Spotting a hook, Malley hung the sling containing a sleeping Hugh from it as Logan handed Raner a promisingly full bag.

Staying in the doorway, the security officer frowned. "Jer and Gabby."

"As I said. Something must have gone wrong outside." Raner'd locked the hidden compartment. Removed Jer's helpful piece of tape. "They'd known the risks and planned ahead. Left me the *Mate* and their son. His name's—" He had to swallow. "They named him Aaron. Aaron Pardell."

His friends stared at him as if he'd grown a second head.

"We can worry about all that later. I need help," Raner said impatiently. "We do," he emphasized, gesturing to the tiny person in the pot.

Malley sniffed. "Your Aaron needs a change. I'll take care of it—you can practice on Hugh first." This as she sailed by.

Raner blocked her. "You can't touch him, not with your hands." Not even gloved hands, he'd discovered. "Use these." He held out the utensils, now wrapped in gauze. They'd do until he could get to the dock and scrounge the parts he needed. Get his own tools. He'd need those.

Malley looked her disbelief. "Because the baby gives shocks? That's impossible."

"No. Because being touched hurts him. See for yourself if you don't believe me." He spread his arms wide and stepped aside.

Malley looked down. "What I see is desperation." Her fingers went to the fastenings of her coveralls only to drop. "There's a warm bottle in Hugh's bag."

Logan eased back and away while Raner crouched to dig through an assortment of strange objects.

"Outside pocket."

Finding it, he fumbled with the lid. Malley took the bottle, flipped the lid open with a thumb, and handed it back. "In his mouth."

"I know that part," Raner muttered. He lowered the nipple, inordinately pleased when tiny Aaron took hold.

Only to turn away and whimper, milk spilling on the blanket.

With a nudge, Malley pushed Raner aside, taking the bottle. "Watch me." She let a drop fall into the still-open mouth, then another. When the little tongue began to move, she slipped the nipple into the baby's mouth, holding it at a slight angle. "Like that."

Raner took the bottle, holding it as he'd been shown in a hand that wanted to tremble. "I can't do this," he whispered.

"You can build a space station. You can do this. He needs to learn, too—there. That's it." To the baby, softer, as Aaron began to suck in earnest. "We should take him to the station hospital." Her eyes shot to Raner's. "Why aren't we?"

"The *Mate*'s his home." Raner didn't dare tell he'd tried to get permission to disembark with the baby—permission refused so quickly he'd had a moment's panic over revealing Aaron's existence at all.

"You said they were lost outside." Logan held out Jer and Gabby's helmets, eyebrow lifting.

"Those are spares," Raner lied. The truth was too dangerous. The way panic was rising everywhere? Anyone who'd landed on a planet would be suspect. To die on one—meant the Quill.

Whether true or not, he wouldn't risk it, or his friends. Raner gave his attention to the baby, feeling Logan's intense stare. "Doesn't matter how good you are," he went on, "space walks are risky."

"You're sticking with that."

He looked up at his oldest friend. "What else could have happened?"

"I'll put these back," Logan said at last.

"Wait." There'd be more questions and not from friends. Raner thought furiously. "Malley's right. Aaron needs medical attention—but not here. My uncle's a neurospecialist on Titan—"

"You can't be serious," Malley objected. "Admin won't let you leave."

"The station can't stop a ship that wants to go—best they can do is detach before there's damage to any connections."

"You do this, you'll need crew—at least one other. Fuel. Supplies. How are you going to pay—" Logan read his face and swore under his breath. "Leland."

"Leland."

* * *

At the chosen time, near the end of second shift and Thromberg's official night, Samuel Leland showed up at the *Mate's* airlock in coveralls, bringing his daughter and young granddaughter. Behind them came a somber group of four, two wearing aprons and clutching small packages Raner later learned contained kitchen knives. On Logan's insistence, none brought luggage. The station, in his words, felt ready to explode.

None were immigrants. These were people Leland had brought to Thromberg to work in his businesses.

They wouldn't be crowded. The Pardells had been more numerous once and the *Mate* had three vacant cabins—vacant once Raner and his new crewmate, Angie Fesson, on loan from the *Haida,* cleared them, putting the pitiful miscellany of personal effects old and newer into the *Mate's* holds.

Leland hugged each of the four, pressing envelopes into their hands. Raner stood by as Leland's daughter argued with her father, urgent and low, urging him to come.

Leland shook his head and stepped back, waving to Raner to close the airlock.

"Wait. You there. Wait, please." As if the quiet words were a signal, figures began to emerge from night-dim corners along the curve of the docking ring. Dozens. Hundreds. Clutching children. Carrying bags. Moving towards every airlock in sight.

Several headed for the *Mate.* "Go!" Leland ordered, seeing them. "Now!"

Raner didn't move. Thromberg was home to stationers and even spacers. It wasn't in any sense to these people. "We can take some." He beckoned to the nearest family.

"The hell you will."

Raner shoved the man out of his way. "Go through the next hatch," he told the grateful parents as they went by him, hustling a trio of young children. An older couple hurried up and he let them board. "That's all we can hold," he told the next to approach, stepping inside the airlock. "Try the *Haida V.* Ask for Captain Nix. Three locks that way." He pointed.

They listened. The ones coming behind didn't hear or didn't care, seeing only a closing airlock and the end of hope. Raner caught a glimpse of Leland being grabbed and tossed aside.

Then the door clicked home. Numb, he keyed the lock.

They were in it now. He hit the emergency undock warning with a closed fist, the alarm shrieking through the door plate. It would give Thromberg time to disconnect—if any stationers could get through what was now a mob.

* * *

Raner sat in the Jer's slingchair, listening to the com. There'd been a brief "Be safe" from Malley before the station feed devolved into a babble of futile protests. It wasn't only the *Merry Mate II* flouting procedures and blowing from the ring. It was every independent starship—even the glittery casino *Aces Adrift* announced it was heading for Earth, filled beyond capacity with those desperate to escape. The captains hadn't planned it. Raner doubted their passengers had either. Survival had become its own imperative.

Fesson wore a headset to follow the ship-to-ship chatter. Her expression had gone from stoic to bleak over the past hour. "*Calypso's Twin*'s cleared the station. Last and slow as a tortoise."

No plan—other than the one forced on them all by the necessities of space travel. Once far enough from Thromberg, the ships would ignite their initiation matrices simultaneously, opening a fissure in normal space through which they'd jump as one to Sol System. They'd emerge at the transit point near Callisto, then begin the week-long trip in-system to Earth. Staying together offered the possibility of mutual aid and rescue; *Twin* wasn't the only ship running on hope and fumes, and far from the only ship overloaded.

The station com crackled. "Raner. Logan here. Glad you got away in time. Sorry to say I was right."

Raner closed his eyes. "Riots?"

"Cropping up stationwide. Stationers upset about losing Outward Five and their jobs. Immies upset because they couldn't get a ship out—and no way the big Earther ships are letting them on board. Admin's ordered the bulkheads closed until people regain their senses—which no one will do locked in boxes. 'Tween us, this keeps up? It'll only get worse. Tell Terracor and EarthGov. They've got to help us."

"I will." Stations were fragile bubbles of breathable air; making them riot-proof hadn't been in the specs. "Keep your head down. Take care of Malley and Hugh."

"On it. You and your boy sniff some real air for me. Logan out."

His boy. Aaron Pardell, sweetly oblivious to the onrush of disaster. Raner checked his watch. "Mealtime," he said, floating up. He'd used his codes to shut down the gravity, conserving fuel—and to keep those not used to space flight in their cabins, strapped to their beds. Against regs; Fesson hadn't argued. "We good here?"

"In sync with *Haida*," Fesson assured him, her former ship setting the course for the rest. She shook her head. "*Twin*'s not looking good."

Raner glanced at the display, seeing the gap. Unless the others delayed, *Twin* would miss the linked jump and have to go alone. "Sync us with her instead," he ordered. "Let Nix know we'll follow in as tight as we can. We're not leaving anyone."

Fesson gave him an assessing look then nodded. "Copy that, Captain."

* * *

Raner slipped his hands into the control gloves. The rig he'd attached to Aaron's pot-bed wasn't fancy—he'd had no time for it—but he'd recalibrated the articulated handlers to gentle and covered the clawtips with tiny socks from the drawer. It looked like a colorful spider. Without gravity, he'd discovered the reason for the pot-bed. A gentle suction kept the baby oriented and on the bottom; a stronger one removed messes.

He fed Aaron, his thoughts on everything else. Had his actions precipitated the riots? Had he said too much—or too little? Was this—any of this—his fault?

"We're synced with *Calypso's Twin*, Captain," Angie reported. The baby gave a slow blink at the new voice. "*Twin* says they'll buy the beer, next port."

"Deal." Raner bent to the baby and whispered, "Hear that, Aaron? Helping each other—that's the key to helping everyone—you've no idea what I'm saying, do you?" Yet. Aaron Pardell had a lot to learn that wasn't in any station manual. He'd have to make teaching tapes—

Raner shook his head. "Don't plan a future till you've the shape of it, Aaron." Might wind up living on Titan, near the research hospital. He'd a message ready to send his uncle when they reached Sol System, giving the barest description of the baby's state. He'd omitted the station. Made up a story of having found the ship in orbit.

Thromberg and his friends were in trouble enough.

After—they'd sell the *Mate* and settle in the cottage he owned on Earth. Become grounders. Jer and Gabby would forgive him.

"I'm a fool." There was no future for Aaron Pardell—for whatever he was—on Earth. Raner used a claw to unwrap a corner of the blanket, revealing a foot and tiny leg. The golden lines hadn't faded. Aaron spat out the nipple and whimpered, as if the exposure troubled him as much as it did the man staring down.

Replacing the blanket, Raner removed the mostly-empty bottle. He put down the cover, securing the pot-bed.

"Transit point in twenty, Captain. You stowed?"

Raner surveyed the small cabin. He retrieved the bottle from its float midair and put it with the others in a bag to be washed. Everything else was secure, another habit to teach the child. "Yes. I'll check our passengers."

* * *

Fesson grinned at Raner as he floated to his seat. "The rest have jumped. We're at four point three and counting. What's it like?"

He strapped in. "Jump?"

"Sol System." Her eyes sparkled. "Never been. That's why I volunteered to crew for you. Finally, an adventure."

Raner found himself speechless.

"Wrong reason?"

"No. No, it's—" Startling, from someone who'd grown up on a starship. But if that was all you knew, Raner thought, stories of the blue ball of Earth must seem fantastic. "—I hope you aren't disappointed."

"Find out in ten, nine, eight—"

He watched the boards. "Confirming *Twin* in sync."

"—confirmed—five, four—translight online—two—one—We're go! We're go! We're go!"

At the first "go" Raner reached forward and pressed the button to cause the *Mate*'s drive to tear a hole in space that would suck them through, an action affecting the control on their sister ship at the same instant.

If either ship's matrix faltered at this point they'd be extinguished without knowing.

The bridge lights flickered off then on again, Fesson gave an exultant "WHOOOP!" and Raner dared take another breath. They'd done it.

Suddenly the *Mate* careened sideways to avoid a collision, her alarm sounding. *Danger, Damage, Thieves!* The com overloaded with a roar like the mob on the docking ring—shouts, multiple, over a drone of incredible words—

"They're firing on us! They're firing on us!"

Stage Five: Skeletonization – dry remains that will linger.

EarthGov Public Statement: The deplorable loss of life in the Callisto Incident is a reminder we mustn't give in to fear. We will defeat the Quill and remove the contamination from our waiting worlds but, until we do, it is up to each and every one of us, here and on our magnificent space stations, to work together.

EarthGov Top Secret Memo: Let Terracor know their stations have to keep their populations in order. If they can't, we'll suspend shipments until assured docking is safe for our ships and crews.

Terracor to Station Admins: EarthGov will abandon you at any provocation. From now on, you are authorized to use whatever measures become necessary to maintain order on your docking rings. You have our prayers.

"Repeat, repeat, repeat. Sync to *Haida V.* All ships ready and GO. Now! Now! Now!"

Strange how the button went down by itself. Even stranger, how slow a motion could be when the result shattered the reality of speed—

The lights flickered off then on. Off again, their faces lit by glows as the *Mate* struggled to restore systems never meant to endure jump twice in quick succession.

Let alone take fire.

Raner silenced the alarm, eyes locked on the displayed idents, each shifting as ships moved toward Thromberg Station. One winked out. Then another.

As for those simply not there—Raner gripped the armrests. "Status of *Calypso's Twin.*"

"I—I don't know." Fesson's cheeks glistened with tears. "We lost sync at Sol—"

"Please see if anyone knows," he told her, forcing himself to be steady. Be calm. It helped when the lights came back on.

Didn't when he spotted an ident abruptly move against the flow, like trash tumbling out of control. The com crackled again. "This is the *Grimoire.*" Was there a faint tremor beneath the stern voice? "Damn Earthers ripped us open—we've a fire below. Need a ride."

"*Merry Mate II.* On our way. Stand by *Grimoire.*" They were closest, tanks still full.

"Captain, she's a freighter. A big'un and tumbling on the long axis," Fesson warned.

Routine. Raner eyed the output with something like content. "I've got it." He took the controls, reached forward to code in the unlawful. "Venting the holds." With the air would go the oddments and small treasures of the Pardells, but it let them bring survivors in through the freight doors, not the airlock.

Gabby and Jer would have done the same.

* * *

Their suits brought the stench of ash into the *Mate.* Ten crew, many hurt, all in shock, and the last to enter the ship proper held the seared stumps of arms to her sides and swore at Fesson, resisting help. "Take me to the bridge. Where's Jer and Gabby?"

Another friend. Senior Systems Engineer Rosalind Fournier. "They're gone, Ros," Raner called out.

"Raner?" She looked for him in the crowded corridor. Actually laughed at him. "Should have guessed."

"Where's your captain?"

Someone else spoke. "She shot him."

Raner stared. Rosalind's attempt to shrug turned into a flinch, quickly hidden. "Bastard got in my way." A round of murmured agreement.

He didn't want to know. The *Grimoire* and her captain were heading for the star; her injured needed the station's hospital. Raner seized Rosalind's belt to tow her to the bridge, leaving Fesson to secure the rest.

* * *

Raner blinked at the com panel, then rubbed his eyes. "Ops, we can't keep sitting out here. I've told you I've seriously wounded people on board—give me something near S17—" Nearest the lift to the hospital—

"The situation hasn't changed, *Mate*. Hold position like everyone else. We've suffered extensive damage. Damage you and your friends left behind—"

The story hadn't changed in three days either. "We're dying, Ops," he said heavily. The *Merry Mate II* had vented a crewmember from the *Grimoire* yesterday—Rosalind insisting they strip the body of anything useful first. "The airlocks have emerg umbilicals. There's no risk to the station." Priority docking went to any ship in trouble and they all were. This was as far from routine as it got.

"Not my call, *Mate*."

Raner swept up the headset. About to switch to private, he caught Rosalind's scornful look. Stationer versus spacer.

They'd die of it if something wasn't done. Raner put down the set. "Benjamin. I know it's you. This is Aaron Raner. Get me the dockmaster."

"Forester's left orders not to be disturbed."

Rosalind lifted an eloquent stump. She'd held open a hatch to save her people from the fire; the ship's medic hadn't been able to save her hands.

She'd given him instructions, if the station remained stubborn.

Raner steadied himself. "Forester talks to me now and in private, or we start aiming our dead at the nearest Earther ship."

"Damn it, Raner."

"*Haida V* has a couple ready to go. Immie children. You want that?"

"Wait. I'll get him."

Time passed, measured in the thumps of his heart, Fesson's quiet voice as she relayed status reports to the waiting fleet of ships. Rosalind leaned back, her eyes pinched shut. She'd refused more pain meds, wanting to be sharp. Nix and the rest—they'd asked him to be their common voice, were listening now. None protested the threat. Were they strapping on jets to deliver the first dreadful message?

"Dockmaster Forester. Raner? That you? What the hell are you doing out there—don't answer. You're fired."

"Captain Raner and I speak for these ships. Let us dock. We've injured—"

"Because EarthGov fired on the lot of you—"

How could he know? "A mistake—"

"Doesn't matter. The Patrol attached a squeal to your ships warning not to let you approach—that you're fugitives. The entire station heard it. There's been more rioting. The population's afraid. No one wants you here."

Rosalind made a cut off gesture; Raner muted the com. "We can't keep the immies on our ships."

He swallowed, thinking of Aaron and Tanya, Leland's granddaughter. Of the others below and on all the ships. Of limited resources driving terrible decisions that mustn't happen, shouldn't be conceived—not with the station in reach.

He unmuted the com. "Forester, let us return our passengers to the station. That'll buy time."

"They chose to leave."

The cold-hearted—"You know you can't stop us," Raner said grimly.

"Check visual, *Captain*. We already have."

* * *

Suited stationers inched over the docking ring, welding airlocks shut. Raner had no doubt the same was happening at the other end of Thromberg, where passenger ships from Earth docked. Had docked.

Fesson handed him her headset. "Captain Nix for you on ship-to-ship."

"On speaker, please." Raner leaned back. "Nix."

"Earth turned on us. Your friends look to finish the job." He'd never heard her voice thick with rage. "We're on our last day of breathable, hear me? Hell if I'll let my people suffocate with air in reach."

The station. He closed his eyes, listening for Aaron. The baby slept, oblivious to betrayal. "I can't get you past sealed airlocks."

"We've grapples. Drills. Tell me where to set my ship down. Where to dig for what we need."

Opening his eyes, Raner searched for *Haida*'s ident among the unmoving hordes. "If you land, the rest will follow. That much mass could affect rotation—tilt Thromberg's solar array—"

"Not if you guide us down. We're going anyway, Raner." Her voice lowered. "It's up to you."

He'd built Thromberg. Protected her these long years. This would too—not that those inside would take it that way.

"Let me warn them first."

* * *

Shadow rolled across the great station and, true to Nix's word, *Haida V* descended first, leading the way. Her nose plowed deep into Thromberg's shield and she wasn't lifting again, ever. Once landed, her crew hurried outside, cutting like bloodsucking insects through the shield and outer wall to the vital pipes beneath.

Dozens followed suit.

Raner'd sent his warning, to clear the level below, then pulled the *Mate* back. As if that made a difference. No matter what the hysterical voices on the com said, the station could take the punishment; no one knew that better. He still felt each impact as if it tore into his own skin.

A voice from behind. "It's our turn, Raner."

He didn't look away from the screen. "We can't do that. I won't."

"Wasn't asking, old friend."

Raner turned. Rosalind Fourier floated in the corridor, crew from the *Grimoire* behind her. Fesson freed herself from her seat and he'd an instant to imagine resisting.

Before giving up. How could he—when the *Mate* herself was running on fumes and he'd people below—

And Aaron. "I'll be with my son," he told them.

* * *

Maybe some of those inside understood that this wasn't an attack, that these were fingers clinging to the only life raft in reach, a life raft big enough for all—

But fear won.

As the *Merry Mate II* came gently down, attaching to the hull next to the airlock Raner'd begged to use and now sealed against him, suited figures appeared at the starward rim, carrying launchers and towing cutters.

And spacers went out to meet them.

* * *

They'd gravity again, being part of the station. Gravity made feeding the baby easier; cleanup stayed the same. Aaron Pardell ate and slept, uncomforted by arms to hold him as Thromberg bled and people died in dark corridors.

Having nothing more to do for the baby, Raner went to those huddled in the other cabins, Leland's family and friends, the immies from the ring. Their eyes pleaded.

As if he'd a way to save anyone at all.

Finally, he found his way back to the bridge, empty once more, and dropped in Jer's chair. He activated the com. "Thromberg. This is Raner on the *Mate*. Can anyone hear me? We have to stop this. Anyone. Please." Raner closed his eyes. Whispered. "Anyone…"

A crackle at last. "Raner? That you? It's Logan."

Adrenalin shot through him, shaking his hands. "Logan! What's happening? How's Malley—Hugh—?"

"They're fine. I've someone here who needs to talk to you."

Another voice, unfamiliar. "Captain Raner, this is Leah Nateba."

He frowned, placing the name. "From Human Resources?"

"I wish. The rest of the board are dead. That makes me Thromberg's Acting Chief Administrator and you the only ship captain willing or able to take my call. You're right. We have to stop this."

"'We?'" Raner choked. "You started it!"

"Losing hull integrity ends it for everyone, captain, and I'm assured that's imminent unless we start repairs now. I'm asking for a ceasefire. Withdraw to your ships."

He could reach Nix. Rosalind was another who had to be in on it. The Smiths. Even as Raner ran through the list he kept talking. "You'll leave the ships alone. Let them keep their hookups."

"If the spacers leave the station and stay on their ships."

Eyes pleading for help— "Our passengers," he countered quickly. "The immies who tried to leave. Take them back."

"How?" Logan interrupted. "Your ships can't move and Earth's scared people stupid. Anyone from outside's a target, ceasefire or not."

"Clear an airlock. We'll slip the immies through a few at a time." He held his breath.

"If you can make that work? Agreed," Nateba stated. "We'll take them back."

"Thank you."

"Don't. Them, Raner, not you. Not ever. Enough here know your part in this."

So be it. "I'll contact the captains."

* * *

"Some of us pretended to work near the airlock. Immies. Stationers without patches. When each bunch came through, we swept them up with us. Good work, Raner."

Station security had turned a blind eye. From the outside, the process had been agonizing: suit up, walk each immie over Thromberg's hull to the nearest still intact airlock, put them inside and take back their suit. Repeat. Repeat. Repeat. Raner'd ferried those on the *Mate*, using Gabby and Jer's suits. They'd seemed numb. Rightly terrified. Tanya's mother, last to go, had hugged him.

Them, not you. Not ever.

Nix and Bolb—no, Bolb had died in Sol—the rest of the spacers appeared glad to stay on their ships. Those below captain had no idea why stationers had suddenly left airlocks unguarded so they could retreat—

Maybe the spacers thought they'd won. Last he'd heard, crews were running cables between ships, creating communication networks, preparing to wait. He'd no idea for what. The ships were derelicts, attached to a dying station.

"Raner? You there?"

"Hugh. You. You're all right? I—can't get news." The silence since the last passenger disembarked—that of itself had meaning. Both sides, in and out, isolating the other.

"Logan's moved us to Outward Five. Says it'll be better. No knowing what's going to happen."

Riots. Famine. More riots. More death. No matter what he did, no one was any safer—Raner put his head in his hands.

"Raner—Aaron—" Sharply. "Is that the baby?"

Cries. He kept hearing them. For how long he didn't know—

"Raner, get up and look after your son!"

"Why?"

A pause. He'd shocked her. Maybe she was gone. He'd deserve it.

But no. "It's what you're going to do," Malley informed him with a warm certainty that filled the empty bridge. "It's what we're all going to do. We're going to take care of each other the best we can and, when this is over, we'll celebrate together. So you get up and do your share right now, Raner. My Hugh is waiting to play with his best friend."

"You can't believe they've a future."

"I believe we make our own. Stop wasting time and check on that baby. Let me know when you need more milk."

"We're Outside." *Them, not you. Not ever.*

"Your friends don't care where you are." Smug. "We'll find a way."

If anyone could—Raner found himself on his feet. Discovered he was badly in need of a shower and fresh clothes—

Those could come later.

"Gotta go, Malley. Aaron's calling."

And their future, whatever shape it took.

About the Authors

JACEY BEDFORD is a British writer of science fiction and historical fantasy. Her Psi-Tech and Rowankind trilogies are published by DAW in the USA. Her short stories have appeared in anthologies and magazines on both sides of the Atlantic, and have been translated into Estonian, Galician, Catalan and Polish. In another life she was a singer with vocal harmony trio, Artisan, and once sang live on BBC Radio4 accompanied by the Doctor (Who?) playing spoons.
Blog: jaceybedford.wordpress.com
Facebook: https://www.facebook.com/jacey.bedford.writer
Twitter: @jaceybedford
Or via her writing website: http://www.jaceybedford.co.uk, which includes a link to her mailing list

ALEX BLEDSOE was raised in west Tennessee an hour north of Graceland (home of Elvis) and twenty minutes from Nutbush (birthplace of Tina Turner). He's been a reporter, photographer, editor, and door-to-door vacuum cleaner salesman. He's the author of THE HUM AND THE SHIVER, THE GIRLS WITH GAMES OF BLOOD, and other oddly-titled novels. He currently lives in a Wisconsin town famous for trolls. Find him online at alexbledsoe.com, @alexbledsoe (Twitter), @alexbledsoewriter (Instagram), and @authoralexbledsoe (Facebook)

GERALD BRANDT is an International Bestselling Author of Science Fiction and Fantasy. His current novel is Threader Origins – Book One of the Quantum Empirica, published by DAW Books. His first novel, The Courier, in the San Angeles series was listed by the Canadian Broadcasting Corporation as one of the 10 Canadian science fiction books you need to read and was a finalist for the prestigious Aurora Award. Both The Courier and its sequel, The Operative, appeared on the Locus Bestsellers List. You can find Gerald online at http://www.geraldbrandt.com, on Facebook as Gerald Brandt – Author, and on Twitter @geraldbrandt.

CHAZ BRENCHLEY has been making a living as a writer since the age of eighteen. He is the author of nine thrillers, two fantasy series, two novels about a haunting house and two collections, most recently the Lambda Award-winning *Bitter Waters*. He has also published fantasy as Daniel Fox, and urban fantasy as Ben Macallan. He lost count of his short stories long ago; a "Best Of" collection will be published in 2021. In his fifties he married and moved from Newcastle to California, with two squabbling cats and a famous teddy bear. He can be found on Facebook, Twitter and Patreon, and at www.chazbrenchley.co.uk.

JACK CAMPBELL (John G. Hemry) writes the New York Times best-selling Lost Fleet series which has been published in English, French, Japanese, German, Finnish, Polish, Czech, Spanish, Hungarian, Greek, Turkish, Hebrew, and Chinese, as well as the Genesis Fleet and Lost Stars series, and the "steampunk meets high fantasy" Pillars of Reality series. His most recent books are *Triumphant*, and the *Empress of the Endless Sea* trilogy. His YA novel *The Sister Paradox* won the 2018 Epic ebook award. John is a retired US Navy officer. He lives in Maryland with his indomitable wife "S" and three great kids. www.jack-campbell.com

Canadian, biologist, award-winning author/editor **JULIE E. CZERNEDA** shares her curiosity about living things and optimism about life through her science fiction and fantasy, published by DAW Books, NY. The 20th anniversary edition of her acclaimed SF novel, *In the Company of Others,* will be released fall 2021 (Philip K. Dick Award finalist; winner 2002 Aurora for Best English Novel). Out next is *Spectrum,* continuing Esen's misadventures in the Web Shifter's Library series, featuring all the weird biology one could ask. Julie is represented by Sara Megibow, of KT Literary. Find more at www.czerneda.com.

ANITA ENSAL has always been intrigued by the possibilities inherent in myths and legends. She likes to find both the fantastical element in the mundane and the ordinary component within the incredible. She writes in all areas of speculative fiction with stories in many fine anthologies out now and upcoming, including *Love and Rockets* and *Boondocks Fantasy* from DAW Books, *Guilds & Glaives* and *Portals* from Zombies Need Brains, *The Book of Exodi* from Eposic, and the novella, *A Cup of Joe*. You can reach Anita (aka Gini Koch) at her website, Fantastical Fiction (http://www.ginikoch.com/aebookstore.htm).

KIT HARDING is a librarian and maker who is excited to be taking these early steps into her writing career! Her work has previously appeared in *We're the Weird Aliens*. You can find her online at https://writerkit.dreamwidth.org/

R.Z. HELD writes speculative fiction, including the *Amsterdam Institute* series of space opera novellas. Her *Silver* series of urban fantasy novels was published under the name Rhiannon Held. She lives in Seattle, where she works as an archaeologist for an environmental compliance firm. At work, she uses her degree mostly for copy-editing technical reports; in writing, she uses it for world-building; in public, she'll probably use it to check the mold seams on the wine bottle at dinner. Website: rhiannonheld.com Twitter: @rhiannonheld

D.B. JACKSON is the author of the novels, novellas, and short stories of the *Thieftaker Chronicles*, a historical fantasy set in pre-Revolutionary Boston. He also writes the *Islevale Cycle*, a time-travel, epic fantasy series. As David B. Coe he has written epic fantasy, urban fantasy, supernatural thrillers, and media tie-ins. He is best known for the Crawford Award-winning *LonTobyn Chronicle*. David has a Ph.D. in U.S. history from Stanford University. His books have been translated into a dozen languages. http://www.DavidBCoe.com; http://www.dbjackson-author.com; http://twitter.com/davidbcoe; http://twitter.com/dbjacksonauthor

MARK D. JACOBSEN is an Air Force officer and professor of strategy and innovation. He holds a PhD in Political Science from Stanford University and has spent his career building and leading teams to tackle wicked problems at the intersection of technology and politics. He also writes fiction and non-fiction about grappling with complex, uncertain futures. He lives in Montgomery, Alabama with his wife and three children. You can find him online at markdjacobsen.com.

SF convention favorites **SHARON LEE** and **STEVE MILLER** have been collaborating since the 1980s, with nearly one hundred works of fantastic fiction to their joint credit. Sharon is the only person to consecutively hold office as the Executive Director, Vice President, and President of the Science Fiction and Fantasy Writers of America while Steve was Founding Curator of Science Fiction at the University of Maryland's SF Research Collection.

Their newest Liaden Universe® novel, Trader's Leap, is their twenty-seventh collaborative novel. Their awards include the Skylark, the Prism, & the Hal Clement Award. More at https://www.korval.com & https://www.facebook.com/groups/16280839259/

JANA PANICCIA is a Toronto-based communications consultant, business writer, and age-group triathlete who carves out time to write speculative fiction between major projects and races. Her short fiction has previously appeared in a number of anthologies, including *Women of War* and *Ages of Wonder*. Jana loves sea adventure stories, and once took a tall ship trip from Norway to Scotland to get a taste of the real thing. It's probably good that she didn't spot any ghost ships. Jana can be found at www.janapaniccia.com, on FB, or on Twitter (@Jana_Paniccia).

ANDRIJA POPOVIC is a native of the Washington DC metropolitan area who indulges in photography, spends entirely too much on books, and occasionally adds to the #NoirAlley Twitter discourse as @andrian6. His stories have previously been published in Daily Science Fiction and the ZNB anthologies ALIEN ARTIFACTS, THE DEATH OF ALL THINGS, and PORTALS. For more, check Biomechanoid Blues (biomechanoidblues.wordpress.com)

KRISTINE SMITH is the author of the Jani Kilian series and other science fiction and fantasy novels and short stories under her own name. As Alex Gordon, she has written the supernatural thrillers Gideon and Jericho. Her fiction has been nominated for the Locus Award for First Novel, Philip K. Dick Memorial Award and the IAFA William L. Crawford Fantasy Award, and she was the 2001 winner of the *Astounding* Award (formerly known as the John W. Campbell Award) for Best New Writer. Visit her website for more information: https://www.kristine-smith.com

GRIFFIN AYAZ TYREE was raised on Star Trek reruns and Iranian folklore, and now writes science fiction in fits and spurts between hospital shifts. He was a shortlisted author in the 2020 Quantum Shorts flash fiction competition and his stories have been featured in Nature Futures and The Colored Lens. He lives in Boston, Massachusetts with his partner and their collection of cold-hardy houseplants.

About the Editors

DAVID B. COE is the author of more than two dozen novels and as many short stories. He has written epic fantasy—including the Crawford Award-winning *LonTobyn Chronicle*—contemporary urban fantasy, supernatural thrillers, and media tie-ins. As D.B. Jackson, he writes the *Thieftaker Chronicles,* a historical urban fantasy set in pre-Revolutionary Boston, as well as the *Islevale Cycle*, a time travel/epic fantasy series. David has a Ph.D. in U.S. history from Stanford University. His books have been translated into a dozen languages. *Derelict* is his third editing project.

http://www.DavidBCoe.com
http://www.dbjackson-author.com
http://twitter.com/davidbcoe
http://twitter.com/dbjacksonauthor

****

JOSHUA PALMATIER is a fantasy author with a PhD in mathematics. He currently teaches at SUNY Oneonta in upstate New York, while writing in his "spare" time, editing anthologies, and running the anthology-producing small press Zombies Need Brains LLC. His most recent fantasy novel, *Reaping the Aurora,* concludes the fantasy series begun in *Shattering the Ley* and *Threading the Needle*, although you can also find his "Throne of Amenkor" series and the "Well of Sorrows" series still on the shelves. He is currently hard at work writing his next novel and designing the Kickstarter for the next Zombies Need

Brains anthology project. You can find out more at www.joshuapalmatier.com or at the small press' site www.zombiesneedbrains.com. Or follow him on Twitter as @bentateauthor or @ZNBLLC.

Acknowledgments

This anthology would not have been possible without the tremendous support of those who pledged during the Kickstarter. Everyone who contributed not only helped create this anthology, they also helped support the small press Zombies Need Brains LLC, which I hope will be bringing SF&F themed anthologies to the reading public for years to come. I want to thank each and every one of them for helping to bring this small dream into reality. Thank you, my zombie horde.

The Zombie Horde: Cyn Armistead, Kerry aka Trouble, Bregmann, Linda Pierce, Beth Lobdell, Beth Barany, Michael Feir, Jennifer Della'Zanna, Michele Hall, Maxim, Erin Kenny, Thomas Bätzler, AlmostHuman, Larry Strome, Chris, Jennifer Berk, Alan Smale, Lorraine J. Anderson, Pulse Publishing, Tomas Burgos-Caez, Kirsty Mackay, Kevin Lowney, Shayne Easson, P. Christie, Old Man Sparck (TyMcC), Aleis Maxim, Melissa Schultz, Richard C. White, Agnes Kormendi, ChristinecEthier, Wendy Schultz, David J. Rowe, A.J. Abrao, S.Jonda, Andy Miller, Vikki Ciaffone, jmi, Randall Brent Martin II, MJ Silversmith, John Senn, Elissa & Wolf Gray, D. A. Nulf, Lutz F. Krebs, Kammi Davis, Tina Connell, Jennifer Flora Black, George Fotopoulos, Christine Budd, Tim Jordan, William Seney, Cheryl Losinger, J. L. Brewer, Graham Robert Scott, Tommy Acuff, Kayliealien, Krystal Windsor, Erin Penn, Susan O'Fearna, Cyn Wise, Heather N. Jones., Bruce Wesley, Mandy Stein, Fiona Nowling, G.M. Persbacker, Bobbi Boyd, Kelly Wagner, Marian Goldeen, Susan Simko, Kevin Niemczyk, Lisa Kruse, Ane-Marte Mortensen, Sure. Julie Pitzel, Dan DeVita, John T. Sapienza, Jr., OgreM, David Gillon, Gavran, Paul McErlean,

Bex O, Samuel Lubell, Henry Herz, Carol Mammano, Walt Williams, Russell Ventimeglia, Levi Qışın, RM Ambrose, Lorri-Lynne Brown, Louise Dimarcello, Shaina Reisman, Leigh Ann Vaughn, Remnant, Dino Hicks, Dylan Larkin, Patrick Dugan, InarisGuardian, Vicki Greer, Sabrina M. Weiss, Ellen Kaye-Cheveldayoff, Kristine Kathryn Rusch, David Bruns, Pat Knuth, Frances Rowat, Olav Rokne, Nirven, Robyn DeRocchis, Vincent Darlage, PhD, Tracy 'Rayhne' Fretwell, E.L. Winberry, TimBlitz, Sachin K Suchak, Lace, Elizabeth Kite, Venessa Giunta, Robert V Riddell, Cory Williams, Dori-Ann Granger, Chris Brant, Greykell (werewulf!) Dutton, Kate Pennington, Tauna Sonn-LeMarbe, Marc Long, Michael Ball, James Conason, Ron Currens, Cassie A Stearns, Rebecca M, Katherine S, Sandra Bryant, T. England, eric priehs, Patrick Osbaldeston, Sheryl Ehrlich, Kristine Smith, Edward K. Beale, CDR, Fionna O'Sullivan, Duncan & Andrea Rittschof, Yankton Robins, Melissa Shumake, BUDDYH, Niall Gordon, Rae Streets, David Zurek, Samantha Sendele, CRussel, Tania Clucas, Michele 'Neverwhere' Howe, Sharan Volin, Amanda DeLand, Caryn Cameron, Jeremy Audet, Christina Roberts, Jasmine Stairs, Doug Ellis, L. E. Doggett, Gregory D. Mele, Michelle Botwinick, Michael Haynes, David Perkins, Margaret Bumby, Eric, _ALR, Michael Hanscom, Michèle Laframboise, writer & artist, Erin Subramanian, Kimberly Lucia, Tris Lawrence, Jenn Whitworth, Michael Halverson, Cindy Cripps-Prawak, Phillip Spencer, Ian Chung, Jarrod Coad, John Markley, Jeff G., Steven Halter, Jim Landis, Meyari McFarland, Chris Gerrib, Evan Ladouceur, Tanya K., Risa Wolf, Mark Carter, Sidney Whitaker, Ed Ellis, Storm Humbert, Chantelle Wilson, Cat Wyatt, Kristin Evenson Hirst, Sean P. Caballero, Camille Lofters, Brendan Burke, Rick McKnight, Jennifer Robinson, rissatoo, Kristi Chadwick, Michael Kohne, Bill and Laura Pearson, E.M. Middel, TF Newbery, Caitlin Jane Hughes, Shadowlight, Michael Abbott, Judith Mortimore, Konstanze Tants, Megan Beauchemin, Deborah A. Flores, Simon Dick, N. Engel, Susan Oke, Juliet Kemp, Colette Reap, Jim Anderson, Ivan Donati, Mustela, Petrina Hartland, M Smedley, Brenda Moon, Justin Pinner, Louise Lowenspets, Juanita J Nesbitt, James Enge, Hephaestion Christopoulos, Jaq Greenspon, Jenny Barber, Mary Alice Wuerz, Yosen Lin, Bryan Smart, Marsayus, Herbert Eder, Piet Wenings, Eva Holmquist, Jim Gotaas, Kelly J. Cooper, Mei Hua, David Lahner, Ash Morton, John Schreck, Ian Harvey, A. Chatain, F. Meilleur, Kimberly M. Lowe, Sarah Cornell, Matthew Egerton, Patricia van Ooy, Robert B Tharp, Jesse Sun, K. Kisner, Karen M, Angie Hogencamp, Blair Learn, Bill Drake, MD, Joanne Burrows, Christopher Prew, Ruth Ann Orlansky, Scott Raun, Carl Wiseman, Camilla Avellar, Cracknot, Anita Morris, Michele Fry, Scarlett Letter, Frank M. Greco, Kortnee Bryant, Doug Porter, Beth Coll, Adam Rajski, Jerrie the filkferengi, Martin Greening, cassie and adam, Rosanne Girton, Megan Lewis, Scott Kohtz, Chad Bowden, jjmcgaffey, Richard Parker, Axisor and Firestar, Elaine Tindill-Rohr, Khinasidog, Wolf SilverOak, Beth Morris Tanner, RJ Hopkinson, John H. Bookwalter Jr., Duncan Shields, Teri J. Babcock, The Mystic Bob, Elektra, Brad L. Kicklighter, Lark Cunningham, Jason Palmatier, Christa Bowdish, Ryan Power, Krystal Bohannan, L.C., Ellie Yee, Anthony R. Cardno, Nick W, Carman C. Curton, Jonathan Adams, Anne Burner, Leane Verhulst, Eleanor Grey, Todd Stephens, Aurora Nelson, GMarkC, Patti Short, Ellen Garner Crawford, Stabby the Unicorn, Alison Sky Richards, Michael Murphy-Burton, Margaret St. John, Sam Stilwell, William Leisner, Nancy M Tice, William Rivera, Jeanne Talbourdet, Megan Miller, Ginevra Marner, Lavinia C, SwordFirey, Jeff Conner, DARIN KENNEDY, Karen Fonville, Ichabod Ebenezer, David DiCarlo, Nathan Turner, Jesse Klein, Jennifer Crow, Kathryn Smith, Robert Gilson, Gotherella Biovenom, Emily Randolph-Epstein, Millie Calistri-Yeh, LetoTheTooth, David Holden, Cathy Green, Chris Huning, EM, Sentath, Michael Axe, Taia Hartman, V Hartman DiSanto, Becky Boyer, Colleen R., Steven Peiper, Nora-Adrienne Deret, Craig "Stevo" Stephenson, Sheryl R. Hayes, Lexie Carver, Jo!, Judith Waidlich, Malcolm & Parker Curtis, Katy Manck – BooksYALove, Tom B., Nancy Holzner, Steve Arensberg, AJ Hartson, Todd Ehrenfels & The Science Fiction Society of Northern NJ, Keith E. Hartman, Timothy Pelkowski, Robin Sturgeon Abess, Aysha Rehm, Heather Fleming, Bruce Shipman, Kathleen Kennedy, Hoose Family, Fred and Mimi Bailey, Brendan Lonehawk, C. C. S. Ryan, Tony Pope, Denise Tanaka, Su Minamide, Marcel de Jong, J.P. Goodwin, Walter Bryan, Ashley McConnell, Stephen Ballentine, Richard O'Shea, Nicole Wooden, Corey T, Brooks Moses, RKBookman, David Mortman, Carolyn Mulroney, Joshuah Kusnerz, Christopher Wheeling, Tania, Jörg Tremmel, Tina M Noe Good, John Green, Jill Crowther-Peters, Richard Leis, Alex Langer, Lisa Short, Marcia Franklin, Chris Kaiser, Ronald H. Miller, Matt Celeskey, Stephanie Lucas, NewGuyDave, Janet Piele, Cliff Winnig, Robert Tienken, Annie Agostini, Steven West, Holland Dougherty, Trip Space-Parasite, Wayne Howard, Helen Ellison, Matt Taylor, Amber N. Bryant, Mark Kiraly, Phoebe Barton, Fred Herman, Brian Burgoyne, Michelle Palmer, Kate Malloy, Camille Knepper, Elise Power, R. Hunter, Gary Phillips, Nick Marone, Benjamin Hausman, Britt Hill, Julia Haynie, Carol Van Natta, Jim Willett, Robert J Andrews II, Anna Rudholm, John Winkelman, Sonya Lawson, Katie Hallahan, Brynn, Michael Barbour, Rolf Laun, Curtis Frye, Jen1701D, Robert Balentine, Jr., James Flux, Shaun Kilgore, Mark Newman, Tibs, Caroline Westra, Robert Zoltan, Kari Kilgore, Carla B, Christine Hanolsy, Marty Poling Tool, Rowan Lambelle, Robert Claney, Kelly Lynn Colby, –Insert Name Here–, Mirranda Prowell, Juli, Kat Hodghead, Anonymous Reader, Jamieson Cobleigh, Carol J. Guess, Keith West, Future Potentate of the Solar System, Bárbara y los Víctors, Dina S,

Willner, Lawrence M. Schoen, Nancy Glassman, Nancy Pimentel, Dr. Kai Herbertz, Undead Auna, Elyse M Grasso, Kiya Nicoll, Simone Pietro Spinozzi, Jessica Enfante, Michael M. Jones, Andrija Popovic, Howard J. Bampton, Connor Bliss, Debbie Matsuura, Craig Hackl, Terry Williams, David Quist, Corky Bladdernut, Olivia Montoya, Steve Salem, William R.D. Wood, Robin Hill, Michael Fedrowitz, Judy Lunsford, Céline Malgen, Katrina Knight, C.A. Rowland, Xploder, Stephanie Cranford, Dave Hermann, Holly Elliott, VeAnna Poulsen, Rhondi Salsitz, Stephannie Tallent, C.C. Finlay, James Lucas, Wilma Lingle, Charles Boyd, Sci Fi Cadre, Heidi Lambert, Greg Vose, Ryan Harron, Cat Girczyc, Danni Brigante, Leah Webber, Morva& Alan, Marco Cultrera, Paul D. Smith, Jenny and Owen Blacker, Michael Kahan, Cara Murray, Chris Matthews, Dorian Graves, Larisa LaBrant, Connor Whiteley, Carl Dershem, Andy Dibble, Tory Shade, Jen Maher, Alex Shvartman